The REPERCUSSIONS of Tomas D

Also by Sam Hawksmoor
The Repossession (Hodder Children's Books) 2012
The Hunting (Hodder Children's Books) 2012

Text copyright © 2013 Sam Hawksmoor
This edition published in 2013
1 3 5 7 9 10 8 6 4 2

The right of Sam Hawksmoor to be identified as the author of this work has been asserted by him in accordance with the Copyright, Designs and Patents Act 1988.
All rights reserved.

Apart from any use permitted under UK copyright law, this publication may only be reproduced, stored or transmitted, in any form, or any means, with prior permission in writing from the publisher, or in reprographic production in accordance with the terms of licences issued by the Copyright Licensing Agency and may not be otherwise circulated in any form, or binding, or cover, other than which it is published and without a similar condition being imposed on the subsequent purchaser.

This novel is a work of fiction. Names and characters are the product of the author's imagination and any resemblance to actual persons, living or dead, is entirely coincidental.

A note from Sam Hawksmoor

The inspiration for The Repercussions began on Anglet beach in France, where the German gun emplacements are still intact 70 plus years on from WW2. A visible reminder of war every hundred yards or so along the French coast. That and finding a picture of my grandfather buried up to his neck in rubble – still alive – from a German air raid on Lincolnshire. This was the second time he had been bombed. The first time was in 1914 when a German Zeppelin dropped a bomb on his home killing his brother and parents. There's a photo of him in his pyjamas standing in his bedroom with the front of the house blown off. So for Tomas D to have this nightmare about being buried alive by German bombs - it comes from a reality.

And all I ask my readers is this:
If you could go back in time to 1941, knowing what you know now, could you make a difference? Who would listen to you? Would anyone take you seriously at all? And what about the one you left behind? If their life changed because you left – would they remember you at all? Or perhaps curse that you ever lived…

Hammer & Tong Publications
http://www.samhawksmoor.com

Hawksmoor

Prologue

The Nightmare

Tomas staggered to the open window. The whole of his attic bedroom vibrated with the swelling sound of approaching bombers. Air-raid sirens were winding up to a crescendo all over the city. Searchlights pierced the sky, their bright beams seeking out the enemy. Artillery tracer fire sped skyward, finding nothing.

Invisible in the darkness, the bombers relentlessly flew towards the city in their hundreds. The night sky was choked with them, a swarm of lethal giant bats. Tomas knew he had to run for the shelter to save himself, nevertheless foolishly remained fixed to the spot.

He remembered all the details. He runs to the shelter. It is packed with anxious people. There's always a girl in a blue smock with a runny nose, a policeman who will soon have his head split open. There will be some man playing a sad tune on a harmonica. The air is stale and filled with dread. Hundreds of eyes will swivel upwards to the crypt's brick ceiling, hoping that this time the deadly bomb won't fall.

He has dreamt this at least twelve times now, and each time the bomb falls he has woken up, choking desperately in his bed.

The bombers are getting closer now, almost directly overhead, the night air quaking with the roar of their massive engines. Then comes the terrible shriek of the high explosive bombs falling over the city and docks.

He must run, save himself. But he doesn't move a muscle. Even though he knows one particular bomb will fall any second now. The one that will completely destroy his house.

He wills himself to stay. It's only a nightmare after all. In a moment he knows he will wake choking, his nostrils filled with brick dust and the smell of freshly spilled blood.

The bomb is coming. He closes his eyes. He is ready.

Tomas hears the shriek of the falling bomb ripping through the night air. He knows he is about to die once more. Last thing he will remember will be the pages on the wall calendar curling and bursting into flames. Somehow he knows that bomb is aimed at him. Whether he goes to the shelter or stays at home – it will always find him.

1

Storm Coming

A sudden clap of thunder rattled the café windows. Gabriella jumped, dropping her book. She glanced up at the blackened sky and wondered where the hell it had come from. She brushed a loose strand of hair from her forehead, realising her heart was racing as she retrieved her book. A week from her fifteenth birthday she was still conflicted about her mother's remark that morning that she was 'almost beautiful'. This coming from her 'almost mother', too busy being a lawyer to cook, or ever attend one of the concerts Gabriella sang in. It went well with her 'almost father', who had been banished from the home after an affair with one of his students. At least she always had Tomas in her life, her one rock in an uncertain world.

She'd already ordered hot chocolate for herself and a latté for Tomas. She breathed a sigh of relief when he finally burst in through Lou-Lou's double doors, all flustered for being late, even though he wasn't really. Embarrassed, she guiltily blew away her sugar doodles so he wouldn't see how childish she was being.

'What's up, Duck? How was the bone-crunching?'

'God, she should work for Army Intelligence. Anyone she tortured would confess anything in five minutes flat.'

Tomas placed his school bag on the floor. He glanced up at the threatening sky, knew he was going to get soaked riding home.

'Did you hear that thunder?' Gabby asked. 'Nearly gave me a heart attack, it was so loud. Twenty-five days of solid rain since Easter. It's May already. I don't think summer will ever come this year.'

'You're always in France in summer.' Tomas pointed out.

'You're coming too this year. I have secret plans to get you there.' She grinned conspiratorially. 'You may have to paint some windows though.'

Tomas raised his eyebrows, wished it were true. He always missed her when she went away. They leaned back to allow the waitress to serve their drinks, muttering thanks.

The osteopath had been tough on him; his legs ached. He knew it was for the best. He'd been riding his bike on a frosty morning, collided with a fast moving van and broken his leg in two places. He had a ton of metal screws inserted into his bones. Lucky to be alive really. He'd just started to ride his bike again, to get fit.

He'd deeply resented being trapped in his attic room waiting for his mother to bring him a cold dinner, or lukewarm cup of tea, or hearing her bleat 'most mothers wouldn't care for their sons like I do', every day, as if she were doing him a favour bringing him food – when she remembered. He still hadn't forgiven her for going away to Spain for three weeks and not making any arrangements to have him fed. If it hadn't been for Gabby he would have starved to death. She'd had to break into his house to save him.

'How was singing practice?' Tomas asked.

Gabby smiled. 'I'm auditioning for *Joseph* tomorrow. I know all the songs. It's only amateur. If they don't pick me it's a fix.'

'You'll ace it. Soon as you open your mouth.'

Gabby grinned. 'That's why I keep you around, Tomas Duck.'

Tomas only let Gabby call him Duck. His real name was Drucker. Named after a German exchange student his mother had met when she was sixteen and left her pregnant. She didn't even know which city he was from.

'You picking up your new glasses today?' Gabby asked.

'Finally.'

'Cool.' Gabby frowned, looking at Tomas' eyes. 'You're not sleeping, are you? You've got those dark rings under your eyes again.'

Tomas shrugged. 'Stupid nightmares. It's all your fault anyway.'

'Tis not.'

'Tis too. You gave me the DVDs.'

At first he'd been reluctant to watch them. He'd never been a war movie fan, preferring sci-fi. But you can get VERY bored lying in an attic room with a broken leg for weeks on end. He'd watched *Guns of Navarone*, then *The Great Escape* and realised that it wasn't so bad. One night the itch inside the plaster was so great he knew he'd never sleep, so he spent a full twelve hours organising the war movies into month and year, so he could watch the war consecutively. It was a total geek thing to do, but he was *really*, *really* bored and it kind of made sense at the time. Gabby's father must have owned every war movie ever made. He lectured at the University on Conflict Studies. Now he'd moved out Gabby rarely got to see her father. Even so, she was lucky. His didn't even know he existed.

'God, I have to write that history essay this weekend. Did you start yours?'

Tomas shook his head. He'd forgotten all about it, what with his nightmares. Something about the industrial revolution and clocks, he vaguely recalled.

Gabby remembered something. 'Alisha said you were planning to be an historian like my father. Is that true? I hope not, Duck.'

Tomas sipped his latté raising his bushy eyebrows.

'I might have told her that.' He said with a smile.

Gabby looked him with surprise.

'She was bugging me about how we all have to plan our futures and I told her I was going to study history at University. I don't remember why. I think I'd just seen *Band of Brothers* or something.'

Gabby grabbed his hand. 'Don't do history. My father is never in the real world. All he can ever talk about is the past. You have to become a journalist, remember? We planned it. You're going to write about injustice and I'm going to be a singer, then when my career fades at 25, I'll go into politics and we'll fight injustice together. It's all planned.'

Tomas loved that about Gabby. She'd decided long ago that they'd be best friends forever. He didn't know what he'd done to deserve that, but they'd been friends since primary school and no one had broken them apart. She was always making him do things he'd never have considered. Flying her giant Eagle kite on the beach in a storm being one. They'd got soaked, the kite fried by lightning and they both came down with 'flu; but now he remembered it as being one of the best days of last autumn.

'I'm worried about your dreams though. Still the same nightmare?'

Tomas nodded.

Gabby sighed. 'War movies are evil. They get inside your head. Maybe in another life you were bombed or died in that shelter. I'm worried your dream is like a bad sign, or something,' she added, a furrow appearing on her forehead. He'd never told her but he loved that little furrow.

Tomas looked back across the coffee shop and the colourful Victorian tiles on the floor and above to the hooks in the ceiling. This place had once been a butcher's shop. Hard to imagine it full of bloody carcasses, but the photo on the wall showed whole pigs hung from the hooks in the ceiling and a row of dead geese in the window.

'I'll dream of kites instead,' Tomas said at last, making her smile.

Gabriella was finishing her chocolate. 'I'm going to drag you to Southsea common this weekend. There's an international kite festival and it's going to be pretty awesome. They're huge, from all over Europe. Tyler and Tabby are going to fly theirs. They made it this winter. It's a giant sausage.'

Tomas looked at her and laughed. 'Sausage?'

'You have to see it. It's twenty metres long.'

'A twenty metre sausage?' Tomas smiled. 'Yeah, I guess I want to see that.'

'Good. I'll be around for you at eleven on Saturday.'

Gabby began to gather her things. She looked up at Tomas and had a sudden premonition that she wouldn't be going to the kite festival with him.

'Tomas, you will tell me if something's bothering you, right?'

Tomas looked at her with a puzzled expression, then smiled.

'I have no secrets from the penetrating gaze of my inquisitor, Gabriella Lamb. She who must know all.'

Gabby smiled, reassured. 'I've invested twelve whole years in you. I just wouldn't really know how to function if you weren't there.'

Tomas shook his head, laughing. She was being dramatic now.

'Go practice singing *Any Dream will do,* Miss Lamb.'

Gabby made a face. She'd forbidden him to ever come to any of her auditions. She never wanted him to see her humiliate herself. She knew just how ruthless and tough auditions were. There was a chance she'd be picked tomorrow, but then again, Sarah Cussins would be there, her deadly rival. Worse, her mother was on the city council and they would help with funding if sweet 'viper jaws' Sarah was chosen. Gabby knew the score. Talent wasn't everything.

'Call me the moment it's all over,' Tomas told her. 'If Sarah wins, I promise we will scour the city for someone with the worst case of 'flu ever and make sure they meet. Deal?'

Gabby laughed. 'Deal.' She felt reassured. Tomas would do that too. She knew he'd do anything for her and she for him. Everyone assumed they were boyfriend and girlfriend, but it wasn't so. They had never kissed. It would be icky. You just didn't kiss your best friend. Not unless you wanted to lose them forever.

'Get going,' Tomas told her. 'My turn to pay. Go before it rains.' Then he remembered something. 'Wait.'

He took a small soft little green rabbit out of his bag and gave it to her.

'For luck.'

Gabby was shocked. 'You can't give me Harold. He's your protector.'

'Give him back after the audition. He'll get you through.'

Gabby snatched him from his hands and cuddled him a moment. 'He will. I know he will. He's the luckiest rabbit in the world.'

Harold had been in Tomas's bag when he had the accident. Gabby was always saying it was the rabbit that had saved him.

She gave him a broad smile and tucked the rabbit into her satchel, leaving his ears to flop out and ran for the door. 'Love you babe.' She called back, and with that was gone.

Tomas sat there with a big grin, really hoping she'd win this audition. Giving her Harold was the least he could do. He knew he'd never have gotten through the last few months without Gabby looking after him. Every day he'd wait for her to come heavy-footed up the attic stairs and liven up his day. She'd bring schoolwork for him to do and gossip about the evil Sarah Cussins, plotting to sabotage her very pink facebook page. Slowly, by just being herself, she'd made him whole again. She was eternally optimistic and happy, and it was infectious. She'd been there the day the plaster came off and it was she who took him swimming every day to get his strength back. His mother couldn't have cared less.

He went to pay. Thunder crashed loudly outside and he just knew he was going to get drenched.

Tomas was examining his new glasses in an estate agent's window. He'd never needed the glasses before his accident. Wondering if Gabby would approve the design, he slipped them back into the hard case.

Thunder rolled overhead and it was growing really dark.

Tomas hesitated. His bike was locked to the railings by Waitrose car park. He'd never get it unlocked and home before the heavens opened. The café was his best option. They wouldn't mind. He was a regular.

Lightning exploded right beside him. He sprinted though crackling, electrified air, his hair standing up with shock. A double clap of thunder followed, so loud it shook nearby buildings. Tomas swung his school bag around his neck as rain fell like stair rods. A car hooted as he dashed across the road, the rain swilling around blocked drains. Lightning flashed again as he jumped across a puddle and he could smell burning – saw a crimson brightness all around him. Rain fell hard around him with an intense hiss of anger, more lightning and thunder followed out of the blackened sky.

He reached the café doors and burst in, slamming it shut behind him to stop the rain coming in with him. He turned around, wiping the water from his eyes, shaking it off his blazer and bag. He realised that his hair and sleeves were singed. He'd nearly been fried out there.

He blinked.

This wasn't the café.

He was in a butcher's shop.

Thunder rolled overhead again and two men in butcher's aprons looked at him with surprise.

'Bit wet out is it?' They laughed. It wasn't even funny.

'Sorry. Thought it was the café. Wasn't looking where I was going,' Tomas told them turning around as if to leave.

The door was exactly the same as Lou-Lou's Café – clearly he had made some stupid mistake.

'Stay lad. Can't have you going out in that.'

Tomas looked back at the butchers and the lone customer in her headscarf and realised he was staring at the same tiling on the floor as in Lou-Lou's. How was that even possible? He looked up. The same hooks hung from the ceiling. This was most definitely Lou-Lou's, but somehow in the brief time he went to get his glasses it had been turned back into a butcher's. Impossible.

'You all right lad? Never seen liver before?'

Tomas realised that the man was chopping liver on the wooden butcher's block counter.

'You're a lucky woman, Violet. There'll be a rush as soon as they discover we've got liver in. Lucky for you liver's off ration as well. Two ounces?'

'I was hoping for more. There's four of us now.'

The butcher pulled a face. 'There's quite a few who'd fancy this. Three ounces and that's it. Fourpence ha'penny.'

'For liver, Mr Braithwaite?'

'That's the price, Violet. There's a war on y'know.'

Tomas stared. He was in a butcher's shop. It was selling meat by the ounce and the woman was dressed like she was from a play or something. He figured that he'd either been hit on the head by lightning or ...

The rain intensified. Tomas turned to look outside and realised with horror that Waitrose supermarket had disappeared. Instead there were houses and more shops. No sign of his bike, or the railings that he'd locked it to. There was only one car parked in the street; a vintage black car flying a sodden Navy flag. There was a horse and cart, the poor horse just standing and steaming as the rain fell on its back.

This had to be his nightmare back again. But he had no recollection of going home, let alone going to bed. He dug his phone out of his pocket. It was 4.45pm. *No Service*. He turned it off, never a good idea to have a phone on during lightning.

'I hope this storm keeps up,' one of the butchers said. 'They won't be bombing us tonight in this.'

'Bombing?' Tomas asked turning his head.

'You sure you're all right, lad?' He sniffed the air and caught the smell of Tomas' burnt hair and cloth. 'Close shave you had there, sonny. Lightning must have wanted you for tea. You look pale. What's the uniform?'

'Millbrook.' Tomas replied, surprised. 'It's been there eighty years.'

'Millbrook College? It's the public school on Elm Grove. For toffs,' Violet declared with a rasp of her cigarette throat. 'It just opened before the war. Eighty years? More like five.'

Five? Tomas was thinking. They were wrong. Had to be.

'Oh, he's a toff,' the butcher remarked with a smirk.

Tomas was annoyed. 'I'm not a toff. I got there on a scholarship.'

The butcher looked at Violet and raised his eyebrows. Tomas was a toff to him at least. Scholarship meant bright and Tomas was bright. Couldn't help it. It was Gabby that had made him enter for the scholarship and her father who'd coached him through it. Another case of Gabby looking out for him.

'Can I ask what today is?' Tomas asked, confused. 'I mean the date?'

'Hear that, Vi? Pay all that money to go to a posh school and he doesn't even know what date it is.'

'I…' Tomas was embarrassed now and prepared to leave.

'It's May the 8th lad.' He turned to the woman as he wrapped the liver. 'Bombing raids on Liverpool and London again last night and pretty much everywhere in between. They say they downed 40 bombers but hundreds got through. It's sinful, Vi. Sinful. If we don't do something about it England will be under the German jackboot by '42, mark my words, and it ain't treason to think it. They'll be back here again no doubt. I've given up replacing the glass in the windows at home.'

'It's 1941!' Tomas felt dizzy with realisation. 'We're at war?'

They laughed at him.

'And it'll be over by Christmas,' the butcher added. They all laughed bitterly.

Tomas was reeling. Surely this was totally impossible. It was May 8th when he left the opticians. It was still May 8th, but seventy-three years earlier. Utterly impossible. He was dreaming for sure.

The air-raid siren began to crank up.

'Bloody hell, talk of the devil. Those bastards. Can we get no peace? Get to the shelter. Away with you all.'

Tomas opened the door and Violet dashed passed him in a rush to get outside.

'Buggers come early. Our boys will be waiting for the storm to end and here they come again. We've suffered enough. There's nothing left standing in the port.'

The butcher grabbed his gas mask box and pushed Tomas out into the rain and locked the door behind him. Tomas began to run, following those who were running towards the end of the street and the Chapel. He saw that some of the buildings around him were in ruins, propped up with huge wooden beams.

The sirens were still screaming in waves, up and down, but the distinct sound of approaching bombers was audible. It was still daylight. Tomas didn't remember any daylight raids in his war movies.

'Come on,' a man in uniform with a whistle urged him. 'Get down to the shelter, boy. Where's your gas mask?'

Tomas ignored him, followed a young girl in a blue smock down the slippery stone Chapel steps and stepped into the shelter.

He knew that smell.

He knew this place.

He had been buried alive here. Twelve times so far.

This was his nightmare. This was where he came to in his dreams. Here was the girl in the blue smock who would sit with him and hold his hand because she was scared. Behind him came in the policeman carrying his torch; he would die when his head split open. In came the woman with biscuits and water.

In front of him would be a naval officer and some woman in a brown coat. It could have been his mother. The officer was reassuring her in a very loud rather pompous voice.

'It's quite safe. This shelter has survived everything they can throw at it. This attack is new, though. Daylight raid during a storm. They knew they'd catch us unawares. Did you hear about Liverpool? Bombed flat it was. Birkenhead too.'

Tomas was in a daze. He took his place on a thick oak side bench, next to the girl. The doors closed. The bombers drew closer and closer.

The air seemed to throb and vibrate as they flew over and water flowed in under the door because it was still raining. Tomas knew that this was no small raid, there had to be a hundred bombers overhead to make this much noise.

'Perhaps they'll fly over. Perhaps they'll go inland,' someone said, shaking like a leaf and crossing themselves.

'No. They'll drop them here,' Tomas answered.

People looked at him in his school uniform and frowned. He guessed no one wanted to hear that. He looked behind him. The poster was there from his dream.

Your Courage, Your Cheerfulness, Your Resolution, Will Bring Us Victory.

The planes were directly overhead now. This was exactly like his dream. They would fly over the Chapel and drop their bombs on the harbour. A navy destroyer would be caught out. He could see the relief on everyone's faces as the bombers passed over. Saw them wince as they could feel the impact of bombs falling a mile further on in the docks. Tomas was aware that people would think it was all over, if it was his regular nightmare. Sure enough a man began playing his harmonica and the woman with biscuits was handing them out to those near her.

'Just like the raid on March 10th. They go for the docks every time,' someone was saying. 'I was there when the Victory nearly burned. Scorched the timbers. Those bastards got no respect for history.' The lights flickered. Someone was crying. A mother was trying to sing a child to sleep.

'We should get under the bench, it's safer,' Tomas suggested to the girl in the blue dress. She was about eleven, he guessed, had snot hanging from one nostril and her leather sandals were sopping wet.

She stared at him for a second, then nodded. She didn't question him. Others, including the policeman, looked at them funny as they crept under the sturdy chapel benches. The girl held his hand. She was shaking. He noticed that she had a small kitten in her bag, which was mewing. That detail had never been in the dream before. Some people put on their gas masks, Tomas thought they looked ridiculous, but then again they didn't know that the Germans wouldn't be using poison gas.

'They'll call the all clear in a moment,' the policeman said confidently.

'Why aren't they firing back? Where's the Ack-Ack?' Someone was asking, their tone more uncertain now.

‘It’s the rain,’ Tomas said. ‘No one was ready.’ He knew that the people manning the mobile guns were changing shifts when the bombers had come and the rain had stopped the line of communication working. Worse, the intercepting RAF Hurricanes weren’t scrambled in time.

Now there was one last piece of the puzzle to play. The lone bomber. The one who flew in five minutes after the others.

He heard it coming before everyone else.

The siren started up again. Someone started to cry. Tomas could see the butcher’s feet all spattered with blood from where he crouched.

Tomas pulled the girl’s head under the bench. ‘Close your eyes and say a prayer. There’s one more bomb to fall.’

‘How do you know?’ She asked.

‘I just know. What’s your name?’

‘Cathy.’

‘Hold your breath when you hear the bomb falling, Cathy.’

The bomber was right overhead. The whole Chapel seemed to shake above their heads. And then they all heard it. The shriek of H.E. bombs falling directly overhead. High Explosives to make everything burn.

Some people began to yell, some to pray. Everyone was looking up at the brick crypt ceiling, wondering how strong it really was.

The blast was immense. The flash of the explosion was just as Tomas remembered. His nostrils were filled with dust and blood and his ears went deaf. The walls and the very floor shook as bricks tumbled with a fierce force on their heads.

And this time Tomas did *not* wake up choking in his bed. But he *was* choking.

2

Buried Alive

Tomas woke.

He wasn't in bed. He wasn't at home. He was cramped and sore under a wooden chapel bench with a mouthful of dust. The air stank of blood and decay and petrol. He couldn't hear a thing, but his ears were ringing. He couldn't see, but he could feel that there was a pair of small hands gripping onto him. The girl with the blue smock.

He stirred – she stirred. Their movements were restricted as the ceiling had definitely collapsed. Brick and rubble had fallen in and everywhere there was the pungent stench of blood. It was pitch black; Tomas discovered it felt weird to be deaf. It made it all seem worse somehow.

Someone shone a dim torch beam across the room and the air was thick with dust. Tomas was looking at the policeman clutching his head – thick red blood pouring down his face. Tomas knew he was probably screaming in pain but he couldn't hear anything.

This most definitely wasn't a dream. No dream could be as graphic as this. Tomas was coughing now; his throat was filled with grit.

The torchlight blinked out, but immediately a chink of light appeared at the door to the underground shelter. Someone was aware they were down here, at least. A great deal of rubble lay either side of the door, he knew it would be hard to clear it away.

The girl was pulling his arm, trying to get his attention.

'I can't hear you,' he told her. It was a strange feeling not to hear his own voice. Was his deafness permanent? He was thinking – how did deaf people even know what they were saying if they couldn't hear their own words?

The girl turned on her torch and immediately Tomas could see her leg was bleeding. There was a dead woman lying on the ground beside them and more dead close-by. Instinctively Tomas took a scarf from the woman and wrapped it around the girl's leg. It would stop the wound getting infected at least. She stuffed her frightened kitten into her pocket.

Tomas realised that almost everyone was dead, or dying or wounded. Only he and the girl had survived intact by hiding under the bench. Thank God for his dream. At least he had been prepared.

This was all new to him from here onwards. No safe dream where he'd wake up in bed. He'd have to act on instinct. He had to get them to the Chapel door or else they'd both die. They crawled forward, lifting bricks and chunks of cement to one side as best they could. They crawled over dead and crushed bodies as well. Tomas was glad he couldn't see them, or hear any cries for help. The stench of blood and other body fluids made them gag. It was an extremely weird sensation moving and lifting without hearing, guided only by a chink of light at the far end.

Tomas wasn't afraid, he realised. He had no time to think about the situation at all. The girl was tugging at his trousers. He turned. She was pointing at flames. Something was on fire at the back of the shelter.

Tomas quickly understood that they had to move a lot faster. He'd smelled petrol earlier.

He crawled faster, moving under wooden beams that could give way at any time. He felt dizzy and was definitely wonky on his legs. The loss of hearing seemed to unbalance him somehow. The girl was right on his tail. Tomas suddenly felt sick. Something stank really bad. His hands were wet. He was glad he couldn't see, but he had the disgusting feeling that they'd just crawled through human entrails.

They were close to the door now. The rubble was loose, but if they removed the wrong piece it could all tumble over them.

He pointed to the girl to get to one side and Tomas started at the top, lifting brick, stone and wood, piece by piece and tossing them back to the gap they had just squirmed out from.

The fire leapt across the room. Tomas stared as blue flames literally jumped and the very air in the centre of the shelter seem to combust.

The girl saw it. She fell to the ground. Tomas dropped down beside her unsure about what to do. The air would be consumed. Everything would bake like an oven and the hole in the roof would draw up the flames and feed them. There was fresh air at this ground level, coming from the partially buckled door. But the more air, the brighter the flame Tomas was thinking.

A brick fell on Tomas's leg. His bad leg. He yelled in pain. Heard his yell. His ears were starting to work again.

More rubble began to shake. He glanced towards the door and realised people were on the outside trying to get in. He scrabbled up and began to remove the rubble again. He had to open a gap for them before the flames reached this end of the room. Another ear suddenly clicked open. With relief he regained his sense of balance and hearing at the same time.

The girl lay at his feet, scared to death.

Tomas head a scream. He turned his head. There was a man leaping up after regaining consciousness and realising he was on fire. He danced crazily for a moment before falling and the flames spread to another corner. The stench of petrol was even worse.

The door budged six inches. Tomas bent down and scooped up the girl, fed her to waiting hands and watched as she squeezed through the gap to freedom. Tomas was bigger. He needed more room.

The flames were getting closer. His back was scorching now. Still he attempted to move rubble so they could get the door open further.

'Get out now, boy. Save yourself.' He heard someone yelling.

Tomas stood on a lump of concrete and squeezed one arm out. Someone took hold of it, began to pull as another was forcing the door open further and suddenly he was free. More hands took him to street level.

Behind him there was screaming and yelling. Dazed, Tomas could see the whole Chapel was on fire and other buildings as well. He quickly realised that he and the girl would be the only ones to get out alive.

'Your blazer's on fire,' someone was yelling and threw him to ground, covering him a blanket. Moments later another person picked him up bodily and took him to a waiting ambulance. They put him down for the attentions of a nurse and looked at him with amazement.

'You the boy who saved Cathy's life?'

Tomas saw the girl wrapped in a blanket staring at him in wonder, her hair matted with blood and grime, her kitten miraculously still alive in her hands.

Tomas said nothing. He was too nauseous. He hurt all over; didn't want to look at his left arm, as he was sure it was badly burned. He looked back at the burning Chapel. It had been a direct hit. As his eyes adjusted to the street, he noticed how old fashioned everything looked. How oddly people seemed to dress. It was just like a scene in one of the war movies he'd seen.

'You got a name?'

The nurse was rubbing stinky stuff that stung like hell on his cuts and bruises.

'Tomas'

'Thomas?'

'Tomas, no H.'

She looked puzzled. 'Thomas without an H.' Then she smiled. 'Well someone's father had a sense of humour. Are they on the telephone, Tomas? We can get someone to call them? Where do you live?'

'Janoway Road.'

The nurse blinked, as if she didn't believe her ears. 'Janoway?'

Tomas nodded, wincing as she dabbed the cuts and burns on his arms.

'Got to bandage your arm, love. Need to keep the air off those burns. Must have been awful down there. Direct hit like that. I saw the bomber. Came in right after the others. Must have known the rain would disrupt everything. Sneaky buggers.'

A man came up in an air-raid warden's uniform. Tomas recognised it from the movies.

'Two bloody lucky kids here then. Where do they live, nurse? Were any relatives with them? I hope not.'

Tomas noticed the nurse go pale. 'Little Cathy here lives on Wilton Street, just around the corner, don't you, pet? Her mum will be along in a minute I suspect, someone's gone to tell 'er.' She glanced at Tomas. 'The boy lives on Janoway Road.' The warden and nurse exchanged worried glances and Tomas picked up on it.

The warden frowned. 'Not so lucky after all.'

Tomas tried to speak but his throat was constricted and dry from all the brick dust. They were trying to conceal something from him.

'Son, you're going to have to stay with the nurse a little longer.'

The nurse pinned the bandage and gave Tomas some water to drink.

'What's going on?' Tomas croaked. 'What date is it?' He asked, still clinging to the hope that it was all a dream.

'Got a bit of concussion have we? Can't remember the date? Not surprised with the roof falling in like that. Fancy them storing cans of petrol in the Chapel. Should know better. Hoarding is against the law.'

She was looking at his blazer. 'Is that..?'

'Millbrook,' he told her. 'New blazer design.'

'Those boys that got killed. They were so brave.'

Tomas suddenly knew what she was talking about. It was part of the school legend. Five boys had enlisted at the beginning of the war and gone into the RAF. All died in 1941. One of the boys had shot down twelve enemy planes and the dining hall was name after him, Leonard Hall.

'Flight Lieutenant Leonard was a hero,' Tomas told her.

'He was a terror, that's what he was. No girl was safe around that school. But he's a hero now,' she told him with a wink. 'You'll be going into the RAF too? How old are you now?'

'Almost fifteen.'

She looked at him and did a double take. 'I thought you were sixteen at the very least.'

The girl suddenly threw up and the nurse lost interest in him.

Tomas was brought a cup of tea in a tin cup by some woman wearing a WVS armband. He said thanks and stared glumly at the burning shell of the chapel. This was no dream. He was sitting in an ambulance in 1941, the war still had four years to go. Five when you counted Japan. They wouldn't even know Japan was preparing for war. Come to think of it, there was a whole lot they didn't know, he realised.

A fireman came to check on him. 'You all right, son?'

'Yes sir. Thank you for getting me out.'

'You did that yourself. Nasty in there.'

'There was a policeman. His head was split in two,' Tomas told him.

The fireman nodded. 'We'll get to the dead soon enough. War can't last much longer. It's you kids I feel sorry for. Living under German rule.'

'We won't,' Tomas told him emphatically. 'I know how it ends.'

The fireman laughed. 'That's the spirit. Tell me off for being pessimistic. Fight them to the bitter end, eh?'

'That's what Winston said, right?'

'That old fart? He'll be the last man standing on the rubble of England and we'll all be dead under him.'

Tomas looked at him with a puzzled expression. Surely he knew Winston Churchill was a hero? This fireman didn't know they were going to win. The war movies he'd seen had been filled with people who were all for fighting to the bitter end.

'I should go,' Tomas told her. 'I have to go home.'

The nurse was busy with the girl who seemed to be having hysterics. Tomas slipped away unnoticed.

He began to walk along Marmion Street, passing shuttered shops advertising Capstan cigarettes. Clearly the soldier smiling out of the poster didn't know they were going to kill him. He looked for his bike again, but he was beginning to accept that it was seventy odd years in the future and lost forever. Somehow he was in the past, alive and bruised, but definitely alive. He wondered how he'd get back. And what about Gabby? Would she even believe him?

He shook his head. No, if he made it back, she'd never believe him. He had to accept that.

An official Army vehicle drove by. He looked around him. That was the difference, hardly any cars on the street. It was getting dark now. There was no street lighting. Not for the next four years anyway.

He turned left on Victoria Road and headed north. He realised he was walking towards Janoway Road. There was no way his mother was there in 1941. There was every likelihood that even the house wasn't there. He knew his road had been bombed in the war. He had even seen the bomber that did it in his dreams. So why was he walking there? Because, he realised, he had to know for sure that this wasn't some fantastic super realistic dream.

All was quiet now. He was surprised to see most of the Victorian homes intact. They were still actual homes, not student flats. No house had double glazing. A few had cars parked in front under tarpaulin – others to his surprise had a pony and trap. He cut across to Campbell Road. All the homes were unscathed; the only damage was a huge hole in the centre of the road and sewage spewing from a drain. Some old man was trying to get his horse and cart around the hole, swearing at the poor nervous horse.

Tomas grew more and more apprehensive as he drew closer to his road. He had no idea what he'd do when he got there. Knock on the door of his old house and tell them that he grew up there? Sixty years in the future? They'd believe that for sure.

He began to worry about bomb damage the moment he reached Delamere Road. All the houses on the left had gone. There was nothing but rubble. His road was next and he knew that he wasn't going to like what he saw.

Finally he stood looking at 112 Janoway and stuck his hands in his pockets. The neighbour's house 114 was intact; the only one still standing in the row. All the windows were smashed, but it was still standing. How crazy was that. His own place was a ruin. Just the outer shell stood, the roof was gone and he could tell further down there had been a fire. A family was camped out in the road piling salvaged furniture onto the pavement. Behind him the man with the horse and cart was coming his way, most likely to pick the family up.

He never knew there had been so much damage. No one said they had rebuilt the house after the war. But then again they had only rented it from the housing association.

'You all right, lad?' Someone asked from across the road.

'Was looking for the people in 112,' he answered.

The man pulled a face. 'All gone. Sorry, son. The boy Rufus was trapped up there. Horrible thing to watch. My sister saw it collapse.'

'Rufus?'

'Sorry if he was your friend.'

Tomas suddenly remembered a tattered boy's diary he had found in a tin box buried in the garden two years before. It had belonged to Rufus aged 10. Neat handwriting; full of complaints about his elder sister who bullied him.

Tomas turned to go, his nostrils suddenly full of decay and brick.

'You want to come in for a cup of tea?' He heard the voice behind him but Tomas kept on walking. He didn't really want to speak to anyone. He was truly stuck back in the past and there was a war on. He had absolutely no idea how he was going to get back.

Suddenly he realised he was hungry. Any money he had wasn't going to be worth anything here and he didn't have a ration book. Or even a home to go to. Finally he realised he was in a desperate situation. *This was bloody real.*

3

Meine Familie und ich

Gabby was late for school. The rain had flooded several roads and the buses weren't working. People said that global warming was responsible but Gabby's mother was of the opinion that global warming didn't stop the council from clearing the drains and it was their fault there was flooding.

She ran into school. It was five to nine and she hated being late.

'You too?' Frances said as they found each other in the corridor. 'I can't believe the floods, Gabby. You ready for the test?'

'Test?'

'German orals today. You're so lucky you get it, but I really struggle.'

Gabby looked at her friend Frances and did a double take. Frances had her hair in braids and she looked completely different somehow.

'Good joke. We don't study German, Frances. In fact, no one does in this school.'

Frances looked at her with surprise. 'We *all* study German. You're the best at it. I just can't get my head around the grammar.'

Gabby dismissed Frances' comments as being a stupid joke. No way was she going to study German. It was bad enough having to learn French.

They entered the classroom and everyone turned to look at them.

'Fräulein Gabriella and Fräulein Frances you are twenty-five minutes late. You will stay after school, you understand?'

Gabby stared uncomprehending at the severe schoolmistress stood at the head of the class. The walls were covered in posters of German images and grammar. Someone had written – freut mich sehr, dich kennenzulernen on the board. Worse – she knew it meant 'pleased to meet you'. She took her place behind her desk and opened up her satchel. Two fat German books fell out and an equally fat German dictionary.

How was this possible? How could she have forgotten she studied German? Or that school started at eight-thirty. She'd discuss this with Tomas later. She looked around the classroom. All the girls were wearing the same uniform as her – dark blue with black stockings.

They all wore their hair in braids and no one wore any make up. How on earth had this happened? How come she remembered none of it, yet knew German. Where were all the boys?

'Hast du Geschwister, Gabriella?'

'Nein, Frau Lister. Ich habe keine Geschwister.'

The schoolmistress nodded, happy with the answer.

'Take out your notebooks. We will have a ten minute test.'

Three hours later lunch was no better. The canteen served sauerkraut and wursts. No mash or French fries. Milk in small glass bottles. At least it was free.

Gabby felt a headache coming on. She only recognised Frances and her mortal enemy Sarah Cussins, who looked thin and emaciated and she didn't even make a single sarcastic comment to her, or refer to the upcoming audition. Usually she just called Gabby 'loser' and laughed, but this was a different girl. Not as pretty as Gabby remembered.

Everyone else seemed to be 'different' too. Hardly anyone spoke in the canteen and if they did it was only in whispers. There was an element of fear in the school and two male teaching staff with short greased hair patrolled the canteen like proud lions, glaring at anyone who even glanced at them. There were no boys here at all. It was a single sex school apparently.

Gabby had no idea of her timetable and was puzzled at the contents of her satchel. It contained heavy English literature and history books and since when had she been reading Goethe? She glanced at the unfamiliar history book. '*The Birth of New Europe 1942-2000*' by Professor G F Lamb. She blinked. Professor Lamb was her father. But he wrote about war. 1942 – 2000? The dates seemed wrong. Surely New Europe started after the war, not during it.

She opened the page to a map of Europe. It was almost entirely German. The Great Third Reich Empire. There was a photograph of Reich Chancellor Fischer who took over in 1998 and was still leader of all Greater Germanica.

'Swotting again?' Frances whispered.

Gabriella looked at Frances and frowned. 'When did we lose the war?'

Frances looked shocked. 'We didn't lose. We joined the Glorious European project. 1942 was the most important year in English history.

'You're giving a speech on the great glory of National Socialism on Speech day remember? Make sure you remind everyone what an evil man Winston Churchill was in trying to keep the war going and encouraging the slaughter of millions of English men women and children.'

'Churchill? But he was a her…'

Frances put her hands over her ears. 'Don't say it. Don't let them hear you say it, Gabby.'

Gabby looked at Frances and realised, as if for the first time that she had never seen this girl before in her whole life. Jessica Howard was her best friend at school, not this Frances. What the hell had happened?

A bell rang. Lunch hour lasted just twenty minutes it seemed.

'History now, gym after,' Frances announced. 'I'm going to beat your brains out in boxing.'

'Boxing!'

History was bad enough but now she had to box? Wasn't that a boy's sport?

'It is the only thing I'm better at than you,' Frances declared with a sly grin.

Gabriella trailed after her to her 'history' lesson.

Maybe, just maybe, she thought, she'd gotten out of bed the wrong way or something. This was just like one of Tomas's dreams. It had to be that. A stupid nightmare. She'd wake up soon enough.

4

Name, Number, ID card

They took him to a temporary police station. With some surprise Tomas recognised the building as his old science block at Millbrook College, now remarkably new. He'd been taken to an underground 'cell', which he recognised as the storerooms in his own time. He'd been surprised to find himself in there with a man with a bloody bandage wrapped around his head. He was dressed in a torn suit, had no tie and seemingly no shoes. His was sleeping on a bench. A single broken light bulb swung from the ceiling and he was left there in the dark, locked in, a tin bucket provided for his 'toilet'.

He'd been stopped by a policeman and asked for his ID card. Tomas had tried to say he'd lost it in the bombing, but the copper wasn't having it and he didn't recognise his blazer. He thought Tomas was acting suspiciously, which Tomas realised was probably true, because he had been wandering aimlessly since he'd discovered his home was bombed. He was hungry too and had absolutely no idea where to go or what to do.

He discovered that all kids were supposed to carry a blue ID document with name, date of birth and address. The Copper had even escorted him back to his address on Janoway Road and seen for himself that his home was destroyed. He was polite, but firm, and told him that he had to take Tomas in (for his protection) and then some 'arrangements' would be made in the morning. Tomas knew what that meant. A foster home, or dreaded orphanage. He had visions of some Dickensian hell with starving brutalised kids. But if he tried to explain who he was or how he got there, they'd lock him up in a mental institution. He'd seen *Twelve Monkeys*. He knew how it went. Awkward or what?

At least they had given him a cup of tea and a tasteless bun.

He was sitting in the musty darkness listening to the man lightly snoring. He was wondering what he could say to anyone to prove he was from the future. He realised that even thinking that they'd listen was stupid. He tried to imagine someone coming up to him and claiming he was a kid from 1941 and he knew he'd just laugh. Even if the kid was wearing clothes from the period. Anyone would laugh.

You'd know it was a joke and that someone had their phone pointed at you filming it to mock you on YouTube or Facebook.

He did have a history book in his bag, but it was mostly about industrial developments and unhelpfully seemed to end in 1960 something. He blinked. His book talked about the First World War, but here they still called it the Great War, as if it was the last. But it wasn't impressive evidence, even if it was printed in 2013. They'd probably think that it was a printer's error.

He had a 32gb memory stick, but they'd never believe he had at least two hundred CDs and movies on there. Besides they'd have to wait like fifty years for someone to invent a USB connection to open it. Worse, *he'd* have to wait like fifty years to hear any decent music. That thought depressed him greatly. Even if he was sort of impressed by swing bands and music from the 40's – he sure as hell hadn't imagined that Glen Miller and Artie Shaw was *all* he was ever going to hear from now on.

He tried to remember what he knew about 1941. The Battle of Britain was already in the past. He knew that much. But what about the Enigma code thing? He tried to remember a name. He'd seen a movie about it and how they broke the German secret codes, but who was it and whom were they playing? He remembered Gabby's Dad, Professor Lamb, had labelled the DVD as 'total tosh', but which people were the actors playing? It was England's biggest secret of the war. Bletchley Park. Great. At least he remembered that. Then he realised with a shock that if he mentioned it he'd probably be shot as a traitor. They'd probably take him out and shoot him anyway for all the stuff he knew – if he could only force himself to remember any of it.

The biggest surprise had been the destruction and the stink as sewers were exposed everywhere. They never showed how smelly England was in the movies. In his nightmares it had always been personal. He'd always known he'd be buried alive in the rubble, but now he'd seen the destruction with his own eyes – he just couldn't believe how people had lived through it. Some had even joked with each other as they pulled people out of bombed houses.

He wondered why they didn't show the pictures of the destruction in class? That would mean something in history lessons, wouldn't it? If you saw your own street in ruins and your granddad lying there dazed in the ruins.

'Tomas Drucker?'

'Sir?'

A cop unlocked the door and dim light from the corridor spread into the gloom of the cell.

'You're for interrogation.'

'Interrogation?' Tomas had instant visions of being held down and water-boarded. He felt an urgent tension in his bladder that hadn't been there before.

The cop moved inside the cell to peek at the other man still lying asleep.

'Some people from London coming down to see him. They'll wake him up, I reckon. Found him unconscious in a bomb crater by the harbour. Couldn't remember anything when he came around.'

Tomas moved towards the door. He realised he had to pee urgently.

'I need to…'

'Lavatory is in the corridor up the stairs, lad. Be quick about it. Don't want to keep Detective Atkins waiting.'

Tomas reflected that at least he wasn't shackled or in chains. He wondered what kind of interrogation he was going to get. He'd seen enough war movies to know they were pretty brutal.

The lavatory was extraordinary. It was beautiful with wonderful Victorian glazed green and red tiles, a high ceiling, a row of porcelain urinals and five separate toilet stalls. No graffiti. This didn't exist in his time. It was a sterile place with a metal trough and big notices about defacing the walls. He wondered why they'd got rid of it. He looked up, saw there were no bars on the windows. He could probably escape if he wanted to, but he knew they'd just pick him up again. He had nowhere to go and no ID. Until he had one of those he was always going to be a 'suspect'.

Then he had to use the toilet paper. What on earth was this brown shiny stuff? You couldn't use this? It had a name printed on it; IZAL. It was like tracing paper. The perforated holes wouldn't tear properly either. He tried to use it, but it was disturbingly unpleasant and completely useless. This absolutely *proved* it was 1941. No one had invented soft tissue paper, yet. His heart sank. This was disgusting. He flushed and wished he could be home, in his own bed, in his own time, with his own bathroom…

The cop knocked on the door outside in the corridor. 'Hurry up, boy.'

Tomas washed, surprised to discover warm water coming out of the chrome taps, even if it was a muddy brown. He used some stinky green soap that appeared to have grit in it, but he was happy to clean his face and hands at last, even if he provoked a scratch on his cheek to bleed again. He was desperate for a shower, he realised. He wondered if they had invented shampoo yet.

'Coming.'

Outside in the corridor again he was pushed up more stairs to a small office. He was told to sit on a simple wooden chair under a bare lightbulb. The windows were all blacked out. He heard clashing bells as an ambulance drove past on the road outside. He noticed the school motto on the wall. Libérer l'esprit et un cœur pur. A clean mind and pure heart. Only now did he wonder why it was in French. Why couldn't school mottos be in English?

Tomas was just thinking he was forgotten when the detective came in and sat across from him on a wonky leather chair. He looked exactly like his science teacher Mr Atkins, with short cropped hair and sticky out ears. He had to be his science teacher's great-grandfather. How weird was that? He took out his pipe, banged it on the table and packed it with some tobacco before taking his time to light it. He didn't take a blind bit of notice of Tomas until he sucked the pipe alight. Tomas wrinkled his nose, unused to pipe smoke or indeed anyone smoking inside. He wondered if the sprinklers would come on then realised they probably hadn't been invented yet either. He checked the ceiling and it confirmed his suspicions. The tobacco smelled vile. The man took a form out of his pocket and spread it out on the table.

'Name?' he asked, finally glancing at Tomas and revealing that he had a sparse moustache over very red lips. It was disconcerting to look at.

'Drucker, Tomas, sir.'

The cop wasn't sure how to spell it. 'What kind of name is that? Eh?'

'I'm not sure I understand, sir.' Tomas remembered to keep using sir a lot because he knew from watching the movies that everyone used to be polite all the time.

'Drucker,' he said, musing. 'You know what rhymes with that.'

Tomas pulled a face. He knew very well what rhymed with Drucker thank you very much. He'd been teased enough in junior school.

'I'm sure I don't know, sir.'

The Detective looked at him and shrugged.

'And your father is?'

This was where the questions got tricky. Tomas decided to face it head on.

'I never knew him, sir. Single parent family.'

The Detective looked at Tomas with a puzzled expression. He'd clearly never heard of a single parent family before. 'You mean you're a bastard.'

Tomas blinked, it sounded so harsh said like that. 'Yes, sir. I suppose I am.'

The Detective wrote that down on his form and took a puff from his pipe again blowing smoke towards Tomas.

'It's not your fault, boy. I'm no hypocrite. There's a lot of toe-rags in this city who don't know their fathers. You look smarter than most of them.' He looked up a moment. 'Your mother?'

'Sandy Tivvet, sir. 112 Janoway Road.'

The man looked at him again and frowned. 'Janoway Road was bombed today. Were you caught in that?'

Tomas remembered to look bad about it.

'No sir… I was in the Chapel when it was bombed. My mother…' he let his voice croak a little and looked away.

The Detective shook his head, now feeling sorry for him.

'It's a bad black day for you, son. I don't know why you're here. They should have taken you to St Mary's orphanage. I'm very sorry, boy. It's hard to appreciate you're left alive when your family is taken like that. Have you eaten?'

'Had a bun, sir.'

He nodded. 'Have to do till morning. We'll get you moved. You go to school here, they tell me.'

'Yes, sir. But …'

'We've taken it over for the duration. They're most likely relocating up the hill to a safer place. No school for you for a week or so until they find a place.'

'How am I to get an ID card, sir? I lost everything…'

'Sergeant Gullet will sort you out. I'll make sure of it.' He looked at Tomas more closely. 'How old are you boy?'

'Fifteen in June, sir.'

Detective Atkins glanced up from his note taking and stared at Tomas. 'You look older. Not old enough to fight yet anyway. War could be over by the time you're sixteen. They're walking over us, destroying everything we have. I hope for your sake we sue for peace before you have to fight.'

'We'll beat them, sir. We can't have peace with Nazis.'

The Detective puffed on his pipe and Tomas could tell that he was considering his remarks.

'You think so?'

'I do sir. We're British. We'll never surrender, you can't make a deal with Hitler.'

'You and Churchill, eh. You think England can take it?'

'I know it can, sir.'

The Detective shook his head. 'I wish I was so sure. What Churchill doesn't see is the panic. He doesn't see the despair, or the bolshie resentment. Most of our city has been flattened, people are living any way they can, most days we can't get enough food or water and … they don't even let us report the crime figures any more, bad for morale, they say. Things are falling apart.'

'But we'll pull through,' Tomas declared. 'I know we'll win.'

The Detective fumbled with his pipe and sighed. 'Well, at least you're a patriot, even if you do have a funny name. I wish I had your faith, boy.' He stood up.

'Go back downstairs. Tell the Sergeant I said you could sleep. We'll get you billeted in the morning and sort out an identity card. You need to carry it around with you at all times. Tie it around your neck. Enough people are getting blown to bits these days and we're not able to identify them.'

Tomas rose and grabbed his bag. A DVD disc rolled out of it and spun on the floor before flopping down on the scuffed wooden floor.

The Detective looked at it in wonder. Tomas's heart flipped. How the hell was he going to explain that!

'What is this?' A coldness entered the room.

Tomas had to think a quick lie. 'My science teacher left this behind when he was called up. Said if I could work out what it was he'd give me an A when he comes back.'

'Did he now. Not many coming back from this war, lad. I wouldn't get your hopes up.'

Detective Atkins came around his desk and scooped up the DVD looking at his face reflected in the shiny metal. He seemed absolutely fascinated by it. He glanced at Tomas for a moment.

'And did you? Work it out, I mean?'

Tomas shook his head. 'It's made with a really light metal. I think it's for a new kind of record player but you can't put a needle on it. It would scratch.'

Detective Atkins was clearly transfixed by it. Little did he know it was a Motown Mix given to him by a kid called Jeff the Coolio, as he liked to call himself. He'd moved on from Hip-Hop to 60's Motown and was trying to convert Tomas to Smokey Robinson and the Miracles.

'I'm confiscating this'. He was staring at the writing on the disc now, trying to read it. 'F -u- j - i film. Video Data. What the dickens is a DVD minus R, do you think, eh?

Tomas shrugged. 'I think that was the challenge, sir. He liked to challenge us.'

'Must be something special. Fujifilm. There's a Mount Fuji but that's in Japan. You think this might be Japanese?'

'I don't know much about Japan, sir. They make good cars, I think.'

Detective Atkins looked at Tomas with interest again. 'Do they now. You ever seen one?'

Tomas shook his head. His mother drove a Polo back home in his time. Almost every parent he knew either had a Japanese or German car. Probably be hard to understand this in 1941.

Detective Atkins looked into Tomas's bag. 'What else have you got in there? Maybe you're a Japanese spy? Is that what you are?

Tomas laughed briefly, then winced. He hadn't exactly examined the contents of his bag in months. Anything could be in there. Besides the history book (mostly unread) and the USB thing, there would be pens, a calculator. Shit that was going to get him in trouble…

The Detective pulled out a half eaten Kit-Kat.

'Kit-Kat. You must be a boy with influence. There's half a Kit-Kat in here *and* its got silver paper wrapped around it. Not seen one of these since the start of the war.'

'I was saving it,' Tomas whispered. Was it a crime to have sweets in wartime? He hoped not.

'I think not, boy. A Kit-Kat is something to be shared. There's two fingers left. I think you know what to do.'

Tomas surrendered his Kit-Kat. The police officer was fair. He broke off a piece for him before he swallowed the rest. 'Got to think of your teeth, boy. Chocolate is bad for your teeth.'

He suddenly looked at Tomas strangely. 'You have very good teeth. No fillings?'

'No, sir. No fillings. It's the only thing I know about my father. My mother liked his teeth.'

Detective Atkins licked the Kit-Kat and wandered back to his desk looking again at the disc. 'You can go back down now. What was the name of your science teacher, boy?'

'Atkins, sir.' Oops, he should have made up a name.

'Was it now. I can check y'know.'

Tomas heart began to race. Wouldn't take long to discover there was no Mr Atkins on staff in 1941. Only when Tomas reached the stairs did he remember his old iPod was in his bag and some pages from a recent *Sunday Times* magazine he'd ripped out a month earlier. It would clearly show the date and cause even more problems. Lucky thing the Detective had found the chocolate first.

He didn't look back. They'd never work out what the DVD was. Ever.

'Drucker?' Detective Atkins called out from his eerie.

'Yes sir?' Tomas half turned to look back up the stairs.

'Get some sleep, boy.'

The man in the cell was awake when they took him back down. He was demanding to see a doctor, which they blatantly ignored. They slammed the door shut again and locked it, plunging them back into darkness. The man lit a cigarette. Didn't even ask if he could smoke. Everyone seemed to smoke in 1941. It was disgusting.

Tomas stared at the man for a moment as the match illuminated his face. He was mesmerised by the red glow of the cigarette as the man drew on it – then blew smoke up towards the ceiling.

'Lost your papers, I suppose.' The man said. He smiled. 'Heard you saved a little girl. Must have been quite an ordeal getting out of that burning Chapel.'

The man spoke with a clipped upper-class accent. He seemed friendly enough.

Tomas shrugged, a little embarrassed.

'So many petty rules now. We say we're fighting for freedom and then they lock us up for a lack of a piece of paper.'

Tomas was concerned they were going to send him to an orphanage. How was he going to avoid that?

'You scared of the dark, son?' The man was asking.

'No. I'm just tired and hungry. Been a long day. You been here long?'

'Too long. You'd think it was a crime to survive a bombing. I was hoping my friends in London would rescue me. Perhaps they think I'm dead.' He chuckled to himself.

Tomas stared at the man in the dark a moment. 'What happened to you?'

'Same bomber that hit you, caught me. I was just walking to the post office and next thing I know I'm being hauled out of huge hole in the road. There's a tram buried in it now. They say almost everyone on board died.'

Tomas had no reply. He felt so tired. He could imagine that tram in the hole though and didn't want to. He could still see the terrified faces in the shelter and it was so hard to think that all but himself and the girl had died there.

He wondered what the time was and pulled his phone out of his pocket and switched it on. 12.05am. There was a text message waiting for him and he opened it up, the glow of the phone illuminated Tomas' face. He was oblivious of the man staring at him.

The text was from Gabby. He felt a momentary elation. If she was still able to send texts maybe he…

'Bet u got soaked. That was one amazing storm. Don't forget Saturday, Mr Duck.' xx Gabs

It must have come before he had changed time. No way a text could get through. But he was happy to have it. He felt stronger somehow and not so alone. He smiled before automatically switching it off. He didn't want the battery to die. He wondered if there would be any way to charge it in 1941. He doubted it.

'What was that?' The man asked.

'What?'

'The thing that glowed.'

'I was just checking the time.'

'What time is it?'

'12.05.'

'You carry a watch in your pocket?'

'It's a …' Tomas sighed. How was he exactly going to explain his mobile phone to anyone? 'It's a phone, it's got the time on it and email and I've got music on it and photos…'

'In your pocket?' The man asked, he sounded sceptical.

'Yes.'

'A phone, you said. A telephone. Without wires.'

'Yeah.' Tomas replied, irritated now. He wanted to sleep.

'Like Buck Rogers?'

Tomas smiled. He'd seen the old black and white Buck Rogers series on TV once. It was hilarious 1930's science fiction. They'd laughed when Mr Atkins at school had shown the spluttering space rockets, but Buck had all kinds of gadgets and even TV, he remembered. A phone in his pocket was just like Buck Rogers.

'Yeah. Just like Buck.'

'And you got a message. I saw you reading something.'

Tomas lay down. He had to sleep soon or pass out. He realised the man had been staring at him pretty hard since he knew he got a message.

'It was a message from a friend. Nothing special. It doesn't matter; I'm probably never going to see her again. Not until I'm about ninety anyway.'

'90?'

'It doesn't matter.' Tomas yawned.

'I think it does.' The man said, drawing on his cigarette again and blowing smoke up towards the ceiling. 'Everything matters, son. What's your name?'

'Tomas.'

'Not Thomas?'

'No H. It's Swedish I think.'

'Or German.'

'Or German,' Tomas conceded. He wished he hadn't checked his phone. Stupid. He hadn't been thinking.

'William Bell,' the man said.

'You're not local,' Tomas stated, as the man crushed the stub of his cigarette on the adjoining wall.

'No?'

'No,' Tomas asserted. 'Your accent …'

'And your accent?' The man asked.

'My accent?' Tomas was affronted. 'Born in Cosham hospital. I'm local.'

'Cosham?'

'It's up on the hill.'

'I see. Well, perhaps you don't recognise a Harrovian accent when you hear one.'

'Harrovian? Is that like Romania or someplace?'

The man smiled, a low disbelieving chuckle escaped his throat.

'You're a little wide of the mark. Harrow is near London. Are all you people so ignorant down here?'

Tomas had heard of Harrow. Seemed to recall something about a school rugby team that had visited.

'That phone of yours. Can you send messages to anyone?'

'You have to know their number and anyway, it doesn't work here.'

'You mean, underground.'

'No. It doesn't work here, now. I mean ever.'

'But you got a message.'

'It was sent before I got here'.

Tomas tried to get comfortable. It was hard to sleep on a wooden bench.

'But you could call someone?'

'No. Not now. Not ever. It's disconnected and like I said, you have to know their number.'

'Use the operator?'

'There's no operator. I need to sleep, really, I'm bushed.'

The man paused a moment then added, 'You're a very strange boy.'

'I'm a very tired boy. I really need to sleep…'

'How many boys do you think there are in England with a telephone in their pocket that sends messages?' Mr Bell suddenly asked.

Tomas sighed. Would this guy never shut up?

'Almost all of them, where I'm from.'

Mr Bell stood up and moved closer to Tomas. Tomas suddenly tensed.

'And where are you from Tomas, without an H?'

'Here. This school. I go to this school.'

'A school with a cell?'

'It's the storeroom in the science block, actually.'

'And all the boys in this school have these devices in their pockets and can call each other?'

'Not here. Not now. Not in 1941. No'

Mr Bell was standing right over him now. Tomas could smell a curious after-shave, quite sour.

'Not in 1941?'

'No.'

'So when? That's a very strange answer don't you think.'

Tomas sighed. Why wouldn't this guy leave him alone?

'In 1941 no one has a mobile phone, OK? I'm not from 1941. I'm from 2013. I've got an old iPhone 4 and you can send emails, instant messages, take pictures, make a video, surf the web, do anything you like on it, watch YouTube. None of this has happened yet and you won't understand any of it. I'm stuck here without ID and I don't know how to get back. OK? Satisfied?'

Weirdly Mr Bell didn't say anything at all for a moment. He moved away back to his own bench. Tomas sighed. Now this guy would think he's in a cell with a crazy kid who thinks he's a time traveller.

'Do you know a Mr Wells?' The man suddenly asked.

'H G Wells? Sure he wrote *The Time Machine* and stuff. He even lived in Portsmouth for a few years. Hated it. My English teacher says so, anyway.'

Mr Bell smiled to himself.

'So you come from the future, Tomas.'

Tomas closed his eyes and tried to sleep again. 'Yes. I didn't ask to. It just happened.'

'Just like that.'

'I was having nightmares about being buried alive after bombing and ...

'But suddenly it was real.' Mr Bell interjected. 'Not uncommon. I have been bombed out of three homes in the last year.

'All I know is that one moment I was getting new specs fitted in 2013 and the next I was running for the shelter in the middle of a bloody war in 1941. No one will ever believe me, but it's true. I swear.'

'I believe you.'

Tomas looked back at where Mr Bell was sitting. He could just make out his shape in the darkness.

'Why?'

'You have a phone in your pocket.'

'I could be lying.'

'A liar would not have so casually checked his phone as if it were the most normal thing in the world.'

'It is.'

'Quite.'

So, because I have a phone in my pocket you believe I'm from the future.'

'What do you know about England in 1941?'

Tomas sighed. He tried to think of the war films he'd seen. He drew a sudden blank. He realised he knew very little about 1941. Or 1942. Or anything. Had he remembered nothing?

'The Germans invade Russia.' It simply popped into his head.

Mr Bell looked at him sceptically.

'You think the Germans will attack Russia, their ally?'

'Ally? I didn't know they were allies. I thought they were communists. Anyway the German army attacks and...'

'You know this how?'

'I can't remember anything else about 1941. Except it's Hitler's biggest mistake.'

'Mistake?'

'They lose. The Germans are beaten back by the Russians. I remember now. It's like Napoleon who was turned back at Moscow, that I did study in history. Same thing happens. They don't prepare for winter, guns freeze, men and horses freeze. Stalin was even told the Germans were going to invade but he thought it was British disinformation.'

'What of the war in Europe?' Mr Bell was listening closely now.

'We win. I have to go to sleep now, really. That's what's so stupid. All these people being killed and bombed and it's all for nothing. We win.'

'It isn't possible, Tomas. Germany controls all of Europe, England has nothing, it is powerless, led by a drunken fool. Germany controls the seas…'

Tomas yawned. 'We win. Germany loses. That's the main thing.'

'The U-Boats? Surely England will starve. Nothing will get through.'

This movie Tomas had remembered. 'No, we beat them too, eventually. Believe me. Germany will lose. England bombs the hell out of Berlin too.'

Mr Bell made sucking noises with his mouth. He didn't seem to believe Tomas.

'And when does this war end?'

'1945.'

'1945! Four more years? Impossible.' He seemed almost angry about it.

'We have to fight for every inch, but Hitler finally kills himself in Berlin and its all over. Millions die, over fifty million world-wide.'

Mr Bell suddenly laughed.

'A nice game, Tomas. A nice game. You are a very patriotic boy. Fifty million people, that would be absurd.'

'It's the truth. No game. The Germans kill six million Jews in the death camps and…'

'Enough. Death camps? Pure fantasy. There will be no attack on the Soviets. Hitler will probably finish off England this summer and then he will control all of Europe. He has no need to attack the Russians. They are poor; they cannot compete. No one will help Stalin.'

Tomas yawned. 'I'm just telling you what I remember, that's all. You don't have to believe me. I just want to get some sleep.'

'How can you think of sleep when there is so much at stake?' Mr

Bell demanded to know.

'I can sleep because I know that England wins. You should be happy. Not many people here seem to think that will happen.'

'I can believe you are from the future, Tomas. But I find it hard to believe Germany will not win this war. Or that it will last four more years. That is too fantastic. You should have a conversation with Professor Wylie in South Kensington. I think he would be most interested to meet you.'

Tomas closed his eyes and thought of Gabby. Felt her hand in his for a brief moment and saw her look of concern. He realised he missed her – he would always miss her.

The next thing Tomas registered was the door opening and the room flooding with light. He realised that he had been asleep. His mouth felt dry and he was stiff and awkward on the bench.

'Right. People from London to see you, William Bell,' a new cop stated, bring out handcuffs. 'You're to come with me.'

Tomas struggled up onto his elbows and watched as the tall Mr Bell walked toward the cop, hands outstretched to be cuffed. He glanced at Tomas as he passed by.

'You see how they treat a gentlemen, son. When you misplace a piece of paper, freedom is already lost.'

'No talking.'

The cop looked at Tomas a moment and then checked a piece of paper in his hands. 'Tomas Drucker?'

'Yes sir?'

'They'll want to talk to you as well, after.'

'Me, sir?'

'Got them all excited with that disc of yours. MI5 men are looking at it now.'

'MI5?' Tomas felt his heart lurch. MI5 existed in 1941? Bloody hell. How was he going to explain that? They'd soon find there was no Mr Atkins at his school in 1941, or Tomas Drucker, for that matter. He was screwed.

The door closed and was locked again. Why had they handcuffed Mr Bell? Just for losing his papers? Made no sense. Tomas closed his eyes again. He still needed more sleep.

It seemed like just a minute later when the door opened again. A man walked in and shone a torch in Tomas's face.

'Wake up, lad. I need to know what you and Herr Belhapt discussed.'

Tomas opened his eyes and then looked away, the torch had him confused. He was exhausted he realised.

'Huh?'

'Belhapt. The German who was in this room with you. What did you discuss?'

'Who? What?' Tomas sat up, his back hurt like hell. 'There wasn't any German in here. Some English toff. Mr Bell.'

'Mr Bell is Wilhelm Belhapt. He's a suspected German spy. Now what the hell did you two discuss? And what is this?'

The man held up the DVD disc and waved it in Tomas' face.

'German spy?' Tomas had a sudden terrible sinking feeling.

'Get up, lad. Come with me. There's some people who want to talk to you.'

Tomas stood awkwardly, his left leg badly bruised.

He felt a wash of guilt flood over him. He'd just told incredible military secrets to a German spy; told him that England would win, that he knew the Germans were going to invade Russia. What else had he said? He couldn't believe he had been so stupid. He'd even heard the man had a slight accent. Harrovian; my foot.

He stumbled; the man caught him.

'You can sleep after we talk, lad. I know you've been through the mill, but we need to know what that man said to you.'

They both heard the air-raid siren start up.

'Damn'.

'Stay here. You're underground. You should be safe. I'll be back in a jiffy.'

With that the man was gone again, leaving the door slightly ajar. Tomas thought of escaping but sat back down on the bench again and lay down. He needed sleep, must have sleep.

The bombers came in – invaded his sleep. His old nightmare took over. He knew the routine now. In ten minutes he'd be up to his neck in rubble. The ground shook, the walls buckled, dust fell, men shouted, a woman screamed.

Tomas heard nothing and heard everything. It was just like his dream.

And then everything was quiet. He didn't hear the all clear. He didn't hear anything. He was asleep and slept for four straight hours.

The door was still open when he woke. Tomas shuffled to the corridor. All was quiet. He saw that there was a lot of broken plaster and pools of water in the corridor. More water was pouring down the stairs.

He needed to go to the bathroom. He mounted the stairs and instantly knew why the elegant Victorian bathroom wasn't in his future. It had been blown to smithereens. Most of the building had gone with it. His school was nothing but a pile of rubble. A dead man lay across some bricks, his head stoved in.

There was no sign of Detective Atkins who had interrogated him, or of Mr Bell, who, he guiltily recalled, was a German spy. He still needed a bathroom. He needed food. He needed home and Gabby. He felt totally lost without her.

He wandered out onto the street. No one stopped him. An ambulance was standing there but no one attended it. He could see several buildings were on fire and some people were standing in the road in dressing gowns watching and weeping.

He took a leak in the alley behind the school. Walking through the short cut to Marmion Road, he came across a dead boy. He looked perfect. Not a mark on him. He was wearing pyjamas. At first he thought the boy was asleep on the path, but he was most definitely dead. He wore his identity card around his neck suspended by some string. Albert Gerald Pitt, aged 12. Tomas paused a moment, looking around him to see who might be watching. He desperately needed an ID card, but no way anyone would believe he was 12, they would know he had stolen it. A car engine started up in a nearby driveway. Tomas left the boy to be found by others and quickly moved on. He wondered if the German spy William Bell was dead, buried under rubble back there in his school. He hoped so. Couldn't believe he'd told him so many secrets. He would have never guessed he was German. Ever.

He wandered onto the road and discovered he was standing near the chapel he'd been dug out of the day before. He needed food. He needed to find someone who would believe him, believe he was from the future. He knew how it ended. He knew some of the mistakes the British had made. He could stop this. He could make a difference. He could save lives.

'Going somewhere, Tomas?'

Mr Bell. The German spy, real name Belhapt, came out of nowhere and grabbed him by the arm and twisted it behind his back, pushed him towards a waiting black official looking car and forced him inside.

A woman grabbed him and held him fast as Belhapt got in and started the engine.

'This is the boy?' The woman asked. Tomas noticed with a shock she wore a plain grey military style uniform. If she knew Belhapt, she was a traitor.

'Yes. I think they are going to find him quite fascinating in London.' He held up Tomas' phone a moment.

'How do you switch this on, boy? I want to see it working.'

Tomas realised that he not only had his phone, but his bag was lying on the front seat as well. He looked out of the window as they drove past a corner shop and saw a poster on a wall.

'Careless talk costs lives'.

He appreciated the irony. He'd come back in time and he was already England's greatest traitor. He suddenly felt sick.

'You're going to be a hero, Tomas. You're going to save England and shorten the war. That's why you've been sent back, my boy. You can save fifty million lives.'

5

The Sweet Shop on the Corner

Gabby stared at Tomas's house, or the space where it used to be. She looked up and down the street to make sure it was Janoway Road. Gone were all the trees save one gnarly beech tree, barely alive. Rows of mostly black VW Bugs were parked on one side, which was strange enough, but in front of her was a huge shabby concrete block of flats. It was brutal. There were more squat blocks like it mushrooming elsewhere in the city. Sure it was good people had somewhere to live, but did the buildings have to be so hostile?

She turned away. If Tomas's home didn't exist, she was beginning to wonder whether Tomas still existed. It was impossible that so much had changed overnight, but it had, she was staring at a whole different city. The skyline was different, she realised. It was disorientating. She began to worry that she had no home to go to either. Yet, surely she had woken up in one?

As she walked away she noted that a few quaint Edwardian homes had survived on the other side of the street, and still had their pretty stained glass upper windows and eyebrows over the front doors. Some people were peering at her from behind their curtains. Well, let them watch, had they never seen a schoolgirl before?

Something was very wrong. A VW drove by, noisy and smelly; she wasn't used to cars belching fumes, and coughed. Tomas would have liked it though. Was always going on about one day owning a VW Campervan and driving them down to Cornwall for a summer. Over her parent's dead bodies, of course, but it was a cool little fantasy they shared. But now she was concerned she'd never see him again.

The rain had finally stopped. She felt warm in the afternoon sun, hoped this was the start of summer at last. She stopped at the corner of her street and stared with surprise. The corner shop was open. It had never been open in the whole time she had lived there and now here it was and the window was lined with jars of sweets and advertising Milka Chocolate. It looked cute and welcoming. She went in.

Gabby paused at the door, inhaling the sweet scent of old fashioned sugary sweets, and noticed it sold magazines too.

'Come in Gabriella, come in, come in, where have you been? I missed you.'

The old woman behind the counter was smiling at her, as if she knew her and indeed, her face did seem sort of familiar.

'Good afternoon, Tante Greta.'

'Ja, you'll be wanting your magazine. I've kept it for you.'

Gabriella stepped towards the counter and the woman produced a copy of 'Berlin-Mädchen'. It looked to be a fashion and gossip magazine in German and English. The fashions were hilarious and the skirts long. She looked into the old woman's face.

'I take this?'

'I put on your father's account. Isn't it wonderful about his medal? You must be so proud of him.

'Medal?' My father gets a medal for being the worst father of the year? She was thinking.

'The Literature prize. His history book. You are lucky to have such a father. They have translated it into German. Professor Lamb will be famous.'

Gabby's head was spinning. Her father had always been interested in history, but this was the first she knew about a book, or that he paid for her magazines. She hadn't spoken to him in almost a year since he'd moved out to live with a girl half his age.

'Well,' she said, at last. 'Of course I'm proud.'

The shopkeeper beamed at her. 'And you'll be looking forward to the class trip to London. It's a privilege to go to London. I haven't been there since the …'

'Class trip?' This woman knew more about her life than she did. How was this possible?

'The Imperial Museum of Culture in South Kensington. It is so beautiful. I remember it before it was renamed, of course, but …' she sighed. 'I was there with Franz. Ich vermisse meinen Mann.'

Gabby understood; suddenly remembered that the shopkeeper's husband had been killed. A riot. She'd been twelve then. Some drunks had beaten him when Munich beat Portsmouth at the Euro-Soccer match. It had been a terrible scandal.

Gabriella somehow knew the old woman was called Greta.

'Which city are you from, Tante Greta?' She called her aunt because it wasn't polite to use the first name.

'Bayreuth.' she answered with pride. 'The birthplace of Richard

Wagner and Field Marshall Robert Ritter von Greim. I remember when I was young listening to the orchestra and choirs as they rehearsed for the Wagner festivals. How I longed to be in that choir. Ach, but not to be, not to be.'

Gabriella glanced at the Bavarian calendar on the wall. May 9th. She suddenly felt overwhelmed by the knowledge that she knew this woman, had *always* known this woman, and yet was meeting her for the first time.

'I am sorry about your husband, meine Tante. You must miss him working here all alone now.'

Greta nodded. 'We came here on the Fuhrer's orders in 1960. He was the Aufseher, the overseer of the Integrated forces. An important job. He loved his job, y'know, bringing everyone together. To be murdered like that. Over a soccer match.'

'Stupid,' Gabriella agreed. She had no interest in soccer at all.

'They shot them all, of course, and closed the pub. I was pleased about that. Justice has to be seen to be done. Gott Sei Dank.'

Gabriella hadn't known that. Shooting them all sounded pretty drastic.

'Thanks for keeping my magazine for me,' she said, backing away.

'You give my regards to Professor Lamb, Gabriella. The whole street is proud of him, I am sure.'

Gabriella made it to the door, the bell pinged as she opened it, just like something from an old movie.

She was keen to go home now. Scared about what other changes she would find. Was her father back? At least he was still a professor. And what of her mother? Was she still at the law office? She realised that she hadn't seen her mother in the morning. She'd been in such a rush to get to school she'd skipped breakfast.

She was relieved to discover her street was much the same. The trees were in their last remnants of pink blossom now, still lining the pavement. She loved this time of year when the street looked so pretty. The houses were all neat and tidy Edwardian homes – no one had built any apartment buildings here, but she noted quite a few Wartburgs, some strange old-fashioned looking BMW's and a fancy Mercedes 300 Sl. Not much changed there really.

'Hi, Gabby.'

Gabriella glanced at a girl cleaning her front door window. Madeline. She'd never said a word to her in her whole existence and now she was all smiles, like they were old friends.

'Oh hi, Maddy.'

'Good to hear about your father, huh. Makes the whole street proud.'

'Yeah, sure. I'm proud,' she replied. Still couldn't make sense as to why he'd get a medal for writing a book.

She finally got home. She had no key, she realised, and it wasn't under the geraniums (which weren't there either). No matter, the door wasn't locked. That was crazy. Who didn't lock the front door? Anyone could walk in and take stuff.

'I'm home,' Gabby yelled. Usually only Stagger answered, her black and white cat. He always waited for her to come home 'cause he knew he'd get a treat at this time of the day.

Stagger stirred at the top of the stairs and mewed.

'You look sleepy… wow… what happened here?'

Gabby was staring at the floral wallpaper that filled the hallway. It was shockingly colourful and she certainly hadn't noticed it being there when she'd left in the morning.

She sat down on the hall chair and removed her shoes as was the custom in the house and stared at the walls. Couldn't get over the pinkness of it all. There was a distinct smell of baking going on too. Some burglar must have walked in and started cooking, 'cause one thing was for sure, her mother couldn't cook to save her life. Everything came from Marks and Sparks ready made. The most she would do was peel off the plastic before micro-waving.

Her mother appeared at the top of the stairs folding a blanket. She smiled.

'Hello, dear.' She was looking down at Stagger, who was now making his way down the stairs. 'He's been waiting for you. We both got concerned, you're usually home by now.'

Gabriella stared at her with astonishment. Her mother, the feminist, was wearing a dress. A floral dress with pleats. Good grief, her mother had legs!

Stagger wanted to be picked up and cuddled and she obliged. He put a paw to her face and she tickled his head (she knew he liked that), carrying him towards the kitchen. He'd want his tid-bit.

'I'm not late. You're home early,' Gabby called out. 'Who's been baking. I can smell something really …'

She entered the kitchen and stood astonished. The kitchen table had three fresh loaves cooling, some scones and a sponge cake. They all smelled fantastically delicious.

Her mother entered the kitchen behind her, smoothing her hair.

'I bake every Thursday, you know I do.'

'You bake bread? No way. You don't even eat bread, you're allergic to wheat.'

Her mother was smiling and filling the kettle with water.

'Nonsense, dear. Now don't go eating it all. There's a couple of buns in the oven that should be ready for you now. Don't burn yourself, Gabby. '

'Buns? You defrosted buns?'

'I made them. You know I did.'

Gabby was staring at the Aga. They had an Aga. A real nice warm kitchen all the time Aga and the whole house smelled of freshly made bread. This was like heaven. It couldn't be her house. Had to be she had wandered into the wrong home. Amazing.

'Wash your hands, dear.'

Gabby set the cat down and looked for the packet of nibbles. There was nothing, but Stagger ran to his dish and found something to eat anyway, so he wasn't aggrieved. She went to the sink and washed her hands.

Her mother lifted the round lid on the Aga and put the kettle on the huge ring to boil.

'When did we get the Aga?'

'Just after you were born. Your grandfather insisted. I told him then that he had to hump the anthracite from the cellar but I must say he was right, it does keep the whole house warm.

'Anthracite?'

'The coal. You've carried enough of it up from the cellar to know what it is, Gabriella. Are you all right, dear, you seem very distracted.'

'I need those buns. We have jam?'

'In the fridge.'

Gabriella stared at the fridge. It had to be the same fridge they used on Noah's Ark, it was so old fashioned. Bosch. German. It figured.

She wiped her hands, found the jar of home made raspberry jam and sat down at the table as her mother took two hot buns out of the oven. This was perfect. Wouldn't do anything for her waistline but who could say no to two freshly home baked bread buns and jam? No one. That's who.

'We have tea. Your father met someone who was importing tea from Ceylon and we finally have some real tea.'

'Ceylon?'

Her mother looked at her with concern. 'The island at the bottom of India. I'm worried, Gabriella, don't they teach you anything at that school?'

Gabby smeared jam into the inside of the buns and took a big bite. It was like she'd never eaten a bun before. It tasted amazing.

'Good buns, Mum.'

Her mother smiled, pleased to be appreciated, surprised to be appreciated possibly.

Gabby noticed the microwave has disappeared. As had the tumble dryer. She wondered what else had gone.

'Oh yeah, what's this about a medal? Greta at the corner shop was saying how wonderful it was Dad had won a medal. How do you get a medal for a book?'

Her mother was beaming. 'Isn't it wonderful? He called me from Exeter. He's giving a lecture there tonight. He'll get ten thousand pounds and an invitation to speak in the Berlin Conference. They are doing a German translation, Gabriella. It will be sold right across Europe.'

Gabby looked at her mother and saw how happy she was and wondered if she had forgotten she'd thrown her father out of the house a year before when she'd discovered he was sleeping with one of his university students.

'Oh and I nearly forgot, I have a class trip to London tomorrow.'

'I know, dear. I'll make sandwiches. You have to be at the school for seven –thirty. You're so lucky. I haven't been there in years.'

'It's not exactly far, mum. You could go up there anytime by train.'

'Perhaps we'll get a permit now your father has won a medal.'

'Permit?' She couldn't figure out why you'd need a permit to visit the capital.

'Visitor permits are rationed, you know that. There has been such a strict curfew since the troubles. You have to have a job there before they'll let you in.'

Gabriella frowned. 'What about tourism? All those people going to see the Queen and the museums?'

Her mother looked away as if she had been reminded of something.

'You know very well that the King lives in Toronto and the museums have been closed for a decade now. You're so lucky to get to the opening of the Cultural Museum. It's a real privilege, Gabriella.'

'The King lives in Toronto? What happened to the Queen?'

Her mother frowned. 'How could you forget? The Royals were

exiled by Prime Minister Mosley, just before he was assassinated by the Free English. Don't they teach you anything?'

Gabriella felt like she ought to know, but everything seemed new to her today. 'If there was a rebellion, why don't I know about it?'

Her mother sighed. 'Perhaps they aren't teaching it. Perhaps they don't want you to know, but I can tell you what happened. They didn't accept the peace of 1942. Fled to Wales, then Canada. They came back and fought a guerrilla war against the government. They tried to seize power in London in 1968 just when the Fuhrer died and they were crushed. In the end, people chose peace, dear. Your father must have explained this to you. It's all in his book.'

Gabriella suddenly remembered the book in her satchel. His book '*The Birth of New Europe 1942-2000*'. He'd won a prize for *that* book.

'When will father be home?'

'You'll see him Saturday. He's taking you to the launch of the new Dreamliner Flying Boat. You are so lucky, Gabriella. It's a marvel. Jet turbines, a flying boat that can take over one hundred passengers all the way to Kapstad in New Afrika in just twelve hours.'

Gabriella nearly laughed, but she could see her mother was serious and quite proud of this fact.

'One hundred passengers to where? Kapstad? Is that in Austria or something?'

'New Afrika, darling. The Germans have expanded so much there. Your father was thinking we might emigrate there. At least they allow English to be spoken alongside German. There is a position opening up in Kapstad University.'

'South Africa is German now?'

'You're too young to remember the terrible war.'

'No one mentioned it to me.'

'Well it wasn't nice. Ethnic cleansing is never nice. I'm not going to talk about it now. Your father can explain.'

Gabriella finished her buns. There was so much to take in; her head was dizzy with all this.

'Mum? Do you remember my friend Tomas?

Her mother looked at her blankly.

'Tomas Drucker, Duck? He ate with us last Christmas. He helped you choose the Christmas tree? I nursed him all winter after he broke his leg?'

Her mother laughed lightly but was definitely confused. 'No dear, I don't remember him. Are you sure?'

'You gave him your old iPhone. He was really happy.'

'A phone? She looked puzzled.'

Gabriella searched her pocket. Her iPhone wasn't there. She felt a rising panic.

'Phone?' her mother queried again. 'Are you sure you're all right, darling? Perhaps you have been studying too hard.'

Gabriella was annoyed now. So everything had changed, but *she* still remembered Tomas, *she* still remembered Africa was run by Africans and *she* remembered she owned an iPhone, goddamnit.

'I have to write a letter,' her mother suddenly announced, getting up from the table. 'Let Stagger out. He's been in for hours.'

Gabby automatically went to the back door and shushed a reluctant cat out. She saw Tomas's jacket hanging on the hook. He'd left it there the day before his accident and it had stayed there ever since.

She suddenly thought of something and ran back to the hallway to find her satchel. She rummaged through it, pulling out gloves, heavy books, her empty sandwich box from two days before and then … one perfect iPhone. It still existed. In this weird changed world her phone still existed.

She switched it on, disappointed to find no new message from Tomas or get a signal, but absolutely relieved it was real.

She walked into the study where her mother was preparing to write a letter. Gabriella was surprised to see so many black and white pictures of herself with her father and some with her mother plastered all over the walls.

'Are you sure you don't remember Tomas?'

She shoved an image of Tomas under her mother's nose, and then pressed play. He began to speak.

'Hi Mrs Lamb. I hope you had a great birthday. Gabby is a saint. Please treat her especially nice, OK; I couldn't exist up here without her. See you when my leg mends. 'Bye.'

Her mother frowned looking at the video of Tomas, then up at her daughter and then at the phone.

'Where on earth did you get this, Gabby? Who was that boy? I hope this thing isn't American. You know American technology isn't permitted. You must get rid of it. Think of your father. You mustn't disgrace him. Especially now he's won the medal.'

'American technology isn't permitted?' Gabby queried, incredulous.

'You know it isn't. There's a trade boycott of all American products and films. Do not show that 'toy' to anyone, you understand. Have some respect for the laws of the land.'

'Toy?'

Gabriella stared at her mother with total astonishment. First she bakes bread and wears a dress, now she obeys rules and hates phones. Who was this person? Not the mother who raised her, for sure.

She hastily switched off the iPhone and turned away.

'I have homework.'

Gabriella resolved to keep the memory of Tomas alive any way she could and to keep her phone secret.

'Supper is at eight,' Her mother called out, as she climbed the stairs. 'Dr Allan is coming with his daughter Heidi.'

Gabriella had no idea who this doctor and his daughter were but she didn't care. What she wanted to know was what the hell had happened, to her life and to Tomas. That was the burning issue of the evening.

6

The Tea Room of Terror

The woman was driving now. Tomas had discovered that this was her job; driving military people around. He'd been hoping for checkpoints on the way to London – anything to stop them, give him a chance to escape, but even when they came across one at Godalming, they were waved through unchecked. After all, they were in an official military vehicle. They weren't to know it was being driven by a traitor and a spy.

The journey took hours. He'd forgotten motorways weren't even invented yet. They crawled through narrow country lanes, passed through Liphook and Haslemere – places he'd seen before, but never like this. Everything looked so shabby; there was no other word for it. At Guildford the roads were a total mess – the result of a bombing raid a few nights earlier. The familiar landmark Cathedral on Stag Hill was just a brick stump covered in scaffolding. At first he thought it must have been bombed, but then he realised it was probably still under construction.

There was a moment when he thought he could escape. They had to fill up and the woman driver was fretting about finding her petrol coupons and Tomas tried to open the back door handle with his teeth, but it proved too difficult and then Belhapt clouted him one and hissed, 'Move another inch and I will cut off your nose'.

Tomas sank back in the seat, resigned to his fate.

Four hours later they were finally approaching London. Tomas was starving, terrified about what this German spy intended to do with him, and he was nursing bruises where he'd been thumped. His wrists were sore and the blood constricted where he'd been tied. Tomas was puzzled that this German was able to travel so easily and so confidently in England, but the fact that he could pass for an English gentleman was part of that he guessed. The police in London probably didn't even know he had escaped yet. Tomas realised that everything worked very slowly in this time.

Belhapt still had possession of his phone and his bag with all its contents. The cutting from *Sunday Times* Magazine had the date on it. It was all the confirmation Belhapt needed that Tomas was indeed from the future, as if the phone wasn't enough. Tomas had no idea what the man was going to do with him. All he could recall now with some feeling of guilt was Gabriella's father telling him that 'a little knowledge is a dangerous thing, Tomas,' and how bloody true that was.

He knew he had to figure a way out of there. So far only Belhapt knew Germany was going to lose the war, and the woman driver, of course, who didn't say much at all. She didn't look the type to believe anything a kid told her anyway. He was hoping the German engineers wouldn't be able to make the phone work. Without a network connection perhaps they wouldn't figure it out. But there was seventy years of technology packed into that phone and if they did understand any of it, could it help them win? He didn't know for sure whether the phone or all the things he knew about the war was the most dangerous thing. He knew, once they started to torture him, that he'd remember a lot more than he could right now. His memory would come back. He had a near photographic memory. He only had to think of a scene in a movie and he could replay it in his mind. He had to keep that from Belhapt at all costs.

Tomas guessed they'd torture him to test what he knew. He'd seen enough war movies to know how ruthless they'd be.

The car slowed to go around a huge bomb crater. He could see a building smouldering in the distance, a smoke trail flowing over the suburbs ahead. He saw some British fighter planes go overhead, surprised at just how noisy they were. He knew they had to be approaching London proper, the sky was full of barrage balloons. The skyline was completely different he realised, no tall buildings. None. This was the London of his history books, smaller, lower and pockmarked with bomb craters and smashed buildings.

Slowing through Putney, the stink of sewage from damaged sewers filled the car and nearly made him sick. St Mary's church by the bridge was bombed and traffic was single file over the bridge that had suffered damage too.

'We'll go straight to South Kensington to the rendezvous point. Professor Wylie will join us there.' Belhapt told the woman.

'What will we say if we're stopped?' She asked.

'We won't be stopped and if we are…' he turned to stare of Tomas, 'the boy will say nothing…if he wants to live. You understand Master Drucker?'

Tomas said nothing. He squirmed in his seat, testing the bonds that held him. They were way too tight; his hands had gone completely dead. He knew he had to get his phone back somehow. If he could just open it up and lose the sim card that might help, swallow it even. They'd never be able to make it work then. Never.

It was dark by the time they reached South Kensington. Tomas couldn't get used to the all the buildings being blacked out and the absence of streetlights.

The woman pulled up across the road from a place called Café Hermitage. Tomas realised with some surprise that they had arrived at their destination. Belhapt was getting out.

He came around to the rear door and let Tomas out.

'Don't even think of running, boy. You'll be a hero now. The boy who stopped the war.'

'I'll do no such thing. You'll lose. Nothing can change that. Nothing.'

But Tomas was no longer sure that was true.

'10,000 volts under your fingernails says you're wrong, my boy. You'll tell us everything you know. I guarantee it.'

Tomas blinked. 10,000 volts! Surely that would blow out his brains? How many volts did they use to electrocute someone in an electric chair? He knew an ordinary plug carried 240 volts and that was bad enough. He remembered getting shocked by the toaster once when he turned a tap on at the same time as touching the toaster when it was on. He'd been flung across the kitchen and blown all the fuses.

10,000 volts would definitely kill him.

He resolved to say nothing, no matter what they did to him. But at the back of his mind he was thinking that he knew way too much. If he had any courage at all, he realised, he should have thrown himself out of the car.

'Thinking about escape, Tomas? Put it out of your mind. You shall not escape.'

They had stopped in Thurloe Street outside some fancy houses. The woman driver – whose name Tomas had failed to learn – wound down her window.

'I have to get back to the Ministry. I'll see you tomorrow, Wilhelm.'

'Don't be late,' Belhapt told her. He looked at Tomas. 'Get a message to Professor Wylie as soon as you can. He knows where to come.'

She nodded and drove off. Thomas noted the name of the car. A Hupmobile. He'd never heard of it. He couldn't see a number plate.

'Ministry? She works for the Government?' Tomas exclaimed. They had a traitor in the heart of British government and they didn't know.

Belhapt smiled. 'You see, Tomas, you still think England will win this war? We're embedded everywhere. The Pro-Peace Movement people are in Government, MI5, the police, and the Army. Just waiting for the right moment.' He untied the rope around Tomas's wrists; as blood began to flow freely again, the pain was agonising.

Belhapt turned him around and began walking towards Café Hermitage. Number 20. Tomas wanted to remember everything in case he escaped and could report this nest of spies. He looked up and saw barrage balloons suspended in the sky. They were supposed to snag bombers as they flew over London but he knew from the films he'd seen that they weren't high enough or effective.

'Don't worry, Tomas, you will be fed before we torture you. I know you must be hungry. The chef is Prussian, old school, trained in the Kaiser's kitchens and a very good cook'

A warden appeared from nowhere, checking that everyone had their lights blacked out in every house.

'Evening.'

'Evening to you, warden.'

Tomas felt Belhapt's hand on his neck and his fingers squeeze a little. Tomas staggered a moment.

'The boy all right?'

'Measles, we think. He has a fever.'

The warden pulled a face. 'Don't want to be having that, lad, can make you right sick.'

The restaurant door opened and Belhapt pushed Tomas inside quickly, nodding at the warden before closing and locking the restaurant door.

It was dark; the man who'd opened the door carried a lamp. Tomas noticed some people were eating by candlelight – they stared at him with annoyance and even though he knew he could shout 'spy', he had no idea if these people were friend or foe.

'To the kitchen, Tomas.' Belhapt whispered in his ear. 'Say nothing.'

Tomas could smell food cooking, the spices in the air made his eyes smart. He was pushed into the kitchen where an older man was stirring a pot and a young boy was cleaning dishes.

Belhapt turned to Tomas. 'Gunther will get you something in a minute. Don't even think of making a fuss. The boy is deaf, he can't hear anything.'

'I need to…' Tomas pointed towards the WC.

'You and me both. Go. Keep the door open. The window is nailed shut.'

Tomas went in – it stank but he was beginning not to care. He needed to pee badly. The toilet was ancient and indeed the window was nailed shut with a plank of wood. The glass had gone, the result of bombing probably.

'Hurry up,' Belhapt barked from the kitchen.

Tomas washed his hands. He could barely make himself out in the mirror, but he knew he looked a mess.

Belhapt made him sit on a kitchen chair when he came out and went in after him. Tomas was left staring at Bismarck's chef and the deaf boy who slyly glanced at him from the sink.

'You like goulash?' Gunther asked.

Tomas had never tasted it but it smelled good, whatever it was.

'I'll eat anything.'

Gunther nodded and began to prepare two large bowls and cut some hunks of grey bread. He saw Tomas looking at the bread anxiously. He tossed a smaller piece to Tomas, who wolfed it down. He had never been as hungry as this, ever.

He heard a toilet flush and Belhapt came out of the WC, shaking water off his hands.

'When will the diners go, Gunther?'

'Soon. It's quiet tonight.'

'Let's eat. We're waiting for Professor Wylie. He's going to be very interested in this boy, I think.'

Gunther didn't know why nor did he ask questions. He was a chef. He served up some goulash in their bowls. He gave Belhapt a glass of white wine to go with his serving.

Tomas fell on his food. For all he knew this was to be his last meal. He'd need to be stronger to resist torture. His brain hurt, he wondered if he could remember anything.

He looked around the kitchen; there were Russian images, empty Russian bottles of Vodka. He didn't understand why Germans were gathered here at all.

Belhapt was looking at Tomas. 'Tell me, Tomas, do you think anyone misses you?'

Tomas chewed on some meat. 'My friend, Gabriella.'

'Not your mother?'

'No.'

Belhapt frowned as he ate. He didn't really like that answer.

'You know you have been missing for over seventy years by this time. It may be no one remembers you at all.'

Tomas ate. Tried not to think about that or the idea of never seeing Gabriella again.

Belhapt looked up at Gunther and pointed at Tomas.

'This boy's from the future, Gunther. He thinks England is going to win the war. What do you say to that?'

Gunther laughed. 'The future? Tell me young man, what is the most popular auto in the future.'

Tomas shrugged. 'Volkswagen, I guess.'

Gunther hooted with laughter.

'Not Morris? Not Austin?'

Tomas looked at him blankly. 'Never heard of them.'

Gunther looked at Belhapt and smiled.

'What is the most popular food?' Belhapt asked.

'Hamburger.' Tomas replied.

'I think perhaps England didn't win, Herr Belhapt.' He turned to go back to the restaurant interior. 'I must attend to my customers…'

He left. Belhapt was looking quite thoughtful.

'Volkswagen?'

Tomas nodded. 'They own Porsche now and Skoda and more'

'Porsche? Ferdinand Porsche is my friend; the Volkswagen is his design. He will be happy to know this.'

Tomas wondered if this was secret knowledge. He guessed not. No matter what he said, it wasn't going to stop Volkswagen making good cars.

'This is excellent goulash.'

Tomas looked at him. 'Why do you speak English so well?'

Herr Belhapt broke some more bread and dipped it into his food.

'My father sent me to Harrow. Then I went to Cambridge. Studied philosophy. A German discipline, you understand. Immanuel Kant, Arthur Schopenhauer, Friedrich Nietzsche, perhaps you have heard of them? Are they studied in your school.'

Tomas smiled. 'I've heard of Nietzsche. I don't think anything good.'

'What do they teach you in school in the future?'

Tomas thought that a good question.

'ICT, that's basically how to use Facebook and social media, which is like impossible to explain. Sex and Relationships, which is a joke. Citizenship which is like boring crap. Science, which could be interesting if we were allowed to blow stuff up, except since the health and safety Gestapo we only watch boring DVDs of other people blowing stuff up. Maths, which is too hard, English language too boring, Gym, self-explanatory. I used to be on the swim team until I broke my leg.'

Herr Belhapt looked at Tomas with astonishment.

'No art? No history? Music? Culture? What kind of education is this?'

'I take history. The rest is extra and my scholarship wouldn't cover more.'

'You used the word, Gestapo.'

Tomas grinned, wiping the bottom of his dish with the remains of his bread.

'People who prevent you from having fun. You should know all about it, Wilhelm. You invented them.'

Belhapt digested this, and how Tomas had called him Wilhelm. He thought of another question.

'How many people live in London, Tomas?'

'Now?'

'No, in your time.'

Tomas shrugged. 'Eight million, I suppose. I don't think I ever learned the actual number.'

'Still the biggest city in the world?'

Tomas laughed. 'God, no. That would be Sao Paulo. Gabby's Dad says its got 23 million. No way would I want to live in a city that big.'

Belhapt was taken aback. 'Twenty-three million in one city? Ridiculous. You could not have such a large city.'

Tomas shrugged. 'I read somewhere that Greater Tokyo would have 37 million in 2020.'

'Weren't you the boy who told me that fifty million people die in this war? Now you tell me that cities will have many millions. Perhaps you don't know the future at all, Tomas. Perhaps you are just a liar and we should kill you now and have done with you.'

Tomas looked at him. The man studied philosophy at Cambridge. How could he work for the Nazis? Made no sense at all.

'The war slowed it down, that's all. There's over seven billion people in the world now.'

'Seven billion? Seven billion people?' Belhapt looked surprised.

'It passed that number in 2011.' He wished he'd never mentioned these numbers now; it seemed to horrify the man.

'And they all eat?'

Tomas shrugged. 'Some starve. We have climate change. The weather's changing. Crops fail. But most people eat, I guess.'

'How many people do you think are in the world now, Tomas, in 1941?'

Tomas pushed his plate away. He needed a glass of water.

'Half that?'

'Two point one billion, I am reliably informed. There is absolutely no way that seven billion people can fit on this earth. It must be hell. Unless they live on Mars or…

'No one lives on Mars or the Moon. They live on Earth. Did I mention the weather is changing? Getting warmer. It rains a lot now in England, or sometimes not at all.'

Belhapt wasn't happy.

'You see, Tomas. You said you wouldn't tell me about the future, but now I know so much already. A painless process, huh? Perhaps we won't have to torture you after all.'

Tomas blanched. Now he wished he hadn't eaten. He suddenly felt quite sick.

'The phone,' Belhapt pulled it out of his jacket pocket and put it on the table. 'Switch it on. Show me how it works.'

Tomas stared at his phone. This was what he really wanted. If Germany had this technology, who knew what they could achieve?

'It won't work here. It only works in my time.'

Belhapt smiled, a patient icy smile. The jokiness was over.

'Switch it on. Show me how it works, there's a good boy.'

Reluctantly he took his glasses out of his case. He was glad to see they weren't scratched. Tomas picked it up and switched it on. As he suspected there was no signal. No message from Gabriella either. It was 10pm May 9th. The stupid cute picture he had of Gabriella dressed as the Easter Bunny was still the first thing he'd see on screen.

'Show me what it does, Tomas'.

Tomas searched for his music store. Found what he was looking for and played *Rita*. It was very raunchy. The least he could do was shock the guy.

Belhapt stared at the screen as it played with total astonishment.

'That is disgusting.' Then 'Show me more.'

'I have the *Muppets* doing *Bohemian Rhapsody*, if you like.'

'Muppets?'

Belhapt looked at Tomas with interest. 'You keep pornography on this device?'

'Porn? This is just stuff off YouTube. She's like in the charts forever.'

'Charts?'

'You don't have charts? Y'know, the most popular singers? Erm,' he tried to think of a German singer but couldn't. 'Frank Sinatra?'

Now he was interested. 'You have Frank Sinatra on there?'

'I'm fourteen, not ninety.' He sighed. 'The future's different, Wilhelm. The future's orange, what can I tell you.'

'Orange? Is there something wrong with the sun? You will show this to Professor Wylie,' Belhapt declared

'The battery will give out,' Tomas pointed out. 'Any moment now. Music videos kill battery life.'

'We can get you batteries.'

'Lithium batteries? I don't think so.'

'Lithium? I don't even know what that is.'

'I didn't exactly bring a charger with me. Wasn't planning on travelling through time when I got up yesterday. I should switch it off.'

An air raid siren started up. Gunther appeared at the door looking worried.

'The cellar,' he shouted.

'I'm not getting buried alive again.' Tomas said.

'Nor I,' Belhapt agreed. 'We stay. Make some tea, Gunther. Coffee if you have any.'

'Coffee? Not seen anything except chicory for months.'

'Then tea. I have to write my report. 'You,' he pointed at Tomas. 'Stay here. Gunther has orders to shoot you if you move an inch. You hear me?'

Tomas didn't think that was true. At least not yet. Not until they had what they wanted out of him.

Belhapt went upstairs whilst Gunther filled a kettle. Tomas had his phone. He quickly wrote a text to Gabby. He knew it probably wouldn't transmit, he knew she'd never get it, but he just wanted to send her a message, know he was thinking of her, no matter what.

'Stuck in 1941. Held prisoner by German spies. They think I can stop the war. I'll never c u again. Just know ur all I ever think about. xx Duck'

He pressed send. It would be the last text he'd ever send and it wasn't even going to transmit.

He thought about adding 'I love you' but he knew she never wanted to hear that. Not from her 'best friend'. It was stupid, she'd never read it. Never know how much he loved her.

The bombers came closer. Ack-Ack guns started up. It was loud, the windows shook, and plaster dust and flecks of paint came down from the ceiling.

'The City again,' Gunther muttered, looking up at the ceiling.

'Don't you care how many people die?' Tomas asked.

Gunther put the kettle on the gas ring and looked back at Tomas.

'They will surrender or we shall invade. The more we kill now, the less we have to kill later.'

Tomas held his tongue; he knew that they never actually invaded. He prayed that that remained true.

Gunther was looking at the clock on the wall. 'Professor Wylie will be here soon.'

'Who's he?'

Gunther smiled. 'You don't know Professor Wylie? He's an important man. Having supper with Mr Churchill tonight. A very important man.'

Tomas's heart sank.

Gunther laid out four cups for the tea. 'You think you have been taken by amateurs, don't you? You have no idea how many of us there are. We are the Government in waiting, Tomas Drucker. You shall be the English hero.'

'I will not.'

'Ja, you will. Dead or alive you will be our hero. I think Herr Belhapt has big plans for you.' The kettle boiled. The sound of the bombers drained away. The danger was over, for now.

7

You Have a New Message

Gabriella was in a deep sleep when her phone beeped on her bedside table. She groaned, it had taken her ages to get to sleep and she didn't appreciate being woken. She suddenly snapped awake. This was the first text she had since the big change. She realised that no one at school seemed to have a phone. But if no one had a phone, who was texting?

She reached out for it with bleary eyes and checked the message.

'*Stuck in 1941. Held prisoner by German spies. They think I can stop the war. I'll never c u again. Just know ur all I ever think about. xx Duck'*

She stared at the screen with amazement. At first she knew it had to be a joke. But then again, it was from Tomas and he'd been missing, almost as if he didn't exist for nearly three days now. *'Stuck in 1941'* Any other time she'd laugh, wonder what he was trying to pull, but she was stuck in this all-new weird German speaking England and that wasn't a joke, not even remotely funny.

Even weirder was him saying – *Just know ur all I ever think about.* Tomas had just told her that he loved her, her best friend loved her. He'd gone and spoiled everything. No wait… 1941? 1941!

No, impossible, crazy. 1941? The year before the war ended. No wait, it didn't end until 1945. Or was it 1942? It couldn't end twice. Made no sense at all.

Tomas was stuck in 1941. How? What had he told them? She closed her eyes a moment. No, this was impossible. No one could go back in time. There had to be another explanation, right?

She heard a toilet flush. Her mother was in the bathroom. Had she heard the phone beep? She was really paranoid about her owning this 'toy'.

She realised she needed to text Tomas back. She frowned as she realised that her battery was almost flat. How had he texted her from 1941? Wasn't that like impossible? They didn't have mobile phones back then, no mobile masts…but then again, now she thought about it, the mobile mast was also gone from the end of her street.

She wrote Tomas a message.

'*Explain this Tomas Duck. Your house has vanished. Everything has changed. I have bloody German classes. Weirder, my mother cooks. No one remembers u but me. What have u done? Can u get back? Tell them nothing. U have to come back to me. Promise me u will come and change everything back the way it was* xxx …:) Gabs.'

She sent it. She wondered if it would ever be delivered and immediately realised she should have told him that the war ended in 1942. There was so much that had changed.

She felt around for her charger. Normally it was plugged into the wall.

Her hands found it but it wouldn't go into the plug behind her bed. She switched her bedside light on. *Now* she was awake. It was almost midnight. She stared at the end of the phone charger. There was a normal three pin plug attached. The socket in the wall was different. It took her a moment to work out what it was. The holes were round. The bedside light was plugged in using a clunky brown round pin plug. Not only had the time changed, but the bloody wiring had too. She HAD to charge the phone, but even non-technical Gabriella Lamb knew a flat pin plug wasn't going into a round hole.

She suddenly leapt up and checked her bag. She'd been carrying her costume in it for the audition. If her phone hadn't changed because it was in the satchel, then maybe it was the same for her bag? The same bag she'd taken to France two weeks before with the choir and had needed an adapter plug. She pulled out underwear and sweaters that should have gone into the wash ages ago and there, at the very bottom, was the adapter. Better yet, it still had a flat pin socket. She teased out the round pins on one side and plugged her iPhone into it. Genius. Crossing her fingers she plugged it into the wall socket. She hoped it wasn't going to blow up the electrics, or her phone. *Charging*. Brilliant! She sat there looking at it, amazed that she had figured it out all by herself.

She left the phone to charge, and fell back onto her bed. Her heart was thumping. Tomas missed her. Tomas probably loved her, definitely loved her in fact. Nothing else was real. None of it. Except the fresh bread maybe. That could stay real.

She pulled a heavy blanket up around her (wondering briefly where her summer-weight duvet had gone) and thought about Tomas. Of course he loved her, it was only natural, but he was stuck in 1941. How stupid was that? How would he get back? Was it a joke after all?

Tomas Duck, it had better not be a joke. This new life wasn't funny at all. Did anyone else still have a phone? She had to find out. Tomorrow; she had a whole list of questions, for tomorrow.

8

Torture

Professor Wylie arrived late. He was not quite what Tomas was expecting. He was dressed in a crumpled white summer suit, smoked a stinky pipe and had nicotine stained teeth, save for one gold tooth. He preened his thick silver hair, spoke like a toff, and paid absolutely no attention to Tomas at all for the first half hour as he conversed with Wilhelm Belhapt. Tomas was now in the upstairs office, strapped into something like a dentist's chair, whilst Gunther wrapped a thin wire around his chest, trailing it back to a weird electrical generator. Tomas was stripped to the waist and the metal bit into his skin.

'10,000 volts will be very painful,' Gunther informed him helpfully. 'You will tell him everything, of that, I am sure. It could cook your heart.'

Tomas looked at him and believed him. He was a chef after all. He didn't know how he was going to resist torture. He had the best intentions, to be sure, but he knew they intended to kill him. He'd seen enough war movies to know that they always disposed of the 'informants'.

Downstairs Professor Wylie and Herr Belhapt were arguing over something. It gave Tomas time to think about his predicament. He could tell the truth, but equally, he could make stuff up. He was from the future, right? They couldn't know what happened. The trouble was he knew he'd get all confused. He wished he'd paid more attention to history or even the war movies he'd watched. Gabriella would know how to do this. She was great at making stuff up and making it sound convincing.

He heard them coming up the stairs. This was it. He braced himself, heart pounding, his pulse racing, he found it difficult to breathe.

Professor Wylie was suddenly in his face; his breath stank of brandy.

'So you think you are from the future, eh?' He laughed, exposing his horrible teeth. 'Seem to have Wilhelm convinced. We shall see about that.' He smiled again. 'It would be a remarkable thing if it were true. But I'm betting it isn't.'

Tomas stared at him, repelled by his smug red-veined face.

'10,000 volts. To encourage you to answer my questions, Tomas. We don't want to use it, but believe me, we will, if I don't think you're telling us the truth.'

Tomas looked up at the ceiling, noting the cracks and the missing pieces of plaster. Belhapt removed his only shoe and his socks and placed his feet on a rubber pad.

'We aren't trying to kill you Tomas. The rubber will ground you, but then again, it can make the pain you will endure a little worse.' He smiled, as if he was doing Tomas a favour somehow.

Gunther stood by the machine, ready to switch it on.

Belhapt stood up again. 'Just tell the Professor the truth, Tomas. That's all you have to do.'

Professor Wylie tapped his pipe on the mantelpiece – regarding a portrait of Joseph Stalin on the wall.

'We're coming to get you, Uncle Joe.'

He turned to look at Tomas suddenly. 'Know who this is?'

Tomas nodded.

'Stalin. He murdered millions of his own people. Don't know much else.'

Professor Wylie nodded. 'Good answer. But of course proves nothing. You know with whom I was having dinner tonight, Tomas? The Prime Minister. He trusts me implicitly. Myself and Professor Lindeman. We advise him on scientific matters relating to the war. Professor Lindeman wants to take the war to Germany. I want to take the war to Moscow. It's a matter of opinion. Do not underestimate me, boy. I shall win this battle. Germany is not the real enemy, Stalin's Russia is. And here we are thinking of giving him all the support he needs. No one seems to realise that he'll come for us next. Communism must be crushed and crushed now. Adolf Hitler knows this. He is a man of courage and will smash Stalin. I tell the PM, let Hitler do your work for you. Stand fast; do not fall for Stalin's lies. You understand? My work is important. And here are you. A boy Wilhelm Belhapt thinks needs my attention. A boy from the future. A boy who says Hitler will lose. That gets my attention. That boy I would like to meet. That boy I will fry until he is dead if he is telling a lie.'

Tomas was trying to understand all this. Winston Churchill put his faith in this man? A man who supported Hitler. Why? Why did he have so much influence? He spoke like someone in one of those old war movies in a clipped, sharp, upper class voice. The man scared him. He believed him when he said he'd fry him alive. This was a man who liked to be taken at his word.

Professor Wylie was looking at the mobile phone and admiring the design.

'Very impressed by the workmanship of your little toy here. Do you know where it was made? Why does it have an half eaten apple on it?

Tomas had never even thought about that. 'I suppose it's made in China.'

Professor Wylie nodded to Gunther.

'The boy thinks we are fools, Gunther. China makes nothing but yak milk and railway sleepers. It could never make something like this.'

Tomas shrugged. 'They sell millions of these every year.'

'Enough about China. What do you know about Operation Barbarossa? Herr Belhapt informs me that you have information…'

Tomas wasn't actually sure he knew anything at all about it, other than a name. He dimly recalled there was a documentary about it in the pile of DVDs Gabby have given him. He hadn't watched it.

'I only know Germany attacks Russia by surprise and…'

'When?'

'June. It was early summer.'

'And the invasion of England?'

Tomas shook his head.

'It didn't happen. Operation Sea Lion. I know Germany planned it, but they couldn't have won. Gabby's father, Professor Lamb, said that they couldn't defeat the British Air Force and without that, they couldn't get across the channel.'

Professor Wylie looked across at Belhapt with raised eyebrows.

'Your boy is well informed. But this does not mean he is from the future.'

He frowned and thought a moment.

'So you are saying England is never invaded? Never surrenders? No peace pact?'

'We win. You lose.' Tomas asserted. 'Nothing can change that.'

Professor Wylie shook his head. 'Impossible. England is finished. The Germans control all of Europe. Soon they will have Russia and the Baku oil fields.'

Tomas shook his head.

'It goes wrong. Germany loses.'

'There is still time to inform Berlin,' Belhapt suggested from the other side of the room.

Professor Wylie laughed. 'They have been planning this a year already. There are four million Axis soldiers committed. It will happen in weeks. It is worrying, I grant you, that a mere boy knows about it. But to stop it? Impossible. Stalin must be defeated.' He signalled to Gunther. 'A little juice, Gunther. Tell me boy, where did you get this information? Who have you been talking to.'

Gunther flipped the switch. Tomas immediately felt a searing pain as power surged through the electric wire and burned his flesh.

He must have screamed and passed out because Gunther was slapping him with a wet towel to bring him around again.

'He's awake.'

Suddenly his phone began to vibrate. Tomas was dimly aware that he had forgotten to switch it off. It was signalling an incoming message.

Everyone stared at his phone resting on the mantelpiece as it vibrated once again.

'It's the alarm,' Tomas whispered, his voice suddenly hoarse. 'A reminder to feed the cat.'

'Cat?' Professor Wylie protested. 'There are cats in this future then?

'And dogs,' Tomas added.

'Ask him about secret weapons,' Belhapt suggested. 'He knows about their secret weapons.'

Tomas felt so dazed by the shock, he didn't think he could remember anything at all, let alone about any so-called secret weapon.

'I only know about German secret weapons.'

Professor Wylie pursed his lips.

'This I want to hear. Tell us, boy. What secret weapons?'

'The V1 and V2 rockets they are going to send across the North Sea to bomb London. I know about them.'

Professor Wylie looked across at Belhapt and frowned.

'Rockets? You have rockets?'

Belhapt was surprised. It was one of the greatest secrets of the war. 'I told you he would be useful. London will find out about them soon enough. They say it will end the war. Constant sheer terror.'

'Wernher von Braun leads the rocket programme. We studied him in class. He led the American space programme after the war.' Tomas didn't mind them knowing German war secrets.

'Space programme?' Professor Wylie was suddenly very interested.

'Who controls the moon?'

Tomas didn't even understand the question.

'No one. They say the Americans went there once, but I'm not sure now. Some people say it was a hoax.'

Professor Wylie turned to Belhapt; Tomas could tell he was unsure now.

'This boy is well informed. How can he be getting this information?'

'I told you, Professor. He comes from the future.'

'But a future where Germany loses the war? It's impossible. They have every advantage. England will be a mere footnote. Once Moscow is defeated, it will be the greatest empire the world has ever known'.

Tomas felt sick. He knew he was burned where the wire had grown hot. Could smell his seared flesh.

Professor Wylie came back to him and stared hard at Tomas.

'If England wins, it must have secret weapons. You must know how and why they win. It is impossible. I know everything that goes on in the war office. I know of no secrets that will defeat the Reich.' He turned to Gunther. 'Remind this boy of what we can do.'

Gunther went to the switch. Tomas hurriedly shouted, 'No.' Then

'What do you want to know?'

'Secrets, Tomas. Tell us all you know.'

Tomas wracked his brains; the nausea was making him dizzy. He knew if they turned on the machine he would die, but secrets? He had no real idea.

'Tom Cruise.'

'Tom Cruise? Who or what is Tom Cruise?'

'He tries to assassinate Hitler. It's a movie but he plays a man who…'

'Tom Cruise is an actor? He plays what man?'

Tomas had absolutely no idea.

'Tell us something else. Something more useful. A lot of people probably want to kill the Reich Chancellor.'

'Rommel,' Tomas remembered. 'He loses North Africa.'

'Field-Marshall Rommel loses? Impossible.' Belhapt snorted. 'Who could possibly beat him? An English General, I think not.'

Tomas nodded. Hoping this wasn't going to do much harm in the future. 'He loses. Montgomery beats him.'

Professor Wylie nearly spat, he was so angry. 'Monty? That pompous ass beats Rommel? Complete utter nonsense. He couldn't beat a …' He looked at Belhapt, then at Gunther. 'I shall have Monty recalled. The Prime Minister has little faith in him as it is.'

'We should have Rommel replaced,' Belhapt mused. 'Although

they have much confidence in him in Berlin.'

Professor Wylie grabbed hold of Tomas's finger and bent them back. Tomas felt a shooting pain. 'And America? Does America come into this war and on whose side?'

Tomas' eyes watered he was in so much pain. The question made no sense. Of course America would come in on England's side. It could hardly come in support of Germany.'

'England.'

'Never. They have vowed to stay out of this war. Roosevelt wants no part of it. He can see which way the world is going.' His fingers were bent back still further and he exclaimed with pain, completely sure they would snap.

'December 7th,' Tomas blurted out.

'What happens on December 7th?' Professor Wylie asked, letting his hand go.

'Pearl Harbour. The Japanese attack Pearl Harbour and sink the American fleet.'

Tomas could see the attack now and Kate Beckinsale looking worried in her bloodied nurse uniform.

'Japan? Japan attacks America?' Professor Wylie exploded. 'Ridiculous, poppycock. That is the most stupid thing I have ever heard.

Belhapt seemed excited though.

'Dec 7th? What year Tomas?'

Tomas had to think about it. He could remember 'a day that went down in infamy' but the year?

'I don't…'

Gunther went for the switch.

'1941. I'm sure.'

Professor Wylie shook his head.

'Why would they do that?'

Tomas had absolutely no idea.

'Why does anyone have wars? Wars are stupid. We're fighting in Afghanistan now and everyone says it's stupid, we can't win.'

'Afghanistan?' Professor Wylie asked. 'Against whom?'

'The Taliban. They are Muslim terrorists. We've been there years.'

'There's no oil in Afghanistan,' Bellhapt declared. 'Why would anyone fight there?'

Tomas shrugged.

'Who is President of the United States now?' Professor Wylie asked suddenly.

Tomas wondered if that was a trick question. 'Obama. He's African-American.'

Professor Wylie looked at Tomas with plain disbelief.

'Black?'

'The first black President. Everyone was really happy when he was elected, the recession was really bad though and …'

'Recession?' Belhapt asked.

'A black American President?' Professor Wylie queried again. 'Impossible.'

Tomas sensed he was upset by this for some reason.

'Professor Lamb says that he was the best President since Kennedy. But he was shot.'

'Kennedy?' Belhapt asked sharply. 'Joe Kennedy?'

'No. JFK. I don't know his whole name.'

'It will be John. I know him. The American Ambassador's son. I met him at an Embassy reception. You are telling me America elected an Irish Catholic to president? Then an African-American? You expect me to believe this twaddle?'

Tomas didn't see the problem.

'Even if I accept that you are from the future, which I don't for one minute, I want to know why you are here? What are the English secret weapons, Tomas?'

Tomas groaned. He was hoping they had forgotten about that.

'Jets. We have jets,' he answered. He knew it wasn't true. Jets flew, but only at the end of the war.

'Jets?'

'Our jets shoot down all of your bombers and rockets and then start attacking your cities. Germany is flattened. Everyone dies.'

Professor Wylie looked at Tomas and smiled. 'Now I know you are lying. The RAF won't support jet development. I know this. Frank Whittle came to see me about investing in Power Jets and to get the PM on side. I told him then he was wasting his time.'

'And the bomb?' Tomas added.

'The bomb?'

'The atomic bomb.'

Professor Wylie went deathly quiet a moment. Finally he had heard something he wanted to hear.

'Atomic bomb, Tomas? See – you have been holding out on us. You know the secret. This is the big one. I know this. Only just a very few know about this, how can a boy like you know anything at all?' Professor Wylie looked across at Gunther.

'You can go now Gunther. I thank you for your efforts.'

Gunther nodded, grabbed his cap, and headed to the door. Tomas felt relieved. Perhaps he'd live through this after all.

Professor Wylie waited until Gunther had left and signalled to Belhapt to close the door.

'Only very few people in the whole world know about this bomb, Tomas.' He turned to Belhapt with a tight smile. 'Congratulations, Wilhelm. I do believe this boy is the genuine article after all.' He moved closer to Tomas, made to grab his fingers again but Tomas clenched his fist.

'I want names. I want places. How many does it kill? When and where do they test it?'

Tomas closed his eyes. He could see the mushroom cloud but whether this was *Akira* or some other movie he'd seen, he had no idea. Worse, he had absolutely no idea of any English people involved. He thought it was American. Would the Germans go full steam ahead with jets and atomic bombs because of what he said now?

'The Führer is very interested in atomic bombs, Tomas. He will be very attentive to what you have to say.'

'I don't know anything about bombs.'

'A minute ago you said you didn't know any secrets. Now you have given us two. I think you know much more than you say. Much, much more. Wilhelm, if you'd be so kind as to flip the switch to help his memory.'

'70,000 people. Maybe a hundred thousand,' Tomas said hurriedly.

Professor Wylie looked at Tomas with keen attention.

'A hundred thousand people killed with just one bomb?'

Tomas nodded.

'That was the first bomb. It was the same as 15,000 tons of TNT. The new ones can kill ten times more. There's enough bombs now to kill everyone on earth twice over. Russia has the most.'

'Russia! The Russians have the bomb!?' Professor Wylie exclaimed.

'A communist spy gives them everything. This I know is true.'

Belhapt frowned and stepped away from the electric machine.

'And this bomb is British?'

'American. But British scientists gave their secret to America. I don't know when but...'

'America has the bomb? Russia? My God, this is not good news at all. And this ends the war?'

Tomas nodded. He didn't add that it only ends the war in Japan. He knew no atomic weapons had been used in Europe, but if that got them excited and made them believe England won, at least that bit wouldn't be a lie.

'And in what year does this happen?'

'The war ends in 1945. Fifty million die.'

Professor Wylie stared at him in astonishment. 'Fifty Million people?'

Tomas nodded. 'Germany is flattened. I told you. You lose.'

'And when Japan attacks Pearl Harbour, Tomas. What do the Americans do?

'They help us fight Germany and they fight the Japanese.' Tomas turned his head to look at Belhapt. 'Millions die in Japan too. The Americans drop the atom bomb on Hiroshima and they fire-bomb Tokyo. I've seen pictures. Their cities are made of wood and burn quickly.'

Professor Wylie was frowning.

'But why do the Americans help England? This I find hard to believe. If only we had persuaded Charles Lindbergh to run for president. He could have won. He would have kept America out of the war.'

Tomas shrugged, he had no idea who this Lindbergh was either. He suddenly felt immensely thirsty. 'All I can see is a picture of Joe Stalin and Churchill and the American President …'

'Roosevelt.'

'No, someone else. Trueman.'

Professor Wylie inhaled. 'Trueman. I remember him. Another…' He swore. 'And Joe Stalin is a winner too.'

Tomas nodded. 'But Churchill doesn't trust him. But then Churchill isn't the Prime Minister. I'm sorry, I haven't studied anything post-war.'

Professor Wylie went to the far end of the room and began to pace. Belhapt give Tomas something to drink. It tasted like cold tea but was welcome nonetheless. Belhapt tried to reassure the Professor.

'We can use this, Professor. I know Uranverein have been researching the uranium weapon and nuclear fission at the Kaiser Wilhelm Institute for Physics. I don't know the details, but I believe they have been building an Uranmaschine – nuclear reactor and heavy water production is already well under way… Hermann Goring has taken a strong interest.'

Professor Wylie shook his head. 'Perhaps it is further advanced than I thought. It is imperative that this information gets back to Berlin. If this boy is right, we go up against the Russians and lose.'

'Like Napoleon,' Tomas said. 'I know he was defeated by the weather.'

Professor Wylie suddenly made a decision.

'I want this boy in Berlin. They must listen to him. They must know the truth. My God, Stalin wins. This is the worst news I have ever heard.'

Belhapt began to loosen the leather straps holding Tomas in place.

'We can get him to Dublin and out by air from there,' Belhapt began as an air raid siren suddenly started up.

'Damn. Another raid.' Professor Wylie declared. 'It is endless, this Blitz.

'Get him to the basement. We can't risk him in the public shelter. I have to go. I need to speak to my friends. This is terrible news. Atomic war. This was my greatest fear.'

Tomas could barely move. The electric shock seemed to have stopped his legs from working and he felt dizzy and sick. He could hear the bombers coming. It sounded like a huge raid and it was getting closer.

'I can't…' Tomas fell in a heap. The room seemed to be going around. His legs wouldn't work at all.

'Get him below,' Professor Wylie commanded as he fled down the stairs.

Belhapt grabbed him under the arms and dragged him up.

'Walk, Tomas. I can't carry you.'

Tomas saw his phone on the mantelpiece and grabbed it, slipping it into his trouser pocket.

The bombers were getting closer; the whole house was shaking now. Artillery started up outside, the noise was deafening, there had to be a gunnery station nearby.

'Go,' Tomas told Belhapt. 'I'm too slow. My legs feel like lead…'

The first bombs began to fall. The horrible scream as they fell relentlessly from the sky curdled Tomas's blood. He had fresh memories of being buried alive already. He didn't want that to happen again.

Belhapt abandoned him. He had what he wanted. Tomas wasn't really needed anymore. He limped awkwardly to the door. Tomas took a deep breath, saw his shirt and satchel on the sideboard and grabbed them too, limping with agony towards the stairs.

When the explosion came, it was as if all the oxygen in the world had suddenly been sucked out of the building. Tomas couldn't breathe. The house lit up all around him and he was momentarily saved by being in the stairwell. A second later the upper windows were all blown in, glass shattering everywhere. He heard someone scream, it might have been him. The stairs juddered and slowly began to sink under him. There was nothing to hold onto. He felt as one with the stairs as his nostrils filled with the stench of high explosives.

'I'm going to die,' Tomas spoke in his head. 'I'm going to be buried alive, again.'

Then there was total blackness.

9

The Imperial Museum of Culture

The bus was packed with excited girls. A trip away from school was unusual enough. To go to London was thrilling; better yet, on an express bus on the toll motorway. London was just one and a half hours away. Gabriella was sitting next to Marsha Gutteridge, whose father was an architect and responsible for most of the plain ugly square blocks of flats that most people lived in now. She was excited that they'd be driving through Guildford and get to see the new Eugenica University built on top of the hill there. Her father had designed it and this would be the first opportunity she had to glimpse it. Important genetic research work happened there about the future of the human race and she herself was planning to study there after school. Improving the nations' racial purity was an important task.

The road was impressive. Four lanes wide of concrete, not one cone to slow them down, and the Hindhead tunnel was amazing, cutting through the Surrey hills and skirting the Devil's Punch Bowl. She noted the signage at the head of the tunnel as they entered. Opened by Prime Minister Sir Oswald Mosley in 1950.

1950! It had only opened in 2011 in her time. Over sixty years earlier. How was that possible?

Marsha grabbed her arm and pointed excitedly towards a hill as they approached Guildford. Gabriella remembered the brick Cathedral that had been there before. She'd sung inside it, on a previous choir trip and remembered the acoustics were odd. Now, in place of the ugly Cathedral, there was an even uglier giant concrete square that dominated the city below it.

'It was Daddy's homage to Albert Speer,' Marsha was trilling. 'Isn't the University building amazing?'

Gabriella had no idea who Albert Speer was and looked away towards the old city as they flashed by. She wondered if any of the old castle and cobbled streets were left. It would be so depressing to be overlooked by such a monstrosity of a building with all those black square glass windows.

'It isn't very sympathetic to the old city,' Gabriella muttered.

Marsha snorted, insulted.

'Who cares about the old stuff? Everything old has to be swept away, Gabby. Daddy says the whole of England has to be rebuilt in the modern style. It will change everything. Too many people look back, not forward.'

Gabriella began to worry about London and the changes they may have made there. She knew from the photographs in her new history book that they had taken the opportunity after the bombing of the war to rebuild London in a new modern European style. She feared that all the historic buildings would be gone. St Paul's would still be there, she knew that, but she worried for the rest of the city.

She wondered about Tomas again. That text. Had it been real? How could anyone go back in time? Surely that was impossible. But here she was, living in a completely different England than the one she grew up in. She realised that she felt a gnawing pain in her heart whenever she thought about him. She missed Tomas desperately.

Fifteen minutes later the driver began to speak on the tannoy.

'We will be stopping at the Putney Toll. The Security Officer will come on board to inspect your IDs and visitor permits. Get them out and have them ready for inspection.'

Gabriella blinked. Did she even have a visitor's permit? Or ID card? She scrabbled in her purse and was relieved to find both documents there. She looked at the photo of herself and nearly screamed. It was hideous. Who had made her wear her hair back like that?

Marsha laughed at her picture. 'I don't know why you don't pluck your eyebrows. It's so weird to leave them to go wild.'

Gabriella looked at Marsha and noticed for the first time that hers were so faint they looked as though they had been drawn on her head. If anyone looked weird, it was Marsha Gutteridge. She wasn't alone though, Gabriella noticed other girls had this look and the pale make-up and tightly braided hair. She knew from her German fashion magazine that this was how Berlin girls looked right now and it had obviously caught on in England. She wondered if there were there any supermodels in this world? Surely there had to be.

'I like being natural.' Gabriella replied. 'I hope we get there soon, I need to…'

'You would think they'd have a toilet on the bus or something,' Marsha said, pulling a face. 'I've been dying to go for an hour now.'

The bus began to slow for the Putney Toll.

Crossing the Thames at Putney was a shock. It was all so different. The old high street where traffic was always blocked had gone and a nice wide tree-lined four lane highway tapered to two lanes before the bridge. The motorway went right to the river. Old Putney had completely disappeared, along with St Mary's church that had always stood guard on the south side of the bridge. Square, hideous concrete blocks had replaced everything and although the river was the same, the skyline ahead towards the city was quite changed. She only realised what it was as they plunged back into the canyons of concrete that lined the New Kings Road. No tall buildings. She had only glimpsed the skyline for a moment and this London was stunted. The tallest buildings were just ten storeys high. And there were billboards advertising Government slogans, such as one showing a fat man eating sausages *'Eat a little less – live a lot healthier'* where buildings should be. The more Gabriella looked, the more certain she was that there was nothing behind the billboards.

At Parson's Green the bus slowed to allow school children to cross and she could see an Underground train go by on the overhead rails in the distance. At least that was still there, but she noted that the buildings each side were all in decay. Even the new ones seemed stained with rust or looked dowdy. This wasn't the London she remembered at all. Where were all the cute little shops and…

'Fulham,' another girl shouted, pointing at a sign. 'This is where they shot the last English rebels.'

Others craned to look but there was nothing to see.

Marsha nodded. 'That's when peace finally came. Five thousand rebels held out there for three months. They were all exterminated to save the nation from civil war. That will come up in the exam, I'm sure.'

Gabriella blinked. Exam? Five thousand English people murdered? She had no recollection. Before she could ask they moved on over a small bridge and they were on the Kings Road where at last shops and boutiques began to show up and all the girls looked with envy at the array of choices.

Gabriella wasn't impressed, however. It was like looking at the sort of shops her mother liked. Everything was quite dull. The fashions were severe, unsexy. The shoe shops had no colour; all was either brown or black. There were a lot of café's and cake shops however, which reminded her that she was hungry.

The bus made a left and headed towards Kensington.

The teacher, Mr Brownstone, got up from his seat at the front and grabbed the microphone.

'We shall be stopping outside the Culture Museum. I shall issue you with your tickets as you leave the bus. Gather in the main hallway and wait for me. We will be spending four hours here. Your ticket will also buy you lunch in the canteen. Lose it and you will go hungry. I will expect you all to act responsibly and gather back in the main hall at three pm. We will then go to the bus and up to Hyde Park for the early evening concert. Those of you in the choir will be taken to the stage area. I will issue tickets for the rest of you on the bus. Is that clear?'

'Yes, Mr Brownstone.' They chorused.

'What concert?' Gabriella asked Marsha.

'The one you're singing in. You aren't with it today, my girl. The Flying Dutchman, in case you have forgotten.'

'Wagner? We're singing an opera?'

'Summ und brumm, du gutes Rädchen.' Marsha sang.

Suddenly Gabriella remembered and began to feel quite ill.

Gabriella seemed to be the only person who knew that once the museum had been called Victoria and Albert. She'd been there with her father and Tomas only a year ago and now she was back and it was called the Imperial Culture Museum. Same place, different name. She wondered if any of the art or furniture was still going to be in there. Her father had been interested in a photographic exhibition on how London had lived though the war. She'd paid little attention to people staring at bombed out homes or digging trenches in Hyde Park. She wanted to go to the fashion section. She'd been writing an essay on changing fashions in British society and this was a perfect opportunity to score an A. Tomas had gone next door to look at dinosaurs in the Natural History Museum. He hadn't any time for art, furniture or fashion, but she remembered he loved dinosaurs.

She emerged from the toilets and wandered towards a gaggle of girls from the bus.

'We're going shopping. Are you coming, Gabriella?'

'Shopping?'

'KaDeWe department store is just down the road and Peek and Cloppenburg. Didn't you know? They're the best.'

Gabriella knew but she hadn't brought any money, but she was torn. She also knew that the best stores down there used to be called Harvey Nicks and Harrods. She wondered what had happened to them?

'I promised to look at the fashion exhibition with Marsha. Perhaps we'll find you in an hour.'

The other girls shrugged. They were excited to be in London for the first time and intended to have an adventure.

'Go. Mr Brownstone is in the loo. Go now if you are going,' Gabriella told them.

They needed no encouragement. They ran off giggling, happy to be off the leash.

Marsha appeared. She'd adjusted her make-up and looked even more pale. Like a ghost. Gabriella thought. She had a museum guidebook with her.

'We have to go to the Heroes of the Nation section first. Then the History of Fashion. Dad says I have to look out for the Future City Living exhibition. He designed most of it.' Marsha added with pride

'Must be nice to have a famous father,' Gabriella told her as they linked arms and headed towards the Heroes exhibit.

Marsha frowned. 'Probably. He never comes home much, though. Spends a lot of time in Munich. That's where the head office is. He only wanted me to go to school there, but Mum refused. She doesn't want to leave England.'

Gabriella suddenly had empathy for Marsha. Her own father had been gone over a year in the previous England. She had yet to meet him in this world and worried what he would be like. Would he still laugh and smile? It seemed to her that smiling was not an option in this world.

'I brought money,' Marsha declared. 'We can go the café after this section. They have excellent chocolate cake and strudel.'

They entered the Heroes of Britain hall. Some names and images Gabriella recognised. Although Marconi was Italian, he did at least invent the radio.

Marsha was a bit disappointed. 'They're all men. First to climb Everest, first to North Pole, first to fly a jet across the Atlantic, they're all men.'

Gabriella smiled. 'That's *such* a surprise. Here's a woman. Dr Hilda Gantree, first to establish DNA of the English Gene.'

Marsha nodded. 'She started the Eugenica University. Amazing woman. Tragic she died like that. Hit by a tram. Hid her deafness all her life. Amazing.'

Gabriella thought that a tad ironic. Someone interested in perfection turns out to be deaf. She turned and saw another exhibit that caught her attention.

Boy Hero – The Boy who Saved England from Destruction.

The boy looked a great deal like Tomas.

'Oh, Tomas Drucker. He's my favourite.' Marsha trilled. 'He's the one who persuaded England to sue for peace with Germany. Saved 50 million lives. He'll definitely come up in the essay, Gabs.'

Gabriella was staring, panic welling in her heart. All the colour drained from her face. She stepped closer. She wanted to read this.

'Tomas Drucker, the boy hero from Portsmouth who persuaded English leaders of the folly of their ways. Drucker personally made sure the traitor Winston Churchill attended the Dublin Peace Conference in 1941 and signed the treaty of co-existence.

'We cannot allow a whole generation to die for the stupidity of our elders. England must join with Germany and unite against Bolshevism. Together we will be strong. This is not surrender. This is nation building. A united Europe under German leadership to save us from total slavery under communism.'

There were *London Illustrated News* photographs of Tomas looking dazed and bruised whilst being pulled out of the rubble. He looked exhausted, his face black with oil, his bag still around his neck, she noted. There were flames right beside him. A very dramatic photograph.

There was another photo of him in smart clothes with some important men. Tomas Drucker with Professor Wylie, Winston Churchill (PM) 1940-41 and Von Ribbentrop (German Foreign Minister 1938-60). It didn't look real, as if they had inserted Tomas into the picture.

The poster stated that Tomas had been buried alive three times and each time vowed to stop the war.

He was the lone voice that shouted 'peace' when all wanted war. His voice called to all young people and they listened. 'We want peace with Germany now'.

German Leader Adolf Hitler heard their cry and reached out to them. He gave England the lifeline it desperately needed. Peace now or total obliteration.

The British Government listened and finally saw the truth. War with Germany was folly. They willingly undertook to join National Socialism and to fight the Soviets. 1942 was the great turning point in world history. Tomas Drucker was awarded the German Cross for his bravery and volunteered to fight on the Russian front. He died, as he had lived, leading others towards the enemy. His body was never found, but to England he remains forever the Boy Hero.

Gabriella?

Gabriella was on her knees. She could hardly breathe. Tears were flowing down her cheeks. Her Tomas buried alive three times. The one thing he was mortally afraid of. Tomas, her Tomas was a traitor. He'd stopped the war. How was that even possible? How could a fourteen-year-old boy stop a war?

'I,' she began but couldn't finish. Tomas was dead. He'd died fighting the Russians.

'Dad says that he probably never existed, but don't say I said that. We have to study him. But Dad says that he was just one of those propaganda things they used to put out to make people happy. I'm glad he stopped the war. Someone had to. I mean, we were fighting the wrong war. How stupid was that.'

'He did exist,' Gabriella wailed. 'He did.'

Marsha was a bit embarrassed. She'd never seen Gabby upset about anything, let alone about a boy who'd died over seventy years ago.

'I'm sure he did. Well, he's our hero, Gabs. From Portsmouth. Nice to know one of boys has something heroic in them. Not like now. I'm going to look for a German husband when I get married. I don't want to get stuck with some spotty weedy English boy.'

'Tomas wasn't weedy. He was honest and a good friend and ...'

Marsha tried to haul Gabriella up off the floor.

'I'm sure he was. Come on, Gabs, people are staring. We have to keep moving. We're attracting attention.'

'I don't care. Tomas is dead. I don't believe he'd be a...' she stopped herself from saying traitor aloud. In this museum he was a hero. A hero for stopping the war.

How on earth had this happened? His phone message had said what '*held prisoner by German spies*'. She hadn't believed him. How could she? Yet here he was, a hero, *dead*, a traitor and yet she could see his face as he emerged from the ruins, she could see his utter exhaustion and a terrible burn across his chest.

Tomas. Please don't be dead. I love you, Tomas Drucker. Please don't be dead.

She allowed Marsha to haul her up. She took out a handkerchief and blew her nose. Yuk, handkerchief? Where were her tissues?

'I can't believe that upset you so much,' Marsha was saying. 'Come on, we need hot chocolate.'

Gabriella allowed herself to be led towards the café and welcomed it. She needed something. Most of all she needed to hear from Tomas.

He was stuck in 1941. She was stuck in the world that he had created. She needed to send him a text. Urgently. *Tomas stop whatever it is you are doing. I hate this world you created. I don't want you to be a hero. Please, whatever you do, don't change history.*

First chance she could get alone she'd send it.

But would he ever get it?

How could a text even go back in time? How crazy was that? No crazier than finding Tomas in a museum. No crazier than discovering her best friend was a traitor, a hero and dead, oh so very dead these past seventy years. No crazier than that.

'Hot chocolate and a blueberry muffin,' Gabriella muttered, not realising she was speaking aloud.

'Chocolate yes, but muffin? What on God's earth is a muffin?' Marsha asked as they drew near the café.

10

In the Rubble

'Here, over here, there's someone over here.'

Tomas heard the voices approaching. His head was spinning, he couldn't move and there was something burning close by, he could feel intense heat on one side of his body. He tried to call out, but his mouth was filled with muck. He tried to move his legs but they were strangely detached, he couldn't feel a thing, worse, he couldn't see either, something stinking of oil was covering his face.

'Up here,' someone was shouting again.

Tomas knew he hadn't been conscious long. He wondered how long he'd been out and what had happened to the people in the building? Were they dead? He remembered Professor Wylie had left just before the bomb hit. He'd still be out there, able to spread his poison.

'Hold on,' a voice was close by now. 'We've got a gas flare here. Tell them to shut the gas off.' His rescuer was right beside him now and pulled away a wooden beam that was pressed up against Tomas' face.

'Surprised you haven't been cooked by now, lad. Can you hear me? Move your hand if you can hear me.'

Tomas wiggled his hand. He could move his head now, but his neck was sore. He was dimly aware that his satchel strap was digging in to his skin. At least he still had his satchel.

'You've got a bad gash on your head, but you're lucky, something is holding you up, don't know what, but we need to get you out.'

Tomas tried to speak, but couldn't, his throat had dried out and everything, mouth, ears, eyes were caked in ash, dust and oil.

He felt hands under his armpits as the man tried to lift him out of the hole.

'You're in one piece, lad, thank god for that at least. More than the other blighters we pulled out.'

Tomas wondered who the other dead people were. Was William Belhapt among them? He hoped so.

'Hold it,' another voice shouted. '*Illustrated News*. Need a picture.'

'Well hurry it up, we ain't safe 'ere.'

'Lift him up a bit. Nice that. Still got his satchel around his neck.'

'Keep your eyes closed,' the man said as he wiped Tomas's face.

'Just dried blood and oil. You'll live. Can you move your legs? Take the bloody photo now man. I have to get him out of the hole.'

Tomas heard the click of a camera, several clicks in fact. His rescuer was slowly extracting him out of the hole, not wanting to dislodge anything suddenly, or scrape him against jagged glass or any protruding nails.

'I'll get his name in a moment,' the photographer called out.

Tomas tried to move his legs again, but the blood was rushing back down his limbs now and he cried out as the worst case of cramp he'd ever had gripped him. He opened his eyes, saw the ambulance man in his tin hat for the first time and a burning gas flare no more than a foot away. He winced as the pain coursed through his legs and cried out again, grabbing his calves.

'Hold on, lad, hold on. Just the blood beginning to circulate again.'

Another pair of hands took hold of him and he was handed over to others who gingerly ferried him to the road below. Tomas held on to his satchel and felt for the phone in his pocket. Remarkably it was still there.

'He's got cramps.' His rescuer called down. 'Get this gas shut off. Where's the fireman?'

Tomas opened his eyes again. He was being carried down by two ambulance men hobbling over debris and broken glass. The pain in his legs was terrible and he was painfully aware of his left arm coming back to life now. One of the ambulance men saw he was conscious.

'Lucky boy. This whole building's going to collapse any minute now, nothing but memory holding it up.'

They carried him over to a waiting ambulance. A crudely fitted out bread van; the bakers name F. Jones Baker still on the side.

Tomas awoke again – realised he must have dropped unconscious for a while. Someone had wiped rubbing alcohol over his face to remove the oil and it was this that had brought him back.

'Awake now, are you?'

Tomas was looking at an unshaven exhausted-looking man still in his dressing gown, with a stethoscope hanging around his neck.

'I'm Doctor Holmbush. You're an interesting specimen, boy. Had an operation on your leg recently. Very neat stitching. Can you speak?'

Tomas saw that his trousers were ripped and he was still shirtless. He looked around for his bag and saw it was safe close by. He indicated his mouth was dry and the doctor asked the ambulance man to give him water. Tomas took a tin cup of water from him and rinsed his mouth and spat out black stuff. He began coughing up a lung full of dust and plaster.

'Got a name?' Someone was calling. 'Need it for the News.'

'Tomas D…' He coughed some more. 'Drucker.'

'D r u c k e r?' The man asked, spelling it out by the letter.

Tomas nodded. 'Tomas without an H.'

'No H?'

The Doctor turned to the man asking. 'He said no H. Now leave him be. He's just been buried alive, for god's sake.'

Tomas drank the remains of the water and sank back against the floor of the van. Only then did he realise how sore his head was.

The Doctor looked back at him. 'We're going to have to get you back to my surgery, Tomas without an H. You need stitches in your head. Want to tell me about the burns around your body? That's pretty nasty. Electric wire burn if you ask me.'

Tomas closed his eyes, aware they were stinging from the rubbing alcohol. They wouldn't focus. His head was spinning.

There was a sudden explosion nearby and shouts of dismay.

Tomas sat up momentarily. The building he'd just been pulled from had collapsed. Had they not got to him when they did, he'd be dead for sure. Heavy brick dust billowed across the street covering everything.

'Let's get him over the road,' the Doctor was saying to someone, pulling him to his feet. 'At least you saved one.'

Tomas felt nauseous suddenly. He doubled over and spewed out across the road. It wasn't pretty.

'Better out than in,' Dr Holmbush declared as he examined the contents and waited for Tomas to finish. 'No blood in it. At least your insides are still intact. You just saved me a lot of trouble, Tomas. Come on, let's get you sewn up.'

Tomas allowed himself to be led across the road towards a much-neglected four-storey white terrace house – its roof covered with a tarpaulin where most of the slate had been blown off in a previous explosion.

Dr Holmbush saw what Tomas was looking at. 'Don't worry, we get by and the rainwater's useful for the plants. We live in the basement most of the time, dry as a bone.'

Tomas saw the bodies then. Five laid out in a line on the pavement, some missing limbs. No one had covered their faces yet. He recognised the chef, Gunther. He didn't look injured at all, but there he was lying dead, his face quite calm. No sign of Belhapt, however.

'Worst raid for months,' Dr Holmbush was saying. 'Well over a thousand dead across London last night, I hear, more probably. My children are exhausted.'

'It's not over yet,' Tomas muttered. 'May 10th is the last night of the blitz.'

Dr Holmbush looked askance at Tomas, uncertain he heard right.

'What did you say, Tomas?'

'It's tonight.'

'What's tonight?'

'I just remembered. They bomb the House of Commons tonight. May 10th. Over 500 bombers are coming. They're going to destroy Westminster Abbey, the British Museum, everything. It's the big one. You have to tell someone.'

Dr Holmbush frowned, puzzled by what Tomas was saying.

'You're just suffering from shock, my boy. Not surprised. Quite a thing to survive a direct hit y'know. Got to get that wound in your head stitched.'

Tomas suddenly turned around and stared at the genial Doctor. He gripped his arm. 'Tell someone, please. I can do one good thing. Please, I remembered. Tell them 500 bombers are coming tonight. Please tell them.'

Tomas stumbled and fell on the grass outside the house. He had a terrifying vision of bombs falling, hundreds and hundred of bombers in the night sky and then nothing.

11

A pretty boy

Gabriella had sung with the chorus on the stage in Hyde Park. She had completely surprised herself that she knew the words in German to anything by Wagner, let alone *The Flying Dutchman* which was all gloomy stuff about some ghost sea captain condemned to roam the sea till Judgement Day unless he could find the love of a faithful woman. It was ridiculous stuff, but she knew the words. What other knowledge and skills did she possess that she wasn't conscious of, she wondered? It scared her a little.

The open-air concert venue was packed with smartly dressed opera fans and as she looked out across the sea of faces she realised that there were no old people. Not even rich old people. At almost every concert she had ever sung at before it was mostly old people in the audience.

She asked Marsha about it when they were changing in the toilets behind the Serpentine café.

'Don't you think it's strange that no old people came to the concert? I mean, you'd think they'd love Wagner and the singing.'

Marsha regarded her with confusion on her face. 'Old people aren't allowed, Gabriella, they're just a burden on the future.'

Gabriella stared at Marsha with horror.

'Not allowed? You loved your grandmother. I know you did. She knitted you sweaters and…'

'And now she's serving the state in the care camp. As long as they work they are useful. My Grandmother had a good life.'

Gabriella was surprised at Marsha's cold tone.

'But she wasn't even old. I mean …'

'You know the rules. When you turn sixty you surrender your home and savings to the state and take up useful work. It's fair. The same will happen to you or me.'

Gabriella watched Marsha pinning up her hair. Sixty was old now?

'We said our goodbyes. She said she was glad to be doing something useful for the nation. The camps are very productive. She makes cushions.'

'Cushions? She was a lawyer. She makes cushions now?'

'Can't have old people doing nothing, can we? It's all about fairness,

Gabriella. You know what used to happen, old people begging on the streets, sleeping in doorways. It was ugly. The camps are better.'

'Camps?' She had no recollection of old people sleeping in doorways at all. In fact, quite the opposite. Old people had homes and places to go and electric scooters…

Marsha didn't want to discuss old people. She pulled a face and pouted.

'I don't care what happens to old people, all right? We have a long time before they put us in the Care Camps. Don't spoil my day, Gabriella.'

'But what if we don't want to go when we're sixty?' Gabriella protested as she washed her face with soap.

Marsha laughed cruelly and drew a finger across her throat. 'That or they make them into that soap you're using.'

Gabriella dropped the soap instantly, staring at in horror.

Marsha laughed again, picking it up and washing her hands with it. 'You're so naïve, you believe anything, Gabby. Anyway, Father says there's too many old people, too many people altogether. But he'll be in Care Camp soon and I won't have to listen to anything he says anymore.'

She smiled, drying her hands. 'Come on, let's get to the café before they scoff everything.'

Gabriella dried her face and ran out after her, uncertain now if Marsha had been joking about everything. But she suspected the camps were true. Until she actually saw an old person, she'd continue to believe it. She paused by the lake, looking out towards the city beyond. Definitely not one tall building on the horizon. This was not the London she knew. Not her time. She wanted everything to go back to the way it had been before. *What did you bloody well do, Tomas Drucker? What did you do?*

'Hurry, Gabriella. There's still some cake left.'

Gabriella followed Marsha into the café, now crammed with fellow choristers. The soloists had their own place to go, of course, no need to mix with the hoi polloi. It was heaving with boys and girls, all surreptitiously eyeing each other up (at least that hadn't changed).

She grabbed two ham rolls, a slice of German chocolate cake and a cup of coffee with hot milk. She realised she was starving and quickly ate them, blowing on the coffee to cool it.

'Did you see him?'

'Who?'

'Daniel Bolsover.'

Gabriella shrugged, a blank look on her face. 'Who?'

Marsha looked exasperated. 'Do you even live on the same planet as me? Don't you watch TV, Gabriella? He's the most divine singer and he's only 18. Got his own show and everything.'

'He was singing with us?'

'No, stupid. He's come to check out the girls. Didn't you see him sitting on the front row?'

Gabriella looked around the crowded café but couldn't see anyone who stood out. So what if he was on TV? Come to think of it, she hadn't even noticed a TV in her home. She wondered what she watched if they did have one. How bad was TV in this world. She dreaded to think.

Marsha was staring at her now, plain envy on her face.

'What now?'

'He likes you. He's staring right at you. God, he has no taste at all. You wear your hair down just to be awkward, don't you.'

'I wear my hair like I've always done.'

'Well don't turn around. His eyes are x-raying you, I swear.'

'When does the bus go?' Gabriella asked.

'You're thinking about the bus? Are you crazy?'

'I need to get some fresh air. I'll see you at the bus. If you like him so much, go talk to him, Marsha.'

'Seven-thirty at the car park. Don't be late.'

Gabriella stood up, finished her drink and then headed out of the door, glad to be out of there. Let them drool over some stupid boy. She didn't care. Marsha was welcome to him.

She strolled away from the lake towards a pretty row of pink rhododendrons. She was surprised to see cute red squirrels stood on hind-legs begging for tid-bits, but she had none to give and they ran away disappointed. She'd never seen a red squirrel, they had always been grey before.

She reflected on her day. Discovering Tomas was a traitor was just plain awful. He'd sold out England to the Germans. She still didn't understand how that was even possible, but she'd seen proof of it in the museum that in this world he was regaled as a hero. She was glad he was dead. He deserved to be dead. This world was impossible but she was in it. And who knew what other horrors she'd discover. Pity the old people having to live in camps. And where were the other people? She hadn't seen one black or brown person. Not one. What had they done with them? She had an inkling, but didn't want to think about that. She didn't want to even let that madness into her brain.

The point was, how to change it all back? Was that even possible?

'Hello?'

Gabriella spun around and found a young, handsome older boy dressed in black, sporting the beginnings of a moustache and goatee. She instinctively knew it was Daniel Bolsover, the singer, despite having never seen him before.

'Oh er, hi…' She was flustered now. He must have followed her.

'I needed to get out of there. Too many people staring.'

Gabriella sighed. She'd wanted to be alone. Daniel was good looking, but she just wasn't in the mood for this.

'You're different to the others,' he said.

Gabriella offered a light embarrassed smile.

'You mean, I'm not staring at you.'

He laughed. She was shocked to see how many fillings he had. His whole mouth was filled with metal. She didn't have one filling. Didn't even know anyone who had fillings.

'You sang well,' he told her.

Gabby just dismissed that with a nervous laugh.

'I was in the chorus, you couldn't tell.'

'True, but I'm sure you did and …'

'I was scared actually. Singing in German. It's hard.'

'Not for me. My father's German. I grew up speaking it. My mother insisted on German in the home.'

'Not fair, that's cheating.'

He laughed again, scratching his neck. Gabriella noticed he had a love-bite there.

'You live in London?' She asked him.

'My mother runs the Central Drama Academy. Have you thought of acting? She's always looking for new talent for TV.'

'Acting? Me?' Gabriella dismissed it. 'I like to sing but I don't think I could pretend to be someone else. I don't think I could even play myself.'

Daniel seemed to like her answer.

'I could get you an audition. There's a scholarship and everything.'

'My father wouldn't approve. He's an academic.'

'I know. Professor Lamb. He won the literary medal this year. You must be proud.'

'You know?'

He grinned, pleased with himself. 'I asked a girl who you were.'

Gabriella inwardly groaned. Now there would be thirty girls on the bus, all seething with jealousy.

'It's a great honour to win the medal. Will you go with him to Berlin for the ceremony?'

Gabriella shrugged. 'I doubt it.'

'I long to see Berlin, that would be so terrific, don't you think?'

'Seeing Hyde Park is quite exciting for me,' she told him.

'Gabriella?'

She turned and saw Mr Brownstone approaching. This could only mean trouble.

'Uh, oh. Teacher alert.'

Daniel was all smiles though, not in the least intimidated.

'I was just congratulating Miss Lamb on her father's success and her wonderful singing.'

Mr Brownstone blinked. He knew exactly who this boy was, even if Gabriella didn't.

'Oh yes, well, in that case… she has a fine voice, fine voice.'

Daniel bowed to her. 'Perhaps we shall see you again, Gabriella Lamb. I shall speak with my mother.'

Gabriella curtsied. She'd never done that before, but it seemed the natural thing to do. She watched Daniel saunter back down the slope to the café. She saw faces watching from the café window as well and groaned.

'Well you certainly caught someone's attention, Miss Lamb.'

'Nothing to do with me, Mr Brownstone.' She looked at her choirmaster with his biscuit crumbs down his waistcoat and sighed.

She suddenly thought of the missing old people again.

'What will happen to you when your sixty, Mr Brownstone? Will you be sent to camp?'

He looked at her with horror.

'Oh no, I'm a party member. Remember that, Gabriella. The National Socialist party looks after its own, you should join. I shall be sent to the colonies, I should think. They always have need of a choirmaster there.'

Gabriella was happy to hear that. As much as she didn't like him, having him melted down for soap wouldn't be fair at all.

'And you, Gabriella? Have you thought about your future?'

Gabriella waked back to the café with Mr Brownstone at her side.

'I'd like to study time. You think there is anywhere you can study time, Mr Brownstone?'

He frowned, treating her remark with serious thought.

'You know, I'm not sure there is, but philosophy has a timeless quality to it. Thinking is a good way to spend four years of your life in University. Might keep you out of trouble at least.'

They re-entered the café and a hundred envious eyes devoured Gabriella. They all wanted to know what Daniel had said to her. Of Daniel she could see nothing.

Marsha bore down on her, urgent questions on her lips….

12

Pancakes for Eight

Tomas tried to look at his head in the mirror but couldn't see the stitches. He sat on a narrow single bed and read the message from Gabriella again then switched the phone off before it completely died.

'*Tomas stop whatever it is you are doing. I hate this world you created. I don't want u to be a hero. Please, whatever u do, don't change history.*'

What had he done? He knew the answer to that. He'd betrayed everyone. He should have just kept his mouth shut. Why hadn't he kept his damned mouth shut?

He looked around the room he was in and sighed. He put the phone into his bag. He doubted he'd ever use it again, let alone send a text. Somehow he had to find a way back to Gabby, but before that, he had to change things back the way they were. Just two totally impossible things.

He looked back at his busy morning. He'd been hosed down with cold water, had most of his hair shaved off so they could do the stitching and been dressed in a shirt and khaki shorts that were at least one size too large.

Later he'd been handed over to one of Dr Holmbush's sensible twin daughters, Iris, and she had taken him in hand. She had all the forms and the all-important Doctor's letter that confirmed he was Tomas Drucker and allowed him to get an ID card. No photograph needed, much to his surprise. They would post it to him within a week – conditional upon enemy activity.

Iris was only one year older than him, but she seemed to him like a woman of twenty-five. Confident, totally in charge, and an extraordinary beauty. Tomas was putty in her hands. She had him down to the Ministry Administration Office, itself in a temporary building on Brompton Road. She had him registered and issued with his junior ration book from the Ministry of Food. (National Registration Number FAKB 344:1) They seemed quite used to her and called her Iris. It seemed she was a regular bringing in her 'strays'.

'When you get a food coupon book, keep it safe because we will need it. They stamp the name of the butcher, baker, candlestick maker in your ration book and it all gets recorded. It's to make sure everyone gets a fair share.'

She also had him registered in the Visitor Record for her address so that her father could collect the 10/6d a week for his board. (A requisition for a new mattress was slipped in too because the previous visitor had wet the bed too often.) She got him a new gas mask, (although she never actually carried hers with her anywhere as it was 'boring'.) She even had him registered for her school and he was issued with a brown label with London County Council School Number 209 written on it and she filled out the temporary school address on Queens Gate.

'Wear this around your neck so they know who you are next time you get blown up,' she told him. 'I'm sorry you're an orphan, but at least you have a place to stay now. Lily, my twin, and I, were evacuated at the beginning of the war. Sent to Petersfield in Hampshire. It was so primitive and backward. They didn't even have hot water or heating, not even a refrigerator. It was like being in the Middle-Ages and they expected us to help them grow vegetables and milk goats. Daddy says that it's important to know how to milk a goat, but I think he was joking. I hated being so cold, although Lily liked hunting for mushrooms. You have no idea how backward some people are. Lily decided after one month of absolute torture we were going home. So we walked.'

'From Petersfield to London?' Tomas was impressed.

'It took three days. Some people stopped for us, but Lily wouldn't get into a car with a stranger. It was bitterly cold too. When we got back Daddy almost cried. I'm not sure Mother was happy. Did I mention she works at the Ministry of Information? She says she writes recipes for the war effort. Although I don't think they could be very good because she hates cooking at home. Lily dances, so I do most of the cooking at home and write for the *Children's Newspaper*. Arthur Mee came to tea with us last year. It's terribly important to keep children informed about the war, don't you think?'

Tomas hardly got a word in, but he didn't care. It was great being looked after by her. He couldn't wait to meet her twin sister, who sounded very imperious.

'I'm making pancakes. Thanks to the bombing Lily grabbed all the milk they left for the restaurant – we have ten whole pints. Don't snitch on us; they get very upset about that kind of thing. Don't tell anyone, especially Daddy. There's enough to make a rice pudding too. Can you imagine that? Of course there aren't any eggs. I do so hate egg powder.

Are you hungry at all?'

'I like pancakes.'

'Well, don't get excited. There's very little flour, absolutely no sugar or lemon. But we do have strawberry jam. Aunt Gemma sends us her jam from Canterbury and she makes tons of it. I think she has a secret stash of sugar. Or did. She keeps getting bombed. War is stupid and beastly. I hope it ends soon.'

Iris took his arm as they walked back towards her house. Tomas stared at the ruins of the restaurant and wondered how he had survived at all.

'The tube train runs under that rubble. It's a wonder they can keep the trains going.'

'Where do you go when there's an air raid?' Tomas asked, noting there wasn't much of a front garden.

'The ground floor is reinforced with concrete. Grandad lived here before us and stored grand pianos here, so he had to have the floor strengthened. The whole house could drop on us and we'd be all right. Just as well, because when next door got hit last week half our roof went. They say it will be months before they can repair it.'

Tomas had found himself back at Iris' house. This was his home now. Quite how it happened he didn't know, but Dr Holmbush had simply accepted his word that he was an orphan, recently arrived from Portsmouth and it had all mushroomed from there.

'We've got eleven bedrooms. Daddy's converted the ground floor into his surgery, but we still have to take people in, to get by. I put your bag in the back room on the second floor next to Lily. There's a bathroom on the first and another toilet on the third.

'This isn't charity, so don't be embarrassed. Daddy will get paid for your lodging and you'll bring your rations in with ours. Every little bit helps.'

'How many are there in the house?' Tomas asked.

'Seven. Daddy and Mummy, myself, Lily, Queenie (who is a bit odd), Helen and Guy, and now you. That's eight I suppose. Quite enough. We can't use the top rooms anyway thanks to the bombing.'

Tomas had never been in such a grand home before, even if it was looking a tad weather worn and battered from the bombs.

'Mother says that helping strays is the best thing we can do for the war effort.'

Tomas nodded. 'Well. I'm a stray and thank you, Iris. You're a great organiser.'

She gave him a big grin. 'Gosh, and you said thank you. A boy actually said thank you. I shall put that in my diary.'

Tomas laughed.

'You have perfect teeth,' Iris remarked, looking at him with studied interest. 'Quite perfect.'

Tomas shut his mouth, embarrassed.

She dragged him down to the basement where she was to prepare lunch.

She pushed him into a tatty brown leather chair, washed her hands and immediately began mixing the pancake mix as she read from a recipe book.

'Not enough flour, horrid egg powder, no sugar, it's hardly going to be a pancake at all. Do you think we could use honey to sweeten it? I have a little honey left.'

'Yes. Do you want me to forage in the ruins of the restaurant? I know they had sugar and everything.'

'Don't be silly. There could be unexploded bombs in there. Besides if there's anything left, the warden would have it by now. They shoot looters y'know. Lily was lucky with the milk.'

'Well, let me mix for you. I'm good at that.'

Iris shook her head and smiled again.

'You just sit there and tell me about Portsmouth. That's where you're from, isn't it? They had terrible times there, I know.'

Tomas settled in his chair, feeling his stitches. He felt they were a bit tight. Twenty-six in all. Must have been a big gash.

'I've been buried alive three times now. I think that's quite enough.'

Iris took that in but made no comment.

'Shout upstairs for me won't you.'

'Shout what?'

'Lunch, of course. Once you start doing pancakes you can't wait.'

'Righto.' Tomas went to the stairs and shouted, 'Lunchtime'.

He heard footsteps and turned back to the kitchen. A sleepy cat crept out of a box by the well worn saggy sofa and stretched its paws.

'Meet Iago. He's a very useful cat. Excellent mouser.'

'You get a lot of mice?'

'And rats. I think he's scared of rats, but he still chases them off.'

A face appeared at the door and slunk into the room, climbing up on a chair. A tiny girl with a pudding bowl haircut, her big eyes staring out from under the fringe.

'That's Queenie. We don't know her real name and she never

speaks.' Iris shrugged. 'She was bombed on the Fulham Road and we took her in last Christmas.'

A boy arrived, thin as a rake, with a vivid scar on his face. He took his seat as Iris plonked a tiny scrap of fat into the frying pan on the stove. It immediately sizzled.

'It's pancakes, as promised, Queenie.' Iris looked across at Tomas and smiled. 'I've been promising pancakes for months. Never have enough flour or milk or something. Thought I'd do it today. Make it special to celebrate your arrival.'

Tomas smiled. Then suddenly couldn't remember where his satchel was and panicked. 'Where's my room again? I forgot where you said.'

'Second floor. Lily put your bag up there and that other thing we took out of your pockets. I'll mend your trousers before we wash them.'

'I'm Guy.' The thin boy told him, holding out a hand to shake.

'Tomas.' He shook Guy's small scarred hand. He realised he'd never actually shaken another boy's hand before. Weird. Everyone was so polite all the time; it was disconcerting.

'Tomas without an H,' Iris added. For some reason she found this intriguing.

'Like Tames,' Guy said. 'No one pronounces the H in Thames.'

'Precisely,' Tomas agreed. 'Why waste an H when you don't have to.'

Everyone smiled, thinking it amusing.

'Where's Lily? Where's Helen?' Iris asked as she poured some batter into the hot pan.

'Lily's coming. Helen's got a headache.' Guy informed them.

'She'll miss lunch.'

'She doesn't care,' Guy told them. 'She was awake 'cause of the bombing all night.'

Iris looked at Tomas and sighed.

'Helen is very nervous. Her mother is in hospital. Got caught in a raid in January. Father's in Tobruk.'

'Fighting the Italians.' Guy added.

'How old are you?' Iris asked Tomas suddenly as she flipped the first pancake.

'Fifteen in June.'

'You look much older.'

'Maybe because I'm nearly bald now. I'm still getting over the shock of them stealing all my hair.'

'Can't stitch with hair on. It'll grow. Daddy says he was surprised your brains didn't fall out.'

Guy laughed, but Tomas didn't think that was funny.

Guy put his hands together and quickly said grace.

'For what we are about to eat, may the Lord make us truly thankful. Amen.'

They all muttered Amens.

'First pancake to Queenie,' Iris called out. 'Open the strawberry jam, Guy and only a quarter of a teaspoon each. Understand? We have to make it last.'

Queenie looked at the pancake and almost cried, she was so happy to see it. And even if there wasn't any sugar or lemon and only a bit of jam smeared over it, she treated it with great respect and ate really slowly, chewing every bit.

'More on the way. Where's Daddy?'

They heard a toilet flush and water splashing in a sink.

'Coming. Just washing my hands. I smell pancakes.'

Lily entered, her hair tied tight in a bun. She brushed past her father as he emerged from the washroom. She smiled at Tomas as she filled the kettle to make tea. Lily wasn't an identical twin. She was pale, quite opposite in looks to Iris, shoeless and wore a blue leotard. She looked haughty, as if she expected people to treat her like a princess. He didn't know which twin was the most beautiful.

'Pancakes. I don't think we've had pancakes since war began,' Lily declared. 'Is this Tomas? And when did you last have pancakes?'

Tomas couldn't remember the last time he had pancakes at all. Then remembered Gabriella had insisted on them on Shrove Tuesday and they'd eaten them so quickly they both had bad heartburn. It hurt to think of her. It was just as painful as the stitches on his head.

'Shrove Tuesday. With lemon and brown sugar. It was just before I broke my leg.'

'You broke your leg?' Iris and Lily asked together.

Dr Holmbush took up his chair at the head of the table.

'Yes, tell us about your leg, Tomas. That was a neat piece of work they did there. St Mary's Hospital in Portsmouth?'

'Yes sir. I was riding my bike in a late frost. I braked, the wheels slid away from me and suddenly I went right under an oncoming van. Dragged me and the bike fifty feet before he could stop. Luckily the van was high off the ground. Broke my leg in two places though. I was in a plaster cast for months. Nearly went mad with boredom.'

'No visible limp. They did a good job of putting you back together.'

Dr Holmbush told him, clearly impressed.

'I guess so. Clean breaks they said. I've got a lot of metal pinning it all together. The surgeon said I was lucky not to break more bones.'

'Fifty feet!' Lily gasped.

'I was wearing my iPod. Listening to ...' He remembered they wouldn't know what on earth he was talking about.

'iPod?'

'I wasn't paying attention. Listening to music in my head. Stupid.'

Iris was churning out pancakes quickly now. Lily put tea on the table for everyone and they all got a mug to drink it from.

'Well, you must have nine lives, Tomas,' Dr Holmbush declared. 'Broken legs, buried alive. I think you can pick out the winner of the Derby this June, eh?'

Tomas smiled. That he understood at least.

'Are you still at school?' Lily asked. 'Ours was bombed and it hasn't re-opened yet. That's why we volunteered at Queen's Gate. Can't let them beat us, you know.'

'Kids are growing up wild all over London now,' Dr Holmbush stated. 'Children need schooling. They'll grow up knowing nothing and turn to crime.'

'My school, Milbrook, was evacuated.' Tomas explained. 'The police took it over for themselves when the police station was bombed, but the school was destroyed two nights ago anyway. So, no school. Summer's almost here though.'

Tomas took his pancake from Iris and reached out for the jam. It was more like a very wafer-thin Yorkshire pudding than a pancake, but it was hot and smelled great.

'Go easy on the jam,' Iris reminded him. 'I'm so sick of rationing. Sometimes I dream of diving into the jam, I want it so much.'

Tomas grinned. She looked so serious.

Iris gave her father a pancake. She looked across at Tomas.

'So you will help us at the school?'

Tomas laughed. 'Of course. What do you want me to do?'

'Help with reading. I teach Mathematics on Monday, English and History on Tuesday, Lily teaches Dance and Gym on Wednesday. They only come three days. They need someone to help with reading skills. The WVS has it on Thursday and Fridays.'

Tomas put WVS through his memory. Women's Voluntary Service.

'I could do that. Might be a crap teacher though.'

Everyone went quiet. Tomas ate on, unaware he had offended.

‘Try not to bring bad language into the home, Tomas,’ Dr Holmbush said sternly.

Tomas frowned.

‘Er… sorry.’ He suddenly realised that ‘Crap’ was probably a bad word in 1941. He wondered what else he’d get wrong.

‘Apology accepted. Iris, this is wonderful. I hope you have enough for yourself?’

‘There’s enough for Mother tonight and at least four seconds now. Who wants seconds?’

Queenie’s hand shot up and a nervous Guy too.

‘Not you?’ Lily asked Tomas.

‘When the chef has eaten, not before,’ he answered. Iris smiled. She liked that answer.

Dr Holmbush was staring. Tomas looked at him with a question on his lips.

‘No, Tomas. I haven’t told anyone. I’m not a great believer in premonitions and don’t like to look a fool. If the House of Commons is to be bombed, it will be bombed. I assure you, no one would be foolish enough to wander its corridors whilst we are under attack.’

Tomas felt aggrieved. He wanted to be useful. He knew he had to atone for what he’d told Professor Wylie. If that was even possible.

Instead he shrugged and ate his pancake, which tasted very plain, not like a pancake at all, but he was very hungry. He realised he could eat ten of them. How was he going to get used to rationing? Everyone looked so painfully thin.

‘What is your best subject at school?’ Lily asked him suddenly.

Tomas frowned. ‘History, I think. I like to know why things happened.’

Lily wasn’t impressed, but Iris nodded with interest.

‘I’d like to know whose fault it is as to why we’re at war. Daddy says it was inevitable. But if it was inevitable, why weren’t we prepared for it? That’s what I want to know.’

‘Mr Churchill warned everyone war was coming,’ Tomas chipped in. ‘I know that much.’

‘But why didn’t they listen to him? Do you think we can survive it, Tomas? You’ve been buried alive three times. Can England take much more?’

‘Now, girls, you know I won’t allow any defeatist talk in this house,’ Dr Holmbush declared. ‘I will have another if there’s any spare, Iris.’

‘Small one coming up.’

Iris handed her father his second pancake.

'We shall have to get you a job in the Ministry, Tomas,' Lily said with a half smile. 'They need someone like you. Mummy says no one really believes we'll survive, but they have to pretend, because of morale.'

Tomas rubbed his head, wincing as he caught his stitches.

'Be very careful what you say,' Dr Holmbush told him. 'Be patriotic if you like Tomas, but don't go making predictions about the war or the bombing. People don't like it. They can easily become suspicious of your motives. No one likes people spreading despondency and alarm.'

Tomas said nothing. He sipped his sugarless tea. He had to learn to keep quiet. He had room and board now. He didn't want to lose it. He knew he had to work out a way to get back home, but until then, he had to work out how to stay alive without pissing people off, and sadly that seemed a very easy thing to do.

Dr Holmbush took out a silver cigarette case and took out an unfiltered cigarette. Tomas watched with astonishment as he put it to his lips and lit up. He was a Doctor and smoking inside, right beside all these kids.

'You smoke, Dr Holmbush? Don't you know about the dangers of passive smoking?' Tomas blurted out, instantly regretting not keeping this thought to himself.

Dr Holmbush looked at him with extreme irritation, but Iris and Lily were on his side, he could tell, even if they looked down at their plates mortified. They had never heard anyone openly criticise their father before, let alone a mere boy.

'I think I'm going to regret taking you in, Tomas Drucker.' He blew his smoke over Queenie, who instantly began coughing. 'If I should live long enough to die of cancer, I'd be happy, but as you can see from the state of London this morning, that's a pretty poor bet right now. And what, if I may ask is passive smoking? I am not familiar with this term.'

Tomas looked at him with astonishment, flushing red with embarrassment. He had to learn to control his reactions somehow and not judge people.

'Everyone inhaling your smoke. It's just as dangerous as smoking, especially for children. Don't they teach that at school?'

Iris and Lily and Guy all looked at him with interest. Queenie too, who was still coughing.

'I'm curious about this school you go to, Tomas. What else do they teach? What else is bad for us?'

Tomas shrugged. 'Everything really. The chemicals in the air and on our crops. We eat poison without realising it all the time. It's a long list. My friend Gabriella knows more. She's a health nut, only eats organic food.'

Dr Holmbush sighed. 'You're right. My wife is always asking me to give it up. Children shouldn't be exposed to smoke, or… I might add, high explosives.' He smiled a little at his sarcasm. 'You don't know how lucky you are, Tomas. Most people don't survive a direct hit.' He continued staring at Tomas, his lips pursed in thought a moment. 'When are you going to explain to me about those burns on your chest? I'd like to know how they got there.'

'Gabriella is such a pretty name,' Iris said suddenly, trying to lighten the conversation. 'Is she your girlfriend?'

Tomas smiled. 'She's my best friend, since we were five.'

Lily smiled. 'That's sweet. Is she pretty?'

'I guess, I mean, yeah definitely. She has a great smile and wild untamed hair. She wants to be a singer.' He looked out of the basement window as a bird perched on the sill. 'She's a long way away now. I'll probably never see her again.'

'She was evacuated?' Guy asked. 'I didn't want to go. Didn't want to leave London.'

'She's …' Tomas wondered exactly how far she was away. Sometimes she was right there with him when he thought of her, sometimes a million miles away. Right now he knew she was angry with him for changing everything. He wondered how bad it was back in her time.

'Canada. She was sent to Canada.' He lied.

Iris seemed quite happy to hear that. 'Well let's hope she doesn't get eaten by a bear.'

Tomas laughed. It was a funny thing to say.

'Your chest? Tomas. I do expect a reply,' Dr Holmbush insisted. 'You didn't get those burns in the bombing.'

'No sir, I didn't. It was just before it. I was being tortured.'

He heard the other kids inhale with surprise.

'Tortured?'

'By Nazi sympathisers. One of them was lying dead on the road earlier.'

'Excuse me for being less than convinced, Tomas, but you're just a schoolboy from Portsmouth. Why would anyone care about you or what you know? I am quite aware of psychological fantasies and such.'

Tomas sighed. He didn't want to get into this at all. He knew no one would ever believe him.

'I'd rather not talk about it sir. I'm not proud of what happened.'

'Did someone really torture you?' Lily asked, showing concern.

Tomas unbuttoned the shirt and showed her.

'Yes.'

'But why?' Iris gasped. 'Daddy's right, what could you possibly know?'

Tomas sipped his tea, all eyes on him now. He knew this could only end in tears and he didn't want it to. He liked Lily and Iris and didn't want to have to leave this house.

'Perhaps Tomas would like to talk to me in private,' Dr Holmbush suggested.

'I'm afraid you wouldn't believe a word I said, sir. It would be pointless. Besides, I promised to help Lily and Iris this afternoon.'

Dr Holmbush nodded, relieved in a way. The boy was curious, and he knew something terrible had happened to him, besides being bombed. He didn't want to press it, just yet.

'By all means. Teaching takes priority in this family.' He turned to Iris.

'He's in your charge. And see if you can get his secret out of him.'

Iris laughed. 'I'll get it out of him, Daddy.'

'But no use of torture, you understand.'

Lily and Iris laughed, thinking that terribly amusing. Tomas just sipped his tea and let it wash over him.

Dr Holmbush rose from his seat. 'Tell me, Tomas, what diseases have you had? Measles? Chicken pox? I have to jot some things down now you are living in my house.'

'None. I had the MMR jab, sir.'

'MMR?'

'Measles, mumps and rubella.'

'In one vaccine?'

'Yes sir.'

'They seem very progressive down there in Portsmouth. Polio? Smallpox?'

'Yes sir. It's compulsory.'

'Is it now? What, if anything, do children die of in Portsmouth then.'

'Most people seem to have an allergy to German bombs, sir.'

Dr Holmbush grinned. It was a good answer. His hand paused by the silver cigarette case. He saw the children staring and shrugged, closing his hand without taking it.

'He'll do, girls. I think you're in good hands.' He began to walk out of the kitchen. 'Don't forget your gas masks.'

And then he was gone.

Queenie got down from her chair and came over to Tomas, tugging on his sleeve.

'Did they burn you to make you tell the truth?'

Iris and Lily were astonished.

'Queenie spoke!'

Tomas let Queenie touch his burn. Her little finger traced it right across his chest. She seemed horrified and fascinated at the same time.

'Goes right around.' She whispered, and then withdrew her hand, adding, 'My real name's Hannah.'

She ran out of the kitchen, her little footsteps heavy on the uncarpeted stairs.

Lily looked at Thomas, still in shock. 'She spoke.'

Tomas nodded. 'Maybe something similar happened to her? You might want to ask her about that, Lily. She spoke for a reason.'

'You think Queenie was tortured?' Iris asked, appalled.

'Parents can do some terrible things to kids. I know that much.'

'Oh dear, that poor little girl. No wonder she's never spoken.'

'Was it really Nazis who tortured you?' Guy asked, very curious now.

Tomas looked at him and shrugged.

'One of them was English, though. I don't want to talk about it really.'

'Are you a member of a secret organisation?' Guy persisted.

Tomas laughed. 'No.'

'But you do know a secret,' Iris stated, looking at him curiously.

'Yes, but unfortunately so do they now.'

Lily and Iris exchanged glances. They both instantly resolved to find out what that secret was. They knew how to get secrets out of boys.

Tomas stood up, feeling odd and uncomfortable in his khaki shorts. He picked up his plate and took it to the sink. He had to try and fit in here, not make waves. Somehow he had to make amends for the information he'd told Professor Wylie. He'd like to pretend that it hadn't had an effect but that text he'd read from Gabriella before lunch gave a lie to that.

Tomas stop whatever it is u are doing. I hate this world u created. I don't want u to be a hero. Please, whatever u do, don't change history.

And he knew, somehow, that what he had said to Professor Wylie had done just that.

But how had everything changed? More importantly, *how* the hell was he ever going to get back?

'Is it a Navy secret?' Lily asked as they walked around the rubble in the street.

Tomas stared at the complete devastation of several buildings in this one street and how everyone seemed to regard it as completely normal. People were piling up bricks and salvaging building materials ready to patch and mend wherever they could. Horse drawn carts were everywhere being used for haulage, and he remembered about petrol rationing. A pack of wild dogs raced across the road arguing about some scrap of meat one of them had in his mouth. The air was filled with brick dust and the smell of burning. It was just another day after enemy bombing in London. The girls didn't seem fazed by it at all. They were utterly conditioned to this.

'No Navy secrets,' Tomas replied at last. 'There can't be much left of Portsmouth Docks after the last bombing and that can't be a secret.'

'Actually it is, Tomas.' Iris stated. 'They never say anything about the ports on the radio or in the newspapers, but we know it must be bad'. She stooped to pick up a book lying in the middle of the road, singed at the edges but otherwise intact. 'Oh, *Our Mutual Friend,* I never read this. It's in good condition too. Look around, are there any others we can salvage?'

Tomas could see that a small bookshop had been burned out as they crossed the road and someone had been trying to save some of the books – leaving them in piles on the pavement.

Lily picked up a brand new hardback. '*Darkness at Noon* by Arthur Koestler. Gosh, this was published last year. Mummy wanted to read it. It's about Stalin's Russia. I think this is a keeper too.'

'We can keep them?' Tomas asked. 'Isn't that…?'

Lily looked at Tomas and sighed.

'If we don't rescue them, someone else will. But if it rains, they'll be ruined. We get almost everything we have in the street now. Look, here's a comic for Queenie. Isn't amazing you got her to talk. She hasn't uttered a word since last Christmas. *Playbox Annual* with Tiger Tim. She'll love it. Wonderful. I feel sorry for the shopkeeper though.

I hope he isn't dead.'

Tomas looked up at the rest of the building and he knew that if the bookseller had been living above the shop he was most definitely dead.

'Find yourself a book, Tomas. You'll go crazy without a book to read. It's the only thing that keeps me sane these days.' Iris told him.

Tomas scouted the mess of books, tossing aside some burned editions. He felt guilty taking one, but they were scattered everywhere and would be lost. And there it suddenly was, the cover was burned, but the pages intact.

'What did you pick?' Iris asked.

'*Farewell My Lovely* by Raymond Chandler. It's almost new.'

Iris snorted. 'Typical boy, detective fiction.'

'I like them. Well, the American ones anyway. Philip Marlowe is pretty cool.'

'Cool?' Lily asked as she slipped her book into her crochet bag.

'Y'know. Smart, sarcastic, cynical tough guy.'

'Oh. Cool is sarcastic and cynical, so that's what you like.'

'And hot?' Iris asked, thinking she was being amusing.

'Hot is sexy.'

Both girls looked at him with widening eyes and giggled, linking arms with him as they made their way across past yet more rubble.

Ahead Firemen were damping down the remains of a clothing shop.

'Oh no, that's Madam Darmentier's shop. She sells such sweet French styled sweaters and dresses … well she did.'

Tomas could see that a whole row of small shops had been either bombed or burned out overnight. The real horror of this war was coming home to him. Businesses burned, people killed, jobs lost, and every night yet more shops or homes destroyed.

'It must be hard getting things you want now, what with clothing being rationed,' he mused.

'Clothing rationed? No. Not that. I didn't hear about that. Did you Lily?'

Lily looked at Iris appalled. 'No. They can't. I mean, they can, but surely not.'

Tomas realised that it probably hadn't happened yet.

'It starts soon. I know it does. Cotton is in short supply. You should probably stock up on things. My friend Gabriella, she had a great Grandma who was in the war and she said the thing she hated most was clothes rationing and not being able to find anything in her size.'

Iris looked askance at Tomas.

'Which war? The Great War? They had clothing rationing then? I don't think so.'

Tomas realised he'd made a stupid mistake again.

'I'm sorry. It's one of the secrets. Believe me, clothing will be rationed soon.'

Lily paused a moment and looked at him. 'You can't possibly know this. Mummy works in the Ministry and she'd know, if anyone did. How do you know, Tomas?'

'Perhaps he's psychic,' Iris suggested with a smile.

Tomas realised that was the best idea he'd heard since he'd got there. He shrugged.

'That's my real secret. You guessed it.'

Iris and Lily laughed. 'You're psychic?' They chorused.

'Did you run away from the Fair, or something?'

'Or the circus? Do you tell fortunes?'

Tomas broke free of them and walked ahead, turning to face them.

'It's not something I can control. I just know some things. It comes to me. Sometimes it comes true and sometimes it doesn't. A psychic can't predict what he'll see. Please don't tell your father. He's a Doctor, he won't believe in anything like that.'

'No he won't,' Iris agreed. 'Daddy only believes in science.'

'But you definitely saw clothing being rationed.'

Tomas squeezed his eyes, scanning the history book he'd read whilst a prisoner in his bedroom at home.

He shook his head. 'It's soon. Very soon. Ask your mother. They have posters called 'Make Do and Mend.' I've seen them … in my mind.'

'Oh, my Lord. Mummy was talking about that two nights ago. Remember Lily? She was asking about a slogan they could use. Make do and Mend. She knows about it and is keeping it secret from us. Tomas is right. We have to stock up on clothes and …'

Tomas took a deep breath. He wondered was it better to pretend he was psychic, a 'freak'? Or tell them he was from the future? He had absolutely no idea which was better or worse.

'And they tortured you to find out what you know?' Iris asked as they resumed walking.

Tomas nodded.

'Were you brave?'

Tomas shook his head. 'No. Sorry. I wish I had been.'

'They burned him, Iris. You would have squealed too.

Iris conceded that. 'Yes. But you said they were English?'

'I can't talk about it.'

An old fashioned London bus came around the corner laden with passengers, many crowded around the open deck at the rear. No health and safety here then, Tomas was thinking. He realised that he wanted to leap onto that bus and look at the rest of London. It was in ruins, he knew, but like any other gawper, he wanted to see it all for himself.

'Can you see if there's a handsome pilot in my future,' Lily asked, taking his arm again.

Tomas smiled. 'Sorry I don't think I can tell fortunes, but I do know you'll break many hearts, Lily.'

Lily laughed. 'Of course I will. Boys are very susceptible to pretty girls.'

'Modest ones too,' Iris added, joining him on the other side.

'There's the school. We won't mention anything about you being psychic. We don't want them to be scared of you.'

Tomas could see the children's expectant faces at the gates. He was going to teach. How weird was that? If only Gabriella could see him now.

Tomas went to bed early. With no electricity and no inclination to try to read by candlelight downstairs, he went up to his room to await the inevitable bombing raid. He wished that he was wrong and he had misremembered, but that date, the end of the Blitz, was stuck there in his memory and he knew it was going to happen.

The twins fretted because their mother hadn't returned. Iris hinted that her mother was not coming home a great deal of late, but at least she was safe sleeping underground in the Ministry building. Tomas got the impression that something else was worrying her about her mother and her reluctance to come home. He sensed that she was worried that her mother may have met someone else and about how it might affect her father.

Tomas had lain in his bed with one blanket pulled over him, wondering if the bombs would fall on Kensington. He stared up at the sky watching and waiting. Iris had insisted he was supposed to have the blackout blind down tight and not let a single chink of light out for fear of prosecution; wardens were very strict about making sure no house showed a light to help the bombers find their way. The electric power had failed at 7pm so there was no risk of any stray lights and besides, it was a very warm night and he needed the air. The chestnut tree in the garden rustled in the breeze and Tomas was also amazed at how quiet the city was. No traffic, no shouting, just the occasional rumble of the underground trains nearby – which had it's own more secure power supply.

He was waiting for the bombers. It was a bright waning moon and he knew that the River Thames would be like a shining path all the way to London for the German pilots. This would be the night Westminster Abbey went up in flames and a million other pieces of history would be consumed by the raging fires and rubble.

The bombers were coming. The night air seemed to throb – even from a distance. The air-raid sirens were beginning to be cranked up right across the city. He realised that he'd done nothing to stop this. Absolutely nothing. He felt utterly useless.

He heard aircraft in the distance. Junkers 88s and Heinkel bombers – he had already become skilled at distinguishing German aircraft engine differences.

Lily suddenly appeared at his door wearing a cardigan over her nightie.

'We have to go to the basement now, Tomas. Bring a pillow and your blanket.'

She disappeared. Tomas leapt out of bed, he had no wish to be buried alive again. He slipped on his shirt and shorts and grabbed his bag. He paused at the door. Would he ever see this bedroom again?

Queenie was on the stairs looking dazed, clutching a teddy bear. He remembered her real name and took her hand.

'Come on, Hannah. Let's get downstairs.'

'I'm scared.'

'Me too. Let's go, huh?'

Tomas scooped her up and he quickly descended the dark stairs, remembering too late that he was still barefoot. Guy stumbled out of a room rubbing his eyes and followed him down.

Iris was making tea. Lily was preparing spaces for everyone to sleep, struggling to see by candlelight.

'Where's your father?' Tomas asked.

'He's coming. He's getting his emergency kit ready. He's always busy after a raid.'

Iris counted heads. Tomas saw a new face squatting in the corner and knew that must be Helen.

'Daddy?' Lily called out concerned.

'Coming.' He shouted down from the ground floor.

The bombers were coming all right. The night air trembled and rumbled.

'How many?' Guy whispered, real fear in his voice.

'Over 500,' Tomas replied. 'This is the night they try to break our will. Every hospital's a target, all the stations, even Westminster Abbey. They'll drop everything they've got, firebombs, they want to see London burn. It's going to be a nightmare.'

Lily and Iris stared at him in alarm, but said nothing. Guy shook. It wasn't what he wanted to hear at all.

Dr Holmbush came down in his dressing gown carrying two medicine bags and a bottle of scotch.

'Everyone settle down. Iris, I think a prayer, don't you?'

Dr Holmbush didn't look at Tomas. Didn't want to acknowledge what he'd predicted earlier was coming true.

The growing noise was terrifying. Outside they knew the sky was coming to life with searchlights piercing the gloom looking for enemy bombers, the ground artillery blindly firing away at them and then soon the inevitable falling bombs.

'May God spare us all,' Iris said softly. 'May God give us strength to face the morning and carry on. May God keep Mother safe and see her return to us tomorrow.'

'Amen,' Lily and her father added.

'Don't you pray?' Lily asked Tomas, noting his silence.

Tomas shrugged. 'The Germans pray to God for victory every time they come. I'm not sure on whose side God really is.'

'That's a shocking thing to say, Tomas Drucker,' Dr Holmbush declared.

'But true,' Iris acknowledged. 'I'm hoping God doesn't take sides though. I've made tea. We still have fresh milk. Help yourselves.'

Tomas grabbed a mug and filled it, adding milk. The hot liquid was strangely comforting in his hands as the moment of doom approached.

'There's more than usual,' Dr Holmbush was saying, listening to the drone of engines in the sky. 'A lot more.'

'Over 500,' Tomas reminded him. 'You'll be busy tomorrow.'

'You can't actually know this,' Dr Holmbush told him. 'You can't know anything. It's just a delusion, Tomas. Stop frightening everyone.'

'We should have warned them. It's going to be bad,' Tomas muttered, finding a space to lie down in. It was going to be a long night. He tried to think what happened next in British history? His mind was filled with images of destruction and confusion.

The bombs began to fall. At first in the distance, then they grew ever closer. Thousands of bombs. The ground never stopped shaking under them. London was burning. Hannah began to sob and Iris comforted her. Lily tried to read by candlelight. Dr Holmbush drank whiskey, wincing as yet more bombs fell. Dust and bits of plaster fell from the walls. Tomas hoped the concrete above them was as thick as Iris thought it was. He realised that he had no idea how all these people had remained sane and so normal in all these weeks of bombing.

Somehow, against all probabilities, in all this shaking and noise, Tomas fell asleep.

Rough hands woke him, shook him awake from a dream where he was on a bus with Gabriella and they were going to Scotland.

Tomas opened his eyes to find a haggard looking Dr Holmbush and a very worried Lily staring at him.

It was early morning, he could tell from the light in the stairwell. A radio was on in the background. That meant the electric power was back.

'How did you know, Tomas? How could you have known?'

One look at the Doctor's face and he knew that all he'd said had come true.

'Westminster Abbey? House of Commons?' He asked.

Lily was nodding. 'King's Cross, Euston, Charing Cross, all the stations, Tomas. The British Museum and the Old Bailey. All gone.'

'The hospitals too. They think there's almost 1500 dead across London and another 2000 injured, at the very least,' Dr Holmbush said.

Tomas noticed he was covered in blood. He'd already been outside attending to the wounded. He was angry, that much Tomas could tell.

'I need to understand, Tomas. How could you possibly know what the targets were in such detail?'

Tomas was angry now and shouted. 'You didn't warn anyone. I told you to warn people. We could have saved lives.'

Dr Holmbush rubbed his unshaven face, too exhausted to argue.

'You know I didn't. Who would have believed me? What was I supposed to say? A strange schoolboy has visions? Lily says you are psychic. Did you tell her that?'

Tomas sat up, rubbing the sleep from his eyes.

'It was easier than the truth.'

Dr Holmbush was staring at Tomas with extreme hostility now. Perhaps angry with himself for not passing on his warning. Guilty, knowing he could have saved lives.

'He has to be psychic,' Lily insisted. 'He saw it all in such detail.'

Iris returned with a bundle of bandages she placed upon the table.

She could detect the tension in the room.

'He's awake then. Can't believe you slept through all that.'

'He's going to tell us how he knew what was going to be bombed,' Lily explained to her sister.

Tomas looked at Iris and shrugged. Dr Holmbush was in no mood for explanations, however.

'Psychic, poppycock. First he claims he has been tortured, and then he predicts precise bombing targets. Impossible I say, unless he knew, unless he knew the targets. Drucker, I believe is a German name. Perhaps your psychic boy would care that explain that?'

Iris looked at Tomas with surprise.

'My father was German,' Tomas confirmed. 'But my mother never told him about me. She didn't even know where he lived.'

Dr Holmbush was even more appalled.

'You're a bastard?'

Iris was shocked at her father's tone. She was crying, Tomas realised.

'Yes sir. I believe that is what I am. My mother never married.'

'A common tart, in other words,' Dr Holmbush exploded.

'Daddy!' Lily and Iris protested together.

Tomas realised that he needed to pee. This scene with the Doctor could only end badly. He was on his way out of this house and he realised with a sinking heart that he really didn't want to go.

'My mother wasn't a good person, sir. I can't pretend she was.'

Iris intervened. 'Leave him alone, Daddy. He can't be blamed for what his mother did.'

'Nonsense. It's all nonsense.' Dr Holmbush shouted. He let Tomas stand up. Tomas realised that he was almost the same height as the Doctor.

'Tell me now, Tomas Drucker. Are you a German spy? I need to know what kind of person I have allowed into my house.'

Tomas stared at him incredulously.

'I'm just a schoolboy, sir. I don't speak German. I don't know any Germans. I just want to survive the war.'

'And what is your next prediction?' Dr Holmbush asked. His tone was mocking now.

Tomas folded his arms. 'It doesn't work like that.'

'And how does it work, Tomas? You need to be tortured first?'

'Yes, sir, torture is one way.'

Iris gasped. She tried to change the subject

'They'll need us to give blood over at the hospital. We should go. I don't know why you're making such a fuss, Daddy. You've been saying for weeks that they'll try to destroy the Palace of Westminster and the stations. They were the only things left standing.'

Dr Holmbush shuffled a step back, realising he was making a scene here.

'I want to know exactly how Tomas knew.' He said petulantly.

'Daddy thinks Tomas is a German spy, Iris.' Lily explained.

Iris frowned 'Daddy, he's psychic. I know you don't believe in these things but…'

Tomas looked at Iris and shook his head.

'I'm not psychic, Iris. I'm sorry, I really wish I were. The truth is even harder to believe.'

Tomas picked up his satchel and began to rummage around in it.

'I'll show you, but you won't like it. None of you will like it.'

'What have you got there?' Dr Holmbush asked.

Tomas pulled out his history book and the cuttings from the *Sunday Times Magazine* and a picture of him and Gabriella posing beside a Ferrari that was parked outside her house one day. He'd forgotten it was there.

Dr Holmbush's patience was wearing thin. 'What is all this?'

Tomas handed him the magazine cuttings first.

'Look at the date, sir.'

Dr Holmbush examined the small print at the top of the pages.

28th April 2013.

He barely registered it. He looked at the headline.

Print RIP in the battle of e-books

'What am I looking at? What does this prove?' He seemed more annoyed than ever.

'I was doing a project at school, on the demise of printed books and...'

'Demise of printed books?' Lily asked. 'What does that even mean?'

'Hardly anyone buys printed books anymore. Not like the ones we found yesterday. You download them onto your iPad or Kindle or whatever and read them on screen. No one thought it would take off so quickly, but in the end it was like a sudden death. Bookshops are disappearing fast. I don't expect you will understand.'

Iris snatched the pages from her father and scanned the words.

'You're saying that no one reads books anymore – in the future?'

'No. They still read, but they prefer electronic books. It's logical. You can store a 1,000 books on one tablet.'

Dr Holmbush was frowning. He had no comprehension of what Tomas was saying.

'What the dickens has this got to do with last night's bombing?'

'Everything, sir. I knew about it because it was history. You are *all* history. Iris, Lily, little Hannah there and Guy. You're all history. I don't come from now…'

Dr Holmbush took another step back.

'Don't say it. You're delusional. Psychotic. My God, we have let a madman into the house. Well, I won't stand for it. You'll have to go. I know it is unfair. It's unreasonable, but you cannot stay an hour longer in this house. There are children here and they need protecting.'

Lily was looking at the photograph of Tomas and Gabriella.

'This is you and your friend?'

Tomas nodded.

'What is that? A rocket?'

Dr Holmbush grabbed the photo, staring at it wildly.

'It's a Ferrari. It was parked outside her house. One of the footballers I should think. They get paid a lot. Well, they used to when Portsmouth was doing well.'

'Ferrari?'

'It's an Italian sports car. It can do around 200 mph. I don't think they existed in 1941.'

'We're at war with Italy,' Dr Holmbush told him. 'This is your proof? A car? I don't even know what it is supposed to prove?'

Iris was shaking her head as she read the *Sunday Times* article.

'I don't even know what these words are. Terabytes? Why do they keep saying Apple? How can an apple be a market leader? What's a Samsung?' She looked up at her father. 'This is an article from the year 2013, Daddy. It means there's a future.'

Tomas winced. 'I hope so. I might have done something to prevent that.'

'What do you mean?' Dr Holmbush asked.

'When I was tortured. I may have altered history.'

'Stuff and nonsense. You're delusional, Tomas. Nothing you do can alter history. It's impossible. I really don't want you in this house any longer.'

'But,' Lily was staring at the history book that Tomas had unpacked. 'Look. Japan declares war on America December 7th 1941. This hasn't even happened yet.'

'Now you're psychic, too,' Tomas told her.

Iris snatched the book from Lily. She was looking at the index.

'My God, Daddy. The war doesn't end until *1945*! That's four more years, We can't live like this for four more years.' Her lips began to tremble, her eyes grew wet.

'It's a fake, a work of fiction, a trick to demoralise us,' Dr Holmbush declared. 'Don't you see? If everyone believed the war was going to carry on like this we would be more likely to want to sue for peace? How many are there, Tomas? How many books did they print? How many more boys like you are out there spreading these evil lies?'

'It's not a lie. There's just me. But it might be out of date now. The man who tortured me got information about stuff they shouldn't know.'

'You were not tortured. You are not in some silly science fiction film. You are a menace, however. That is what you are. You think Iris and Lily could carry on if they thought this bombing would last another four years?'

'It doesn't. It ended last night. I told you. The Blitz ended on the night of May 10th 1941. Everything changes from today. Hitler isn't going to invade us. He's going to invade Russia.'

'You can't know that. You can't know anything, you're just a boy.'

Lily was looking at the photograph again.

'Gabriella is pretty. She's wearing jeans. They are very … hot.'

Tomas smiled and took the photo back. He didn't want to lose it.

'Hot?' Dr Holmbush remarked, not understanding. He turned back to Tomas. 'I want you gone, Tomas. Have your breakfast and go. I don't care where, just go.'

'No,' Lily and Iris shouted. 'He's from the future. He has proof.'

Tomas shook his head.

'Your father's right. I didn't realise that if I reveal what happens it could affect how you deal with the present. I should go. It's my fault. And Dr Holmbush is right. Anything can be faked. You can't know if the Germans printed this.'

Iris was checking.

'It was printed in China! China, of all places. They don't even speak English, do they?'

'Ah, well,' Tomas explained, 'that's because everything in 2013 is made in China. It's the world's second largest economy, bigger than Japan even and they make everything else.'

Dr Holmbush groaned.

‘That’s stupid. Don’t say any more. You are just contaminating their minds with your foolish madness.’

Tomas sighed and packed away all the other things.

‘I want to thank you for taking me in, Dr Holmbush. I appreciate it. I really do. You are very nice people.’

‘Don’t think I won’t report you to the…’ he wasn’t quite sure who to report it to, actually.

‘Thanks to Professor Wylie, it’s all going to change anyway,’ Tomas sighed.

Dr Holmbush grabbed his arm.

‘What you do mean? Thanks to Professor Wylie? How do you know him? One of the most respected academics in all of London? You dare to involve his name in all of this?’

Tomas winced; he was hurting his arm.

‘That’s mummy’s friend,’ Lily said. ‘She’s always going to see him. He can’t be who you mean…’

‘Professor Wylie tortured me. He’s a Nazi-sympathiser, the Fifth Column, I think people call it. It’s always the people you least suspect.’

Dr Holmbush narrowed his eyes at Tomas. ‘He is the foremost academic in this country, a man who advises Winston Churchill and you are accusing him of treason? Do you have any idea what you are saying? What the implications of that are?’

‘Yes, sir.’ He could see that Lily looked disappointed in him now. ‘I’m afraid you can’t trust anyone. They have sympathisers everywhere, in MI5 even, and they are all waiting for England to fall. Your mother may not realise…’

‘You do not even mention her name,’ Dr Holmbush snapped. ‘I will not let you poison my children’s minds.’

Tomas shrugged. Iris handed back his history book to him but he pushed it back towards her.

‘Keep it. It might make sense later. It’s too heavy to lug around.’

Iris was about to protest, but she could see how sad Tomas looked. She didn’t know why, but in that instant she knew he was telling the truth. (Even if she was disappointed he wasn’t really psychic.)

‘Have your breakfast first. I’m making porridge.’ She told him.

‘Feed him then get him out of my sight,’ Dr Holmbush said tersely and walked up the stairs. ‘I’m going to get dressed. People will need help out there. People worth saving.’

‘I have to go to…’ Tomas whispered suddenly and ran to the downstairs bathroom.

Lily and Iris looked at each other for a long moment.

'You believe him?' Lily asked.

Iris nodded. 'How would a boy fake a book like that? *A Sunday Times* magazine from 2013? Impossible, but it's here, Lily. We could learn a lot from him.'

'You could learn a lot from him, you mean. He's just a boy. He doesn't really know anything.'

'He can stay at the school. There's that room at the top.'

Lily nodded. 'The children liked him, at least.'

'Don't tell Daddy.' She snatched a look at Hannah and Guy quietly waiting for their porridge. 'You don't say anything either.'

'Is he really from the future?' Hannah asked softly.

Iris shrugged. 'He says so.'

'You think he's got a time machine?' Guy asked.

Lily laughed. 'Ask him.'

They heard the toilet flush. Lily looked at Iris again.

'I'll get his shoes. Daddy won't want him upstairs again.'

Lily left, running bare footed up the stairs.

Tomas rejoined everyone in the kitchen.

'I need my shoes…' he began.

'Lily's gone to fetch them,' Hannah informed him. 'Have you got a time machine?'

Tomas smiled, sitting down at the table.

'Don't ask me how I got here. That bit I just don't understand at all. There was this storm and …'

'A storm?' Iris asked, serving him a dollop of porridge that looked a lot like cement. 'Sorry, no sugar. Don't use all the milk.'

Tomas looked at the porridge and forced himself to eat it. He realised that it might be a while before he ate again.

'I'm sorry if I upset everyone, Iris.'

Iris shook her head.

'I believe you. I want to know more. I want to know how people live in the future. I want to know how we survive this war. I can't believe it will last four more years. There won't be anything left to bomb. It'll be just like *Things to Come,* did you see it? H G Wells' film? He predicted the war would last years and years and all of London would be rubble. We watched it at the film club last year. It was so depressing. Lily hated it.'

Iris shook her head. 'It was ridiculous. They shoot people off into space with big guns. Daddy said gravity would crush them in an instant.' She paused a moment. 'You sure it was Professor Wylie who hurt you?'

'Goatee, silver hair, vain, strokes his hair a lot, a gold tooth.'

Iris frowned. 'That's him. Daddy said he's important… but he hates him really. Lily thinks mummy is having an affair with him. Daddy does too, but he won't say anything.'

Tomas was appalled.

'I'm sorry, Iris.'

'Go to the school. There's a room up at the top where we go for breaks. You can stay there. If you volunteer in the kitchen you'll get food and when your ID card comes I'll bring it to you.'

Tomas nodded.

'I don't want to get you into trouble.'

'You need a friend and you have to promise you'll tell me everything you know about the future. Who knows, I could write science fiction stories and they would all come true!'

Tomas laughed.

'Yeah. For now. Unless Professor Wylie has his way.'

Lily came down the stairs with his shoes.

'Mummy's home. You'd better go, Tomas.'

Tomas took the shoes from her, quickly putting them on. He grabbed his bag, pulling the strap over his shoulders.

'Is there a back door?'

Lily nodded. 'But it's stiff, there's lots of broken glass and stuff out in the alley.'

'I hear we have a guest,' Mrs Holmbush was saying as she descended the stairs.

Tomas stared at a beautiful elegant woman with flowing auburn hair, wearing a black smart jacket and skirt. She could see exactly why Lily and Iris were so pretty. She stared at him for a second, making a judgement no doubt, then turned to face Iris.

'Is there anything to eat, Iris, my darling? I'm exhausted. Spent the night in the basement of the Ministry again. London is ruined. Just about everything is destroyed. It's just too awful, my dears. I should have sent you away to the country weeks ago.'

'Pancakes, Mummy? We saved you some of the batter from last night.'

'Pancakes? Luxury. My goodness, don't you girls know there's a war on?' She laughed lightly.

Mrs Holmbush took a small packet out of her handbag and handed it over to Iris. 'Coffee. It's already ground. Fresh this morning. I couldn't resist. Your father certainly looks as though he needs it.'

'Was it bad? Was the Ministry bombed?' Lily asked.

'Flattened. We will have to find somewhere else to work. I cried when I saw Westminster Abbey in ruins and the debating chamber at the House of Commons is gone completely. It's devastating, my dears, so much blood and so many dead people. My shoes are ruined.'

She took off her jacket and sat down on a chair to remove her bloodstained shoes. She glanced up at Iris again.

'I hope there's enough food for my friend. We're starving.'

Tomas looked up as more legs descended the stairs. His heart skipped a beat as he saw who it was. The man didn't seem surprised to find Tomas there at all.

'Well, if it isn't Tomas Drucker. Still alive I see.'

Lily looked at Tomas, the surprise writ large on her face. He glanced at Iris and she understood in an instant what she had to do and darted quickly towards the backdoor.

'Run Tomas, run,' Iris shouted suddenly. 'Run.'

Tomas didn't need telling.

Mrs Holmbush stared opened-mouthed as Professor Wylie tried to grab him. Tomas evaded his grasp, running to the back of the kitchen.

'What's going on?' Mrs Holmbush shouted.

'You're not going to get him,' Iris shouted as she tried to push open the stiff back door. Tomas crashed into it and forced it open, squeezing out through a gap and outside before anyone could stop him.

Professor Wylie stared at Iris – seething with anger.

'You don't know how dangerous that boy is. Damnation, child. I must find him.'

He turned and raced up the stairs.

Iris and Lily faced the growing wrath of their mother who still couldn't make any sense of all this. Iris quickly hid Tomas' history book under the old leather sofa.

'What on earth has been going on here? You will tell me now, girls. Who was that boy?'

'He's from the future,' Hannah declared. 'He's gone back to his time machine.'

13

May 11th 2013 Launch Day

Gabriella had woken hours earlier after a restless night. She realised that she was nervous about meeting her father again. She hadn't seen him in months. Not only that, now she was in this other 'world' she didn't know what to expect. Before he left, he'd always been encouraging her in her studies. He'd never let her slack off and he'd been very supportive of Tomas too. She knew he liked Tomas and it was her father who'd coached him for the scholarship to Millbrook. Perhaps, she realised, he knew just how much she relied on Tomas and how close they had become a long time before she did. He was just making sure he had the same kind of opportunities she would have in life.

But now – in this weirdness, how different would her father be? She'd seen her mother go from lawyer to homemaker and that was just totally freaky. Feminism had just never happened. She was this bread-making homemaker who discussed recipes. She hadn't even known how to cook before. Pizza delivery was on speed dial.

Gabriella stretched and pulled the sheets off her. Sunshine was streaming through the window. It was going to be a perfect May Saturday. They would be driving to Southampton for the launch of the new flying boat. That at least would be a change.

She showered, washed her hair and looked for the pretty white cotton dress she'd bought in the sale at Primark in January. Then she looked again. Where were all her summer clothes? The stuff in her wardrobe was hideous. She wouldn't want to be seen dead in any of it. What was anyone thinking? Who exactly had chosen this stuff? Her mother? Had to be.

She rummaged through her wardrobe trying to find something that would be halfway presentable and took out a white blouse and a light blue pleated cotton skirt with little diamond motifs on it that was possibly acceptable in a retro kind of way. She couldn't believe the shoes either. Open toed sandals or plain white dorky plimsolls. Did she own nothing decent at all?

Depressed, she stuck a grip in her hair to pin it back a little and grabbed her tiny Topshop cardigan with pearl buttons. That at least still existed, if only because she'd been wearing it on the day Tomas disappeared.

She discovered it was only eight o'clock when she got downstairs. She fed the cat and let him out. No one was up, which was a relief. She remembered her father hated getting up on Saturday mornings – at least that hadn't changed

There was mail. A ton of it, all addressed to her father. The newspaper was stuck in the letterbox. She dragged it out and wondered when they had started getting the *Daily Telegraph*. '*Anarchy in Spain – Terror bombing in San Sebastian and Vigo by separatists. President Clinton opens second front in fifteenth year of Sino-War*'

Always war. People learned nothing.

'You're up early. Excited?'

Gabriella jumped. Her father was standing on the landing above her in his pyjamas. He had a moustache. He'd never had a moustache before.

'Hi Daddy.'

'Get the kettle on. I'll join you for breakfast.'

Gabriella smiled. He actually seemed quite normal. The same, even.

'Congratulations on your medal,' she remembered to say.

He took a little bow. 'I'm just grateful someone read the book. Now get that kettle on. Be down in a moment.'

Gabriella went back into the kitchen, much relieved. She'd been deathly afraid he'd be – well, different.

She toasted her mother's bread buns, made sure there were at least three sorts of jam on the table and made fresh coffee. She realised that she hadn't actually had breakfast with her father in over a year. A long time.

He came down wearing a tweed jacket and brown corduroy trousers. Made him look older. Like a professor. The moustache took some getting used to, but at least his smile was the same.

'Hmm, smells good. Your mother's been baking again.'

'She bakes every Thursday now.'

'Well she's good at it. How are you? It feels like I haven't seen you in ages. You've grown, I swear, and I like what you've done with your hair. Much more natural. I hate the way everyone seems to wear it tight around their heads now.'

'When did you grow the moustache?' Gabriella asked.

He looked at her with surprise.

'I've always had a moustache.'

Gabriella said nothing.

'You excited about the launch today, Gabby? The first turbo-jet flying boat. The Fantastdampter can fly to Lake Ontario in just seven hours, non-stop. Bet you'd like to visit Toronto.'

'Fantastdampter?' She didn't know this word.

'Dream Liner if my German is correct.'

'Sounds better in English.' She'd meant to find out more about the plane but had forgotten.

'Mummy said it was designed for the Africa route.'

He nodded, buttering his toast.

'Well, I was leaving that for the surprise.'

'Surprise?'

'There's a possibility of a senior post at Kapstadt University. We might be going to the Cape. You'd love it, Gabby. Southern Africa, or Südafrika as they call it now is the fastest developing country. The new electric Trans-African railway is almost complete, all the way to Cairo. They are crying out for settlers from Europe and it's going to be an interesting future there. Dr Schmidt is investing in the wine industry in Stellenbosch. New machines that can pick all the grapes – solves the labour shortage in one blow. Astonishing.'

'Labour shortage?' Gabriella asked cagily. She seemed to recall an Africa teeming with people.

'The pandemic wiped out millions. It was a great tragedy.'

'Pandemic?' Gabby asked. She knew nothing about this.

'It was a new kind of 'flu. Began shortly after the atomic tests in the Sudan – although the scientists denied there was any connection. It developed a new lethal strain in the Congo, then spread everywhere before they could contain it. Populations crashed. It was one of the world's greatest disasters. Ports and airports were restricted for years.'

'Did any white people die? Or did it only affect the Africans.' Gabby asked. She was suspicious of everything now. How convenient to have a pandemic in Africa to get rid of anyone you didn't want there.

Her father looked at her sharply. 'No need to be so cynical. It was a natural occurrence, Gabby. No Berlin dark arts involved, and yes, it affected everyone, of all colours and religions, including devastating the wildlife. It took almost a decade to restore order. The Cape was the first area to recover. It's safe now, if that's what's worrying you. Just think about living somewhere warm, Gabby.'

'But it's thousands of miles away.'

'Six thousand miles actually. It would be an adventure.'

Gabriella realised she knew nothing about this Africa.

'I take it you haven't actually read my book, or you'd know all this.'

Gabriella shook her head. 'Not yet.'

Her father looked momentarily peeved. 'Well you can easily remedy that, Miss Lamb. But for the record, since Germany took control, poverty and disease have been practically eliminated. The German Congo provides our copper. Rhodesia and Südafrika are the richest and most stable protectorates on the continent. The wheat you eat right here in this bun probably comes from there. Nigeria is rich since they found all that oil. As the German Chancellor said, all Africa ever needed was a strong hand and discipline and it would bloom.

Gabriella recognised the code words immediately. Strong hand meant so much more in German speak. She wondered how many Nigerians were rich and sharing that wealth.

'And the Africans? What about them?' She feared the worst.

He looked at her for a long moment then shrugged.

'You can't stop progress, Gabriella. It's swim or drown in this world. They lost the war, the pandemic took its toll. The survivors have jobs and a stake in the future. That's what is important.'

'But what does that mean, exactly.'

'Evolution is all about survival of the fittest. We have to learn to live within the rules.'

German rules. Gabriella said nothing more. She poured coffee for them both. She resolved to read his book, but instinctively knew she wasn't going to like what she found in there.

'Daddy, do you remember my friend, Tomas?'

He looked at her a moment, confused. Almost as if he did remember for a second – then shook his head.

'Thomas? No.'

'Tomas, without an H.'

'Like the boy hero. Tomas Drucker, you mean.'

Gabriella stared at him – surprised that he didn't make the connection to Tomas, her friend.

'Yes. Tomas Drucker. You don't remember him at all?'

He looked at her, puzzled, as he added sugar.

'He was a boy in the war. Long before I was born.'

'He was buried alive in a bombing raid. I saw *London Illustrated News* photos of him in the Cultural Museum.'

He suddenly remembered she'd been away to London.

'Oh, yes. How was your London adventure? Your mother says that the concert went down well. It was on the radio.'

'It was?'

'You don't quite seem all there today, Gabby. Didn't you sleep?'

'Bad night. But Tomas, I saw him in the heroes section and…'

'Without him the war could have dragged on for months longer, years even. He probably saved millions of lives. Some kind of hero, I suppose.'

'I don't understand what happened. How a boy could even talk to anyone in Government or make contact with the Germans? Wouldn't he have been considered a traitor?'

'Hero or traitor? Sounds like a good essay topic.'

'That's the essay title.' Gabriella told him quickly to appease him. 'Please can you explain how it actually happened?'

He looked at her for a moment to make sure she was serious, then nodded.

'When we're driving to Southampton, perhaps. Meanwhile take a breakfast tray up to your mother. Give her a treat. She hasn't had breakfast in bed in a long time, I bet.'

Gabriella nodded and began to butter some toast for her.

'When would we go to SüdAfrika? And when did they rename it?'

'After the war a lot of places got renamed, to the victor the spoils and all that. We'd go in December, I should think. The academic year starts in January there. But it isn't confirmed yet. I have found a nice school for you though. St Cyprian's. I'm told it's the best in the city.'

Gabriella said nothing. She hated moving schools. She'd have to make new friends again and she'd be in Africa. What on earth would that be like?

She gathered all the breakfast things up for her mother and a mug of coffee. Her father was right, her mother hadn't had breakfast in bed in a long time. It would be a treat.

They were on a narrow two-lane road jammed with cars. It was going to take forever to get there. The air was foul with smoking car exhausts.

'Can you tell me now. About Tomas Drucker, I mean, and why exactly we lost the war? The truth, Daddy. Not the stuff they say in school.'

Her father frowned, uncomfortable with her question. He sighed.

'He made Hitler realise that although he hadn't defeated England militarily, there were enough people there who wanted peace. The Pro-Peace party was growing all the time and had many influential people in it. Lloyd George, a former Prime Minister tried to have Churchill dismissed for his lack of leadership in the war but had been defeated in parliament. Viscount Halifax, a prominent appeaser, was working behind the scenes with other important figures. Nevertheless, all that stood between peace and continued war was Winston Churchill. The German Chancellor had sent Rudolph Hess to negotiate with the Pro-Peace movement but Churchill had him locked up, he was never allowed to speak.'

'But where does Tomas come into all this? It makes no sense to me.'

'It's what happens next. Tomas makes contact with the Pro-Peace deputy leader Professor Wylie and he makes a representation to Churchill on Tomas' behalf.'

'That's it? A boy protests and Churchill just sees him and then agrees to a peace?'

'The official version is that Churchill discovered that the Pro-Peace movement was much bigger and more widespread than he thought. England was so demoralised by the relentless Blitz, he knew he had to negotiate peace or face the utter destruction of the country. A million homes in London had been destroyed in just eight months. Never mind places like Portsmouth and Coventry.'

'And the unofficial version?'

Her father smiled momentarily concentrating on the road.

'This isn't something you can put in any school essay, all right?'

Gabriella nodded.

'Professor Wylie discovered that the German military were much more advanced on atomic weapon development than hitherto was believed. He privately revealed to Prime Minister Churchill secret information sent to him by Foreign Minister Von Ribbentrop. It detailed the atomic weapon being developed by scientists from the Kaiser Wilhelm Institute for Physic. The German military were going to 'test' the first bomb on London in the autumn of 1941. They projected that just one bomb could kill at the very minimum around 70,000 to 100,000 people.'

'And that's why Churchill signed the armistice?'

'Yes. Churchill was forced to come to the table to sign a peace agreement.'

'But the bomb might not have even been real.'

Her father nodded. 'You're right. In fact, German scientists such as Max Born, Robert Oppenheimer, Robert Frisch were already working with the Americans at the same time and they, not the scientists in Germany, would be the first to make an atomic weapon. It was Frisch who first calculated the critical mass of U-235 needed for an explosive. As you know they did use their bomb against the Japanese in 1946.'

'So the German threat against London was a bluff.'

Her father nodded. 'In the end they demonstrated the first successful German atomic bomb in the Sudan in 1947.'

Gabriella blinked. 'What about all the people there, the animals and …' She was appalled.

'They tested in the desert, Gabby, not on cities. They aren't monsters y'know. They are developing Africa. The place to be right now is German Angola, since they discovered oil. They are building a six-lane autobahn all the way to Pretoria, or New Germanica as they call it.

'And Tomas Drucker started all this?'

Her father shrugged. 'He was more of a symbol. Some historians think he was used as a propaganda tool by the Pro-Peace movement and Professor Wylie. He 'volunteered' to fight against the Bolsheviks and was never seen again. He's not really important, but he was clearly a hero. Not a traitor. If he existed at all.'

'Of course he existed.' Gabriella protested.

'I'm not sure. When you look, and I have researched it, there's precious little information about him. No family. He just popped up out of nowhere, didn't belong to any organisation, it was as if the German propaganda machine had invented him.'

Gabriella couldn't believe her father, who had known Tomas practically all his life, doubted his existence.

'And then Churchill resigned?' She asked.

'Well, of course. He was a warmonger. He wanted to fight to the last man standing. Germany wanted England to stand with them against communism. When Prime Minister Mosley took over everything changed, as you know. Reconstruction began. The Empire was rapidly dissolved and America retreated into isolation, along with Australia. The New Europe under National Socialism has been the greatest contribution to world stability. For the first time there are no countries at war with each other anywhere in the world.'

'Except Spain.'

'There's always some separatists who want to be difficult. I'm sure the Spanish government will regain Catalonia and the Basque country in time.'

She looked at her father a moment.

'Why did we give in so easily? We could have beaten Germany. The English people had already survived the worst.'

Her father glanced at her again and made a face.

'We'll never know, Gabriella. There's only ever one outcome in history. You can't go back and change things. If they'd kept Winston Churchill as Prime Minister maybe he could have battled through; if the Russians had resisted the German onslaught; if the Americans had come in on England's side, instead of just fighting Japan in the Pacific. There are a lot of maybes. England chose peace with Germany. We can't change that.'

Gabriella bit her lip. She resolved to send Tomas another message. Avoid anyone called Professor Wylie. Somehow or another he had to change history back again.

Her father began to slow. Suddenly there were a lot of police up ahead and military vehicles with flashing yellow lights. Cars in front of them were being forced to turn around.

A military policeman approached and her father wound down his window, automatically showing his party card ID.

'Problems officer?'

The officer examined her father's ID and handed it back. 'We've got a terrorist incident in Southampton. You're going to have to go back to where you came from. City's sealed off now.'

'No way around to the coast? We're heading to the launch of the new flying boat…'

'All roads sealed off, sir. You'll have to go back. There won't be anything launched today.'

Three ambulances came screaming by on the opposite side, lights and sirens flashing as they headed towards the city.

Gabriella could see the look of concern on her father's face as he turned the car around.

'Terrorists?' Gabby asked. She wondered what they had done.

'Communists, probably. You would think with all the controls, the police and army, that no one could get away with anything.'

'Perhaps some people don't like all the rules.' Gabriella said quietly.

'Blowing up schools and hospitals is not just about not liking the rules, Gabby. They want to destroy the state. They want chaos. The Germans defeated Russia decades ago, but communism is like the cold virus, it keeps on living.'

'It's not on the news.'

'It's never on the news. No one is allowed to report it. They don't want people to know there's any resistance to state authority.'

'But there is resistance?' Gabby asked.

Her father nodded. 'No one knows how widespread it is, but little incidents keep happening all over England. Perhaps we'll be safer in Africa.'

'Resistance is futile.' Gabby remarked, suddenly remembering Tomas' old t-shirt.

Her father glanced at her. 'Yes, probably. Sorry we didn't get to see the launch. Perhaps a walk on the downs and lunch in Winchester?'

'Can we go there? I thought we needed permits.'

'We have the freedom of Hampshire, Gabby. We can go anywhere we like in our own county. The Wykeham Arms does a nice lunch. No communists allowed.'

Gabby smiled. Seeing Winchester again would be good, but she was thinking about resistance…

14

Dead Battery

His phone was definitely dead. Tomas felt utterly depressed about it. He was cut off from Gabriella forever now. It was beginning to feel as if this was going to be a permanent situation. No matter how stupidly impossible it all was – he was probably stuck in the past forever and he had absolutely no idea how to get back.

He knew Professor Wylie had people looking for him. They had followed the girls to the school and searched it up and down, but he'd found a way up onto the roof and slept the night there, too scared to go down. Luckily he could survey all from this vantage point. He desperately wished his phone worked for another reason, he badly wanted to take photographs of the incredible devastation around him. He was in awe of the destruction that had devastated London. The Pioneer Corp was busy everywhere – clearing away rubble, making way for cars and buses to get around the huge bomb craters in the roads. As far as the eye could see the German bombers had done their worst. In the distance St Paul's still stood proud over the city. Some of the larger buildings in the city still smouldered, smoke drifting eastwards across the ruins. They wouldn't have had nearly enough water to put out the flames in so many fires. Nearby, the Victoria & Albert Museum was badly damaged, and many of the buildings immediately around him had their roofs blown off. Yet, right in the middle of this chaos normal life continued. He could see mothers hanging out washing between one ruin and another. Finally he understood the British Blitz spirit.

It was around ten o'clock, a warm sunny morning. His stomach rumbled. He realised that he was incredibly hungry and wondered if he dare go down to wash and raid the kitchen. He knew Lily or Iris would come for him eventually, but they'd know Professor Wylie's people would be watching them like hawks. He realised that he might starve to death before they got around to coming to the school again.

He decided to risk it, climbing down the ladder back into the top room. Someone had been here for sure, the little bed had been flipped over, the bedclothes scattered over the floor. He realised he had made the right choice to sleep up on the roof. Glad he'd hidden his bag up there with him. Warily he made his way down the stairs to the bathroom in bare feet to avoid making any noise, ready to run at the slightest sign of trouble.

There was no hot water, but he found some scraps of soap. He removed his bloodied bandages and was able to wash his itchy head, at last. He realised that he should get a cap if he wanted to blend in and cover his scars. He missed his wild untamed mop of hair. Bloody scabs washed off into the sink, but he was happy to see in the mirror that he was beginning to heal. He wondered who would remove the stitches and if it would hurt?

He removed his shirt and examined his bruises. He hardly recognised his upper body. He had cuts on his face, slowly healing to broad scabs now and harsh blue bruises on his neck and shoulders and ribs from being buried alive. The scarring from the electric wire was still vivid around his chest. That wasn't going to heal in a hurry. He desperately wanted to clean his teeth. All the little normal things he took for granted at home were denied to him now. He wondered if anyone had even thought of electric toothbrushes or whitening toothpaste yet?

He dressed and went down to the kitchen. He could hear someone was busy down there. He hoped there might be fresh bread or cereal to eat.

The cook, a large perspiring woman with swollen feet and hair stuffed under a red headscarf, looked at him with suspicion at first. She was stirring a big pot of something she called Brown Windsor and hungry as he was, he didn't think he could face it.

'You can find some bread and cheese in the larder. Friend of Lily and Iris, y'say?'

'I'm helping them with the kids now.'

'Kids? Thieving little monsters I say.'

'They're OK. Can't believe what they've all been through.'

The cook nodded. 'My Susan and Michael slept through most if it. I'm there praying for God to help me get through one more night and there they are just lying in the shelter fast asleep as if it was the most normal thing in the world to have bloody death and destruction fall from the sky every night.'

Tomas cut himself some unappetising greyish looking bread and took a chunk of stinky cheddar to go with it.

'I think it's over now. The bombing, I mean.'

'Well I hope you're right. We couldn't take much more and that's a fact.'

Tomas was thinking about his phone again.

'You think if I left my battery out in the sun it would charge it?'

'You got a dead battery? For a torch is it?'

Tomas shook his head. 'It's a special kind of battery. I need to recharge it.'

The cook smiled, revealing a broken front tooth. 'Now that's an idea for the boffins. Rechargeable batteries! Why hasn't anyone ever thought of that before, I wonder. When I think of how we have to throw them all away when they're dead, such a bleedin' waste.'

Tomas nodded, sniffing his food before stuffing the bread down his throat and chasing it down with some water.

'If you want to get more life out of your battery, love, it's not so difficult. You just need a potato.'

Tomas laughed. 'Potato?'

'Scoff all you like my boy, but if you've got a dead battery, a potato will fix it.'

'How?' Tomas realised he was desperate enough for a solution to listen to her, no matter how improbable.

'You put the battery into the potato, right? Then you put it into an ice-box for about fourteen hours and there you go.'

'Ice?'

'You have to freeze it.'

'Cook, if there is one thing I have learned since being around here, absolutely no one seems to own a fridge.'

The Cook looked at him with eyebrows raised. 'Well, I'll have you know that there was a Prestcold Refrigerator in this school only last week.'

'And now?'

'The Head took it home. He was afraid it might be destroyed in the bombing.'

Tomas smiled. In other words the Headmaster stole it. A fridge would have been so rare in any home. Even Dr Holmbush didn't have one.

'So you don't know where any ice is?'

The Cook smiled.

'You need to see Rosie's.'

'Rosie's?'

'The ice cream shop. It's just down the road.'

'Ice cream? There's a war on. They still make ice-cream?' Tomas was astonished. The cook didn't seem to think this was unusual at all however.

'It's summer, darlin'. You want the Germans to stop everything? We need ice-cream.'

Tomas smiled. He picked up a large potato from a basket on the table.

'Do I peel the potato first?'

The cook smiled. 'Just cut a hole in it, stick the battery in.'

Tomas nodded, found the largest spud he could, sliced it in half and cut a space in it for his battery.

He could see the problem right away. The phone was sealed tight. You weren't supposed to ever get at the battery. The screws by the dock connector were

a: impossibly small and b: tiny Pentalobe screws that he was pretty sure hadn't been invented yet. He was not yet defeated though.

'I have to go find my bag.'

'You'll need some string,' the cook called after him. 'To hold it all together.'

'Left or right to Rosie's?' Tomas asked at the kitchen door.

'Right. You can't miss it. Tell them Mrs Manse sent you.'

A school bag contains many things. Calculator, bits of broken biscuits, post-it notes of something really important that you can't remember why or who, and if he was really, really lucky, a small set of screwdrivers he'd bought to fix his phone if it ever went wrong and anything else that was impossibly tricky to fix.

His bag was stashed under a sheet of metal. He began to rummage, emptied everything out. Found some chewing gum. Couldn't ever remember buying any. Two pound coins, a book of second class stamps, his school library card and slipped between the pages of his *Neverwhere* paperback, an iPhone 4 liberation pack. Unused. Still intact. He had wanted to open the phone up and see what was inside and never quite got around to it. Without these miniature screwdrivers he'd never get it open.

It took longer than he thought, nearly lost the teeny tiny stupid screws, but he got the battery liberated. Then screwed it back up 'cause he knew he'd lose the screws otherwise. Replaced the screwdrivers back in the bag hoping it would all still be there when he needed it. No way he'd get the battery back in there without them.

The street was more chaotic than he realised. Broken water mains, gas leaks, crumbling walls and smashed cars. It was a wonder London continued to function at all.

An old man with holes in his shoes was pushing an ice cream cart and ringing a bell.

'Ice cream. Tuppence a roll.'

Tomas caught up with him at the corner.

'You Rosie's?'

The unshaven old man with a frayed shirt collar looked at him and frowned. 'Do I look like a Rosie to you?'

Tomas smiled. 'Sorry. I mean I'm looking for Rosie's shop.'

'What shop? This is my shop. You want an ice-cream or not? Tuppence.'

Tomas realised that he very much wanted an ice-cream, but he had no money.

'Actually I just need to freeze this potato.'

The ice cream man looked down his nose at him as if Tomas were mad and it might be catching.

'I'm trying to recharge this battery, y'see.'

'Why didn't you bloody well say so. Damn war. You can't get anything these days.' He pointed back the way he'd come.

'Number 18. It's in the passageway.'

Tomas grinned. 'I never knew they sold ice-cream in the war.'

'And soon they won't, lad. Can't get the cream, never mind the sugar. Bet the bloody Germans are eating ice-cream in this heat. Bet they don't go short.'

Tomas nodded and ran off. A little surprised that the man knew about the battery trick. There was so much to learn about this London.

He found the passageway and half way up it, a beautiful old brick courtyard filled with ice cream carts outside a small factory building. An old sign declared this was Rosetti's Ice Cream Emporium – The Best Italian Ices. Rosie's equalled Rosetti's. Another sign on a window declared that Rosetti's was now under *Exclusive British Management*.

Tomas heard a woman tunelessly singing a song to herself. He approached with caution.

The woman ignored him at first. She was mixing a fresh batch of ice cream in a huge metal vat, stirring the mixture in by hand. It looked like hard work. He watched as she added something sticky and red to the mixture, the heady aroma of strawberries filled the room. All the while she stirred she smoked a cigarette, some of the ash drifting into the mixture, not that she seemed concerned at all.

'If you think you can get a free one, you can piss off right now,' she told him after he'd been watching her for a few minutes.

'Mrs Manse said you could help with my battery.'

She looked at him sharply. 'She did, did she?'

'I got a potato.'

She was trying to size Tomas up. He noticed she was wearing Wellingtons. For some reason he thought that amusing.

She wiped her brow and wiped her hands on her apron.

'Don't just stand there then, come and stir. I'm sick of this. First there's no vanilla. Then no sugar, now there's no electricity and we have to stir this lot by hand like it's the Middle-Ages, and now they say they can't supply any more milk. I mean, why bloody bother to make ice-cream when there's a war on? I don't bloody know. We're not a 'priority industry' they say.' She vaguely pointed outside. 'You tell that to the kids out there wanting their ice-creams this summer.'

Tomas came forward and she showed him how to stir. It was a lot tougher than it looked. Strawberry ice-cream. Who would have thought it?

'Normally got a machine to do this. When Signor Rosetti was here, they wouldn't have dared to cut off our supplies. He'd have cut *them* off. Me, they couldn't care less. They want us to make it with soya flour. I told them Signor Rosetti would rather die than make it with soya.'

'Where is Signor Rosetti?' Tomas asked in all innocence.

The woman looked at him as if he was thick. She lit another cigarette and watched him stir a moment.

'Make sure you get the mixture in smooth, make bigger circles. Come on, you can do it. With luck you'll have muscles like mine after this.'

Tomas snuck a look at her arms, but they didn't seem overly muscular. It was probably a joke.

'Give me your potato then. I'll pack it with the ice. Should do the trick. With luck the electricity will be back on soon. Mrs Manse all right, then? She's had it rough. Her old man was taken prisoner in France. Couldn't get on the boat at Dunkirk, could he. Bad leg. Signor Rosetti liked her. She wrote to the Government on his behalf, she did. Fancy sending an old man like him off to the Isle of Man. But no, they had to round up all the Italians as if they were spies. Signor Rosetti only cared about ice-cream. His brother had seven cafés. They took him and all his family. Poor bastard.'

'But why would you round up all the Italians?' Tomas asked.

'You do know there's a war on, right? If they're going to round up the Germans, got to take the Italians too. Stands to reason. Can't get a decent coffee in London now to save your bloody life.'

She impatiently held her hand out for his potato. Tomas handed it over.

'You won't lose it? It's a special battery. Only one like it.'

She laughed. 'They're all bloody special now. It's safe. Mind you come back for it tomorrow. I might get hungry.'

Tomas continued stirring as she made her way across the room to a walk-in fridge. She opened it and he saw it was filled with blocks of ice and milk churns.

She put his potato right inside the room. She didn't come out right away. He heard her chipping away at the ice and she emerged with a large block quickly closing the door behind her.

She saw him staring.

'This is most likely the last batch of ice cream I'll ever make. The dairy won't supply milk, I can't get any more cream or butter and no one has any custard powder either. There's no more sugar after this and I'm not going to use that powdered milk, am I? It'll be eggs off the list next, and you can't make smooth ice cream without eggs, can you? We haven't got any ice-cream sellers left, except Bill and he's on his last legs too. Need the bloody power back on and soon. I have to get this lot heated up first before we can freeze it. Making ice-cream is a dicey business at best. You know how hard it is to stop it all from separating? Got to be done just right. I'm probably going to join the Land Army. Sick of being bombed. Nice cushy job on a farm somewhere in the country where there's no cows. That's me.'

Tomas left an hour later when the electricity came back on. His arms ached from stirring, but he finally felt useful. He hadn't mentioned to her that the war was going to last four more years. It would be a long time before she'd make proper ice cream again, that was for sure.

Iris was waiting for him in the playground. She looked pleased to see him and he realised that he was happy to see her and felt not a little guilty about that.

'I was thinking you should get away. I have two pounds. We could send you to Devon. I have an Uncle there with a farm and he needs workers. A good place to hide and I could come down to see you. Mummy doesn't want us to stay in London any longer.'

Tomas frowned. Devon sounded nice an' all but …

'You don't understand, Iris. I have to get back to my own time. I don't belong here.'

'But how? You don't even know how you got here.'

Tomas made a face. Precisely! He had no idea how or why or anything.

Iris frowned. 'Is it the girl you left behind?'

Tomas blinked. He realized she was asking something else entirely. She wanted to know if Gabby was more important than her.

'It's not about Gabby, it's not about you. It's me, Iris. This is 1941. I come from 2013. I mean, we aren't at war like you are. It's pretty rubbish right now actually with strikes and the world economy going pear shaped. I'll never be able to pay to go to University and there's no jobs and no one can afford to rent or buy, but I'm pretty sure there's some kind of cosmic rule I'm breaking being here.'

'Cosmic rule?' Iris asked, the beginnings of a smile on her lips. 'The Cosmos is so strict about that kind of thing I should think.'

Tomas could see she was mocking him now.

'If it were you suddenly transported to my time wouldn't you want to go back to your sister and your Dad and stuff?'

Iris shook her head. 'It would be the world's best adventure.'

Tomas considered this. Yes, maybe, but in his experience of time travel so far it seemed to involve torture, bombing and being buried alive.

Iris took his hand and led him across the yard to the street beyond. 'Come.'

'Where?'

'I know someone who writes short stories about the future.'

'Like you want to.'

'He's trying to get his stories published.'

'He is? I was hoping it was H G Wells, 'cause only the bloke who wrote *The Time Machine* is going to believe anything I say.'

'I told you, he's dead. Arthur lodges at Mrs B's house. She teaches history at and takes in lodgers. Arthur was bombed out in a raid two months ago and I helped him move his books. He didn't care about anything he owned except his books on the stars.'

Tomas walked beside Iris, his hand still held tight in hers and it felt good. He realized that Iris had kind of taken him over. He didn't mind that either.

They reached a tall end of terrace town house with a Victorian turret at one end. A man was sitting in the topmost turret window smoking a pipe, the sash window help up with the help of a chair.

'That him?'

Iris waved to the man and he waved his pipe at her.

'Can we come up? I've got someone you should meet.'

'I'm writing.'

'I think you should meet Tomas. He knows a lot about the future.'

Tomas could see the man was less than interested.

'Five minutes.'

Iris smiled and pulled Tomas towards the steps into the house.

'Does he teach too?' Tomas asked as they mounted the stairs. He could see they had stacks of firewood all the way up the stairs on every floor. They were prepared for winter in this house.

'I think he works in the Ministry of Pensions. Mummy says it's full of writers now. Although he's trying to get into the RAF.'

'Pensions?' It didn't sound very promising.

Iris reached the top landing and climbed over the many boxes of books left in the way. She rolled her eyes, clearly getting these books up here had been a heavy chore. A lot of them seemed to be on electronics Tomas saw.

She knocked on his door. He took his time to answer and even then only opened the door a crack.

'What?' Tomas saw a tall man with a pale face and spectacles.

'Tomas is from the future, Arthur. He wants to ask you a question.'

Arthur looked at Tomas sceptically; saw his wounds, and you could see he wasn't impressed.

'What year?'

'2013,' Tomas told him, wishing they weren't here. This was ridiculous. He'd be just another person who wouldn't believe and couldn't help.

'Is man living on the moon?'

Tomas shook his head. 'We went once or twice.' He tried to remember stuff about the space programme and the only moon movie he'd ever seen, Apollo 18. He'd almost been scared watching it, he remembered. 'Didn't work out well for the crew. The Space Shuttle burned up too. No one up there. It's just a rock really.'

'Just a rock?' Arthur exploded. 'Just a rock!'

Iris stood her ground. 'I think you should talk to Tomas. It might help with that book you're going to write.'

'Who wins?' Arthur asked, still keeping them on the threshold.

'Wins?'

'The war. You're from the future it seems. You must know.'

Tomas wasn't so sure about that anymore. 'I don't think I'm allowed to say anything. There are rules in time travel. I'm not supposed to say anything that could change things…'

Arthur opened his door a little bit wider. Tomas' answer interested him at least.

'You'd better come in. Don't touch anything.'

Iris led the way into his stark bedroom, a lone poster of '*Things to Come'* the only decoration on his wall.

They had to sit on the floor and Arthur went back to his window and rolled a cigarette. An uncomfortable silence lay between them for a moment until he licked the paper and got the fag lit, blowing the harsh smoke over his two young guests.

'Tomas wants to know how to go back.'

'Back?'

'To the future,' Tomas told him. '2013.'

'Any proof?'

Tomas shook his head.

'Well then. Do I sell my novel on Space Travel to the Stars?'

Tomas has absolutely no idea. He didn't know who this Arthur was and besides anything he wrote now was going to be ancient history by 2013. 'It that the one where they get on a space ship that travels faster than the speed of light?'

Arthur nodded. 'Einstein's is right. We can't get to the stars unless we can go faster than light. We have to migrate to the stars and other galaxies.'

'Faster than light? Won't that mean you get to where you're going before you left?' Iris asked. A perfectly reasonable question she thought.

'Like time travel,' Tomas chipped in.

'Is that what you did? Arthur asked with a smirk.

'I have no idea how I got here. There was a big storm. I ran into our usual café to get out of the rain and suddenly it was a butcher's shop in 1941.'

'No time machine?'

'No.'

'And you've no proof.'

Daddy says his stitches in his leg are very advanced,' Iris pointed out.

'Stitches?' You could tell he wasn't impressed.

'I broke my leg.'

'Tell me about Jet Engines, Tomas. I am very interested in Jets and range finding technology.'

Tomas relaxed. He felt a bit more comfortable talking about jets.

'Rolls-Royce make huge jet engines. The Airbus can take about 600 passengers. They fly at over 600 miles an hour at 30,000 feet. You can get from London to New York in about five or six hours.'

'Six hundred passengers?'

Iris smiled she could see Arthur was finally growing interested.

'Rolls-Royce?' Arthur queried. 'You are sure about this? They make cars.'

This Tomas was absolutely sure about. 'Well Rolls-Royce and Bentley are both German companies. I think Volkswagen owns Bentley and BMW own Rolls –Royce. The jet engines I'm not so sure about.'

Arthur buried his face in his hands. 'Oh my God, we do lose the war. I knew it. I absolutely knew it.'

Iris looked at Tomas for confirmation. 'Rolls-Royce is German? You're sure?'

'Well yes, but I know they make Rolls-Royce cars in England because I went on a school trip to the factory at Goodwood.'

'Goodwood? The racecourse?' Arthur protested. 'That has to be pure nonsense. How could they build a factory there? Is there nothing English at all?'

Tomas had to think hard about that.

'What about Space Stations? At least tell me there are space stations. People live in space?'

Tomas shook his head. 'There was a space station, but the Americans had to close it down, I think, when they cancelled the shuttle programme. I think the Chinese are going to be launching one soon, though.'

'The Chinese? Arthur exploded again. 'In space?'

'Or the Russians, but they've got financial problems too.'

Arthur was looking disappointed again. 'Tell me one good thing about England that you absolutely can't live without.'

Tomes had to think hard about that.

'My smart phone.'

'Phone?'

'He means telephone.' Iris explained.

Arthur blinked. 'I don't understand.'

'Everyone on earth has a phone and you can talk face to face with them or text or instant message them via Facebook or Google, and you absolutely have to have at least one thousand friends and you can send them stuff or share your favourite music or photos or whatever…'

'Everyone … on… Earth?' Arthur queried, mouth agape.

'Just about.'

But the cables. It's impossible. There wouldn't be enough copper wire, you'd be falling over cables all the time. Impossible.'

Tomas held his hand up. 'I've already told you too much. But you don't need wires if you've got satellites in space.'

'Space!'

'Yes, space.'

'So the future is space and satellites. I knew it!'

Tomas nodded. This bloke really was desperate for the future to be about space.

'And you want to go back there.'

'Yes.'

'Can you help him get back?'

Arthur shook his head. 'Time travel is impossible. Absolutely impossible.'

'But…' Iris began.

'But nothing. The future is space. That is all and man leaving this planet for a better one.'

'You won't help?'

'Iris I thank you for bringing me such an entertaining boy, but even you can see what he says must be impossible.

'Rolls-Royce make cars, not jets, and they'll always be English. Can you imagine anyone driving German cars in England ever again after all this bombing? It would never happen unless…'

'We lost the war?' Iris whispered.

'That's not true,' Tomas began, but then again – he wasn't so sure anymore.

'I've heard enough.'

Iris signalled to Tomas it was time to leave. Tomas was already at the door. No one was ever going to believe him. He knew that now.

'That went well.' Tomas said, somewhat dejected, as they walked back towards the school.

'Does he really become a famous science fiction writer?'

Tomas shrugged. 'I've never heard of him. But if you write down what I told him you'll be famous instead.'

Iris squeezed his hand tight. 'Oh I intend to. I'll remember every word.'

'Don't forget that everything is stored in the cloud now.'

Iris looked up at the sky frowning. 'How?'

Tomas grinned. 'It's a meta thingy cloud. Electronic. There's trillions and trillions bits of information and no one has enough storage space so they put it in the cloud. And don't ask me to explain, because I don't really know what the hell it means either.'

Iris shook her head. 'Your world must be so complicated.'

'It is. There's too much choice of everything. Whatever it is, cars, tablets (that's mini computers you can read books and watch movies on), food, clothes, music. There's too much pressure to choose a brand. And every brand says something about you, so people judge you. That's why I won't wear anything with labels. Even *then* they judge you for not wearing a label. You can't win.'

Iris studied his face, trying to decide if he was joking with her or really conflicted. She decided 'conflicted'.

'Good luck writing about the future, Iris. Just image a world where everyone gets what they want, but they don't really want it. Upgrade anxiety. That's the future. Everything you buy goes out of date exactly one week after you bought it.'

'Seriously? I have no idea what you are talking about, Tomas.'

He laughed, taking her arm. 'Nothing lasts, no one cares.'

Iris frowned. How was she going to remember any of this? Was he telling he truth?

'If you were going to buy a present for your friend back home from here, what would you get her?' Iris asked.

Tomas' mind went blank. What on earth would Gabby want from 1941? He had absolutely no idea. Not the clothes, nor the shoes. Couldn't even play the 78's. He couldn't think of a thing.

'She likes new things,' Tomas said finally. 'Don't you?'

Iris smiled. Yes, she liked new things. Might be a while before she saw any though.

At school that afternoon a teacher hadn't turned up and Tomas was drafted in to talk to a class of nine year olds. He told them about how the dinosaurs were made extinct by a change in the weather after a giant asteroid crashed into the Gulf of Mexico. He felt on safe ground here; his time in the Natural History Museum hadn't been wasted, nor the years he'd spent collecting pictures of every pre-historic creature he could get hold of. The kids seemed interested at least. By three o'clock he had them all noisily zooming around the room pretending to be Pterosaurs, swooping down on innocent creatures and snapping them in half. They didn't get much reading practice though.

Of Lily and Iris there was no sign. He ate the Brown Windsor soup with the kids and discovered it was almost palatable. Most of them would have eaten anything, they were so hungry. He watched them be collected by parents and smiled as the kids still continued snapping and snarling, pretending to be pre-historic beasts.

The stars came out that night. Tomas was back on the roof, huddled under a thin scratchy blanket, watching the sky and listening to a nervous city still sleeping in their Anderson shelters, waiting for the bombers that were probably no longer coming.

It was much cooler than the night before and twice, as he shivered under the blanket, he thought about going down the ladder to the single bed. He knew he couldn't risk it. He wished Iris was there to talk to. He worried for them. It was no fun to discover your mother was seeing someone else. He felt sorry for Dr Holmbush too. He knew he'd never persuade him that he was from the future, and he couldn't blame him for finding it so impossible. He thought about how he'd react if someone claimed to be from the future. Maybe not so negative, but certainly he'd be sceptical and want some proof. He briefly wondered if anyone else had ever time-travelled before? How had they coped? Had they wanted to help or change things or just been laughed at?

Something flickered to Tomas' right. An electrical short in a building maybe? He'd seen how scary the wiring looked in this school building and he was surprised anything worked at all considering, never mind health and safety. Bright blue sparks caught his attention again and a low electrical hum. He scanned the tallest building in the area and he caught the flashes again. He counted the floors. Eighth floor. No blackout. Maybe they thought no one could see, but someone was experimenting with an electrical device in that building. He made a mental note to find out something about the place in the morning.

He turned to his left and saw a fire had broken out in Chelsea. He could see a fire-engine snaking its way towards it around rubble and potholes in the road. How the heck could the driver see anything without full beams on?

Sometime around two a.m. Tomas finally fell asleep.

He woke early, a warm sun breaking through clouds. His legs felt stiff, lying on such a hard surface wasn't easy.

'Battery.' He called out to make sure he remembered.

Once again in the tiny top room he found there was a note for him stuck to the underside of the roof cover lid. It was very discreet. Clearly whoever had put it there wanted to ensure only he found it.

T

Mother's gone mad. She's not coming home anymore. Daddy is very upset and keeps smashing things. (He doesn't blame you and he's not angry with you any longer, even if he refuses to believe anything you say.) He says you have to have your stitches out in two days by the way.

Lily says the kids love you and I think you have started a Dinosaur craze.

PW has spies everywhere. He seriously wants to find you. If you get this, meet me at 'Farewell My Lovely' ten o'clock.

I x

Tomas smiled. Farewell My Lovely he guessed would be the burned out bookshop. He didn't know what time it was exactly but he knew it was early, he had a few hours before ten yet.

He found some milk and some of yesterday's grey bread in the kitchen, which he toasted and covered with something called greengage jam. It wasn't as bad as it sounded.

Tomas didn't dare risk leaving by the main school gates in case Wylie's henchmen were watching out for him. He reasoned that as long as Lily and Iris kept him as their secret he was safe. He climbed over the back wall and landed in a narrow mews, which must have been for the stables at the back of the big houses at one time. He realised an incendiary bomb must have landed here recently. Many of the exterior walls were charred and personal possessions lay where they had landed in the middle of the cobbled lane. He picked up a penknife and found a cap that fitted perfectly and thin black sweater from the pile, something to help him get through the chilly night.

There was no one at Rosetti's ices. The door wasn't locked either. The fridge was still working and he could see that the woman had cleaned all the metal vats till they shone. He felt sorry for her, trying to keep a business going when they wouldn't even let her buy the ingredients. How many other places were like that?

He found his potato frozen hard, too hard to pull apart. He shut the fridge and wrote a note to say thanks. He mused on how if they'd left an ice cream shop unlocked back in his time it would have been cleaned out by the morning with not a scrap of machinery left either. Here no one seemed to lock anything, everyone was incredibly polite and trusted each other. Just when had all that changed?

Tomas wandered for a while, feeling safer now his head was

covered. He'd be just one more kid in the streets. Without CCTV they couldn't track him either.

Walking aimlessly he could see that some rows of houses were completely untouched by the bombs, with avenues of trees proudly displaying the last of their blossom. Other streets were visions of a blasted hell with wrecked homes, shattered trees and cars lying upside down in huge craters. It would take years to put all this right, he realised.

A woman lay on the pavement on Brompton Road. She was playing with broken dolls. Her hair was loose, her skirt tied with a rope. He couldn't see her face. At first he thought she was horsing around, then, as he watched and listened for a moment, he realised she was talking to the dolls as if they were her children. A man came out of a house and patiently spoke to her in a calm voice, then picked her up to carry her back inside the wrecked home. He seemed resigned to this. Tomas realised that everyone was coping, but some better than others. He wondered if he would have been sane if he had endured nine months of bombing and death every day?

An hour later Tomas entered the burned out bookshop and, looking around, immediately wondered if this was such a good idea. The wooden beams on the upper floors were still intact, but nothing looked safe. He noted the bookshelves had survived the fire, most with books still on them, the spines burned but the pages within too tightly packed to burn. Such a waste.

Iris wasn't here yet. He still didn't know what time it was precisely but knew it was around ten o'clock.

He made his way across the rubble to the back of the shop, not wanting to be seen from the road. He'd walked past the sign that said '*Dangerous Structure – Unsafe to Enter*', and this was probably not the best idea. He made sure not to touch any of the supporting walls or doors. Anything could set it off.

Tomas moved some blackened wood beams from the rear of the shop and to his surprise discovered the cellar door was intact. Scorched to be sure, but with luck the cellar would be safer from prying eyes than the ground floor.

He pushed open the door and it swung wide. Remarkably there was a candle and box of matches in a nook ready to use. To think a fire had been raging outside this door and the matchbox wasn't even scorched or candle melted.

He lit it and made his way downstairs, wondering what he'd find.

He did have a passing thought that it would be a stash of naughty pictures, but was happier to find he was in a dusty map room. There were rows of long pigeonholes, each filled with a rolled up map. Abyssinia, Mesopotamia, Rhodesia. He'd never even heard of these places.

There were footsteps above him.

'Tomas?' He heard faintly through the wooden ceiling.

'Down in the cellar. Don't touch the walls, OK? It's unsafe.'

He could hear Iris gingerly making her way over the rubble to the back of the shop. He set the candle down on a wide map table where a huge wall-sized map of Italy was spread out, for all to see. That's when he spotted the banknote. Five whole pounds lying under a glass paperweight. The banknote itself was enormous. At first he thought it was fake, it was so fancy and big, but he swiftly folded it into his pocket. Five pounds meant a lot to him. Gave him options. The bookseller wasn't going to miss it, that was for sure. He had bigger things to worry about, if he was still alive.

He saw Iris's bare tanned legs first. He realised for the first time that she had very nice legs. The rest of her appeared and she gave him a big broad smile, mixed with relief that they had finally reconnected.

'Nice cap. You look almost normal.'

'Thanks, I think.' Tomas said, then immediately frowned. 'Hey, what happened to your face?'

Iris immediately flicked her hair forward to cover it.

'Nothing.'

'Nothing? I can see finger marks.'

Iris could hear the real concern in Tomas' voice. She pulled a face as he went to greet her. He pulled her towards him and gave her a huge hug. He felt as though she hadn't had a hug in a very long time.

'Did your father do that?' He asked softly.

Iris looked offended. She pushed him away and fiercely shook her head. 'He'd never do that. Never.'

Tomas didn't know what to say. She looked very upset he'd even brought it up. Finally she relented.

'My mother lost her temper. She wanted me to tell her where you were. She's besotted with that old man. He's sixty at least. What is she doing mooning around after him? She's got Daddy. Daddy is like an angry bear and keeps locking himself in the study where I know he's drinking. Lily is crying all the time and Mummy wanted us to come and live with her at Professor Wylie's house in Holland Park.'

Tomas took Iris's hand and squeezed it. 'I'm sorry she hit you. I know it's all my fault.'

'Yes, it is. You will have to make it up to me.'

Tomas looked at her sharply, then saw she was teasing him. They were OK again.

'You weren't followed?'

'I'm sure I was. Lily swears a man with a broken arm has been following her for two days now. I think I confused whoever it was following me at South Kensington tube station. I hope so anyway. I came to find you last night and…'

'I know. I was on the roof.'

'On the roof?'

Tomas nodded.

'Oh, I want to go on the roof too. Can you see much?'

'Right over London. It was pretty cold though. I managed to nick a sweater for tonight.' He indicated the blue v-neck he was wearing. 'Not sure how long I can hide out there.'

'I have a plan to get you to Milton Keynes.' Iris said. 'It should be safe there.'

Tomas laughed; he had a sudden image of concrete cows in a field. 'Milton Keynes? Why would I go there?'

'Daddy's brother works there. In some place called Bletchley I think. He owns a huge mansion and…'

'Bletchley?' Tomas suddenly remembered one of the war movies he'd watched. 'Bletchley Park? You're kidding, right?'

Iris shook her head.

'That's the most secret place in the whole war, Iris. You mustn't say anything about it. *Ever*. I'd forgotten I knew. Oh my God. If Wylie gets me and I told him about that we'd lose this war for sure. I can't go there. It's too dangerous.'

Iris hadn't a clue as to what Tomas was talking about.

'It's just a big old house. I've been there. Nothing happens in Bletchley. I promise you.'

Tomas furiously shook his head. 'You are so wrong.'

They both heard footsteps overhead. Iris looked at Tomas with panicked eyes and Tomas quickly turned to snuff out the candle, licking his fingers to make sure there was no smoke.

'Quick. Under the map table,' he whispered in her ear.

They followed the intruder's footsteps as he went deeper into the bookshop.

'You sure she came this way?' A voice called out.

Tomas realised with a chill that he knew that voice. Wilhelm Belhapt. It seems he hadn't perished in the tearoom as Tomas had thought.

'She entered.' Someone called back.

'Well she's not here now. Wait, there might be a cellar.'

He heard Iris' heavy breathing. She was afraid. There was no way out. How stupid of him to come down to the cellar.

'Lie flat. Absolutely flat. Don't breathe,' Tomas hissed.

He slipped the map of Italy off the table and pulled it over them, wishing it wouldn't make so much noise. They both lay as flat as possible on the cold dusty concrete floor, the map covering as much of them as possible.

They both heard Belhapt's footsteps on the wooden stairs. Tomas wondered what the map lying on the floor looked like. Whether their feet were sticking out. A bloody ostrich would have a better plan.

Belhapt swept the torch around the cellar, paused on the map lying on the floor under the table. Everything was tidy save that. Someone had left here in a hurry. Perhaps during the bombing. There was no sign of Tomas or the girl. His informer must have been mistaken, or she'd left again when he'd run to the phone to get him. He thought he could smell candle wax but there were so many smells in here from the fire he dismissed it.

'Alles in Ordnung? (You all right?)'

'Ja. Es war reine Zeitverschwendung. (Yes, this was a waste of time.)

Belhapt turned and went back up the stairs.

Tomas listened keenly as he made his way back over the rubble.

Neither of them moved an inch. It could be a bluff. They might wait across the road for them to emerge.

'Just stay put,' Tomas urged her. 'Give them time to get bored.'

'They were German.' Iris whispered. 'I can't believe they were speaking German.'

'You can speak German?'

'No, but it wasn't French, was it. They're really after you, Tomas.'

'I know. Shush. Just stay calm.'

They lay there for at least another twenty minutes. Cold, their nostrils filled with dust. But they didn't move a muscle.

'I need a hot bath,' Tomas said at the end of it.

'Me too.' Iris replied, suddenly blushing, glad he couldn't see her face.

‘I think we can get up now.’ Tomas said at last.

‘Hell, my arms and legs have gone to sleep.’ Iris complained

Tomas pulled the map off them. He realised they didn’t need the candle anymore, sunlight was shining through tiny cracks in the flooring above.

Iris sat up, brushing herself down, spitting out dust and coughing.

Tomas scrabbled up and then pulled her up after him.

‘You’re right. I need to get away, Iris. We can’t risk them finding me. Is there anywhere else I can go, besides Bletchley?’

‘For how long?’

Tomas shrugged. He had no idea.

‘That, or get me to see Winston Churchill. Let me tell him what I know first, before Professor Wylie gets to him.’

Iris frowned. ‘I have no idea how to do that. He’s not going to see a schoolboy. He’s not going to believe anything you say. No one in authority will. Unless, of course you’ve got Professor Wylie at your back.’

Tomas reluctantly agreed.

‘Which is why I have to get away.’ He grabbed her hand and pulled her towards the stairs. ‘And you should come with me.’

Iris stopped dead looking at him in complete astonishment. But didn’t let go of his hand either.

‘What did you say?’

‘We should disappear together. Before something bad happens. I shouldn’t have come into your life and I know I’m only going to mess it up, but I want you to come with me.’

‘What about Gabriella?’

Tomas blinked. ‘She’s there. I’m here. I’m stuck here forever. One day when I’m ninety I’ll take the bus down to Portsmouth and knock on her door and give her a heart attack, or I’ll have one falling down outside her house. But we can never be together. Ever. I’m lost to her and she to me.’

‘Is that like when you have a thrombosis?’

‘I forget, you’re a Doctor’s daughter.’

‘I’m also the sensible one, Tomas Drucker.’ Tomas noticed she was blushing slightly. ‘I’d love to run away with you, but I might remind you that we are children and children in this time don’t usually get to stay in hotels or rent flats or get jobs or do anything but live under hedgerows until they are discovered and forced into orphanages and made to drink very awful soup.’

'Soup?'

'Soup. Awful Brown Windsor soup. If I'm not mistaken.'

'That's bad,' Tomas agreed, remembering eating some the previous night in the school kitchen. 'So what's the plan?'

Iris made a decision. 'Hot bath. I come up with all my best plans in a hot bath.'

'I'm up for sharing a hot bath.' Tomas grinned.

'Sharing!' She wrinkled her nose. 'You're a stinky boy. You get to go second.'

'Sharing saves water.'

'And have you see my awful blue knickers? This will never happen in your lifetime, Tomas Drucker.' She laughed, but never once let go of his hand.

He pulled her up the stairs and they faced the rubble together.

'Any sign of the Germans?' She whispered, nervously looking both ways

'No, but I know who one of them was. MI5 were looking for him earlier. You think you could show me how to use a public phone?'

Iris looked at him a moment, unsure if he was joking or not.

'It's complicated. Button A and Button B. I've never used anything but my mobile. And remind me to try the battery out. I'm almost scared to try it in case it doesn't work.'

Tomas finally took out the frozen potato, well on the way to defrosting now.

'Oh goodness, *that* was what was in your pocket.'

'It's not what you think.' He separated the two halves of the potato and took out the battery. 'Got to get my phone working again.'

'It's not going to work. You can't possibly call the future. Can you?'

Tomas shrugged. 'Not even sure what the hell I'd say if I could. Come and get me? Very few people own a time machine y'know.'

'No, I didn't know. But thanks for telling me.'

Tomas grinned. The road was clear. She took his hand again and they headed south towards her Aunt's house where he was assured they had scads of hot water.

15

The Missing

She didn't recognise anyone in the school library – with luck, she hoped they didn't recognize her. This wasn't schoolwork. This was a mission.

She'd woken at four a.m. in a total sweat. Gabriella had realised that she'd been ignoring the truth of her new world. Wasn't facing up to all that must have gone on.

It had been triggered by a conversation with her father on the way home. His casual remark about the twenty-five million people in Great Britain. She hadn't even registered it at first as numbers were never her thing.

But at four a.m. she had suddenly remembered she'd left a Great Britain that had at least sixty million people in it and was well on the way to seventy million by 2020 according to predictions, she seemed to recall.

Twenty-five million sounded – well, small. Less than half. She had to wait until after Maths and Physics before she could get to the library, but she was determined to find out exactly what had happened to the British population. It made no sense for such a low figure if the war had ended in 1942. Millions would have survived the war, not died. So what had happened?

Life without the internet was ridiculous, tedious and frustrating. You had to go through books, find one fact and then go to another and not all the books were in the reference library. So many were 'out for recovering', which she was beginning to think was a euphemism for being shredded or something.

'What are you looking for, exactly?' The librarian had asked when she'd requested her fourth, difficult to find book.

'Population figures for the UK from 1900 to the present day.'

The librarian looked at her with surprise.

'I don't recall that being a topic under discussion this term,' she replied acidly.

Gabriella was about to give a sarcastic reply but remembered this librarian would report her for that.

'It's a quality of life issue for the school magazine. *Room to Grow for Everyone*.'

The librarian was taken aback, but shrugged. 'I'm glad you girls are finally showing an interest in the magazine. You should be writing the articles, you know, not leaving it to the teachers.'

'I know. I keep saying to people that we should be more proactive.'

The librarian frowned. 'Proactive? Is that even a word, Gabriella?'

'It is now. Do you have any statistics on population?'

'There might be something.'

Gabriella gave her best fake smile. 'Please look for it, I have to go to German classes at 2pm.'

It was a very suspicious librarian who handed over a dusty reference book to her a quarter of an hour later.

'You have to view it at the counter. It's restricted.'

'Why?'

'That's what the sticker says on the front, see?'

Indeed that was exactly what it said. 'Restricted Access'

Gabriella opened it up. It was pretty stiff. She doubted anyone had opened it in years. She noted it was printed in 1996. Recent enough for her research.

Population statistics in the UK. 1901-1995 (Date of last Census)

Gabriella scanned the opening remarks:

In 1900 the population of the UK was around 20 million. By the end of the century, the population will have increased by five percent to 25 million, and it is estimated GDP will have risen fivefold.

She looked more carefully: Someone had scribbled in pencil a correction on the first figure to 38. Not twenty million but thirty-eight million in 1900 and then another amendment: By the end of the century the population will have *decreased* by 12 percent. See page 248

She flipped to page 248:

Depopulation of UK cities: The Economically Active Citizen Programme 1950-59

The success of the Care Camp programme for Seniors saw a rapid reduction in economically inactive UK citizens and a greater distribution of wealth and fair-housing for all, under the auspices of the National Government Re-Location Scheme.

Aided and abetted by the great polio pandemic of 1955 and the reoccurrence of the terrible African 'flu of 1958/59, which saw a sudden drop in children needing schooling and supplemental medical services. NHS rationing was finally abated in 1960 as the UK population reached a manageable and self-sustaining number. As prosperity was regained, numbers began to rise as survival rates for children rose under the mass vaccination programme of 1960-1962. By 1980 the UK population was approaching 24 million and steadily growing.

The Berlin Population Directive of 1971 proposed a European-wide population maximum for European protectorates. The surplus population and emigration initiatives were initiated to repopulate Africa. In 1973, when Australia and New Zealand sought protection from the Asian Communist threat and came into the Euro-zone of influence, another opportunity for Germanic peoples to prosper and expand came into existence.

Again someone had pencilled in a question: *how many million children died in the British compulsory and subsequently lethal vaccination programme? Seven million or more? An accident or deliberate part of state depopulation planning*?

Gabriella closed the book without taking any notes. She sensed that she could be in trouble for even requesting this book, never mind reading the scribbles in the margin. Certainly someone knew that the figures were doctored. Worse, there was no-one she could talk to about this. Her father didn't seem to want to admit that anything could be wrong. Was this all because Tomas went back in time? It made her dizzy just to think about it. British children deliberately infected with a lethal disease. All the old people made to disappear. The Germans didn't need to bomb the country once they had it under their control. They reduced the numbers so it wouldn't be a threat. Got rid of all the old people so no one would remember what it was once like.

Gabby realised that because of her connection to Tomas she could be the one person left who remembered the truth. (Besides the person who wrote those notes in the margins.) She wondered who that might be.

'I don't think this book has been opened in a long time. Who was the last person to request it,' she asked the librarian in a jokey kind of way.

The librarian, who had no sense of humour at all, looked at the book, then the request list on it, then back at Gabriella.

'Dr Lamb, in 1997. I think he ordered it actually.'

Gabriella blinked. Her father?

'Dr Lamb?'

The librarian shrugged. 'A Dr Lamb was working here in 1997. Is he a relative?'

Gabriella realised that the librarian didn't know who her father was.

She also realised that she had no idea what her father used to do in this time. There was no University of Portsmouth. She meant to ask him about that.

'Must be,' Gabriella told her. 'Thanks for your help.'

'That's why we're here.' Came the answer.

Gabriella sat in German class, confused and alarmed at what she had read in the library. The fact that her father had also read that book and was clearly the one who had added the questions in the margin meant that he either knew the truth or at least suspected something.

An hour before she was due to go home the summons came from the Headmistress, Dr McIvor. Gabriella Lamb was to go to the office at four. Her heart sank. It had to be the requests she had made in the library. And the lie she had told about the essay. The Head never called you in, unless she was going to mete out some dreadful punishment. Everyone stared at her, some with a smirk, others with pity. They all lived in dread of ever being called up to the Head.

She didn't have long to wait. No sitting in the corridor, to be seen by all, as a humiliation. She arrived and was surprised to be ushered in promptly. She sat on a chair staring at a poster on the wall of a young girl sitting on a mushroom with the words, 'Give me a child until she is seven and I will show you the woman she will become.'

Gabriella sensed it had a sinister meaning but could not exactly say why.

The head was a woman of around fifty with severe scraped back black hair, bushy eyebrows, no make-up and she wore a suit that was tailored enough not to be a man's. Even in summer she wore harsh cloppy black leather shoes, and she had an odd way of staring at you that instantly made you distinctly uncomfortable, even if you hadn't done anything wrong. Dr Heather McIvor busied herself with a letter and didn't look up to acknowledge Gabriella's presence until she finished it and signed with a M cut so deep it nearly tore the paper.

'So, we have taken an interest in history, have we?'

Gabriella suddenly realised that the interrogation had begun.

'It was curiosity, Dr McIvor.'

'And we all know what happened to the cat, don't we?'

'Yes, Doctor.'

'And now the truth, Gabriella.'

Gabriella frowned. She wasn't even sure what was true anymore. She sighed.

'We were discussing in history the other day about how many

people lived in England before the war and the number was so different to what I thought I knew, I wanted to look it up. I mean, a lot different, Dr McIvor.'

Dr McIvor stared at Gabriella a moment, then did something miraculous. She smiled.

'I like you Gabriella. You have spirit. You are questioning. I know some of the staff don't like it when a student questions things, but if you can't question when at school, when can you? You have done nothing wrong, Gabriella.'

Gabriella noticed the reference books she had been looking at were now stacked on a table in the corner. A hunch told her they wouldn't make it back to the library.

'Did you know that I was one of the lucky children who survived the second great African 'Flu pandemic of 1959? I was born in the February and almost all the newborns at that time died. It was a terrible time in the British Isles. I'm told that a million children died that year, on top of many millions the year before. It swept through Europe and Asia. My mother succumbed. My father developed pneumonia and had to have me adopted, as he couldn't cope. I was one of the lucky ones, Gabriella. The population of Poland crashed and it took hundreds if not thousands in Germany too. No one could stop it. Then, as suddenly as it had come, it vanished.'

Gabriella stared. She had no idea about all this and felt awkward.

'You have no idea what life was like then. You're right we should teach about it. I don't even know why we don't. We were lucky to be under the guidance of the Reich, and we didn't go under, unlike some countries. There were shortages of doctors, nurses, teachers, railwaymen, everyone and every business was affected. That's why one can never quite rely on things like population statistics. Yes, it is true that there used to be more of us. But, at least, we are well now, our nation's health is taken very seriously.'

Gabriella bit on her lower lip wishing she could disappear. She felt she had to ask the one question however, no matter the consequences.

'I can understand that many children died of polio and flu. It must have been terrible, but did *all* the old people die?'

Dr McIvor shook her head.

'That's a ridiculous notion, Gabriella. All the old people were sent to the Care Camps. Our old people are cared for with love and affection and all of them perform useful lives. As indeed I shall when I am sixty.'

'And if you didn't want to go?'

Dr McIvor gave her a thin smile. 'Who wouldn't want to go to a place where you will be fed and kept warm and looked after? Nonsense. Everyone goes.'

Gabriella smiled back, hoping it looked genuine.

'You wanted to check facts for yourself, Gabriella and that is the mark of a good student. I admire that in you. Just like your father. And look at how well he has done. You can go now, Gabriella. Keep up your studies and if you have questions like this in future, my door is open. Never be afraid to ask questions. Dismissed.'

Gabriella stood up, curtsied and left. Hardly able to believe she had got out of there without a punishment of some kind.

She ran to the girl's room. She realised that she felt sick with tension.

Moments later Dr McIvor's assistant entered the headmistress' office.

'You called, Dr McIvor?'

The Head handed her the heavy reference books that Gabby had been reading.

'Burn these.'

'Burn them?'

'Make sure *all* the pages burn, Daphne. Do not think of going home until they are completely destroyed.'

Daphne curtsied, taking hold of the heavy reference books.

'That will be all.'

Dr McIvor watched as Daphne struggled out of the room with the books, her face totally impassive. She picked up the telephone and dialled a number. A voice answered after only one ring.

'I want a list of all Gabriella Lamb's friends. I want all her conversations at school recorded.'

She replaced the receiver and briefly allowed herself a bitter smile.

16

Running Hot and Cold

They had passed Onslow Square Billets where all the men slept from the Blitz Repair Squads. All empty awaiting their return. They'd be busy for a few months yet. Tomas knew from a school project that over a million homes had been destroyed in London in the eight months of the blitz. A lot of rubble for the Pioneer Corp to clear.

'When the bomb fell on Thurloe Street,' Iris was saying, 'it was so loud I could feel all my teeth and bones at once. It was horrible, Tomas. Lily screamed so loud it broke Mother's precious vase. She was really cross, but it wasn't Lily's fault.'

They came to a halt outside a huge mansion house facing Onslow Gardens. It was impressive as long as you ignored the fact that most of the windows had been blown out and were now shuttered or covered with wooden boards. There was a huge crack from top to bottom in one exterior wall. Iris explained that a bomb had just missed her aunt's house, and she'd been very annoyed as it had totally ruined a dinner party she was throwing.

'My Aunt B is incredibly rich and the war is a terrible 'inconvenience', that she is determined to ignore.' Iris explained. 'She can be rude, so please don't get upset.'

Tomas grinned. 'At least she sounds interesting.'

A battered and dusty Bentley stood in the driveway – its roof crushed by a huge chimney pot. The bomb damage was clearly recent, but it hadn't stopped daily life continuing inside the house, as he could hear piano music playing loudly.

'Aunt B runs a ballet school in the house. She's married to Lord Milner. He's something important in the government, but I don't know what he does. No one does, really.'

'You sure we should go in?' Tomas asked.

Iris seemed surprised by his reluctance.

'Aunt B is my mother's sister. Lily studies dance here. We come and go all the time. They don't see many boys, so ignore any rude stares.' Iris jumped over a pile of broken glass and plaster by the wide marble steps. 'You should have seen this house before they bombed the street. It was so beautiful. It has eighteen bedrooms. Someone famous lived here, I think, he owned lots of West-End theatres, then went very bankrupt in the last war.'

Tomas followed her, staring at the cracks in the walls, some so large you could see through to the inside.

'You sure this house is safe?' Tomas asked, pointing to where one wall look close to collapse, supported by one heavy log jammed up against it.

'Aunt B wouldn't have her classes here it if wasn't, silly.'

Tomas wasn't so sure.

'Anyway, Aunt B won't leave it. She's *very* headstrong. Worse than mummy, actually.'

Tomas believed it. Iris grabbed his hand and dragged him over the threshold. The front door was missing and a workman was trying to fix it on a makeshift bench in the hall, shaving long strips of wood off one edge.

Tomas stared in wonder at the entrance hall. It was truly huge. A grand staircase rose upwards with intricate dragon tails wound around the balustrades. Dusty portraits of famous rich dead people in assorted wigs were fixed to the walls, some hanging askew after the recent bombing. The ground floor was inlaid black and white marble in an intricate geometric pattern, and there was a vast stone fireplace with seats around it on one side. He'd never been in anything so elegant before.

'Come on, the bathroom is on the second floor.'

Iris pulled him after her all the way up the wide staircase.

'If we bump into Aunt B, don't panic. She knows all about you. She won't bite.'

Tomas glimpsed a huge ballroom off the first floor where several girls danced on their toes, whilst an old man with wild white hair was bashing away on a grand piano in the corner.

How many other houses were big enough to have ballrooms in them, he wondered? He stopped to stare, eyes wide at the opulence of it all.

Iris was amused by his reactions.

'Lord Milner is very rich, or he was, I think. He keeps saying the war will ruin him, but I don't believe it. He owns gold mines in Africa and other places.'

Tomas absorbed his surroundings, noticing how bad the damage was everywhere. Lord Milner would need a lot of money to fix the house, that was for sure.

'You'll have to wait in here,' Iris told him pushing him into a changing room.

It boasted a life-sized mosaic mermaid on the floor and was tiled all the way up to the ceiling on one side, and there were walk-in mahogany cupboards filled with a man's clothes hanging inside.

'I'll run the bath and go first – you'll only dirty the bath.'

Tomas was about to protest then figured she was right; he was pretty stinky.

'Take off your clothes and grab a towel.'

Tomas blinked.

'Now?'

Iris laughed. 'No silly, when I'm gone. Take them off, find a towel and I'll call when it's your turn.'

'What if anyone comes in?'

'They won't. This is Lord Milner's bathroom. Please don't touch anything.'

Iris abandoned him and Tomas did as he was told and took his clothes off. He didn't like what he saw of himself in the mirror and tried to avert his eyes.

He found a copy of *The Times* on a chair and was amazed at how thin the paper was and how few pages it had. He struggled to make sense of it, as the front page didn't seem to have any news on it at all. Inside it was full of war news and shortages and new government regulations. Monumentally boring. He was about to put it down, when he saw a photo of Professor Wylie standing with Winston Churchill surveying war damage at Waterloo station. It depressed Tomas to have proof that Professor Wylie really did have Churchill's ear. It made him all the more determined to stay out of his clutches.

Iris called to him a few minutes later.

'Tomas!' She hissed.

He dropped the paper and went to the door, remembering to pull the towel around him.

He opened the door and there she was, lobster red from the hot water, a towel around her head and another wrapped around her slender body.

'It's very hot. Wash your head, but be careful of your stitches. I put the soap on the side. I'm going to get dressed now. Be as quick as you can.'

Tomas grinned as she squeezed past him, steam coming off her body.

Iris paused a moment, looking at his chest and the scars with awe and concern. 'I'm going to find something to put on those scars. Aunt B will have ointments.'

Tomas shrugged. He wasn't thinking about his scars at this moment. Iris suddenly smiled, aware of their semi-nakedness and how Tomas was looking at her.

'Get in the bath, Tomas. I'll see if I can find you a clean shirt.'

Tomas sighed and turned towards the steaming iron bath. It would be good to be clean.

He was just enjoying the soak when Iris returned.

'I'm not peeking,' she said walking in, averting her eyes. He noticed she was already dressed, her damp hair held up by a purple ribbon.

Tomas placed a flannel over his middle, attempting modesty.

'Aunt B says I have to put this in the water and you have to stay soaking in it for ten minutes.'

'What is it?'

Iris poured the liquid into the water, still averting her eyes. 'Stir it around.'

'It stings, Iris.' His eyes began to water.

'Aunt B said it would sting.'

'Well it stings a lot.'

'Did you wash your head?'

'Yes. I know how to wash, Iris. I shower every day back home.'

Iris looked down then and saw how dirty the water was.

'Really?'

'Most people do, I think. A bath uses too much water.'

Iris retreated to the corner of the bathroom and looked at the cracks in the wall, noting that the fig tree outside was forcing a new growth up through the hole.

'Is it working yet?'

'What?' Tomas could barely see the vapours were so toxic.

'The liquid I put in the water?'

'I can hardly breathe. What on earth is it?'

'It's what they make the girls bathe in to heal their feet. They get very bruised and sometimes bleed and this is supposed to help.'

'If I pass out, you'll have to drag me out of here.'

Tomas struggled. He felt dizzy. It was powerful stuff and it really stung on his cuts and bruises. His eyes were streaming now.

'I don't think I can do ten minutes, Iris.' Tomas winced. This was seriously painful. He began coughing.

'The girls do.' Iris mocked.

Tomas frowned. Clearly these Kensington girls were made of tough material.

'You sure you put the right amount in?' He coughed again, keeping his eyes closed.

Even Iris was finding it hard to breathe now. She realised that she may have heard her aunt's instructions wrongly. Perhaps using half the bottle had been a mistake.

'Iris, I have to come out NOW,' Tomas gasped, leaping up out of the bath and trying to find his towel through weeping eyes.

Iris had to find it for him, her own eyes painfully watering now. She found him and Tomas plunged his face into the towel.

'Ow, ow, ow.'

Iris realised she was in the bathroom with an entirely naked boy for the very first time and neither she nor he could see a thing.

'I think I used too much liquid.'

Tomas poured cold water into the sink and plunged his face into it, bathing his eyes.

Iris did the same moments later.

Together they stumbled out of the bathroom, gasping for air, Tomas not caring a fig for his nakedness. Every part of his body stung like hell now.

Iris had very red eyes and could see Tomas was being very brave. His scars and cuts were bright red and had to be smarting like bee stings.

'I'm sorry. I'm sorry…' she kept repeating.

Tomas put the towel over his head and dashed back into the bathroom. He pulled the plug in the bath and turned on more water to splash over his raw skin. He urgently needed to wash off whatever Iris had tried to kill him with.

He emerged a few minutes later, exceptionally clean and a little calmer. Iris was nowhere to be seen. Tomas found she'd left him clean grey shorts that almost fitted and a fresh shirt that was only one size too big. He was grateful for both.

Someone knocked on the door.

'Yes?'

'Master Tomas, Lady Milner expects you down for luncheon in ten minutes.'

'Lunch?'

'Yes sir. I have found you new shoes and have left them outside the door.'

Tomas shrugged.

'Thank you.'

He got no reply. He realised they had servants. Even in war, rich people had 'staff'.

Iris was waiting for him at the bottom of the stairs on the first floor. Her eyes were still red. She looked sheepishly embarrassed, not her usual confident self, 'guilty', Tomas thought to himself.

'I was only supposed to put in two drops. Aunt B says it's lucky you're still alive. You are still alive, Tomas?'

Tomas grinned. 'You know what? I can't feel a thing now. Whatever it was kind of worked. Almost worth the pain. I feel as though my whole body has been starched or something.'

He took both of her hands and leant forward to kiss her lips.

'I forgive you.'

Iris didn't want to let go of his hands, and so badly wanted him to wrap his arms around her. She closed her eyes, holding onto the moment.

They did not know it, but a pair of eyes was watching them from the second floor, and the expression on the face was not a happy one. Lily frowned, her lips pursed. Iris was far too close to Tomas. Far too close.

Iris pulled away and turned leading Tomas down a corridor.

'Aunt B is having lunch in the breakfast room. The dining room is still a wreck.'

Tomas winced as he walked. It was true he sort of felt better for the 'treatment', but everything, including his head, tingled now and it was an odd sensation.

'I have to write down everything you know about the future,' Iris declared as she walked ahead. 'If I'm going to write science fiction novels, I want to know everything that happens.'

'I hope you realise that's cheating,' Tomas pointed out with a smile.

Iris pouted a second, presenting a very serious face.

'I'm going to be a famous writer, Tomas. I've decided. I shall call my first book "Confessions of a Time Traveller as told to Iris Holmbush by Tomas Drucker"

Tomas laughed, then shrugged. 'Could use a better title, I think. Besides, things might change.'

'No getting out of it, Tomas. I'm going to find out everything you know. It will all come true and everyone will think I'm a genius.'

Tomas laughed.

'Maybe people won't want to know how everyone becomes obese and how there are so many people in the world it's doomed to be crushed by climate change. People won't believe anything you say, Iris.'

She paused outside a doorway.

'Obese? Everyone in the future is fat?'

'Not everyone, I guess. But tons of kids and adults do no exercise, they just watch TV, eat junk food, surf the web and grow so large they have to widen the aisles in the supermarkets and build bigger car seats because they're all so fat. I blame genetically modified food. It gets fed to the animals and we eat the animals and suddenly everyone weighs 20 stone.'

'What's a supermarket? You're just making things up now to make me write silly nonsense.'

'Not so. It's true. I swear it.'

'Your Gabriella isn't obese.'

'No, she isn't. Thin or fat. It's a lifestyle choice, like sex. You can be gay or straight or whatever and no one cares. The future isn't what you expect. At least, no one cares if you're a bastard in the future.' He realised he was still angry about that. Tomas glanced at a portrait of a General on a horse. 'Also, you'd need to know about all the wars after this one, in Asia and the Gulf, as well as all the technology changes. I mean, it's hard to have secrets in the future. Your own computer spies on you.'

'You're going to tell me everything. I want to know more about the pill.'

'The pill?'

'You said the other day that the pill changed everything.'

'Oh that pill. Well, it did. Women could decide when they got pregnant and then it sort of caused a whole sexual revolution sparking feminism and …'

'See. That's exactly what science fiction is. I can write about the sexual revolution.'

Tomas smiled. He loved Iris' optimism.

The door suddenly opened.

'Sexual revolution? Do tell, Iris dear. When does it start and where do we queue?'

Aunt B stood in the doorway. She was almost identical to Iris' mother and just as beautiful. Twins run in families, he realised. Her hair was tied up above her head with a blue ribbon and he could see where Iris had copied the style. She was wearing a black leotard with a small pink cardigan around her slim shoulders. He guessed she had been dancing with her students.

'Come on in. No lurking in corridors. Is this the future boy you tried to kill? I said two drops, Iris. Two drops.' She wagged her finger at Iris and Iris blushed. 'I'm surprised he didn't dissolve. My maid tells me the whole of upstairs stinks.'

'Sorry, Aunt B.'

Tomas entered what he surmised was the breakfast room and was surprised to see that it was round, with French doors leading onto a small balcony facing the garden at the rear. A salad lay in a large ceramic bowl on table centre and there was a freshly baked loaf besides.

'Where's Lily?' Iris asked.

'Eating with the girls. They all complain I make them eat lettuce and radishes, but at least it's all fresh. Harris, our gardener, has converted the whole garden to vegetables and salads. We'd starve without him, I think.'

Aunt B was studying Tomas carefully all the while.

'Good looking boy, Iris.' She said with relish. 'I've heard all about you, Tomas Drucker.'

Tomas smiled, embarrassed and awkward all of a sudden, not sure where to look.

'So, find a seat. Eat some rabbit food. As much as you like. It grows like weeds out there.' She waved nonchalantly towards the garden.

Tomas found a seat and Iris sat close by, handing out plates to all.

'How can I be so sure you really are from the future, Tomas?' Aunt B asked him. 'You have Iris convinced, but how could you convince me?'

Tomas shrugged as Iris put food on his plate.

'I can't prove a thing, I'm afraid.'

'Professor Wylie is convinced,' Iris chipped in.

'And Lily tells me that my sister and the Professor are going to try and convince Mr Churchill to surrender to Germany. Is that correct?'

Tomas looked at Iris. He realised that he didn't know what side this sister was on.

'Yes. I think that's their plan,' Tomas agreed, cautiously. He nibbled on some salad.

'And why would he do that, do you think?'

'Because he's going to lie about the bomb,' Tomas told her. 'It's my fault. I told him that the Americans use the atomic bomb to end the war in Japan and…'

'We aren't at war with Japan, are we?' Aunt B looked at Iris for some kind of confirmation of that. Iris shrugged.

'Not yet. They declare war in December.' Tomas pointed out.

'Do they now.' She seemed to find that detail amusing for some reason. She leant forward, her curiosity piqued now. 'Tell me more.'

'Professor Wylie is going to lie to Mr Churchill and say that Germany has the atomic bomb and they'll use it against London and kill 70,000 people. But they haven't. All the German scientists who build it are in America, not Germany.'

Aunt B narrowed her eyes as she chewed on a spring onion.

'This bomb really exists in your time, Tomas? It can really kill 70,000 people at once?'

Tomas held her gaze a moment. 'Yes.' He paused a moment before adding. 'America has them, China, England, Israel, even India, Pakistan and Iran I think. I think they can kill twice that many people these days. More probably. America and Russia have over 1200 bombs each, I read somewhere.'

He could see that Aunt B didn't believe him.

'I doubt that one bomb could kill so many' She said, pulling a face. 'Impossible. And this … what did you call it, Pakistan? I've never heard of it. Or Iran come to think of it.'

'You haven't? It's right next to India.' Tomas realised he had no idea Pakistan didn't exist in 1941. 'I think Iran used to be called Persia.'

'And all these countries have these terrible bombs and kill each other with them?' Aunt B asked.

'Well, no. They could, but they don't use them. They can't use them. At least they haven't yet.'

'So we have weapons in the future that people are too afraid to use?'

Tomas nodded. Aunt B was bright. He could see she was sizing up both him and his answers.

'And *why* don't they use them?' She asked, being provocative now.

Tomas thought about that for a moment.

'Radiation. It's poison. The bomb kills a city with the blast, but then you get poisonous radioactive clouds and even more people die and get sick and develop cancer…'

'And clouds don't respect borders.' Aunt B added, musing.

'Exactly.'

Aunt B looked at Iris, who was nervously watching their exchange.

'Iris, how many boys do you think you could dig out of the rubble, who know about atomic bombs and radiation poisoning?'

Iris smiled. 'Just the one.'

Aunt B poked her fork at a radish, eventually spearing it and lifting it towards her mouth. She paused a second to ask, 'And Professor Wylie is convinced you are genuine?'

Tomas shrugged.

Iris chipped in first. 'He wants to get hold of Tomas desperately. He has people looking for him everywhere, Aunt B. You won't say anything, will you? You won't tell him Tomas was here today?'

Aunt B just smiled at Iris and nibbled on a lettuce.

Tomas took a slice of bread to eat. 'I think his German friends will make up some details of the Nazi bomb they don't have and he'll use that to convince Churchill it's real.'

'And you think our Mr Churchill and the whole War Office are so gullible they will believe this?' Aunt B asked.

'It's already happened.' Tomas explained. 'The moment I came. My friend back home sent me a message. Everything has already changed.'

Aunt B seemed confused. 'Someone sent you a message? How?'

'On her phone.' Iris chipped in.

'Her phone? Now you have lost me. Even if I somehow accept Tomas is from the future, but you also claim he brought his telephone with him. It's laughable, Iris. Where's the wire?'

'No wires in the future,' Tomas said. 'The future is wireless.'

Aunt B shook her head. She had heard enough already.

'Iris may have told you that I teach ballet, Tomas. It's hard, it's exacting, it doesn't require much science. But I know when my leg is being pulled. Wireless. We have wireless now and believe me it has wires.'

'Wires are for the electricity. Radio is broadcast without wires. That's how my phone works. Only my battery died.'

'He's telling the truth.' Iris protested.

'And I love you for believing him, Iris. I really do. But I don't think you have to worry. Our Winston is not a fool. He's not gullible and I am sure he takes everything Professor Wylie says with a pinch of salt.'

'There was a photo of him with Mr Churchill in *The Times* today,' Tomas said. 'He has a lot of influence.'

'As does my husband. Unfortunately for you, dear Iris, Lord Milner does not believe in the fantastical, or the future, and certainly not that anyone could ever time travel.'

'At least tell him that William Bell is working for Professor Wylie. I know that he's a wanted German spy.' Tomas explained.

Aunt B laughed. 'Now you are being ridiculous. Willie Bell dined here just two weeks ago. He's terribly good company. German spy, my foot. He's an excellent shot. My husband loves his company when he goes shooting.'

'He's a spy. He was the one who kidnapped me in Portsmouth and brought me to Professor Wylie.'

'If that were true, Tomas, we should certainly cross him off our Christmas card list, but it is patent nonsense. Willie is a friend of England. He'd do nothing to harm it.'

Clearly agitated now, she stabbed and ate one more radish.

'Eat your lunch, but Iris, your trust in Tomas here is misplaced. I'm sure he's a nice boy and he means well, but I don't think he's the genuine article. He may need some help. I know your father thinks so.'

Iris sighed. 'He's a time traveller, Aunt B. You should listen to him. He can help.'

Aunt B smiled politely as she stood up from the table. 'I'm sure he can dear. Now if you don't mind, I have students to teach.' She put out a hand to Tomas. 'It was nice meeting you, Tomas. Will you be staying in London long?'

Tomas detected some sarcasm in her voice.

'I have no idea, I'm afraid.'

'Well, don't outstay your welcome. Got to go. Enjoy your lunch, my dears.'

She swept out of the room leaving Iris and Tomas staring at each other.

'Better eat,' Tomas suggested. 'We might not get to see salad again for a while.'

'Or bread. They make very good bread here.' She cut them both some thick slices.

They left a quarter of an hour later, passing by Aunt B's office on the ground floor. She was speaking on the telephone, her voice clear and sharp echoing into the marble hallway.

'The boy is clearly mad. Time travel is impossible, isn't it? You should hand him over to the authorities. They can treat him. They can do wonderful cures for people like him now. It's Iris I feel sorry for, she's so convinced.'

Iris took Tomas' hand and they walked out of the house without another word.

Tomas looked at Iris and noticed Iris's eyes were moist. She made no sound, no fuss, but he could tell she was disappointed. He felt guilty her aunt didn't believe him, but not at all surprised. He tried to reassure her.

'It's hard for people to accept things they don't understand, Iris. Even I wouldn't believe anyone who claimed they were a time traveller! There's a series of movies back in my time called *The Terminator*. A humanoid robot goes back in time to kill the mother of the man who will grow up to be the leader of the last humans who fight them – so he'll never be born.'

'Robot?'

'Well first he's an evil robot, then in the sequel he's a guardian robot. He doesn't look like a robot though, he looks like a body builder, y'know, muscle man.'

'And people watch this?' Iris doubted he was being serious.

'There was even a TV series.'

'You're not a robot.'

'No. I'm not even a very good time traveller. No one believes me except you and the Germans.'

Iris hugged him momentarily. 'That's because I have an imagination,' she said. 'Besides, you didn't show her your history book. That might have persuaded her.'

'I doubt it.'

'Can you get to the school on your own? I have to go queue for rations otherwise there won't be any dinner.'

Tomas nodded. 'Take care, Iris. Don't let your Aunt upset you. If I had an aunt, she wouldn't believe anything either. At least I survived you nearly killing me.'

'I'm sorry. You're never going to forgive me, are you?'

Tomas grinned, placed his cap on his sore head and kissed her lightly on her lips. 'I already have. Go. I'll see you later maybe.'

'I'll bring soup later tonight.'

'I'll be on the roof. It's safer.'

She nodded, reluctant to leave him, but knew she had to get the rations.Tomas watched her go. He glanced back at the mansion house. He wondered who the aunt had been talking to on the phone and if they'd send people to lock him up? Time to leave London most likely. Tomorrow for sure. He decided to make himself scarce for a while.

17

For A Shilling

The Victoria and Albert Museum was smouldering, the overnight damage to the roof was devastating and Tomas briefly wondered about all the beautiful objects and art inside. Lily had said that they had taken most of them to a secret location outside London, but the biggest surprise was a large hand painted sheet hung up by a side entrance. *'Yes we are open to Visitors'.*

It was true then, this wartime Blitz spirit. Health and Safety would have shut it down forever in 2013, that was for sure.

'Give me a hand, lad.'

Tomas was passing Brompton Oratory, the Catholic Church, amazed at the destruction to the houses around it. Bedrooms were exposed to all, curtains and clothes flapping in the wind, fallen masonry everywhere. Official cars and lorries drove around the debris as if it was all quite normal.

Tomas turned and saw an old bloke in a flat cap and wearing brown overalls, struggling with a large piece of furniture. He quickly went to the man's assistance and together they got it into the back of his old Ford van.

'Want to earn a shilling, lad?' The man asked, wiping the sweat from his brow. 'Help me move this lot and I'll pay your bus fare back home as well. I'm getting too old for this lark.' He looked at the stitches on Tomas' head. 'You been caught in the raids?'

Tomas smiled. 'Got buried up to my neck. Been bombed in a shelter too. I think Hitler's got it in for me.'

'You and the rest of us.' The man replied revealing a fresh scar on his right arm. 'Shrapnel. Eating my supper when the window blew in. Put me right off my pie, it did.'

Tomas grinned. Helping the man would get him away from the area. Iris's aunt's phone call had unnerved him. She clearly thought him mad.

The man paused a moment as they watched a barrage balloon going up just beyond Exhibition Road.

'Not much use, but I suppose they have to try,' he muttered. 'Come on, I have to fetch an ornate mirror down from the third floor before this building collapses.'

'Is it safe?' Tomas asked, following the man into a five story Georgian home.

The man scratched under his flat cap and laughed. 'Safe? You want safe, you better catch a train to the Highlands of Scotland or somewhere. Nowhere's safe now. 'Mr Blake' – that's me – Sir Ralph says, 'We have to save what we can. The Nazis may not care for civilization but we very much do.' He grinned. 'Of course he's much too busy to save civilisation himself. It's the likes of me and you who've got to take the risks.'

Tomas followed him up the grand stairs, the green carpet slightly soggy under foot from a burst water pipe, some water still trickling out. He could see where pictures had already been taken off the walls and the marks left on the Chinese patterned wallpaper.

'Nice to know the rich folks get it in the neck, just the same as poor, eh?' Mr Blake added, stepping over fallen plasterwork. 'Taking all this to an underground storage warehouse in Bread Street. Sir Ralph has his office there and thinks it might be safer underground. Not so sure myself, the city is almost a wasteland now. They'll never get it rebuilt, I reckon. My missus says London is finished. We'll have to build a new city somewhere else.'

Tomas didn't say anything. He knew London would be rebuilt. He didn't want to have to explain how he knew, though. He was happy to help the man; at least he'd get to see how bad the city looked after the bombing.

'It's heavy, lad. Seventeenth Century mirror. The bloody Nazis don't care a fig for history or art. Fancy bombing the V&A. I'd like to send Hitler a few bombs of my own. There'll be nothing left to save soon. Makes you wonder what the hell we're fighting for.'

Tomas took his end of the gilded mirror and staggered towards the stairs. It was very heavy. The old man may have looked thin and fragile but he was certainly strong. Tomas struggled to keep his side up.

'You all right there, lad? Getting a bit red in the face.'

'I'll be fine.' Tomas gasped, his arms and muscles straining like hell.

The little van was weighed down with all the rescued pieces of art and furniture. Tomas didn't see how on earth it could move, it was so heavy, but somehow it got going. They slowly made their way around debris and diversions and joined the stinky buses belching smoke and official cars moving towards the city.

Tomas could only gawp in wonder at the terrible destruction. It seemed impossible to him that people could go on living in this, but Mr Blake explained to him that the underground was still running despite everything, and behind the boarded up windows and shattered walls business still went on.

'Can't give in now, can we. No matter what they bloody throw at us.'

Oxford Street was blocked with rubble, but Mr Blake skilfully threaded his way down alleys and little short cuts as if he was quite used to this journey.

'Bourne and Hollingsworth is open despite fresh damage last night,' Mr Blake said, a hint of pride in his voice. 'Selfridges is still open too. Not that the likes of me shop there. You all right, lad? You're a quiet one.'

'Just can't believe what I'm seeing, Mr Blake. I've seen pictures, but seeing it for real. It's...' Tomas didn't really have the words for what he was feeling. Astonishing, incredible, amazing – none of them seemed right somehow. He'd had no idea of the total destruction or of how people were just carrying on as if it were an everyday thing.

'We'll make it. Mark my words, this won't be forgotten in a hurry.'

Tomas nodded. Mr Blake was right about that at least.

Mr Blake's composure changed as they finally reached Bread Street. He swore as they pulled up outside the remains of St Mildred's. 'That's pure history gone there, lad. The poet Shelley married Mary Wollstonecraft Godwin here. It seems to me Hitler's got a map of every one of Sir Christopher Wren's churches and decided to bomb the lot. This tower won't survive, they'll have to pull it down. Look on this, lad and weep.'

Tomas recognised Wollstonecraft name. *Frankenstein.* He'd even tried to read it when Gabby had lent him her dog-eared copy. History wasn't just buildings, it was the people who had used them too.

They went down a steep ramp underneath an office building, down three floors. The place was filled with crates and cars on jacks and other possessions.

'Is this deep enough?' Tomas asked.

'Survived the bombs so far. Other than dragging everything down to the underground, this is as safe as things can be right now.'

Tomas helped him unload, stashing all the valuables into a wooden crate marked with the owner's name. He watched as Mr Blake nailed it all shut and slipped a bolt through the door for good measure.

‘There’s a night watchman, but best to make sure, eh?’

Mr Blake gave him a big smile, exhausted from his efforts, but happy his task was done. ‘Sir Ralph will sleep easier tonight, I reckon. Come on, I promised you a shilling but I think we both deserve a cup of tea first.’

Mr Blake took him up the stairs to a canteen. Tomas drank tea so strong you could stand a spoon in it and reluctantly ate some bubble and squeak, because Mr Blake reckoned he needed fattening up. All the people around him were pale faced, dressed in grey, talking ten to the dozen, living as normal life as they could. The air was thick with tobacco fumes, no one even blinked in the fug.

‘Sir Ralph’s in insurance. Not a business I’d like to be in right now,’ Mr Blake said, sliding a shilling over to Tomas and adding three pennies for the bus fare. Tomas picked the coins up, immediately surprised at just how heavy they were.

‘Mind you get home before the bombing starts tonight. You don’t want to get stuck in a shelter overnight, your parents will fret. Where do you live anyway?’

‘South Kensington. Bunking there for a while.’

‘You’d be better off outside London completely. My nephews were sent to Lincolnshire. Which is a laugh on my son Harold, as they’re busy turning the whole county upside down for the RAF. Best not talk about it I suppose. Loose talk an’ all that.’

Tomas nodded and pocketed the coins. Catching a bus back would be a new experience.

‘Is there a library near here?’ He asked, standing up.

‘Library? You like to read, lad? There’s one on Cheapside, I think. Out of here, turn left and walk straight up and then turn left again on Cheapside. Bit of a walk, but you’ll find it.’

Tomas smiled. ‘Thanks, Mr Blake.’

‘I’m the one who should say thanks. That bloody mirror nearly did my back in. Lucky thing you were there.’

The library was hopeless. He was directed to a reference section with tall stacks of books, some covered in plaster dust and other debris from the cracked ceiling. The librarians were wary of a ‘child’ wanting to look at these precious tomes, and didn’t seem to think he should be in there at all

‘What exactly are you looking for?’ One imperious woman asked, oblivious to the fag ash dribbled down the front of her grey jacket.

‘I’m doing a project on Time-Travel.’

‘This is the reference section.’ She told him with a sneer. ‘Fiction is over there.’

‘I’m studying the *science* of time-travel,’ Tomas insisted.

The woman bared her yellow teeth at him. ‘There is no science in time-travel. It is twaddle. Utter twaddle. You’re wasting my time.’

Tomas ignored her. She obviously wasn’t going to help.

He couldn’t make sense of the numbers, or that you had to go to a tall wooden chest of drawers filled with index cards with yet more numbers on them. The Dewey Decimal system of index numbers and letters was beyond his comprehension. Ten main classes each subdivided into ten divisions, and each division into ten sections, giving ten main classes, 100 divisions and 1000 sections. You couldn’t just look up ‘Time Travel’ because all it gave you was Wells. H.G (Fiction: Time-Machine). The closest he could get to anything useful about ‘time’ was Einstein’s field equations, which made no sense to him either. He didn’t know why he’d hoped a library might give up the secrets as to how and why he’d ended up in 1941. The reference on weather or Electrical Storms was no better. Certainly it had no explanation as to how he’d been transported back in time. ‘*See Auroral mechanism – Forms and magnetism – Solar winds and the magnetosphere*’ No thanks. Searching for information using actual books took forever, and they were ridiculously heavy and dusty and each question he had meant he had to look for another volume.

After he’d searched seven tombstone-heavy books and got absolutely nowhere Tomas realised that no library in 1941 was going to help him get back to 2013. Someone suggested an encyclopaedia and he was ‘helpfully’ directed to the ‘Children’s’ Encyclopaedia, which had just about realised that ‘flying machines’ existed and was published in 1933. How people did any research without Wikipedia and computers was beyond him. Living in the past was like living in slow motion. He had to accept that he was in England forever, and if he was here for good, he had to disappear so Professor Wylie couldn’t grab him. Didn’t matter where. Iris was right. He could work on a farm, they’d need people and he’d get fed at least. It was a plan of sorts.

‘We’re closing now.’ Someone called out to him from the far end of the room.

Tomas sighed. He followed others reluctantly shuffling out of the library, blinking as they emerged into the late afternoon sunshine. Men were preparing for the next raids, putting up shutters against the windows. Tomas noticed that there was precious little glass in any of them.

He went to look for a way back to Kensington, wishing he'd asked which number bus he was supposed to take. As he waited in a long queue, he glanced up at a forest of barrage balloons rising in the sky.

Someone steered him onto a bus going towards the King's Road, and that would have to be close enough. The windows were covered in netting to prevent broken glass causing damage during bombing. Tomas was glad it was still light because he had no idea how the bus drivers could steer the bus at night without headlights. It was crazy. Cars and buses had covers on the headlamps which would let just a slit of light to escape.

He wondered what Gabby was doing at this moment. She'd be amazed at the stuff he'd seen since he'd gone back in time. It didn't seem right that this was an experience they'd never be able to share. Truth was, they'd never share any moments together ever again and that made him feel down. He wondered if he could leave her a post-card for her to find one day. Stupid idea. Where would he leave it? What would it say? 'Having a lovely war. Wishing you were here?'

She was more likely still cursing him for changing everything. What a fool he had been for thinking he could be useful to anyone. He was the stupid kid who'd changed history. Now he'd be living under Nazi rule. He cursed himself as well.

It was around ten o'clock that night by his reckoning. Tomas could see the clock on the church tower was still showing a quarter to five. Most of the clocks had stopped around the city, certainly no one ever rang the bells anymore. He was up on the roof, the blanket wrapped loosely around him as he lay back watching the stars and planets. Mars was in place, appearing orange, to the right Orion and above it Taurus. He sighed. Tomorrow would be a difficult day. He realised he'd miss Iris. He felt the same way for her as he did for Gabriella. He knew that was kind of wrong, but he was beginning to accept he was never ever going to see Gabriella again, so it wasn't cheating – was it?

He snacked on some stale crackers he'd found in the kitchen earlier. It reminded him of a time he'd been sick for a week when he was about eight years old and all he could eat was dry crackers. It was strangely comforting to remember that. Even then, he recalled, Gabriella had brought him things from her home.

He suddenly remembered his phone battery. He'd been strangely reluctant to even re-insert it into the phone in case it hadn't charged.

He was ready for disappointment. He quickly found his bag again and carefully went through the whole fiddly process of unscrewing and replacing the battery, blowing on the points to make sure there was no dirt on the connectors. He put it all back together again saying a quick prayer that this would work. Working in darkness with such tiny screws wasn't easy. Twice he panicked he'd lost them. Finally it was done.

He pressed the start button.

Absolutely nothing happened.

What had he expected? Ask a cook for advice and you get stupid answers.

He shook the phone and gave it a light tap on the deck. Maybe he hadn't cleared all the fluff out, but he didn't want to reopen it again and get more dirt in there, or risk losing the screws.

He pressed the button again.

His phone came back to life. It was three-quarters green, no less. Potato's worked! Thank you Cook! He wondered how many times he could repeat that little exercise. There was no signal, of course, but he felt better knowing it worked.

'Hey'?

He looked up sharply. Iris' head popped up through the hatch.

'Hi. Welcome to the stars.'

She hauled herself up through the hole and carefully pulled the hatch cover back to cover her tracks.

Tomas got up to greet her and she fell into his arms and hugged him tight.

'I brought soup, as promised. It's not very hot now, but it was when I left.'

Tomas grinned and took the flask from her.

'Come and share it. I pinched some crackers from the kitchen.'

He led her back to the blanket and they snuggled up together, their backs against the chimney stack.

'You're a star watcher? Do you know their names?' She asked.

He looked at the stars again, pointing to the right a little. 'That's Orion, but I never really got their names. I mean, does Taurus look like a bull to you? I think not.'

Iris stared at the sky. 'No, it doesn't.' Then laughed, snuggling closer. She felt happy and safe with Tomas, something she hadn't felt in a long time.

'I can't believe how clear the sky is and how many stars you can see. There's so much light pollution now in our cities I almost never see the stars. See, the Milky Way, everything. Absolutely never see this in my time. I'd have to go to Chile to get a really clear view.'

'Chile? South America's Chile?' Iris asked.

'Yeah. I'm not kidding. When you look at pictures of earth taken from space, it's a mass of light. Crazy waste of energy.'

'They can take pictures of earth from space? Gosh, there's so much I want to know about your time, Tomas. You're right, though. Before the war and blackout started, I never saw the stars much either.'

She suddenly remembered the letter in her pocket.

'This came for you today. You finally have an ID card.'

She dug it out and handed it over.

Tomas stared at the envelope a moment, impressed that letters still got delivered at all, then folded it over and slipped it in his breast pocket. He didn't know why but he felt simultaneously elated and depressed by it. It felt good to be 'legal' but it also made everything so permanent.

'That helps. Thanks, Iris.'

'Helps?' She detected a change of mood in him.

He sighed. 'You're right. I have to go away. It's too dangerous for me to stay here and I can't live on this roof forever. Your aunt was right too, Iris. Either people think I'm a spy or they think I'm bonkers. I need to go somewhere where I don't tell anyone anything and just keep my head down. If I can't find a way back home, I'm here forever. I need to start thinking about what I can do.'

Iris felt dizzy. She hadn't expected this and it hurt, but then again, he was only being logical. 'I don't think it's safe for you to be on the roof here tonight, Tomas. Lily made a decision today. She's going to live with Mummy. She moved to Aunt B's tonight and we had a terrible row about you…'

Tomas squeezed Iris' arm, he could feel her sadness about this.

'I'm sorry, Iris. My fault again. I'm sorry about Lily. Can't believe she'd leave you. Are you going to stay with your father?'

She nodded, tears welling. She didn't even know how to talk about this. She felt betrayed by Lily. They were sisters; they should be staying together.

'Come with me,' Tomas said. 'I don't know where I'm going but …'

Iris buried her head onto his shoulder and he could feel her hot tears on his chest.

'I wish I could. I truly wish I could.'

A bright blue arc light flashed abruptly in the building opposite. They both watched in fascination as it strobed for a second or two, then settled down to occasional popping flashes.

'Why haven't they got the blackout covering the windows?' Iris complained.

'They have. Those are very bright flashes. Someone has been experimenting with electrical equipment for days now. I was going to ask you about the building. Is it a secret government place?

Suddenly his phone lit up and incoming messages started to signal their arrival with the familiar ring.

Iris stared at it astonished. 'Your phone. It's working.'

Tomas stared at it in wonder. 'I know.' Three messages had suddenly appeared.

'It really re-charged. And wow, look, I have a signal.' He looked across to the building with the flashes. 'It has to be connected to whatever is going on in that building, Iris.'

'What do you mean?'

'Someone is experimenting with radio frequencies in this spectrum. Has to be why the texts are coming in. You sure you don't know what goes on in that building?'

'I think it's an MOD building, they took it over when Whitehall was bombed.'

Tomas opened the first text.

'It's from Gabriella!'

'*Avoid someone called Prof Wylie. He will betray you and England. G x*'

'That's a message from Gabriella? In the future?' Iris was excited by the very idea of texting, never mind that this was coming from the future.

'Yeah,' Tomas said, as he opened the next text.

'She knows about Professor Wylie?' Iris remarked. 'I don't understand.'

'Wait. There's more.

'Tomas, please don't tell PM about the bomb. I hate this world you created. Change it back. L G'

Iris read it, overawed by the significance of it.

'This is terrible, Tomas. This means everything you said is really true.'

Tomas opened the last text, sent just moments before, according to the time.

'We're going to Cape Town to live. Please txt me. Are you still alive? They say you died on Russian Front? G x.'

'Reply to her. Quickly, whilst you can.' Iris demanded. 'Tell her you're alive, tell her you love her.'

Tomas looked at Iris for a trace of sarcasm, but she was being sincere.

'Tell her about me. Tell her that I'll come and see her one day. Before she goes to Africa.'

Tomas did exactly that.

'Am still alive but Prof W hunting me. Too late re-bomb. No Russian Front yet, will try to avoid. I love you Gab, but don't wait, I can't find way back. One day Iris H will come to see you. She will tell you what happened to me. I will always think of you. Lolz xx T Duck

He sent the text.

'We can send messages to the future,' Iris whispered in awe. 'That is so incredible.'

The flashing in the building had momentarily subsided. Tomas realised he was hungry, and opened up the flask to drink the soup.

'Will you really go and see her?' he asked. 'You'll be a little old lady by then.'

Iris grinned. 'She'll be so shocked to see me.'

Tomas nodded. He pointed to the building across the way. Even in the darkness they could see smoke pouring out. The blue arc lights flashed again and they both distinctly glimpsed a man opening up all the windows to let the smoke out, momentarily raising the blinds.

'Want to see Gabriella?' he asked suddenly. Iris looked confused, then hurriedly nodded.

'Come closer.' She huddled up to him as he swiped the screen again, searching for the clip of Gabby fooling around in a hat shop.

'Hey, do I look cute or what? J'adore ma chapeau, c'est tres chic n'est-ce pas?'

Iris watched the video clip with fascination and amazement.

'She's beautiful, Tomas. She speaks French.'

Tomas felt a strange tug at his heart. He'd never ever see Gabriella again. This was all he had of her. Three video clips and a bunch of silly photos of her flying her kite on a windy day.

'We should go,' Iris said. 'Daddy will wonder where I am. You should come with me. Lily threatened to tell them where you are.'

Tomas held her tighter, feeling her slim body under his arm.

'Not yet.' He put the cap back on the flask. 'This might be our last time together. There's so much I have to tell you and if you're going to be this famous science fiction writer, you need to know a whole lot more.'

Iris looked into his face and took a deep breath.

'I *will* be a famous writer, too. Everyone will be astonished at how much I know about the future.'

'Listen. Everything will be smaller, except people. They will get bigger and taller, except the girls who starve themselves to look thin.'

'Am I supposed to understand that?'

Tomas grinned. 'Just remember electronics small, people big. And films will be in 3D and the price of a two bedroom flat in London will be over a million pounds in 2013. Oh yeah, and social networking will be huge. No one will live in space though, although we'll all wish we could go to other planets. Tons of species of animals and birds will disappear as we cut down all the jungles to grow trees to make palm oil to power cars, and just about everything you eat or drink or breathe in causes cancer. Everyone will think you're a genius if you get all that in.'

'My goodness. I don't even know what any of that stuff means. How old will I be in 2013? I don't want to get old, ever.'

'Sadly, that's something they haven't fixed, but they're working on it. There's millions of old people riding around on electric scooters… no one really gets old until they're over seventy and …'

'Now I know you are just teasing me.'

'It's true. People live twice as long as they used to.'

'And diseases? Daddy says they'll have cured the common cold and ...'

'No. That makes too much money for the people who make the medicines. They'll never cure that. But smallpox and polio and a whole host of things virtually disappear. But then we got some new ones. HIV, which completely destroys your immune system and then we have flu pandemics.'

'Oh I know about the Spanish Flu. We had that in 1919. Millions of people died. It's going to come back?'

Tomas nodded. 'You need to know about other stuff too. How we all eat frozen food and live off pizza and coca-cola is huge all across the world.'

Iris held his hand and squeezed it. 'I don't want you to leave. I need to know so much more.'

Tomas kissed the side of her head. He didn't want to leave her either.

'I wish I could come with you, Tomas. I really do.'

Tomas nuzzled her ear. His heart was in two places at once. With Gabby in the future and right here with Iris, her small hand gripping his fingers so tight, her heart beating wildly. Was he being bad?

She turned to face to him, pulling him towards her and they kissed. Her lips burned hot and trembled and he tugged her still tighter to him, and was scared at how badly he wanted her. He slipped his arms around her.

The air-raid siren split their air with a sudden scream – searchlights pierced the sky and in the distance the distinct drone of approaching German bombers was coming from the East.

They broke apart, both gasping for breath, keenly aware how intense their feelings were for each other and how dangerous it was to be up on the roof. Iris didn't want to look at Tomas, she could hardly stand, she felt so dizzy. Her first kiss and it had to be wrecked by a damnable air-raid. Tomas felt light-headed. The air-raid ruined everything. He could barely let Iris go, he so badly needed to feel her close to him.

He pulled her up beside him and they stood looking eastwards. Tomas was confused.

'I don't understand it. The Blitz is over. They are supposed to have stopped bombing London already.'

They watched barrage balloons being winched up into the air, both aware of the danger, but horribly reluctant to part from each other.

'We need to get to a shelter,' Iris said.

Tomas was looking the other way, the electrical machinery was sparking bright blue arcs again and they hadn't pulled the blackout blinds down. He realised that whoever was in that building was not running some legitimate Government experiment, they were actually guiding the enemy.

'That's acting like a beacon to the bombers. God, Iris, who is in that building? You have to find out! I think they're communicating with the German bombers, guiding them in. Promise me you'll tell someone to check on it.'

Iris didn't need persuading. She could see the arcing equipment and brilliant blue flashes from the eighth floor window. It was clearly not an accident. Had they been guiding the Germans in all this time?

Tomas's phone vibrated again with an incoming text but there was no time to read it. They had to get off the roof.

Something made Tomas glance west. He saw just a flash, then heard a sudden roar as a Spitfire flew overhead at full throttle, another in close pursuit.

'We have to stay. I can shoot this.' Tomas shouted, excited.

'Shoot it? With what?'

'My phone.'

'It's a gun too?'

'No, I can film it. I have to film it.'

The bombers were approaching, a course bearing right towards them, the ack-ack already uselessly pounding the sky.

'They are coming right here,' Iris shouted, growing nervous now. 'You're right, someone is signalling them.' All her instincts told her to run, seek shelter, but Tomas wasn't moving, the boy who had been buried alive three times wasn't scared.

The searchlights were looking for the bombers.

'I think there's enough light, I can get this,' Tomas shouted over the ever growing intensity of the bomber engines. He flipped the phone and starting hunting for the bombers on zoom. He followed the searchlights up until he found one and paused his finger on the record button.

'This will be so cool. Keep an eye out for the Spitfire, Iris. They are going to attack in ten seconds.'

'How do you know that?'

'Because it's all going to kick off right here. Watch the sky.'

How he knew this, he had no idea, but he wanted a record of it.

The bombers were almost overhead now. He pressed record.

The Spitfire swooped in, training its tracer fire between the bombers that relentlessly seemed to keep on towards their target, oblivious to their fate.

Tomas followed one Spitfire as it found its mark and flames spurted from one Heinkel engine. Then, as the bomber returned fire, the Spitfire abruptly exploded.

He heard Iris shout in horror behind him.

'Run. For God's sake, run!'

She grabbed him and pulled him the full length of the roof as burning debris fell from the sky.

Tomas had got the shot he wanted, pocketed the phone quickly, scanning the roof for a way down. Behind them a burning aircraft wing plummeted into the school roof, crushing everything, falling deep into the school building, the impact knocking them off their feet. Tomas realised that had he been sleeping in the top room he would be dead by now for sure.

Above them three of the bombers were still heading west, but two were on fire, limping now and exposed to ground artillery.

Iris picked herself up, pointed to the Spitfire pilot floating down – his parachute had opened. He was drifting towards the river.

'That was incredible. I can't believe we saw that.' Iris was shouting over the sound of the rapidly burning school.

Tomas took her hand. He was excited, but suddenly quite concerned. 'How do we get down, Iris?'

They had reached the furthest end of the roof and looked down towards the playground.

'I don't know.'

Tomas glanced back, the last blue arc flash dazzled him momentarily before it ceased entirely and the same man was hurriedly pulling the blackout blinds back down.

Tomas remembered he'd had a text just before the bombers came and dug the phone out again.

He showed it to Iris.

'Iris Holmbush! My God Tomas, she dedicated all her novels to you. Tell her to write me. I need to see her now! Stay alive. Change it all back :) *Please! x'*

Iris was shocked, feeling goosebumps on her neck. 'She's talking about me. I'm really going to be a writer, Tomas. I told you'.

Tomas switched the phone off and pulled her towards him hugging her hard.

Fire engines could be heard approaching. It was too late, this school was going to burn down to the ground. They both could feel the heat building under them.

A part of the roof collapsed to their left and a shower of sparks cascaded into the sky.

'We have to find a way down now! There has to be a fire escape.'

Iris followed, not daring to look down, as he ran along the edge.

Flames were gushing from the ever-widening hole behind them. At the furthest edge Tomas could see the fire escape below. They'd have to jump down a floor to get to the platform.

'I'll go first. Then you lower yourself down. I'll catch you.'

'Won't it hurt your leg?'

Tomas shrugged. 'They pinned it together well. Time to test it, I think.'

He jumped, grabbing the rail to stop himself tipping over and grazed his hands. It hurt like hell and he swore loudly, but nothing broke.

He turned around and Iris was already dangling above him, ready to drop.

'I'm here. I'm here. Let go, Iris.' He told her. 'Let go now.'

She dropped into his arms and they fell together, nearly rolling off the edge in the process.

'Shit. Hold on. No time to…'

The top floor window abruptly shattered and flames flared out practically roasting them. Iris screamed. Shards of broken glass had pierced her back and Tomas shouted with pain as glass cut him too. There was no time to think. They scrambled up and ran down the rusty metal steps of the fire escape, aware that the fire was spreading rapidly throughout the school now.

Tomas struggled with the last ladder that had to be lowered to the ground and clearly hadn't been moved in a long time. Tomas felt his left hand was wet and realised that it was covered in blood. Iris stood behind him looking nervously into the school, scared that this window too would suddenly explode.

He kicked hard and the ladder came free at last and dropped to the ground. He made Iris take it first.

He joined her in the playground where Iris grabbed him.

'My back is …' she felt the blood on his hands. 'Tomas, you're bleeding too. We have to get it treated.'

'I'll find an ambulance when they arrive. Go home. Your Dad can treat you there, he'll be worried about you. How bad is your back?'

'I don't want to look.' She pulled a small handkerchief out of her skirt pocket. 'Here, wrap this around your hand. Where will you go now, Tomas?' She hated to leave him.

'Rosie's. The ice cream shop. You know it?'

She nodded, relieved he wouldn't be going far.

Tomas picked some glass out the palm of his hand and wrapped the handkerchief around it, grateful for anything to stop the bleeding.

'When will I see you again?' Iris asked nervously. She clung on to his shirt – she wanted to drag him home with her and hide him there. 'I'll come to find you tomorrow. We have to think where to send you.'

'I'll be fine.' He grabbed her and kissed her on the lips again. 'Tomorrow, I'll see you tomorrow. Go.'

Police and fire engines were very close now. Burning wreckage fell nearby showering them with sparks and he pushed her away.

'Go. It's not safe here.' He turned Iris around and made her run.

She paused at the corner to wave goodbye, but he had already disappeared. Irish had an awful, sinking feeling she was never going to see him again.

Tomas glanced back once, heard her running, saw her giant shadow on the brick walls as the flames illuminated her. It would an image that would stay with him forever.

He made it to the rear wall, some burning debris smouldering close by. He hauled himself up and lowered himself down. He hoped he would be safe now. He had to get his hand dressed, but he realised putting some distance between him and the school was his first priority.

Flames from the burning school shone brightly over the cobbled mews lane. He looked up again at the building where the transmitter had been signalling the Luftwaffe planes. He wondered if there was a back way up to it. He *had* to find a way to destroy it. He ran up the side of the building looking for a way up, or a fire escape, but there was nothing but the slab side of the building, not even any windows at street level. The only way in was through the front door.

Suddenly he thought he saw movement behind him in the archway that led to the main road, a cat shrieked somewhere and a milk bottle tipped over.

Then, under the archway – he saw Lily, shining red in the reflected glow of the flames. She saw him and stopped in her tracks with surprise. Without any hesitation she raised her arm, pointed at him and shouted, 'He's here. He's over here.'

Tomas stood rooted to the spot. He couldn't believe it. Lily really had betrayed him. He hadn't wanted to believe it.

A huge black car raced through the archway and came to a halt just feet away from him. Tomas thought of running, but he knew the mews was a dead end. He looked back at the school wall and realised it was too high to climb up from this side.

'Tomas Drucker. You have been a very difficult boy to find.'

Tomas spun around again and there was Professor Wylie, stepping out of a black Rolls-Royce and behind him coming out of the front door of the transmitter building was Wilhelm Belhapt, his arm in a sling. He knew at once that he was the man he'd glimpsed opening the blackout blinds on the eighth floor of the high building, signalling the German pilots.

'Don't move,' Professor Wylie called out, as Tomas turned back, poised to run. 'There's no escape, Tomas.'

Tomas turned his head. Lily had vanished, but in her place two men waited in the archway, blackjacks in their hands.

‘You’re just in time, my boy. We have a flight to catch to Dublin. There are a lot of people very keen to meet our young hero.’

‘I’m no bloody hero of yours,’ Tomas declared, realising in a sickening instant that he’d never now be able to help Gabriella and change things back. He had little choice but to go with them.

‘Get him a bandage,’ Professor Wylie instructed Belhapt. ‘I don’t want him bleeding on my leather seats.’

18

The Visitor

Her father was packing when she got home. Gabby was surprised. He hadn't mentioned he was going anywhere so soon. He was staring at the closet trying to decide on which tie to wear. The exact opposite of the father she knew before, who didn't even own one tie.

'I'm going to Berlin. I would have liked you and your mother to come with me, but they only sent me one ticket.'

Gabriela leaned against the wall of her parent's bedroom and wondered why her mother wasn't helping him pack. She always did the packing before.

'Your mother is upset.'

'Why?'

'We will be going to Africa a little earlier.'

'Why?'

Her father looked down and sighed heavily. Clearly this was not something he wanted to explain right now.

'Is everything all right between you two? I mean…' Gabby began but trailed off as she could see he looked unhappy.

Professor Lamb gave her a half smile. 'It's nothing like that. Don't jump to conclusions. We still love each other and we both love you. Have no doubts about that, Gabby. I have the possibility of writing a history about the Southern German Africa zone. They want me to get started on the research before I start my teaching post.'

Gabriella understood.

'And that means I'll be leaving my school.'

Her father nodded. 'Yes. I'm sorry. That means leaving friends behind. That's what's worrying your mother too. She depends a lot on her friends and I suspect she doesn't think she'll make new ones. Are you cross with me? You'll get a couple of months off and you can explore the Cape and…'

Gabriella thought of Tomas. What if he came back? How would he find her again? Simultaneously she realised that he was probably never coming back and even if he did, the world had changed so much he'd hate it and it was all his fault anyway.

Her father was looking at her.

'You look confused…'

'Africa is fine by me, Daddy. The sooner we go the better, actually.'

He looked relieved.

The front doorbell rang. They both looked at each other as if expecting the other had a visitor.

'I'll go,' Gabriella said. 'You want some tea? I was going to make some.'

'I have to finish packing,' he glanced at his watch. 'I'm running late.'

Gabriella went down the stairs heavy footed, her emotions racing up and down the scale. Africa would be exciting, a big change in her life. Leaving her school would cause no heartbreak at all.

There was a man in a peaked cap standing outside the front door. He looked like a chauffeur.

'Afternoon Miss. Is this Miss Gabriella Lamb's residence?'

Gabby looked at the man with surprise. Why on earth would anyone wearing a chauffeur's uniform visit her house?

'That's me.'

The man smiled briefly before turning back towards the car.

'Miss Iris Holmbush would like to visit with you, if she might take up some of your time.'

Gabriella stared at him in astonishment. 'Iris Holmbush, the writer? She wants to see me? Iris equalled Tomas. Her heart began to beat a little faster. The last text she had received from him had been about Iris.

'Of course. I was just about to make tea.'

'I'm sure she would love to have tea. Miss Holmbush has been wanting to visit you for a long time now.'

Gabriella stared as he went to the Mercedes Benz and opened the rear door.

A gloved hand appeared, then the frail form of a very old lady. He helped her out, gave her a cane and she approached Gabriella with an awkward smile on her face. Gabriella realised this was an actual old person, the first she'd seen. They weren't all dead then.

'You're even more pretty than Tomas said you were, my dear. Please forgive me for being so slow. You have no idea how long I have waited to speak to you.'

Gabriella stared, felt her temperature suddenly spike and then she was falling and falling.

She awoke and discovered she was lying on the sofa and her father was serving tea to the old lady. It was not a dream. Worse. If this old lady was Iris it meant that Tomas really was long dead, or at the very least, just as old and wrinkled.

'You're back with us, at last,' Iris said, smiling.

Professor Lamb, looking quite concerned, wiped Gabriella's face with a damp cloth.

'You gave me quite a turn, young lady. Can you sit up?'

Gabby sat up – flushing red, embarrassed she had fainted like that.

'I'm sorry,' Iris said softly. 'I must have given you quite a shock.'

Gabriella took a deep breath. She wished her father wasn't there, she wanted to ask so many questions. He was hovering by the door now.

'They're coming for me soon, Gabby. I have to finish packing. Will you all right now?'

'Yes, Daddy. I'm sorry, I ...'

'I'm not sure you're eating enough, y'know. Your mother...'

Gabriella cut him off quickly. 'I'm fine. I eat like a horse. I just had a shock, that's all. Go finish packing.' She turned to Iris to explain. 'Daddy's off to Berlin to receive a prize.'

'I know. Congratulations, Dr Lamb. Don't worry about your daughter. She's in good hands with me.'

Her father offered an embarrassed smile, grateful to be released. He left.

'That's how I found you,' Iris explained to Gabby. 'Your father's award was mentioned in *The Times*. I have looked for you a long time y'know. It was so hard to wait all this time. I knew I couldn't come to see you until Tomas had gone. I knew the date he disappeared from your life, but of course he never told me your surname.'

'But if you knew it was going to happen you could have stopped it happening, couldn't you?'

The old lady contemplated that a moment. 'It's very complicated. But until he left here and arrived back in 1941, the future or, is it the past?... hadn't changed. I'd be just some strange old lady who'd knock on your door and tell you Tomas was about to travel back in time. You would have thought me utterly mad, I think. Besides, until yesterday's newspaper I never knew your surname, or where you lived.'

Gabriella stared blinking at Iris, understanding at once that what she said was true. She would have thought she was mad. She tried to imagine this old woman being the same age as herself, but struggled with the concept.

'Did you not have to go into the care camps? You're the first old person I have seen since…'

'Since Tomas travelled back in time, you mean.'

Gabriella nodded, glad Iris brought it up first. Her chauffeur was sitting at the other end of the room drinking tea and eating some cake. He wasn't interested in the conversation, but glanced at his charge from time to time to make sure she was comfortable.

'Yes. Since Tomas disappeared.'

'I'm a party member. Reluctant party member, I might add. My mother was important for a time when she married General Huber. Then my sister Lily married a German politician and I had no choice but to join. By then of course I was a young woman and England had already changed forever.'

Gabriella didn't want to know all this. She wanted to know about Tomas.

'Did you marry Tomas?'

Iris laughed, putting an elegant gloved hand to her mouth as she did so.

'No, dear. I only saw Tomas very briefly in my life, but he made a strong impression.'

'Your books. I read two of them. I loved those stories. My mother says they are science fiction, but I know them as the real future, the one I used to belong to. You didn't get it all right but it was fun to read them.'

'Well I was lucky to be in print at all. Writing novels about Germany losing the war is frowned upon. I was called all kinds of things, but my sister Lily protected me. All out of print now, of course.'

'And Tomas?'

'That's who I've come to talk about. All in good time. He was desperate to receive messages from you, y'know.'

'They got through?' Gabriella felt reassured suddenly.

'I saw some myself. The very last night I saw him… alive.'

Gabriella braced herself for bad news.

'Then it's true, he's dead.'

Iris sipped her tea.

'Oh, I'm sure he's dead. I'm eighty-seven now. He'd be…'

'Eighty-six.'

'There are very few of us old timers left now. Clive, that's my chauffeur, he says he's seen only one other old person in his lifetime and I know that wasn't Tomas.'

'How did you find him?' Gabriella asked.

'He was buried alive in a building across the road from our house. He said he'd been tortured by Professor Wylie. We didn't believe him at first. He had been hurt quite badly, but Daddy, who was a doctor, stitched him up and I made him pancakes.'

'Pancakes?' Gabriella could just imagine him eating pancakes.

'Terrible pancakes. No sugar, hardly any flour and stolen milk. We thought it very grand though.' She smiled, remembering.

'Tomas told my father about the terrible bombing that would come that very night and of course he didn't believe him. Then when it happened Daddy accused him of being a spy and Tomas had to confess he was from the future.' She looked very sad but Gabriella could tell that she really wanted to tell this story.

Gabriella felt tears coming. 'Did you believe him?'

'Daddy didn't. I did. He was so different. And he had a history book printed in the future and his phone. Lily was sceptical of course. We set him to work talking to the children at the school. He was very good with the children, they adored him.'

'Tomas was teaching?'

'He was quite natural. Mostly about dinosaurs I think.'

Gabriella laughed. That was Tomas, he could talk forever about pre-historic monsters.

'But Professor Wylie desperately wanted him. He had people looking everywhere for him, Tomas had to sleep on the school roof to escape them.'

'The roof?'

'That was the last time I saw him. It was the last bomber to attack London that year and there was a dogfight. Tomas filmed it on his phone. I begged him to get off the roof, but he was so excited to film it.'

Gabriella shook her head in wonder. 'Sounds like him. He was obsessed with bombers.'

'Tomas had just shown me messages from you and I made a vow then, if I lived long enough, that I'd come and see you one day.'

Gabriella said nothing. She watched as Iris fumbled in her handbag and withdrew a small black and white photo.

'Lily took this when he was sleeping in our house. I only found it a few months ago when I was going through her things. She died, last year, when she was visiting her son in Canada.'

Gabriella stared at the photo of Tomas with a bandage around his head. He looked so bruised and exhausted.

'What happened to his head?'

'He was buried alive three times y'know. That part of his history is true at least.'

Gabriella touched Tomas' face. She turned away a moment, tears rolling down her cheeks. She couldn't stop them. He was gone forever. Thank God she was going to Africa to start a new life. She'd have to forget him.

'The school was burning. He saved my life that day. I would have died on the roof if he hadn't got me down. He sent me home. He had to look for a new hiding place and that's when it happened.'

'What?' Gabriella looked back, drying her eyes with her sleeve.

'I saw my sister Lily. She told me straight to my face that I wouldn't be seeing Tomas again. I didn't know what she meant at first. I had to warn Tomas. He'd gone over the wall at the back of the school and I raced to find him.'

'Where was this?'

'South Kensington. I have lived there all my life.'

'And the school was on fire?'

'A part of a burning Spitfire fell on the school. We were so lucky not to have died ourselves. I raced around the back, but I was too late.'

'They caught him?'

Iris sighed. 'I'm afraid it was Lily.'

'Lily?'

'My sister. I didn't know it at the time, but she was jealous. I had brought him to my aunt's house for a bath that day and Lily had seen us leaving holding hands.'

'Holding hands?' That was a surprise; Gabriella felt a twinge of jealousy.

'It's my fault. I'm afraid I was very smitten and …'

Gabriella shook her head. So that was why Iris had dedicated her books to Tomas. She was jealous of the young girl Iris must have once been, but then again poor Tomas had every right to hold a pretty girl's hand. They weren't even going out, just 'best friends' after all… but she did feel a momentary pang of jealousy.

'I arrived at the entrance to the mews. I saw Professor Wylie standing besides Tomas and Herr Belhapt was there too. Tomas had no chance. I had to hide as two of his henchmen appeared. They carried blackjacks. They would use them too. Lily never said a word to me about it after that night, but I knew, she had betrayed him.'

'Because you held his hand?'

'Lot's of reasons. My sister sided with my mother; who was having an affair with Professor Wylie. It's complicated. Wylie was the one…'

'Who persuaded Churchill to surrender England to the Germans.'

'He used Tomas to do it.'

'My father says the Germans didn't even have the atomic bomb then.'

'Your father is right. But that hardly matters now. Tomas believed that Professor Wylie was experimenting with radio microwaves in the Gannet building and this was guiding German bombers into London or passing on target information at least. They were on a similar wavelength to his phone and that's how you were able to communicate.'

Gabriella stared. 'Really? I had been wondering about that.'

'My father did the right thing and called the authorities and they raided the building the next night. Herr Belhapt was caught along with two other pro-German sympathisers, but it was all too late. We didn't know it then, but Professor Wylie and German intelligence had already persuaded Churchill of the potential power of the bomb and history was about to be changed forever.'

'And Tomas?'

Iris shrugged. 'Professor Wylie snatched him. Lily confessed she betrayed him years later. She might have been jealous that he preferred me, I suppose.'

'You really liked him, didn't you?'

'Yes. But it all seems so silly, but I was fifteen – he was the first boy I had ever really kissed and …' She sighed.

'My mother went to Berlin with the political transition team. Lily went to ballet school there.'

'And you?'

'I stayed with my father and started writing. My first story was published when I was sixteen. Even then I wrote about the future. The future Tomas showed me. Or at least what I thought was his future. I imagine it was all foolish nonsense really.'

'And you never saw him again?'

'No. Never. Nor Professor Wylie.'

'And him volunteering to fight on the Russian front?'

'Definitely untrue. Lily knew what had really happened – she promised to tell me one day, but she never did.'

'So you don't really know?'

'No.'

'So he could have led a normal life? He could be alive, like you.'

'Perhaps. But I don't think so. I never understood why he didn't ever write to me. I never left the family home.'

'Perhaps he couldn't?'

'Or he met someone else.' Iris suggested. 'He was a very good looking boy.'

Gabriella shrugged. The Tomas she knew would have written to her. After all she had held his hand. He was very old fashioned.

'So there is absolutely no trace of him?' Gabriella asked, disappointed.

'You never got another message?' Iris asked.

'None, but I only got the message about you two days ago, remember.'

She sighed, looking away a moment, her eyes quite moist. 'Professor Wylie would have taken Tomas' phone. He was fascinated by the phone, he wanted to know how it worked.' She grinned momentarily. 'That's why everyone in my books carry phones. Tomas gave me that, at least.'

Gabriella fell quiet a moment, heavy with her thoughts about Tomas lost back in time, trying to imagine Iris as a young girl.

'He tried not to change history, Gabriella. But he couldn't stop it. The moment he went back he was bound to change things.'

'There haven't been any other time travellers, have there?' Gabriella asked. 'I keep thinking about why it had to be Tomas. I know he was always dreaming about being bombed, but why was it him that went back? And how? Did he explain that?

Iris put down her tea cup and nibbled on a piece of cake. 'No. I don't think he knew how it happened. Perhaps there were others? How would we ever know? I have always been curious as to why and how it happened, Gabriella. Did you ever know of anyone who went back in time before? In the world you used to inhabit.'

Gabriella shook her head.

'No, I mean, people went back in time all the time on TV, but that was just fiction. In real life it was as impossible, as it would be here.'

Iris frowned.

'So why Tomas? Why 1941? What do you think happened?'

Gabriella shook her head then remembered something.

'You want to see Tomas? I have him on my phone.'

Iris' eyes lit up.

'Yes. Oh yes.'

Gabby jumped up and ran upstairs. Her phone was hidden, but fully charged. The very least she could do was show Iris what Tomas was like. She'd been waiting all these years to talk about him.

She was back in minutes. Iris hadn't moved. She sat there on the sofa, her eyes closed. They opened again as Gabriella sat down again, switched on her iPhone.

'Don't tell anyone I have this.'

Iris's eyes opened wide. 'I shan't. Oh, I'm very excited. I might need my heart pills.'

The chauffeur was up in a trice and came over to administer them to her. Gabriella realised that Iris was not only old, but also probably very rich. Her books must have sold millions when they had been in print.

She found a clip of Tomas fooling around playing air guitar.

Iris watched amazed.

'It's Tomas. It really is Tomas.'

'Wait, I have another clip. When he broke his leg. He's in bed and here…'

Iris watched as Tomas was lying with his leg in plaster suspended above the bed. He was talking to Gabby.

'And I heard the bombers approaching. The whole house was shaking and I wasn't scared. I mean, I knew the bombs were going to fall and I knew I was going to be buried alive, but it was so real and somehow I knew I wasn't going to die.'

'You have to stop watching these DVD's, Tomas. Really. I mean it. They are really getting to you.'

Tomas smiled and the video abruptly stopped.

Iris was crying now. She waved her chauffeur away.

'I'm all right. Don't fuss. I'm so happy to have seen him again, that's all. Poor dear Tomas…'

Gabriella handed Iris a handkerchief to dab her eyes.

'I always thought there was a purpose to this. His travelling back in time and accidentally changing history. He did change history didn't he? He always insisted that in his time Germany lost the war. That was true, wasn't it.'

Gabriella nodded.

'Everything was different. But only you and I know this, Iris. I don't understand that either. Even my Father doesn't seem to remember, nor my mother. Just me.'

'Because you were connected to him.'

'I wish …'

'What?'

'It's not a good world, Iris. Many terrible things have happened. My Father is taking us to Africa, but it all changed. The England I remember had lots of people in it and old people too, tons of them, and people of all colours and religions and it wasn't illegal to be gay and you didn't need a special pass to go from one city to another. It wasn't a perfect world, but the music was better. The music was definitely better.'

Iris smiled.

'My world. It sounds like my world. They never liked my books. They taxed all my earnings from America so much I might as well not have sold a single copy, but I get still get letters from readers via Canada and they say the same as you. We live with an iron grip around our throats and just because they let us breathe, it does not mean we are living.'

Gabriella looked at Iris then leaned forward and hugged her. Iris was surprised but hugged her back, her frail arms around Gabriella hardly making a dent.

'That's for bringing Tomas back to me,' Gabby said. 'And I'm sorry this happened to us.'

Iris pulled back and looked into Gabriella's eyes.

'I would give up all my success, Gabriella, in a second if it meant that we could change history back again.' She glanced at her chauffeur who was reading a magazine, not listening to them.

'Go to Africa. Gabriella. Find yourself there. They tell me it's different. I hope it is true. Make it true. Never forget Tomas or what history might have been. Promise?'

'I promise.'

19

Dublin Bound

Someone told Tomas that he was flying on a DH 89 Dragon-Rapide. In the darkness he'd glimpsed the double set of wings and heard two incredibly noisy air-cooled engines driving the propellers. Inside he saw that there were six rather flimsy seats and one for the pilot who was already seated, glancing at a map on his lap.

One of Professor Wylie's men had put Tomas in the back and tied him to the rear seat, then pulled a curtain to cut him off from the rest of the travellers. Someone important was getting on and they didn't want him to see. He prayed and hoped that it wasn't the Prime Minister. If it was Churchill then already everything was lost and Professor Wylie had won.

He wasn't sure where they were, but it was definitely West London and a private airfield. They took off almost immediately. The plane moved forward with an incredible roar from the engines and rose quickly, banking left and heading West. Tomas saw nothing below them out of the window until they rose above the clouds and the light of a waning moon reflected on the wing. They were running without lights in or outside. London and its surrounds were truly blacked out below. Tomas felt acute despair. He knew that once they landed in Dublin he'd be handed over to the Germans and that would be that. They'd torture him for everything he knew and then probably kill him.

The flight was incredibly bumpy, and the aircraft seemed to be easily buffeted by the wind. He began to feel nauseous with the motion.

Professor Wylie came to the rear of the plane after they had been flying about an hour. He peered around the curtain and stared at him. His face was quite sinister in the pale moonlight.

'I feel sick,' Tomas told him.

Professor Wylie pulled a face. 'You'll have to hold it.'

'Haven't you got a paper bag or something?'

'No.'

'You don't need me'

Professor Wylie looked at Tomas without pity. 'I told you; they're interested to meet you in Berlin. They have a lot of questions for you. You're going to be a hero, Tomas.'

'Is that the Prime Minister in the front?'

Professor Wylie smiled. 'You think the Prime Minister would fly in this tub? Without a fighter escort? Prime ministers are not so easily prised out of London. We have a former Foreign Secretary with us. He understands the situation we are in. One cannot have a serving Minister meeting with the German Ministry of Foreign Affairs- even in Dublin, there are spies only too keen to pass information back to London. But he will, in this instance, hear the evidence and take it back to the Prime Minister. Diplomacy, Tomas, even when at war.'

'Why would he believe them? You know the Germans haven't got the bomb.'

'He already does believe me. A little knowledge and a lot of fear can go a long way. Don't you understand? German intelligence has already presented convincing evidence to prove they are just weeks away from successful testing. Thanks to you, Tomas. Besides, you really think Germany wants to continue this war? Von Ribbentrop is keen to re-establish a truly cordial relationship between British and German peoples. He made many friends with important people here before the war. He has a genuine affection for London and the King.'

'You really think that the people of England will surrender after all the bombing they have been through and survived?'

'When they discover about the terror to come, Tomas. Yes, when they are told about the terrible fire that can burn 70,000 people with just one bomb. They'll see sense. I guarantee it.'

The plane lurched again and Tomas felt his stomach flip over.

'The bomb doesn't exist. Churchill will discover that. He isn't stupid.'

'That's the risk Churchill will have to take. He already fears the worst. He will blink and the war will be over. You, Tomas will become the hero you deserve to be.'

Tomas closed his eyes, he was definitely going to be sick any moment now.

'You need to sit down, Professor,' the pilot called back. 'We're encountering a lot of turbulence.'

Professor Wylie let the curtain fall and returned to his seat.

Tomas suddenly vomited and it splattered all over his shoes. Then he puked again, spewing hard and painfully, amazed at how much came out. He was suddenly sweating and felt terrible, but the force of lurching forward had created a space between the ropes that bound him to the chair. He realised that he could probably wriggle free.

The plane suddenly plummeted down into an air pocket before jerking up again. Tomas almost went flying, restrained only by the ropes that bound him. He heard others shouting with pain as they had banged their heads on the bulkhead.

He puked again and heard others doing the same behind the curtain. The cabin was beginning to smell pretty bad.

Tomas moved from side to side and the ropes finally fell off him. He was free to move. He began to work on the rope around his wrists with his teeth, wishing he could have some water to rinse out his mouth. Sweat poured into his eyes. He edged forward and wiped his face on the curtains.

The plane bucked again and something came loose behind him, falling onto his back. Lifejackets. The knot finally came away and he shook his hands free. He grabbed one of the lifejackets and put it over his head, tying it as best he could. If this plane was going down and he survived, he would float at least.

Up ahead someone was shouting. Tomas pulled the curtain to one side to peek, just as a bolt of lightning flashed. He glimpsed the pilot wrestling the controls, and the other passengers hanging on for dear life; most of them violently vomiting. The wind was battering the plane hard now and Tomas could tell they had drastically slowed as the engines struggled to make any headway.

Another flash of lightning revealed the extent of the tower of storm clouds outside the window. Tomas realised that this was no ordinary gale, the clouds extended high up above them and sheet lightning rippled through them. If they flew into this storm the wood frame plane would be smashed, he was sure of it. A sudden vivid flash exploded, sending red lightning way above storm clouds. Tomas stared at the impression left on his eyeballs of a giant jellyfish of light.

'Can we set down somewhere?' Professor Wylie was shouting to the pilot.

'I've never seen such a storm in all my life,' the pilot shouted back. 'Did you see that Sprite? That's a huge amount of energy. We shouldn't be flying in this. Hold on tight. We're over the Irish Sea. I'm going to try and fly under the clouds.'

Tomas held on as tight as he could. He felt the lifejacket and wondered if it had any buoyancy at all. It was solid, cork probably, not something you blew up with air. He definitely felt better for having thrown up, but was still sweating and nervous. Weirdly he was thinking that maybe it was best for everyone if the plane crashed and they all died. At least Professor Wylie wouldn't be around to persuade Churchill of his crazy plans.

He understood what the pilot was trying to do. He couldn't climb over a storm this big. Only jets could go that high, propeller driven planes of this time had to go where the wind was least. If that meant sea-level, then that's what he had to do. Even though they were getting lower and lower, the wind didn't let up and it seemed to continually batter them, a fierce driving rain beating on the windows now.

Tomas fell forward suddenly, grabbing the curtains for support that came away from the bulkhead. He was wrapped up in it now and sliding along the floor in a river of vomit.

The plane violently lurched again as Tomas tried to untangle himself. As he dragged the cloth off his head he heard an ominous bang and looked out over the portside wing. Lightning had struck the engine and it was on fire. They began to lose height almost immediately.

Someone tripped over him and went sprawling, knocking his head on the edge of the metal seat. Tomas didn't know who it was, but he could see now in the glow of the flames that he was adjacent to the door. He hauled himself up into the nearest seat and began to look for the door handle. They were flying so low, maybe he could get out; trust his luck to the sea. If he drowned, well at least the Germans wouldn't have him and that was the better kind of hero in his mind. Then he had a moment of clarity. Jumping out was a coward's choice. *He had to make sure Professor Wylie died with him.* He realised that it was his duty to get the plane to crash.

Another flash of lightning revealed Professor Wylie sitting just ahead of the door, his head in his lap as he groaned with sickness.

The pilot was grimly trying to keep the plain aloft, flying just fast enough not to stall.

Tomas took his chance.

He ran towards the pilot and leapt on the controls, forcing them forward and the aircraft into a steep dive. The pilot screamed at him to get off, his voice filled with panic. Suddenly another of the passengers fell on top of Tomas and the pilot, the man's face pressed up against the cockpit window. The pilot's controls seemed to buckle under the weight of the three men. The aircraft was plunging straight towards the sea, as everyone screamed and shouted in panic.

Tomas was in extreme pain, the metal controls were digging deep into his chest, someone was trying to pull him off, but he knew it was over. He closed his eyes in the final seconds, he was taking them all with him. *'Now I really am a bloody hero, Gabby. This crash is for you.'*

The aircraft seemed to flip under as it plunged into the foaming sea. It felt like hitting concrete at speed. The wings were ripped away instantly from the fuselage. Tomas yelled with shock as the fuselage ploughed down into the freezing sea. The cockpit windows smashed, seawater surged in over them all and Tomas suddenly lost consciousness.

Tomas was drowning. It was dark, but somewhere close an engine was momentarily still burning nearby. The wooden frame of the aircraft seemed to have disintegrated around him. He experienced an intense pain in his chest and yet all the pressure holding him down was suddenly gone. He kicked and realised that he was no longer surrounded by anything but water. He was moving up towards the surface, his left arm now in pain as if it had been struck by something hard. Gasping for air, he broke through the surface of a wild sea and fantastic wind. Bits of the plane were coming up with him and he grabbed at something that seemed to float. A metal canister. It didn't matter what it was, he was somehow alive. He felt his chest, knew he was cut and bleeding, but in the darkness could see nothing. He tied the lifejacket more securely around him, conscious of a shooting pain in his arm now, and clung on to this canister. He was freezing, he jaws began to chatter and he shook with the shock of what he'd just done. He'd killed men. Traitors to be sure, but he'd caused the death of others. He knew there would be consequences.

Tomas looked around for more survivors. It was unlikely; he'd been the only one wearing a lifejacket. He wondered if anything else might float up to the surface but the wind and the huge rolling waves were quickly taking him away from the crash zone.

Tomas realised he was miles from anywhere; his chest and left arm hurt like hell now. The wind whipped at his face and spray lashed his skin. The wind had to be blowing a hundred miles an hour at the very least. He couldn't believe he'd survived the crash only to drown at sea. How stupid was that?

The life jacket was heavy, barely kept him afloat, but he was alive in the freezing cold Irish Sea – for now. He was thinking that it was nearly June, should the sea be this cold? He turned around 360 degrees; there was no horizon, it was dark, no stars were visible as the wind and clouds obscured all. How far was he from the coast? Which way the current? Where was he headed? How long before the cold got him or would he just starve to death? Had anyone else survived? He doubted it. These were the thoughts that quickly passed through Tomas' mind.

Tomas made his legs move to try and keep warm. But it was hard in the life jacket. He tried to get on top of the canister, but he just rolled right off and would have lost it completely had he not tied it to the lifejacket. Was he going towards land or further away? He hadn't a clue. Who would rescue him? Who on earth would be out on the Irish Sea at night, in wartime, in a terrible storm? And what about mines? Were there mines?

Tomas knew it was a miracle he'd survived the crash. Had it been flying at the normal height of 16,000 feet he would have died for sure. A huge wave rolled under him and lifted him up and then down once more. It was truly scary at the bottom of the trough before he was again swept up.

Overhead thunder cracked and lightning snapped like a whip. He tried to think of Iris and then of Gabriella, but he was too tired to do that. Although the cold water numbed the pain in his arm, he was beginning to wonder if he had pulled it out of its socket. He could still move his hands, which was a relief, but the spreading pain in his upper left arm and shoulder worried him.

He awoke suddenly, spluttering. *Mustn't sleep, mustn't sleep*. The canister wasn't helping. He needed to be out of the water. He knew he'd lose consciousness soon, he already could barely feel his body. Hypothermia would take over. The early dawn light was visible in the East. He was extremely cold now. He untied himself from the canister and tried to swim in a circle around it, ignoring the stabbing pain in his shoulder. He had to keep his circulation going. He noticed that the wind was calming down, the sky softening. The storm was over at least.

Tomas realised the chances of being rescued were practically zero. He turned and his memory flashed up Lily's face at the exact moment she had spotted him and raised her hand to betray him. He still didn't understand why she had done that and it hurt.

He cursed himself for thinking he could help anyone, or that his knowledge of the war could be useful. Time travel totally sucked, that was for sure. If he ever got back he'd … what? Tell people? No way. No way he was ever going back anyway.

Tomas tied himself to the canister again, his fingers barely able to move at all. He was freezing, but the sun was up and under a clear blue sky he could feel some warmth on his face. He brought his legs up so he was floating just below the surface in the faint hope the sun would warm all of him. Stupid idea. The warm sun on his face just made it worse somehow.

The sea was now almost flat. Hard to believe that just hours before it had been churning wildly. He heard the throbbing of an engine, but although he turned right around, he could see absolutely nothing. The horizon was empty. Had he drifted to the open ocean? Was he going to end up in the Pacific? or on the coast of Scotland? He had no idea which.

A glint of sunlight caught his attention.

The engine noise was not like any he had ever heard before. He couldn't put a word to it. He saw a glint of sun on metal.

The conning tower of a submarine passed him by, submerging slowly. It was cruising by, no more than a hundred yards away, creating less than a ripple in the water as it submerged. Had he been closer he could have hitched a ride. But was it British or German? He had no idea, saw no markings. He realised that he no longer cared. He almost smiled at the idea of jumping onto it as it went down and banging on the tower. Would they have stopped? Or would he have been dragged down with it? Nothing seemed to make sense anymore.

Tomas continued to lie in the water, maximising his exposure to the sun, desperately trying to keep his legs up by making circling movements with his arms. His shoulder pain was easing or was it simply that in the cold water he couldn't feel anything anymore?

A school of fish swept by him, he felt a thousand mouths tugging at his clothes to see if it was edible. He had to splash around him to scare them off. He didn't want to be fish food just yet.

He realised with a growing fatalism that that was exactly what he was becoming, fish food. Were there sharks in the Irish Sea? He was pretty sure there were …

The next thing he was aware of was a hook under his life jacket, pulling him towards a boat. Hands were grappling with him, hauling him up and over into a fishing boat. He was barely conscious but all around him he heard Irish accents.

'And where the hell have you come from, Boy?'

'Is he a pilot?' Another asked.

'Not unless you have children flying now.'

'Is he dead?'

'He's breathing.'

'Does he have any money?'

Tomas opened his eyes. The two fishermen stepped back.

'Water,' Tomas croaked.

'Well now, I reckon he's English.'

'Throw him back,' another voice suggested, but no one did and he lay on the deck like a stranded herring.

'He wants water.'

'Give him some whiskey. He'll need it. Lord knows how long he's been out here in the water.'

Tomas felt liquid being poured down his throat. Felt it burn. He gasped, nearly threw up, it was so disgusting. He opened his eyes again and coughed. He discovered he was naked and a man in thigh-high fisherman's boots was rubbing something absolutely vile into his skin.

'Wintergreen, boy. This stuff will warm the dead, believe me.'

Tomas could believe it. His skin was on fire. He was alive but on fire inside and out.

One of the men wrapped a blanket around him then and explained that they weren't going to return to port until they had their quota of fish. He picked Tomas up, and dumped him in the corner of the small wheelhouse and made him drink some hot black tea. It was warming and although Tomas wanted to speak, almost immediately afterwards he fell asleep. They hadn't asked how he got there and he didn't tell.

Tomas awoke. Someone was cooking. A kettle was screaming on a gas ring and the fisherman looked down and nodded, registering that Tomas was stirring.

'Hungry?'

Tomas realised that he was starving.

'It's just soup. Fresh tea on the way.' He ducked his head out of the wheelhouse. 'The boy's awake. You got his clothes?'

A moment later another man brought his clothes. They had dried out in the sun and Tomas quickly put them on, aware that he still stank of wintergreen and the clothes stank of fish. They gave him a mug of soup and when he was completely finished, someone poured tea in the same mug. Tomas didn't care. As long as something went down.

He noticed they were heading towards land. The sun had already set and darkness was approaching.

'Brought us luck. Best catch in a long time,' one of the men said.

Tomas nodded. He was pleased for them.

'You'll be needing this, I suppose.' Another of the fishermen said as he handed over the ID card, still in its envelope. Tomas didn't open it, he knew all the pages would be stuck together. His name was faintly visible on the envelope, however, and that might be useful in persuading an official he was not a refugee. He was dreading having to explain how he came to be in the sea.

None of them asked him anything. The man called Derry gave him back his still unspent five-pound note that he'd carefully dried. Tomas tried to give it to him as thanks but he put up his hands and shook his head.

'Can't spend English money here. No one would take it.'

Tomas remembered that he'd been on his way to Dublin and realised that British pounds were probably an insult or something. It was a reminder to be cautious.

They entered the small fishing port in darkness. Just one streetlight lighting the way, although Tomas noted a pub was lit up at the quayside and loud singing was coming clear across the water. Eire wasn't in the war. They didn't have to use blackout, or close the pubs. He remembered they were neutral in this war.

Derry took Tomas aside as they docked.

'You'll wait for my sister. She'll put you up for now. You can call whoever you want in the morning.'

Tomas nodded and watched as the men efficiently landed the baskets of fish. He was surprised to see a man come out of the pub armed with a clipboard and begin to inspect the catch.

'Good haul, lads. Fetch you a good price I reckon.'

Several people came out of the pub then and Tomas watched with astonishment as the catch was auctioned off right there and then to a small group of men who'd walked over with him. He couldn't believe how fast the auctioneer talked or how quickly the baskets of fish were taken away after money was given to a woman in a shawl by a makeshift table.

All in all it took less than twenty minutes. The men who had rescued him looked exhausted, but happy, then without even a glance at Tomas they wandered off towards the pub.

'Derry says you'll be needing a warm bed,' a voice announced behind him.

He realised it was the woman with the shawl. She had finished her work and the table was stowed away already.

'Name's Shannon. You got a name, Sinbad?'

Tomas smiled briefly at the name she had given him.

'Tomas.'

'Well come with me, Tomas. Any idea how long you were out

there?'

Tomas shook his head and followed her. The fishing village was quaint, dark, with few homes showing light. Shannon walked ahead of him slightly at quite a lick, a large fish wrapped in newspaper under her arms.

'You from any place I'd know?' She asked when they reached her cobbled street. Tomas noted a very old dusty Citroen 2CV parked outside it with flat tyres.

'I was living in Kensington, but I was born in Portsmouth.'

She looked at him, frowned but made no comment. She let him into her cottage. It was a simple whitewashed affair with little furniture or decoration, not very homely at all. She led Tomas into the primitive kitchen and he sat down at the long table, noting the mousetraps set by the larder.

'I hope you know how lucky you are. Being adrift like that in the sea. God knows someone must love you. I'd not lay odds on surviving out there.'

'You hear of a aircraft crashing near here last night?'

'Plane crash?' Shannon looked at him askance and Tomas could tell she didn't believe him. She put the kettle on and used a bottle opener to get the cap off the milk. He hadn't seen milk sealed like that before.

'You sure no one talked about a crash?' He wanted to make sure.

'If you crashed at sea, only the sea knows what happened, Tomas.'

Tomas sighed and felt depressed. He wanted to be sure Professor Wylie had drowned. The flight had been secret. So it was unlikely there would be a rescue mission. In public at least.

'You hungry? There's some fresh bread on the table. Have some bread and jam.'

Tomas sat down and cut himself a slice of dark brown bread. Looked good too. Obviously there was no rationing in Eire.

'I've got no butter, but the strawberry jam's homemade. Derry keeps promising me a fridge but I've never seen it yet.'

Tomas looked around the kitchen. She was right, she had no fridge, but there was an ancient washing machine in the corner with a mangle attached.

Shannon pointed to the stairs.

'There's a bedroom in the loft. If you need to go use the pot. Not many luxuries in this place. Another thing Derry was going to do.'

'Does Derry live here too?'

'God no. Derry is shackled to Catherine O'Malley and she barely lets him out of her sight. I'm surprised she doesn't go out to sea with him, she's so possessive.'

She smiled. 'There's a telephone in the village if you need to call someone tomorrow. You'll find sheets and blankets upstairs.'

The kettle boiled and she made them both a mug of tea, adding the long-life milk to both cups.

'If you wanted sugar I'm out of that too.'

Tomas was getting used to tea without sugar. He took the mug from her hands and set it down on the table.

'It'll be trout for breakfast. I'm going to cook it now and we'll have it cold. That all right with you?'

Tomas smiled. People ate kippers for breakfast, so why not trout?

He spread jam over his bread and ate. He hadn't quite appreciated how hungry he was. He wanted to call Iris, but try as he might he realised couldn't remember her landline number. They'd been stored on his iPhone which was now lost forever. He wondered if the operator could find Dr Holmbush's number and how much it would cost to call, assuming one could even call London from Eire. Then he remembered he only had a five-pound note and probably couldn't spend it here.

Tomas made his way upstairs carrying the mug of tea. Even though he'd slept most of the day, he was exhausted. A hot bath would have been nice, or a wash to get rid of the wintergreen, but at least he had a bed to go to and it was highly unlikely to be bombed. He examined his chest. Only a scratch but the bruising was massive, all purple and black. The same on his arm, which hurt like hell when he lifted it above shoulder height. He realised he'd been dead lucky to survive at all.

Tomas had drunk his tea and glanced at a book left beside the bed called *Finnegan's Wake*. Clearly he wasn't going to sleep; his mind was wide-awake. He tried to think about what he would do. He had no plan. It might even be best if he contacted no one. Let everyone think he was dead. Lie low. Maybe work with the fisherman if they would let him, just for a while, until people forgot him. He could write to Iris and tell her he was OK. But then again, he didn't want it to be intercepted and one of Professor Wylie's people find out where he was.

He was puzzling over this when he heard someone talking. Heard a shot.

He went to the stairs and listened. There was music. Shannon must have the radio on. He was about to go back to bed when he heard American voices. If one thing was sure about the radio in London at least, he almost never heard anyone with an American voice.

Curiosity overwhelmed him and he put on his trousers – still stiff from the sea water and stinking of fish. He walked back down the stairs.

The kitchen was empty. The old battered Robert's radio silent.

He went to the half open living room door.

Shannon was watching TV. Humphrey Bogart was pointing a gun at a blonde girl who didn't look too happy to see him.

'*I could turn you over to the cops now, lady, but I don't like cops, I don't like what they might do to a lady like you, so you'd better tell me where you hid the body lady 'cause you don't want to see me get mad. Who can tell what I might do*?'

Tomas smiled. He liked the old detective movies. Then realised something astonishing. Shannon was watching a black and white film on TV! Did Eire have television in 1941? His heart began to beat a little faster. Where was he exactly? What year was it?

He turned back to the kitchen and searched for the newspaper that the fish had come wrapped in. The kitchen stank of fish now, the trout was sitting cooling in a dish on the stove.

The newspaper was in the bin. He pulled it out and took it to the base of the stairs and the light coming from the loft. *The Irish Examiner* February 2014.

His heart flipped. He was back. *He was back.* He had been gone nine whole months somehow, but he was back!

But which world was it? The one he left, or the one Professor Wylie created?

The newspaper didn't seem to enlighten him much. The headlines were about banks and scandals and fishing quotas. There was an advert for a strange shaped new Citroen he didn't recognise and something about the Euro.

'Tomas?'

He looked up. Shannon was staring at him, surprised to see he was looking at the newspaper from the bin.

'I didn't know what the date was.' He explained sheepishly. 'Sorry, didn't mean to disturb you.'

The music from the film was playing in the background as it ended.

'I never saw that film,' Tomas added. 'Watched a lot of Philip Marlow films.'

'If Humphrey Bogart washed up in the Irish Sea I'd give him more than bread and jam.' She said with a wink. Then she looked at him more seriously. 'But you're too young to know who Philip Marlowe is.

'You never spent four months in bed watching DVD's.'

Shannon looked at him confused.

'DVD's?'

Tomas's heart missed a beat again.

'You don't know what a DVD is?'

'No. And you know American films are banned in England. So how do you know about Philip Marlowe?'

Tomas blinked. 'Banned?'

'You know they are. Where are you really from, Tomas?'

Tomas shrugged. 'Portsmouth.'

He desperately wanted to call Gabriella – wanted to hear her voice, have her tell him what had happened.

'When did the war end?' Tomas asked suddenly. He realised his legs were shaking. He didn't really want to hear the answer to the question.

'You don't know?'

'Please. Just tell me.'

''41 or early '42. I forget. The British capitulated. They knew they couldn't win, not against the atomic bomb.'

'And America?'

'America? It's always at war. My father grew up in New York. Sent us back home here to save the boys from fighting in Asia. We're poor, but we're still alive. More than you can say for a few million others.'

'But didn't they defeat Japan in 1946?'

'Where did you learn your history, Tomas? It's the terrible war against Communist China that's draining them of life and hope. Over fifteen years now.'

Tomas sat down on the stairs. Everything had changed. But he'd crashed the plane. Professor Wylie was dead. He'd *not* been tortured by Germans. How then had he changed so much history?

'I've only got this five pound note and I know it's worthless, but do you think you could let me have something so I can call a friend?'

'Now?'

Tomas nodded, laying the five-pound note on the table.

'I really have to call a friend.'

'Is she pretty?' Shannon asked.

Tomas smiled. 'Yes. But she might not forgive me.'

'Girls are more forgiving than you think,' Shannon told him going towards her purse. She glanced at the five-pound note on the table.

'I know someone who'd give you a lot of money for this. This is a genuine five-pound note? From before the armistice?'

Tomas shrugged. He guessed it was.

'You're better off than you thought, Tomas. Here, take some coins. If you're calling England they'll sting you.'

'How does the phone work?' He stared at the coins not recognising any of them.

She looked at him with wonder.

'You really aren't from Portsmouth are you? Go, make your call. Dial 100 for the operator and they'll put you through. The phone's by the dock. You'll have to give it a knock, sometimes it gets a bit fuzzy.'

Tomas nodded then remembered he needed shoes and a shirt.

'Was there ever an air crash at sea near here in 1941, do you think?'

'We'll ask Gerry Dacre. He's lived here since time began. He'll be in the pub. Never leaves until they throw him out.'

Shannon grabbed her shawl. Clearly she intended to come along. Tomas ran upstairs to get his shirt. He could hardly believe he was going to call Gabriella. He was excited and fearful at the same time.

Shannon disappeared into the pub when they got there. Tomas wrestled with the phone. You had to put money in to get to the operator and then when you gave the number in England, you had feed more in before she'd connect you. How she knew how much he'd put in he didn't understand.

He heard the phone ringing. The English operator answered. She repeated the number wanted. There was a terrible pause.

'That number has been disconnected.'

The money disappeared. The phone went dead. Gabriella's number had been disconnected. What did that mean exactly?

He was numb. Upset. Disappointed, sick actually. He had been so excited to hear Gabriella's voice.

Shannon was standing there with a shrunken old man who was clearly a bit worse for wear.

'In 1941, did you say?' Shannon asked Tomas, as he came out of the phone box.

'May 25th 1941. A De Havilland twin engine DH 89. Did it crash near here? There was a really big storm.'

The old guy was staring at Tomas, his eyes small cracks in his wizened face. Tomas did not hold out much hope.

'You mean, when Professor Wylie was killed, along with a Minister from London. Caused a major scandal that did. No one ever knew what it was doing here.

I remember that. It was a terrible storm. The plane crashed into the sea, killed all of them outright. Bodies washed up no more than a mile from here. Remember it as if it were yesterday.'

Tomas sighed. 'That's because it *was* yesterday.'

He looked at Shannon and turned away. He wanted to be alone now. Gabriella had gone. Where had she said she was going? Africa. How was he ever going to find her there? Professor Wylie *had* died, so *why* had history still changed? History should *not* have changed – it was impossible. He hadn't been tortured by the Gestapo. He'd done the right thing, crashed the plane. History should have stayed exactly as it was. Why had it changed?

'Are you all right, Tomas?'

'No.'

'She wasn't there?'

'No.'

'Better come home. Get some sleep. Maybe things will make more sense tomorrow.'

Tomas didn't think they would. He wished he'd drowned now. All he wanted to do was find his way back to Gabriella and have her not blame him for changing history. He couldn't even do that now. He was alone in a time and a place he didn't belong.

He allowed Shannon to take his good arm and walk him back. The old guy was sitting on a barrel by the harbour wall – still remembering, but no one was listening.

'I think you have some explaining to do in the morning,' Shannon was saying.

Tomas wasn't sure he had any explaining left.

20

The Gardens – Kapstadt

Gabriella lay on the green lawn under the shade of a huge spreading oak tree. It was stupefyingly hot. Late March in the Cape seemed to be completely airless. There was no breeze on this side of the mountain and she was exhausted, even though it was just nine-thirty in the morning. The whole family had been unable to sleep the previous night and the temperature hadn't dipped at all. Now here was yet another bright hot sunny day beginning. She never thought she'd miss rain and snow but today she did.

'Gabriella?'

'I'm in the garden.'

Her mother appeared, dressed for tennis. She had adapted to the new lifestyle here best of all, taking up tennis and swimming and lunching with the ladies of Tamboerskloof. Her father would be at the University library or having coffee with some of the professors he'd met there. All of them worried about the new anti-communist activities by the hated PSS. Almost anyone who didn't agree with the government was being labelled a communist sympathiser. University staff were a target in particular. Her father didn't even want her to go into town. Nowhere would be safe until after the election some two months away.

They had been living in the Cape six months already and almost everything about their lives had changed. Gabriella, however, hadn't quite found her footing. The school was better than she had expected, and friendlier (as long as you didn't talk politics). Everything about the city was beautiful, from the architecture, the whitewashed homes with bright red bougainvillea crawling up the walls, to the zinc rooftops, which, when it did actually rain, echoed like massed drums and deafened your ears. She loved the trees, the bright flowers and purple trumpets on the gnarly fig trees. She was constantly fascinated by the cloud that hung over the mountain like a tablecloth, ever renewing itself around its wispy edges.

Gabriella wasn't sure anyone should be allowed to be so happy. Not in this world, under these rules and there were rules, lots of rules about who you could be friendly with or be seen with, even if many people seemed to ignore them. At least there were still old people here and Malays, as well as French and Germans, of course. Everyone neatly in their own separate areas in the cities or their 'homelands' elsewere. Apartheid applied to everyone. *Apart We Are All Equal* – the slogans declared on Government posters. They had settled in the English area, yet just two streets away the street signs were in German and nearby, in Oranjezicht, in French. It was too weird. The schools were segregated by race, language and religion. The only place you met anyone 'different' was in the Mall, or downtown in the big department stores on Adderly Street.

'Oh, there you are.' Her mother handed Gabriella a letter. 'Shouldn't you be in school?'

'My first class isn't until eleven and I've got a match this afternoon, Mother.'

Her mother beamed. 'I'm so glad you got picked for the hockey team. Best way to make friends.'

'Or get beaten to death. They are *very* competitive.'

Her mother laughed and turned to go. 'Make sure you wear a hat, dear. This heat is so oppressive. And put some cream on. You're getting so brown I hardly recognise you sometimes. Oh yes, we're taking your father to dinner tonight at the Mount Nelson. I hope you remembered it's his birthday. He's going to be upset turning forty. Men hate turning forty.'

'Present already given. He almost glanced at it at breakfast.'

'Don't be like that, young lady, he's a very busy man.'

'Quite.' Gabriella sighed.

Her mother hovered, glancing again at the letter. 'Who do you know in Ireland?'

'Ireland?' She squinted at the letter. Then frowned. It was post-marked Cork. Cork, was most definitely in Ireland. She knew absolutely no one in Cork. She watched her mother leave and heard her talking to someone in the hallway.

Suzanne arrived, her new best friend at school. She sauntered into the garden dressed for tennis. Tall, blonde, very sporty and not at all similar to any friend she'd had before. She was irrepressible. Suspiciously she was carrying a towel. 'God, I can't take this heat, Gabby. Freak weather. Hotter than January. Can't face school today. We're going to the beach. I've organised us a ride.'

Gabriella was definitely tempted. But school was strict about absences and they'd most certainly write a note to her mother if she failed to turn up. Nevertheless Clifton Beach and its icy waves beckoned.

'I don't know, Suzanne. Daddy doesn't think I study hard enough and …'

'Is he mad? You already have a reputation as a swot. I doubt you could get higher marks if you tried. Come on. Third beach. David and Sebastian are bringing the volleyball. Get your cossie…'

Gabriella grinned. It *was* very hot and the sea would be deliciously cold.

Suzanne spotted up her letter. 'I never saw an Irish stamp before. Pretty.'

Gabriella looked at the letter more carefully and her heart suddenly did a back flip. A little pen and ink squirrel had been drawn there. *Tomas*. It couldn't be. It wasn't possible. She looked again at the handwriting. Why hadn't she spotted that immediately? It was most definitely Tomas's scrawl.

Suzzanne noticed the change in her.

'My god girl, are you ill? You've gone all pale. It's way too hot to have goosebumps. Are you alright?'

Gabriella could hardly speak. She just seemed to be staring at the letter.

'It's from Tomas.'

Suzzanne shrugged. She knew nothing about Tomas. Gabriella had kept him secret. Tried her best to leave him behind.

'A boy! Ooo … you kept him quiet. Aren't you going to open it?' Suzanne asked, very curious now.

'I'm scared to. I'm scared, Suzanne.'

Gabriella carefully examined the letter again. It must have come by sea to have taken so long. She'd had only a very few letters since leaving England. Two from school friends, one from her old school library demanding she paid a thirty pence fine for a book she hadn't returned and a card from Iris Holmbush to wish her Happy Christmas. That was it. Now here was a letter from Ireland.

She opened it carefully and unfolded the single sheet of paper; a photo fluttered to the ground and fell face down.

Suzanne picked it up.

Gabriella put up her hands to her eyes. 'Don't show it to me. Don't even look at it.'

Suzanne was staring at the picture completely puzzled, then back to Gabriella. This boy was very important to her new friend. Obviously the one she'd left behind. Suzanne was intrigued.

'He's old, isn't he,' Gabriella was saying, almost shaking. 'He's like eighty years old. Tell me he's old and wrinkled.' She fell back on a chair in despair. She realised she was being stupid, but couldn't help herself. She was in shock. Tomas was alive and he'd be oh my god *87 years old* by now at least. He'd be like Iris Holmbush. She couldn't bear it, she felt dizzy and sick. She didn't want to even think about him being old. Better he was dead than old …

Suzanne was staring at her and the photo.

'I think it must be the heat. You need to get into the shade, Gabs.'

'What does he look like? Tell me honestly. What does he look like?'

Suzzanne smiled coyly. 'All I can say is that if he's coming here don't think you're keeping him to yourself, Gabriella. He looks divine. Look at you. Keeping this sailor boy secret all this time. You're a dark horse, girl. Got to watch you.

'I'm going to the beach. Have a sleep or something. Come down later to swim. Promise? And don't tell anyone you saw me today. Promise?'

Gabriella nodded, barely listening, still reluctant to look at Tomas's photo.

'Thanks for asking me, Suzanne.'

'I'll keep your sailor secret, Gabby. But if I see him before you, may the best girl win.'

Gabriella pretended to laugh. She heard a car horn sound outside the garden wall, Suzanne's ride was here. Swimming would have been good, but she had to read a letter. A very important letter. She realised her hands were shaking as she picked it up.

Dear Gabriella,
First of all I'm sorry. I am VERY sorry I didn't manage to change things back. Believe me I tried. I crashed the plane carrying Professor Wylie; I am certain he didn't survive. I don't know why it didn't change everything back. Please accept my apology, I never meant for this to happen. I really didn't.

Gabriella felt dizzy. Never mind the heat. This really was a letter from Tomas! He was alive; he was actually alive and back in her time!

I was saved by some Irish fishermen and they took real good care of me. I have managed to get some money together and there's a promise of a job as cabin boy on a ship coming to the Cape. I shall

only post this letter if that's coming true.

Please don't blame me, Gabby. I am coming to you in the hope that you will forgive me and because you are the only person who matters to me in this world. I called your number and they said it was disconnected. It was the worst moment of my life – so I really hope this letter finds you. A Professor at Cork College is a big fan of your father's book and that is how I got your address.

If you haven't stomped on this letter by now and are still reading, please don't fall in love with anyone else before I get there.

I have to go on board the ship now. I hope this letter finds you and that you are still my best friend. Perhaps together we can think of a way to change things back or at least make sense of it. I am on my way on the Neuschwanstein Kastell freighter. Please be there when it docks.

T. Duck xxx

PS: I know you must hate me for changing everything but PLEASE give me a chance to explain…

She finally stared at the black and white photograph of him grinning, wearing a sailor's cap. There he was, young, the same as ever and smiling right at her. Her heart began to melt. All her fears and apprehensions vanished. He was right. Together they would change things, make sense of everything. Suddenly she was crying. She re-read the letter 'I crashed the plane…' She shook her head. What terrible desperate thing had happened to him that he would chose to deliberately crash a plane and risk almost certain death? How on earth had he survived?

Gabriella wiped her eyes and re-folded the letter. She wanted to put it in a safe place. Didn't want it to vanish. All thoughts of the beach disappeared. She decided to go down to the shipping office immediately and find out when the Neauschwanstein Kastell was due in port. She suddenly felt stronger. Tomas was coming and now her life would start to make sense to her at last.

She stared again at the tiny passport photo and more tears fell. Suzanne had to think she was mad, but she no longer cared. She was no longer alone. She wasn't the only one who *remembered* anymore.

A shadow passed over the lawn. She glanced up and saw a black-breasted snake eagle soar overhead towards the mountain gliding on the thermals. She took it as a good omen and smiled. *Tomas was coming to her*. Her Tomas – and he was all hers.

21

Last Word

Proclamation Series 66. GGA 2014
By order of the Office of the
Governor General of Cape Province
From henceforth all citizens must carry their passbook with them at all times. It must be date stamped by officers of the Public Safety and Standards Police (PSS). All citizens are required to produce your pass upon request from authorities. Failure to do so will result in a fine.
(Maximum penalty of 3000 RM) and
imprisonment of no less than 30 days.
Note: Only legally registered citizens and visitors of the Cape Province may apply for a passbook

Gabriella stared at the sign on the bus with annoyance. Petty rules. Paranoia. She longed for the world she used to live in before Tomas disappeared. A place where everyone got along; race and politics didn't matter. Well in England at least. These PSS cops could stop anyone and arrest them for practically anything. She hated them and their shiny black uniforms and silly hats, and the way they leered and strutted around 'protecting' people's morals. As if. She'd seen them drinking at the back of the bottle store in the Gardens terrorising anyone who dared to criticise them. Morons – just because they belong to Neu Bruderbund.

Tomas would need a passbook and ID. How would he get them? Where would he stay? Suzanne had a poolhouse at her Camps Bay home, but she couldn't trust Suzanne to keep her hands off him. She was boy mad. Worse, her own parents didn't even remember him.

And what of Tomas? What about all the things that had happened to him? He'd crashed a plane, for god's sake! How different was he now?

'You'll need a passbook, son.'

'What?'

'To land. They're very particular. Name, religion, race. Take it from me, if you want to stay here, enrol in a German class first chance you get. They'll like that'

Tomas stared at the mountain range he'd just learned was called the Zwölf Apostel (12 Apostles). He frowned. All he'd thought about these past weeks was getting to Gabriella and finding her. Somehow he didn't think he could even begin to put things right without her at his side. He'd never once thought about all the legal stuff, passports, ID.

Radleigh, the First Engineer sighed. He'd befriended Tomas during his weeks aboard. Been heartbroken over a woman in Lorenco Marques and Tomas had kept him from killing himself, made him stay sober too. He felt protective over the boy now they were about to dock in the Cape.

'I know a Chinaman in Salt River. He can get you a passbook made up.'

Tomas frowned again. 'That'll cost, right?'

'True, but beats a fine, 30 days in the clink and deportation afterwards.'

Tomas nodded. He had to take this stuff seriously. He was nervous Gabriella wouldn't see him. She had every right to blame him for the all the changes in her life. She might even hate him.

He was genuinely scared of what she would say or do. But one look at the mountains and the endless blue sea, he was sold on it. Been that way all the way down the coast. Africa was beautiful.

'Get a photo done. Several, passport sized and go see him. Charged the last First Mate 200RM, but he's good and quick. Got watermarks, genuine German paper, everything. You'll only get a permit for 48 hours when you disembark here and they will come looking for you if you don't get back on the ship.'

Tomas nodded. The Engineer was being a friend, helping him out. Had to appreciate that.

'Got an address?'

Radleigh pulled a moth-eaten card out of his wallet and showed him it.

'Memorise it. If the PSS find this on you you'll be interrogated. Believe me, you don't want that.'

Tomas had vivid memories of torture. He really didn't want that at all.'

'Chi Xi. 47D Lower Rochester Road.'

'Tell Chi, Jowett sent you. That's all he needs to know. Nothing else. Don't mention the ship by name, or the ports we've been into.'

'Why?'

'They might be listening. This might look like paradise to you, Tomas Drucker, but you're walking into a minefield. They've had over sixty years to perfect apartheid and exported it everywhere the Germans wanted to divide and rule. Pits every community against the other. Perfect distraction. Eats away at the soul. I hear they got a new paranoid Governor General. Sees Reds under the bed everywhere. My suggestion? Be English. Ditch the surname, OK? I know it's your name an' all, but be someone new. Something plain, that suggests nothing at all. Smith or Brown or Jackson. Something they can't pin something on. Y'understand?'

Radleigh suddenly stiffened. The Captain was strolling on deck.

'Boy, (Tomas had been 'boy' from the day he came on board) I need my uniform pressing and my shoes shined.'

'Right away, Captain.' Tomas ran off sharply. He'd be on duty till the moment he was paid off.

Gabriella showed her passbook at the dock gates and was waved through with a clutch of noisy good time women, all chatting excitedly, just waving their passbooks at the bored security guard. Gabriella was embarrassed. Did the guard think she was a prostitute too? But then, why else would a single girl be rushing to meet a plain old freighter at Alfred dock.

Gabriella watched the women, wearing bright tight blouses and revealing skirts and high heels, jabbering excitedly as they went on before her, never even giving her a glance. They were there to grab the sailors money before it was wasted on booze, or on any wives and hungry kids that might be waiting somewhere. They were there to have 'fun' and sailors knew how to spend.

Gabriella was nervous, almost sick with worry about what Tomas would be like. She had no idea of what she would even say to him. Except maybe, how the hell did you get back and why is everything still crazily WRONG.

A diesel shunter chugged past her, hauling a few empty freight wagons behind it towards the docking ship. A crane was swinging around ready to unload. She had no idea things happened so fast. From a distance she saw customs officials boarding the gangplank, almost to the second it swung over to the pier.

By the time she reached the vessel crew members were already disembarking to the delight of the assembled girls who whistled and vied for their attention, showing off their charms. Some men readily embraced them; others tried to skulk past, not so ready to part with their earnings. An officer followed with a large kitbag on his shoulders. He teased the girls a little, but there was an impatient tight-faced tall women waiting for him beside a Mercedes sports car. They had no chance.

Of Tomas she saw nothing. It had been almost forty minutes now. Had she got the name of the ship wrong? She was nervous to ask, didn't want to draw attention to herself, but almost everyone who was getting off was gone already. She stepped into the sunlight, staring up at the ship wondering whom she could ask…

'You're a shy one,' a man said.

Gabriella turned and saw this portly officer of about 35 with a bushy beard and realised with horror that he thought she was one of *those* girls…

'Oh my g-god,' she stammered, blushing. 'I'm not…'

The man laughed at her and suddenly Tomas popped out from behind him shouting 'Surprise'.

Gabriella stared at him open mouthed. Tomas was tanned, taller, grinning like a Cheshire cat and astonishingly good looking. She had never actually realised that.

'This is who you came to see?' The officer asked Tomas.

Tomas introduced them with a grand wave. 'This is First Engineer Radleigh. Radleigh meet Miss Gabriella Lamb.'

Gabriella smiled. She could see they were friends, despite the man being older. The officer was staring at her, bemused.

'Well, I can see why he sailed half way around the world to find you, Miss Lamb. You've got yourself a fine boy here. You take care of him now. He's never once stopped talking about you. Practically talked my ear off.'

Gabriella wasn't listening. Suddenly Tomas was in her arms and they were hugging and then abruptly she was sobbing, hot tears rolling down his neck.

She couldn't speak. Tomas clung on. They kissed, trembling tentative kissing and she cried some more, tasting hot salty tears.

When she wiped her eyes the engineer was long gone. They were alone on the dock in the sun. Tomas didn't say a word, neither could she, but they clung on to each other. Each thinking that now, at least there were two of them to remember the past. Two had to be stronger than one. Just had to be.

They finally began walking back towards the dock gates. Tomas carrying a small bag of possessions on his shoulder. Gabriella felt so strange to be beside him again, yet it was so wonderfully normal and right. She remembered something she'd brought with her, something he should see. Proof on a Roneo copy. She handed it to him without a word and he glanced at it, frowning.

JOIN US
AND SMASH COMMUNISM

Tomas D spoke for England and stopped the war.

He gave his life for Peace.

You too can be a hero. Safeguard Your Afrika

Join the Neu Bruderbund. Be our Eyes and Ears.

Root out the Communists in our midst

They might even be posing as your friends!

Join US and Smash Communism forever

Tomas stared at a picture of someone who looked a lot like who he used to be, wearing a uniform he had never worn – a young soldier smiling out of the poster.

Finally Gabriella found the courage to speak. 'I don't know what you did, Tomas Duck, but somehow we have to undo this.'

Tomas glanced at her as she wiped her eyes. They were approaching the gate and they'd be wanting to see the passes.

'This isn't me, Gabby. Doesn't even look like me. It's all fake.'

'I know that. Besides even *you* don't look like the Tomas I used to know. You've grown.'

Tomas took her hand. 'You too. You're beautiful, Gabs. Amazing actually. Have your eyes always been violet? I …' he turned away blushing.

'Now I know you're a fake. Tomas Duck never noticed my eyes. Not once.'

'Passes,' the bored gate guard demanded as they stepped up to his booth.

Gabriella waved hers under his nose but he was more interested in Tomas.

'Drucker, Tomas Christian?' He called out reading his pass document with some surprise.

'That's me.' Tomas stayed cool. The Captain had made sure all his paperwork was correct. Had offered to keep him on if he decided not to stay. The ID photo was rubbish, taken when he'd first signed on. He wondered if that would be a problem. Or the famous name. Radleigh was right – he had to ditch the name.

'Any relative of the Boy Hero?' Tomas detected a sarcastic tone.

He shook his head. 'Just wish my Dad had called me something else.'

The Guard laughed. 'Yeah. Hard living up to a bloody hero, right?'

He produced a big time and date stamp and clamped it down hard on the thin document.

'48 hours. Don't lose it. They're doing raids everywhere looking for illegals and communists. Best be back here before it expires. The PSS can be right bastards.'

Tomas nodded seriously, thanking the man with his eyes. Pocketed the pass and arm-in-arm he and Gabriella walked out of the gates towards the city.

'Where are we going?' Tomas asked, breathing a sigh of relief.

Gabriella was all smiles now. 'First we have to celebrate. You won't believe the coffee shops or the stores. I have a ton of places to show you.'

Tomas relaxed. He couldn't believe he was really here. It was like they hadn't spent more than hour apart. They were still Tomas and Gabriella, after all that had happened. Only better. He felt good basking in her smiles, dizzy in fact.

'I want to know everything, Tomas. Everything that happened to you. About Iris too.'

'You know about Iris?'

'She came to see me in Portsmouth. First old person I'd ever seen in this wonderful new bloody world you created.'

'No way. And I said I'm sorry about this bloody world. I'm stuck here too.'

Gabriella shook her head. 'We can argue about that later. Right now I want to hear your stories. Iris waited years and years to see me. She and I are the only two people who remember you. How weird is that? We're probably the only ones who know the real future – which is even more depressing.'

Tomas nodded.

'And how did you get back? That's what I'm dying to know.'

Tomas took her hand and squeezed it. 'Find me a place to have coffee and I will confess everything.'

'We're heading there now.' She turned her head towards him and narrowed her eyes suddenly. 'You really think I'm beautiful? You never noticed before.'

Tomas shrugged. 'There's a whole lot of things I never noticed before, Miss Lamb. Now I see everything.'

'You're dreadfully thin. But definitely taller.'

'Grew two inches in the last three months I think. Radleigh measured me.'

'You're a freak, Mr Duck.'

He grinned. 'Yeah, that much I can agree.' He was looking up at the mountain from where they stood and Adderley Street ahead, the giant department stores beckoning. 'It's beautiful.'

'You haven't even seen the best parts. Wait till you see the beaches. Warn you though, the water is freezing. There are penguins, it's so cold.'

'Penguins?' Tomas thought she was kidding. He couldn't help but feel insanely happy holding her hand as she led him towards her newly adopted city. He noticed that the street signs were a mixture of English, what he guessed was Afrikaans and German.

She could see he was thinking and taking in all the signs and people.

'Where are all the…?' Tomas began.

'Don't even say it, Tomas. Whoever it was, they don't exist now. You can't talk about it. My father is discovering the whole past has been rewritten. They don't like his research at all here. He's protected because he was commissioned by important people in Berlin; but you'll have to fit in fast. No one talks politics at all. *Ever*. We're English, we have our quarter here and out in the suburbs, but the German immigrant suburbs are expanding.' She sighed. 'You think we can ever change it back?'

Tomas was looking at a vast statue of Governor General Rommel at the foot of Adderley Street. There was an inscription at the base. 'War without Hate wins Minds and Hearts'. He wondered what that meant exactly. In a different world the Field Marshall had been charged with treason and taken his own life rather than face a trial. In this world he'd been made Governor.

'It's bigger than us, Gabby. The stupid thing is, I thought by making the plane crash I'd end it. I really thought I'd change everything back.

I've thought and thought about it. What was that one thing I did? Might have been all of it. Just me going back and telling that German spy about my phone. That could have been it right there. Something I did, or said, changed everything. I was so bloody stupid, Gab. So stupid.'

'Don't say anything more, OK? I want to hear it from the beginning. Don't jump to the end. Leave nothing out, Tomas.' She took both of his hands and clasped them together. 'Listen to me. If it can change once, it can change twice. I swear it. We have to figure it all out.'

'I've only got 48 hours,' Tomas said. 'You heard the guy.'

Gabriella shook her head, pulling him on again. 'If you think I'm ever going to let you out of my sight ever again, Tomas D – you can think again. If we have to stay here, we have plans remember? Graduate school, University.'

Tomas shook his head. He didn't think any of that would happen anymore.

'Somehow we have to make you legal here.'

'Radleigh told me about a Chinaman who can forge documents. Foolproof, he said.'

Gabriella frowned. 'Can he be trusted? You get caught, Tomas, the jails here are brutal. Everyday you read about someone who's fallen out of a window and died during interrogation. They are obsessed with Communists for some reason. Daddy says there aren't any. It's just something they're doing to keep everyone frightened and in check during the election. Everyone is so suspicious of everyone else they aren't going to think about all the other shit going on. They arrested a teacher for making students write an essay on the Russian revolution.'

'That's history.'

'Not here it isn't. There's nothing before the war in 1948.'

'There was a war in '48?'

Gabriella shrugged. 'That's when Germany finally 'Liberated' South Africa. Once they had the atom bomb for real they blew up the Sudan to prove it, then threatened to blow up everyone else. It was the first war where practically no one died.'

'Unless you count the Sudan,' Tomas muttered quietly.

Gabriella nodded. 'Here we are…' She pulled Tomas back suddenly and hid behind a parked van. Her heart racing.

'What?'

'PSS. They're raiding our coffee shop.'

Tomas turned his head. Saw black uniforms emptying out of an armoured police vehicle and rushing into the small coffee shop on

Greenmarket Square. People were walking out with their hands on their heads. Guns pointing every which way.

'Look away.' Gabriella said tersely.

Tomas didn't need to see more. He took her hand again and they headed up a side street away from the scene.

'Welcome to paradise,' Gabriella said.

'What were they looking for?'

'Communists. I told you. There's an election coming up. They're building the fear. Same bloody party wins every time but…'

'Anywhere we can go that we won't get arrested?'

She had to think fast. 'Maybe. Keep walking.'

Tomas felt the heat from the pavement, saw the beautiful buildings all around him and felt a familiar bitterness. Could ALL of this have happened because of him? It just didn't seen possible. Yet…

'You ever read 1984?' Tomas asked.

Gabriella looked at him, then suddenly remembered. 'Orwell, right? I'd forgotten it. I was supposed to read it, but I… God, I bet he doesn't even exist in this world. I bet a whole lot of writers and artists don't exist anymore. Shit, Tomas, we have to remember so much. We bloody well have to.'

Tomas was beginning to realise that.

Gabriella saw a PSS car at the top of the street disgorging armed officers and dogs. Anxious now she pulled Tomas into a doorway of a nearby art gallery. What the hell was going on? She'd never seen so many cops. 'In here. It's stuffy and safe.'

Across the marble lobby they glimpsed an inner courtyard and small sunny café with shaded tables. They casually sauntered in and sat down. The people around them looked well dressed and very respectable. They probably didn't approve of how Tomas was dressed in a thin sweater and faded jeans.

'Daddy meets people here for coffee. Boring but safe, I think.'

Tomas was looking at the obscure artwork on the walls. Blobs of colour saying nothing. Nothing to upset anyone. Especially the PSS. A blonde waitress approached, her hair tied tightly around her head Bavarian style. She didn't smile.

'Two cappuccinos please.' Gabriella ordered. 'And some banana cake.'

'No lattes?' Tomas asked Gabby as the waitress left.

'No one has even heard of them.' Gabriella whispered. 'Haven't seen a muffin in almost a year.'

Tomas smiled, looking around at people talking in hushed voices whilst unseen birds cheeped in the ivy on the walls. No communists here, he reckoned.

'Start now, from the beginning, Tomas. Don't leave out a thing.'

'It'll take forever,' he protested.

'I ordered cake. Spill it, mister. Now.'

Tomas made a face, leaned forward across the table, drawing breath. 'It began in Lou-Lou's.'

'Our café?' She was surprised.

'Only it wasn't a café anymore. It was suddenly a butcher's shop and there was this terrible storm outside, remember?'

Gabriella remembered.

'I was running from Specsavers to get out of the rain, it was pelting it down and suddenly all this lightning was dancing around me and ...'

Gabriella was listening, watching his face, excited and nervous to be with him. How was it possible he'd grown into this beautiful boy with such interesting scars. She never wanted to be parted from him ever again. She took his hand as he spoke, barely able to comprehend the words he was saying.

'And you didn't feel anything?'

'Not till the bomb fell on the crypt. That's when I knew it wasn't my nightmare anymore. That's when I knew it was for real. Death stinks, Gab. It really stinks.'

The outer doors to the art gallery suddenly crashed open. The place was filled with armed PSS cops. Some people behind them panicked. Began to run for the high walls.

The PSS cops were yelling at everyone, guns poised, police dogs at their side. Gabby grabbed Tomas's hand hissing. 'Pick up your bag and follow me!' She dragged him to the nearby ladies toilet, ignoring other women in there, some crying, some hiding, scared to death.

'Find a window, Tomas. Get us out of here, *now*.'

Tomas didn't hesitate. Entered a cubicle, climbed up and kicked open a small window. He turned to grab Gabriella. 'Leads to an alleyway.'

He pushed his bag through and then Gabby, heard her land safely. Some other women wanted out as well but none of them were thin enough by Tomas's calculation. He followed Gabby, scrabbling up the wall, squeezing through, dropping down into the alley beside her.

'Why are we running? We didn't do anything.' Tomas asked, picking up his bag.

Gabby took his hand. 'You don't understand. Someone in the gallery must be a suspect. They'll arrest everyone there, Tomas. We could be in jail for months. It's like a virus. They sweep everyone up and just hope they get a big fish. Just pray we can get home.'

Tomas held Gabby back from heading to the end of the alley. He knew the PSS would be waiting there.

'Here, in here.' He kicked a door open and they entered a small car park and delivery space behind a store. Empty cartons and all manner of stuff were stacked ready for disposal. He took her hand and swiftly walked towards the gates, looking out to see what was what in the street.

'Radleigh taught me something when were in Zanzibar,' Tomas whispered in Gabby's ear. 'Own the street. No one will tackle you if you own the street.'

Gabby searched Tomas' face. He'd changed. Changed a lot.

'You were in Zanzibar?'

'Take my arm,' Tomas whispered. He pointed towards a bookshop across the road. 'We're going there. Like we don't know anything that's going on. We're just not interested, OK? I'm going to leave my bag behind the garbage cans. We can come for it back later.'

Gabriella nodded, nervous as hell. Amazed at this cool confident boy on her arm.

They strolled arm in arm like young lovers towards the bookshop. A PSS vehicle was parked no more than ten metres away, a dog handler poised to pounce, but Tomas held his nerve, they didn't waver from their aim of the bookshop.

Gabriella realised she urgently needed to pee. Not good timing at all. Somehow they made it to the shop and even went inside. Only then did she look back. Saw with horror they were carrying someone out of the alley. The man looked all bloody. Might be already dead.

They watched the PSS officers escorting some of the people from the art gallery into the waiting black windowless vans. Tomas felt bad for them. All this time he'd only thought about finding Gabriella, never once considered the world she was living in.

'You still owe me coffee,' Tomas whispered in her ear. He discovered she was shaking. Gabby looked up into Tomas' face. 'I'm scared.'

They stepped out of the shop. Stood in the shade of a tree as the PSS vehicles drove away. Tomas took her into his arms and held her. This bit, this them, he didn't want to change. Ever. But everything else, there just had to be a way.

'Let's get my bag and find a quiet place to talk. These cops can't be everywhere at once.'

Tomas had a sudden thought. 'We don't have to stay here, y'know.'

'What do you mean?' Gabby stared at him confused.

'The ship's heading for Rio. Then Florida. You could sign on. The cook quit and believe me, he couldn't cook, he really couldn't cook.'

Gabriella looked at Tomas as if he were mad, but saw he was being serious.

'Leave? Africa? Mum and Dad?'

'South America is free. So is America. No fascists. No communists.'

Gabriella was stunned. Tomas had come all this way to find her and now he wanted to leave. Take her with. Was that even possible? Would she even consider it? What about school?

They went back across the road. He retrieved his bag and pulled out something to give her. A pebble. A glass pebble. She looked at him, uncertain about how to react.

'It's a diamond,' he said, finally producing his old smile. 'This is what they look like when they dig them out of the ground. The Captain said it would be worth a lot if we had it cut and polished.'

'Where did you get it?'

'Pulled a man out of a burning bar in Alexandria. He insisted I have it.'

'You were in Alexandria? Like in Egypt?'

They began walking towards the older part of town. Gabriella was beginning to realise that she didn't know this Tomas at all. It was if he'd grown up without her. It hurt. They weren't ever supposed to be separated. Had never been part of her plan.

'Here. We can have coffee here,' Tomas decided on Loop Street. They were walking along an unmodernised Victorian street with laced metal balconies and dimly lit second-hand bookshops and antique stores. It was strangely comforting. The café was run down, tiny with just six tables, not at all the kind of place Gabriella had wanted him to see. 'They have cake too,' he added with a smile, pointing to the strange looking pastries hidden under glass to protect against wasps.

Gabby sat down on a rickety wooden chair. The place was definitely authentic. She sensed she was not in her zone anymore. The owner was Portuguese, seemed happy to see customers, making a fuss of them. She made an excuse and went to the toilet, dreading what she would find. Her head was about to explode. Leave Africa and her parents?

Rio? Cook? Crazy, crazy stuff.

Tomas watched her go, ordered coffee and cake and watched the world go by. He felt disappointed. Not by Gabriella, who was the same as ever and made him happy to know she was perfectly her old self. But seeing the PSS cops, the fear in people's eyes and knowing that this society was infected with paranoia, made him feel doubly guilty. It smothered him like a black shroud. All this was his fault.

An old woman was watching him from the corner of the café. He'd not noticed her when they came in.

'Want your future told, sonny?' She rasped, her accent heavy.

Tomas shook his head. Nearly laughed. He knew all about futures. Wondered if he even had one in this world.

Gabriella looked strange when she returned, stared at him hard, her lips drawn tight. 'I think you should go to the loo, Tomas. Go now.'

Curious, Tomas got up without a word, followed the signs to the toilet at the back. The old lady in the corner was watching him very carefully, as if she knew who he was.

The Neu Bruderbond poster was in the toilet. His fake smiling face in uniform. Now he saw it close-up, the photo didn't resemble him at all. He guessed it didn't matter which boy they used – no one would know what he really looked like.

Someone had scrawled in large black ink over the poster:

Tomas D - Fxxxing Traitor
The bastard who became a hero
and lost us the bloody war

Tomas didn't react. It was true. His name was a piece of history now, endlessly used as a propaganda tool any way they wanted. Whoever had written this knew the truth. He *was* a traitor. He wasn't upset, because this meant that someone in this city remembered the world the way it was supposed to be. If there was one, there would be others, right? Perhaps he should stay. Try to find them. But then again – how?

When he rejoined Gabriella, their coffee had arrived and some sticky cake. Gabby leaned in and whispered. 'There's an old lady in the corner who thinks you're the boy in poster. She wants to tell your future.'

He nodded. 'I know.' He turned and gave the old woman a brief smile.

'I told her that you were taking me far, far away to a place where they don't need heroes anymore.' Gabby said quietly.

Tomas stared at her a moment registering her words. 'You mean?'

'You do know I can barely boil an egg, right?'

Tomas was grinning suddenly, his heart beating wildly. 'Rio? You'll come to Rio? You'll go with a traitor?'

Gabriella shrugged. 'Whatever you did, I know you didn't mean to. Iris told me that they used you. Tortured you too. Is that true?'

Tomas lifted his sweater for a second. The scarring was still a vivid crimson.

Gabriella's mouth dropped open, she looked back into his eyes, wondering just what else they did to him. She leaned into him and they hugged again, as if it was for the first time.

'Daddy will kill me.' Gabby whispered into his ear.

'We'll send him a letter.' Tomas told her. 'After we've gone. Let him know you're safe. You have to do that.'

She nodded. 'And we'll change it all back somehow, right, Tomas?'

Tomas hoped it was possible. He'd changed history, the guilt of it was a heavy burden. He sipped his coffee. 'The Captain said that history only needs a tilt and it can all go the wrong way. I wanted to tell him everything, but he wouldn't have believed any of it.'

'Then tell me. Tell me now. I need to know, Tomas. Everything. I can't help us change it if I don't know what happened.'

Tomas drew breath and finally began to tell his tale.

Ende!

Further information

1: For London Blitz bomb damage details see:
http://www.bombsight.org

Source Wikipedia 2013: Blitz of London and the UK

The Blitz (from German, "lightning") was the sustained strategic bombing of the United Kingdom by Germany during the Second World War. Between 7 September 1940 and 16 May 1941 there were major raids (attacks in which more than 100 tonnes of high explosives were dropped) on 16 British cities. Over a period of 267 days (almost 37 weeks), London was attacked 71 times, Birmingham, Liverpool and Plymouth eight times, Bristol six, Glasgow five, Southampton four, Portsmouth three, and there was also at least one large raid on another eight cities. This was a result of a rapid escalation starting on 24 August 1940, when night bombers aiming for RAF airfields drifted off course and accidentally destroyed several London homes and killed civilians combined with Churchill's immediate response of bombing Berlin.

Starting on 7 September 1940, London was bombed by the Luftwaffe for 57 consecutive nights. More than one million London houses were destroyed or damaged, and more than 40,000 civilians were killed, almost half of them in London. Ports and industrial areas outside London were also heavily attacked; the major Atlantic sea port of Liverpool was the most heavily bombed city outside London, suffering nearly 4,000 dead. Other ports including Bristol, Cardiff, Hull, Portsmouth, Plymouth, Southampton, and Swansea were also targeted, as were the industrial cities of Birmingham, Belfast, Coventry, Glasgow and Manchester. Birmingham and Coventry were heavily targeted because of the Spitfire and tank factories in Birmingham and the many munitions factories in Coventry; the city centre of Coventry was almost completely destroyed.

The bombing did not achieve its intended goals of demoralising the British into surrender or significantly damaging their war economy. The eight months of bombing never seriously hampered British production, and the war industries continued to operate and expand. The Blitz did not facilitate Operation Sea Lion, the planned German invasion of Britain. By May 1941 the threat of an invasion of Britain had passed, and Hitler's attention had turned to Operation Barbarossa in the East. In comparison to the Allied bombing campaign against Germany, the Blitz resulted in relatively few casualties; the British bombing of Hamburg alone inflicted about 42,000 civilian casualties.

Several reasons have been suggested for the failure of the German air offensive. The Luftwaffe High Command (Oberkommando der Luftwaffe, or OKL) failed to develop a coherent long-term strategy for destroying Britain's war industries, frequently switching from bombing one type of industry to another without exerting any sustained pressure on any one of them. Neither was the Luftwaffe equipped to carry out a long-term strategic air campaign; it was not armed in depth, and its intelligence on British industry and capabilities was poor. All of these shortcomings denied the Luftwaffe the ability to make a strategic difference.

The Luftwaffe and strategic bombing

In the 1920s and 1930s, the air power theorists Giulio Douhet and Billy Mitchell espoused the idea that air forces could win wars by themselves, without a need for land and sea fighting. It was thought there was no defence against air attack, particularly at night. Enemy industry, their seats of government, factories and communications could be destroyed, effectively denying them the means to resist. It was also thought the bombing of residential areas would cause a collapse of civilian will, which might have led to the collapse of production and civil life. Democracies, where the populace was allowed to show overt disapproval of the ruling government, were thought particularly vulnerable. This thinking was prevalent in both the RAF and United States Army Air Forces (USAAF) between the two World Wars. RAF Bomber Command's policy in particular would attempt to achieve victory through the destruction of civilian will, communications and industry.

Within the Luftwaffe, there was a more muted view of strategic bombing. The OKL did not oppose the strategic bombardment of enemy industries and or cities, and believed it could greatly affect the balance of power on the battlefield in Germany's favour by disrupting production and damaging civilian morale, but they did not believe that air power alone could be decisive. Contrary to popular belief, the Luftwaffe did not have a systematic policy of what became known as "terror bombing". Evidence suggests that the Luftwaffe did not adopt an official bombing policy in which civilians became the primary target until 1942.

The vital industries and transportation centers that would be targeted for shutdown were valid military targets. It could be claimed civilians were not to be targeted directly, but the breakdown of production would affect their morale and will to fight. German legal scholars of the 1930s carefully worked out guidelines for what type of bombing was permissible under international law. While direct attacks against civilians were ruled out as "terror bombing", the concept of attacking vital war industries—and probable heavy civilian casualties and breakdown of civilian morale—was ruled as acceptable.

Throughout the National Socialist era, until 1939, debate and discussion raged within German military journals over the role of strategic bombardment. Some argued along the lines of the British and Americans. Walter Wever, the first Chief of the General Staff, championed strategic bombing and the building of appropriate aircraft for that purpose, although he emphasised the importance of aviation in operational and tactical terms. Wever outlined five key points to air strategy:

1. To destroy the enemy air force by bombing its bases and aircraft factories, and defeating enemy air forces attacking German targets.
2. To prevent the movement of large enemy ground forces to the decisive areas by destroying railways and roads, particularly bridges and tunnels, which are indispensable for the movement and supply of forces
3. To support the operations of the army formations, independent of railways, i.e, armoured forces and motorised forces, by impeding the enemy advance and participating directly in ground operations.
4. To support naval operations by attacking naval bases, protecting Germany's naval bases and participating directly in naval battles
5. To paralyse the enemy armed forces by stopping production in the armaments factories.

Wever argued that the Luftwaffe General Staff should not be solely educated in tactical and operational matters. He argued they should be educated in grand strategy, war economics, armament production, and the mentality of potential opponents (also known as mirror imaging). Wever's vision was not realised; the General Staff studies in those subjects fell by the wayside, and the Air Academies focused on tactics, technology, and operational planning, rather than on independent strategic air offensives.[18]

In 1936, Wever was killed in an air crash. The failure to implement his vision for the new Luftwaffe was largely attributable to his immediate successors. Ex-Army personnel Albert Kesselring and Hans-Jürgen Stumpff are usually blamed for the turning away from strategic planning and focusing on close air support. However, it would seem the two most prominent enthusiasts for the focus on ground-support operations (direct or indirect) were actually Hugo Sperrle and Hans Jeschonnek. These men were long-time professional airmen involved in German air services since early in their careers. The Luftwaffe was not pressured into ground support operations because of pressure from the army, or because it was led by ex-army personnel. It was instead a mission that suited the Luftwaffe's pre-existing approach to warfare; a culture of joint inter-service operations, rather than independent strategic air campaigns.[19]
http://en.wikipedia.org/wiki/The_Blitz

2: For an extract of Sir Winston Churchill' s speech to the nation on June 4 1940 read the next page:

'I have, myself, full confidence that if all do their duty, if nothing is neglected, and if the best arrangements are made, as they are being made, we shall prove ourselves once again able to defend our Island home, to ride out the storm of war, and to outlive the menace of tyranny, if necessary for years, if necessary alone. At any rate, that is what we are going to try to do. That is the resolve of His Majesty's Government-every man of them. That is the will of Parliament and the nation. The British Empire and the French Republic, linked together in their cause and in their need, will defend to the death their native soil, aiding each other like good comrades to the utmost of their strength. Even though large tracts of Europe and many old and famous States have fallen or may fall into the grip of the Gestapo and all the odious apparatus of Nazi rule, we shall not flag or fail. We shall go on to the end, we shall fight in France, we shall fight on the seas and oceans, we shall fight with growing confidence and growing strength in the air, we shall defend our Island, whatever the cost may be, we shall fight on the beaches, we shall fight on the landing grounds, we shall fight in the fields and in the streets, we shall fight in the hills; we shall never surrender, and even if, which I do not for a moment believe, this Island or a large part of it were subjugated and starving, then our Empire beyond the seas, armed and guarded by the British Fleet, would carry on the struggle, until, in God's good time, the New

World, with all its power and might, steps forth to the rescue and the liberation of the old…

Home Security

We have found it necessary to take measures of increasing stringency, not only against enemy aliens and suspicious characters of other nationalities, but also against British subjects who may become a danger or a nuisance should the war be transported to the United Kingdom. I know there are a great many people affected by the orders which we have made who are the passionate enemies of Nazi Germany. I am very sorry for them, but we cannot, at the present time and under the present stress, draw all the distinctions which we should like to do. If parachute landings were attempted and fierce fighting attendant upon them followed, these unfortunate people would be far better out of the way, for their own sakes as well as for ours. There is, however, another class, for which I feel not the slightest sympathy. Parliament has given us the powers to put down Fifth Column activities with a strong hand, and we shall use those powers subject to the supervision and correction of the House, without the slightest hesitation until we are satisfied, and more than satisfied, that this malignancy in our midst has been effectively stamped out.'

Sir Winston Churchill June 4 1940

Sam Hawksmoor is the author of

The Repossession

An intense, edgy thriller for readers who love suspense, action and romance. **Paperback:** 495 pages

Publisher: Hodder Children's Books 2012
ISBN-13: 978-0340997086

Thirty-four kids are missing from the mountain town of Spurlake B.C. No one ever hears from them again. The town community is considering electronic tagging all their children. Meanwhile, Genie Magee (15) is imprisoned behind bars at home by her mother, who claims her soul is possessed by the Devil. The Reverend Schneider leads all night vigils to pray for the missing kids' souls, to stop a sickness in the town that seems to drive the kids away. Genie has almost given up. Does anyone even know she's up here, starving herself to nothing? She knows she's slowly going crazy, seeing visions, beginning to think she is as mad as her mother thinks she is. As stormclouds gather over the mountain town, Rian, Genie's boyfriend, has not forgotten her. He plots a daring attempt to break her out and steal her away from Spurlake forever.

'The Repossession... will blow your mind and keep you guessing until the very end'.

A Dream of Books SJH

Winner of The Wirral 'Paperback of the Year'
and
Bronze Winner of the ABA Awards
and
Finalist at the Leeds Book Awards 2013

The Hunting

Order from Amazon now or your local independent bookshop

Publisher: Hodder Childrens Books 2012

ISBN – 13: 9780340 997093

Genie and Rian had miscalculated. They had expected to return heroes. Unmask the evil Reverend Schneider, expose the Fortress experiments that had killed so many runaway kids. Instead there's a $10,000 reward on each of their heads. Genie and Renee are being hunted for the secret that only their DNA can reveal. Roadblocks ahead. Mosquitoes in the air that can shut down their brainwaves. They must flee down the wild unforgiving river with armed hunters in pursuit. Denis is waiting for Genie is a cold dark place as the other kids lay dying. He urgently needs her help to resist The Fortress. They can't run forever. Soon they will have to turn and fight for their very right to exist.

'I loved The Hunting. It's a great story with a very cool premise. If you like your books fast-paced, thrilling, ambitious and thought-provoking, you'll definitely love this one!'

Evie Seo – Bookish-blogspot

Made in the USA
Charleston, SC
26 November 2014